A Touch
of Temptation

What Reviewers Say About Julie Blair's Work

Never Too Late

"This was an excellent story. Every moment of this book was a joy."
—*Rainbow Awards 2015*

Making a Comeback

"*Making a Comeback*, by award-winning author Julie Blair, is…a poignant story of love, loss, and love regained. Music—specifically jazz—is at the heart of this book, and the love of music and its beauty infuses every scene. …This is a complex and multi-layered love story. Though unabashedly a romance, it is so much more. The writing is masterful and paints memorable characters with deft and sure strokes, exploring internal and external landscapes with great attention to detail. The prose is complex and well-edited, and I liked that the love scenes are off the beaten, formulaic path. They truly capture passion and add a very special layer of tender love to this wonderful read, which may best be savored with a good glass of wine and your favorite music playing."—*Curve Magazine*

"This story is definitely a roller coaster ride with soaring highs, gut-wrenching vertical plummets, and it is not to be missed. Plus all the sublime musical complexities put this book in a rarified world usually not open to many in life, yet here everyone gets to live the magic as two women make a comeback!"—*Rainbow Book Reviews*

Visit us at www.boldstrokesbooks.com

By the Author

Never Too Late

Making a Comeback

A Touch of Temptation

A Touch of Temptation

by
Julie Blair

2016

A TOUCH OF TEMPTATION
© 2016 BY JULIE BLAIR. ALL RIGHTS RESERVED.

ISBN 13: 978-1-62639-488-9

THIS TRADE PAPERBACK ORIGINAL IS PUBLISHED BY
BOLD STROKES BOOKS, INC.
P.O. BOX 249
VALLEY FALLS, NY 12185

FIRST EDITION: MAY 2016

THIS IS A WORK OF FICTION. NAMES, CHARACTERS, PLACES, AND INCIDENTS ARE THE PRODUCT OF THE AUTHOR'S IMAGINATION OR ARE USED FICTITIOUSLY. ANY RESEMBLANCE TO ACTUAL PERSONS, LIVING OR DEAD, BUSINESS ESTABLISHMENTS, EVENTS, OR LOCALES IS ENTIRELY COINCIDENTAL.

THIS BOOK, OR PARTS THEREOF, MAY NOT BE REPRODUCED IN ANY FORM WITHOUT PERMISSION.

CREDITS
EDITOR: SHELLEY THRASHER
PRODUCTION DESIGN: SUSAN RAMUNDO
COVER DESIGN BY G. S. PENDERGRAST

Acknowledgments

Thanks to Radclyffe for offering me the opportunity to be part of her extraordinary publishing company. Thanks to senior editor Sandy Lowe for making sure this story started in the right direction (and for the pink hammer). Thanks to the talented and dedicated staff at Bold Strokes Books who shepherded my story into a polished book with a beautiful cover.

Again, working with my editor, Dr. Shelley Thrasher, was a privilege and an education. Thanks for treating my work with care, patience, and a keen eye for detail.

This story had a new, and at times daunting, set of challenges. I wouldn't want to undertake any writing journey without the guidance of my writing coach, Deb Norton. Her story wisdom shows on every page.

Beta readers Ginny, Greta, Suzy, and Pamela graciously read many drafts and provided invaluable feedback. Liz provided expertise from her many years as an attorney. Besides my beta readers, I'm grateful for friends and family who provide encouragement and common sense when needed—Dena and Susan, Patricia, Jac, and Summer.

And perhaps most important of all, thanks to all of you who sit down and spend some hours with this story. Your support of lesbian fiction keeps it alive and thriving.

Dedication

To Suzy, for joining me on this journey and bringing a healthy sense of humor with extra wisdom and a side order of unwavering support.

Prologue

Kate Dawson woke as if swimming through rolling surf. Hot. Why was her bedroom so hot? She untangled herself from the sheets and went to open the window. Uh, oh. She rushed into her bathroom and barely made it to the toilet before her stomach heaved. No! Not today. Not. Today. Bracing one hand on the vanity, she held her forehead, squeezing the pounding headache. Dizzy. Shaky. What had she eaten last night? Soup and a sandwich her gran made. That couldn't be it.

She turned on the light and snapped her eyes shut against a spike of pain. Opening them gingerly, she tucked hair behind her ears and stared at herself in the mirror. Bags under her eyes she was used to from long hours finishing up her last semester at Stanford and then studying for the bar exam. Skin pale. Cheeks red. Not good. She splashed water on her face. Rinsed her mouth with mouthwash. Took a few sips of water and then swallowed repeatedly to keep it down. No! She couldn't be sick. She wouldn't be sick. First day of the California bar exam began in…she walked to the bedroom and squinted at the clock on her desk…five hours. Not today. Please.

She picked up her phone and read the text from Nic, her best friend, and study partner. Another of the MBE practice questions they'd been blitzing on this last week of prep, sending texts when they weren't studying together, challenging each other as they had throughout law school. She read the question again. She knew the answer. They'd gone over this yesterday. Damn it. She couldn't pull it through the fuzziness in her head.

She tugged her sweat-soaked tank top off and put on the Stanford sweatshirt lying on top of the law books on the bed. Went back to the bathroom and took Advil, praying it stayed down. She crawled under the covers, chilled, and curled onto her side, scrunching the pillow under her head. Pressing her hand against her stomach, she took deep breaths to calm her racing heart. This would pass. Stress and nerves. Sleep it off. Mind over matter. Like when she ran. Focus on the goal. Block out the discomfort.

She woke with a start when her alarm chirped. Hot again, but the headache was tolerable and she wasn't queasy. She took a lukewarm shower, dressed in comfortable business attire, and applied extra makeup to hide her flushed cheeks. She took two more Advil and put the bottle in her purse. She'd take more at the lunch break.

Her legs felt rubbery as she walked down the hallway toward the stairs. Toast and coffee. She could keep that down. She had to leave by six to pick up Nic. There would be heavy traffic across the Bay Bridge to the Oakland test site. No, wait. Nic was picking her up. No, they'd decided she was picking Nic up. Why couldn't she think straight?

Halfway down the stairs she gripped the railing with both hands as a wave of dizziness rolled through her. Taking deep breaths, she willed it away. Focus. She was so close to reaching the goal she'd worked for all her life. Passing the bar exam was the final hurdle. She *would* take the exam. She *would* pass. She *would*. Focusing on each step she made it down the stairs and set her purse on the credenza by the front door. Her flats tapped across the marble entryway, quieted through the carpeted living room to the formal dining room.

She dropped onto her chair to the right of her father's place at the head of the table. She could picture him in the white shirt and polka-dot bowtie he always wore to the office. He'd come down at five thirty every morning to eat breakfast while reading *The Wall Street Journal*. When home she'd loved to join him, talking business and world affairs and law. God, she missed him. He'd been killed a year and a half ago, hit by a car as he walked across an intersection on his way to the office. She put her hand over her stomach as nausea flooded her. Deep breaths. *I. Am. Fine.*

The French doors to the patio opened and Kate's gran marched in. Regardless of place or time of day, marching was the best way to describe her no-nonsense strides and perfect posture. She was dressed in a navy suit with starched white shirt, her gray hair in its customary bun. She'd had to come out of retirement after her son's death to resume managing Dawson Law Firm, one of the oldest estate-planning firms in San Francisco. "Good morning." She squeezed Kate's shoulders and kissed the side of her head. "You feel hot. Are you all right?"

"Just nerves." Kate's mother flounced into the room, dressed in her morning attire, a kaftan, pale blue. "She's never sick. Certainly not on such a monumental day." She sat across from Kate at the long, highly polished table. "You could have gone lighter on makeup today, Kate."

Her gran put her palm to Kate's forehead. "You have a—"

"I'm fine." *I. Am. Fine.* Kate squinted. The light from the windows hurt her eyes. "Coffee and toast," she said when their cook appeared. Whatever this was it would wear off. It had to.

"I didn't know you were joining us for breakfast, Katherine." Kate's mother stirred sugar into the cup of tea the cook set in front of her.

"I'm not, Cecelia." Her gran lived in a cottage at the back of the large property she owned in the Pacific Heights district of San Francisco. Since Kate's father's death, she rarely joined them for meals in the main house.

"Oatmeal," her mother said. "Cream and brown sugar with it." She opened the *San Francisco Chronicle* set by her placemat.

The cook caught Kate's eye and gave a slight shake of her head. Pointing out that the brown sugar and cream negated any benefit of the otherwise low-calorie meal was a lost cause. Her mother was on a perpetual diet, although her weight was on a perpetual climb.

Her gran put a small black box on the table. "I am proud of you."

Kate opened it and lifted the gold Cross pen from the red-velvet lining. She read the two names engraved in identical italic font. Phillip Dawson. Her grandfather, who'd started Dawson Law Firm in 1941. William Dawson. Her father who'd taken the helm upon his death. Turning the pen she saw the newly added name. Kate Dawson. Her throat tightened as she rubbed her finger over the names.

"Phillip took the bar exam with this pen," her gran said. "We gave it to your father the day he started the exam. I'm passing it to you in the same spirit of hoping the practice of law brings you much satisfaction."

"Of course being a lawyer will make Kate happy," her mother said, not looking up from the *Chronicle*. "Your father would be so proud of you, following in his footsteps."

"Oh, Gran." Kate hugged her and then pulled away as her usually comforting floral perfume made her stomach roll.

"Good luck, today," the cook said, setting a cup in front of Kate.

She sipped cautiously, hoping the coffee stayed down. She needed the fuzziness in her head to clear.

"Oh, look." Her mother handed her the *Chronicle*, open to the society page. "Sylvia Peter's daughter is engaged. Not a flattering picture. We'll have yours done professionally. I do hope Todd proposes soon. The best wedding venues book so far in advance. I was thinking—"

Kate stood. "Have to go." She steadied herself for a moment with a hand on the back of the chair. Nauseous, and her head throbbed. Pressing her palm to her stomach she walked from the dining room. *I. Am. Fine.*

"Remind Todd and Nicole that I'm taking all of you out for dinner tonight," her mother called out.

Her gran followed her to the front door and out to the circular driveway. "Let me drive you."

Kate continued to her car as a chill shot up her back. "I'm fine." Tossing her things on the passenger seat, she slid behind the wheel of the red BMW Z4, a graduation present from her mother. She wanted to rest her forehead on the steering wheel. Instead she started the ignition and put it in gear.

❖

Noises seeped into Kate's awareness as if from the far end of a tunnel. Echoey. Strange, rhythmic sounds. Machine sounds. Panic rose. When did she fall asleep? Where was she? Her eyelids felt glued in place and she was so, so exhausted. Why couldn't she remember taking the bar exam? A groan escaped. She hurt. Everywhere. Bad in her hips and lower back. Someone held her hand. Too hard to focus... drift back to...

"Kate?"

Beckoning. But she was so tired.

"Kate."

"Gran." She could barely hear her own voice. It was gravelly and her throat felt like sandpaper.

"Open your eyes." Her gran squeezed her hand.

She knew better than to disobey that voice. She forced them open a crack. Dark except for lights blinking on screens above her, casting the room in a bluish tint. Not her bedroom. "Where..." The rest of the question took too much effort.

"UCSF Medical Center. ICU." Her gran's usually placid face was creased with worry.

"What—" She tried to sit up. Winced at the pain.

"You passed out and ran your car into the Monterey cypress at the end of the driveway."

She didn't remember anything past...what was the last thing she remembered? "How long?" She let her eyelids close.

"Four days."

Tears rolled from the corners of her eyes. "Missed...it." She tried to swallow. Mouth dry. Tears flowed faster as memories of that morning formed in her mind. Missed the bar exam. Noooo.

"The important thing is to get well." She stroked Kate's forearm.

She forced her eyes back open. "What...happened?"

"Viral infection. Went to your kidneys."

"Kate? Oh, Kate. Thank goodness." Her mother's voice from the doorway. Too loud.

Shhh, Kate thought, but couldn't muster the energy to say. She winced when her mother took her hand. The one with the IV in it. She peeked up at her and tried to smile.

"You scared us. Hundred-and-three fever. They put you on dialysis for—"

"Cecelia." Her gran's voice was sharp. "We don't need to bother Kate with details. She needs rest."

"I'll call Todd. He'll want to come right over. And Nicole. Poor dear was so exhausted I had to send her home."

Rest. Yes. She closed her eyes, vaguely aware that they continued to talk. She squeezed her gran's hand. Soft. Callused from working in her garden. Every time she'd floated up she remembered this hand holding hers. She'd failed. It hurt more than the physical pain.

Chapter One

Kate woke with a start. Sweaty. Cheeks hot. No! She jerked to a sit and the blanket slipped to her lap. Her racing heart calmed a notch. Blanket. That's why she was hot. She was on the settee in Gran's cottage, not a hospital bed. She looked over to the wingback chair where her gran sat, studying her over the rim of her glasses, wisps of gray hair escaping her bun. "How long was I asleep?" She tugged the gray Giants sweatshirt off.

"Snoring since the top of the second." The Giants game must be over because the TV was off. Weak daylight came through the window behind the settee. Her gran removed her glasses and set them on the yellow legal pad on her lap. Her black Giants cap was gone, but she still wore the black team shirt, long sleeves pushed up to her elbows. She fixed Kate with her piercing lawyer stare instead of her supportive Gran look. "Good thing one of us had enough sense not to go to the game."

Kate was annoyed when she'd suggested they watch it on TV. Crucial game against the Dodgers with only two weeks left in the season and the Giants fighting for a spot in the playoffs. Season ticket holder for decades, her gran had taken her to games since she was a child. They never missed important ones. "I'm fine."

"That's what you said before you crashed your car."

"Can we not talk about it?" The awful morning of the California bar exam the last week in July. Hospitalized for ten days, half of that in ICU.

"I'll stop talking about it when you start taking it seriously. You need to rest, not gallivant all over the city like you did yesterday."

"Lunch and a little shopping. I'm fine." Okay, the all-afternoon outing had left her exhausted. "It was important to Mother." A Saturday ritual for them. She shivered. Hot one minute, chilled the next. She didn't put the sweatshirt on lest her gran worry more than she already did. The doctor had assured her she'd return to normal with no long-term consequences, but five weeks out of the hospital and she wasn't even close.

"And running again? Honestly, Kate."

She looked away from the withering stare. She'd gone out this morning determined to do a mile. A measly mile. She used to do five easily. She hadn't made it around the block. "Is it wrong to want my life the way it was?"

"That's not something you can force."

"I hate feeling like this." Tired. Fever and nausea that came and went for no reason. Concentration nonexistent. Made studying for the next bar exam impossible. In June she'd graduated valedictorian of Stanford Law School, class of 2014. Now she couldn't stay awake for a Giants' game. "I hate that I let Father down. And Granddad. And you. Giving up your pro-bono projects. Taking over the firm." Her gran's return to retirement was now delayed. The next bar exam wasn't until February.

Her gran's face softened. "You could never let me down."

"Did the Giants win?" She gave in to the chill and put her sweatshirt on.

"Lost four to two." Her gran rubbed the bridge of her nose and put her glasses on.

"They're blowing it." The Giants' chance of winning the division was slipping away.

"Their perseverance is being tested. They had things too easy for most of the season. They're having to dig deeper to reach their goal."

Kate suspected there was a point for her. She was spared from having to think about it when someone knocked on the front door. She shared a look with her gran. Undoubtedly her mother, who lived in the main house at the front of the property but rarely came to the cottage. She went to the door and opened it.

"I had to tell you the good news." Her mother pressed her palms together in front of her. "The cocktail fund-raiser for the supervisor is on. His wife called me personally to accept our invitation." Politics wasn't her usual arena, but she'd used her sorority connection with their county supervisor's wife. "We must begin planning immediately. Tonight."

"Not tonight." Her gran stepped beside her. Sunday-night dinner and a movie, just the two of them, was a tradition since her childhood.

"Well." Her mother shifted her shoulders. The new outfit she'd bought yesterday hung beautifully on her. She was an expert at stylishly concealing the extra thirty pounds she bemoaned but did little to lose. Her hair was a lighter brown than usual, with golden highlights, although always styled in the pageboy she liked for its versatility. "I assumed helping Todd with his political aspirations was a priority. I went to a lot of trouble."

"Which I appreciate," Kate said. "Tomorrow. I'm free all day."

"I suppose we can work with that. We'll want to hold it at the Top of the Mark, of course." The bar atop the Mark Hopkins hotel had been her mother's favorite place for drinks. A few blocks from the offices of Dawson Law Firm in downtown San Francisco, her parents had met there often for cocktails before dinner or the theater. "Your father would have done anything to ensure you have the life we wanted for you." She dabbed under her eyes with her fingertips and waved Kate away when she stepped forward to offer a hug. "Oh, don't mind me."

"Is there anything else, Cecelia?" her Gran asked.

Her mother folded her arms. "We need to meet with the florist to order arrangements for the party." Her annual day-after-Thanksgiving party, a large, lavish affair that required months of planning. "We'll work that into our outing." She turned and walked across the porch, down the stairs, and onto the path that led through the garden to the main house.

Kate closed the door, stifling a yawn.

"Honestly, Kate." Her gran shook her head.

She looked away. Now that she was done with school, it was time she took an active role in helping with the social events her mother hosted throughout the year.

"Let's eat." Her gran went to the kitchen.

"Sure." Kate ignored the flash of nausea. It would pass.

Her gran set bowls of minestrone on place mats on the oak dining table, a vase of fresh flowers from her garden in the center. She buttered a piece of sourdough bread and handed it to Kate. "You need weight back on you."

She stared at the thick layer of butter but didn't argue. You didn't argue with Katherine Dawson. She forced herself to eat in spite of her queasy stomach. She was fine. To prove the point, she took a second helping of soup. They talked baseball, and when they'd finished eating, she cleared the table and washed dishes while her gran heated oil in a pan. A movie was incomplete without popcorn.

Kate went to the living room and looked through the collection of old movies. "*Bringing Up Baby*?" she asked over the sound of the popcorn pinging against the pan. A screwball comedy. Light and fun.

"Hard to find fault with Cary Grant and Katharine Hepburn."

Kate took her spot on the end of the settee, sinking into the soft cushion and curling into the rounded corner with the blanket over her legs. Her gran had relinquished the main house to her only child and his family twenty years ago after her husband's death. She'd renovated the caretaker's cottage at the back of the large property she still owned, turning it into a cozy home. Dark-wood antiques, lots of books, minimal but comfortable furniture covered in plush, warm-toned fabrics. Growing up, Kate had spent almost as much time here as in the main house.

Her gran set the bowl of popcorn on the end table along with her nightly glass of port. Settling in her wingback chair, she pointed the remote at the small flat-screen on the sideboard, bracketed by vases of flowers. She'd given up the house, but the gardens around it remained her domain.

Kate could quote most of the dialogue, but for as many times as she'd seen *Bringing Up Baby*, it still made her laugh. Partway through, her phone signaled a text from her best friend, Nic. Her pulse jumped as she read it. "Boys went ring shopping! Weddings next summer!" She put her hand over her chest as a moment of panic shot through her. She'd known Todd most of her life and dated him the last seven years. She knew they'd be married after finishing law school. Why did it land as a surprise?

"Anything wrong?"

"Nic says Todd and Brian went shopping for engagement rings. At least something in my life will stay on schedule."

Her gran studied her for a long moment. "Staying on schedule sounds like an excellent reason to marry." She returned her attention to the movie and turned up the volume.

Kate's thoughts drifted to things she didn't want to think about. She'd gone home with Todd last night. They'd made love. He was tender and gentle, as always. He'd come. She hadn't. As always. She liked kissing. Cuddling and talking afterward. But intercourse hurt. And she'd never had an orgasm. At least she didn't think she had. Wasn't it just supposed to happen? If only she'd spoken up the first time they had sex. Or the second. Even the third. But now…how did you tell your boyfriend it wasn't as great for you as it was for him. She pulled her focus back to the movie. She was being ridiculous. There was more to a relationship than sex. Todd was a great guy. She was marrying him. Period.

"There." Her gran used the remote to freeze the picture on the screen. "The look on Susan's face." She used the main character's name.

"You mean that starry-eyed look?" Common to movies of the thirties, it looked a bit silly on Katharine Hepburn.

"I've never seen you look at Todd like that."

"It's make-believe." She stared at Hepburn's face, trying to imitate it. How did she force that look?

"It's a representation of what happens when you feel passionately for someone. You love screwball comedies," her gran said a few minutes later as the characters played by Hepburn and Grant chased a pet leopard and a dog, slid down a cliff, and fell into a pond. "Why is that?"

"They're fun. The characters do silly, spontaneous things that make no sense, but in the end it all works out."

"As opposed to your carefully planned, orchestrated, scheduled life where your mother has your future husband's political career mapped out before you have a ring on your finger."

"Life isn't a movie." For a moment she wanted it to be. A place where anything might happen.

"Do you love Todd in that way?" She pointed a finger at the screen. "Like you can't live another minute without him?"

Everything about Katharine Hepburn's face was soft and adoring as she gazed up at Cary Grant. "No. Is that what you want to hear?" Kate pushed the blanket aside. Hot again.

"Then why would you marry him?"

"We're good together. The way my parents were. Compatible. Isn't that enough?"

"Only you can answer that."

"I'm not meant for great passion, Gran. Trust me." Her heart sank with each word.

"Everyone is meant for great passion. It can be difficult. Impossible. You can choose to walk away from it. But until you've experienced it, don't discount it."

"I'm glad you had that with granddad. Not all love is like that."

"I did not have that with Phillip. I loved him deeply but not with great romantic passion. I married him knowing the difference."

"And you had a great marriage. I rest my case."

"Now I'm truly worried about you. Your brilliant mind would not throw out such a sloppy defense if you were thinking clearly."

"I'm scared."

"Thank you. That's the first honest thing I've heard you say in a while."

"Twenty-five-year-olds aren't supposed to almost die." She swallowed hard. She hadn't spoken those words out loud, but they'd been in her mind, jabbing at her. "Everything's different. Not only my health. I do the things I used to do, but I feel like I'm just going through the motions." She let the shuddering breath out because she couldn't stop it. Maybe she didn't want to. She'd always been able to talk to her gran. "I can't shake the fear that I'll never get back to who I was." Like her cells had been changed against her will.

"You'd be a fool not to be affected by your illness, and you're no fool. Your life has taken an unexpected turn, as did mine at your age."

"What happened?" It must have been around the time she graduated from Columbia Law School.

"A story for another day. Instead of fighting so hard to be who you were, take this as an opportunity to reevaluate where you are and where you want to go."

"You don't approve of Todd."

"He's a fine young man. I'm not sure he's right for you."

"Why haven't you spoken up?"

"I hoped you would figure it out on your own."

"I've never questioned marrying him." Her voice sounded scared. Little-kid scared.

"Consider this my standing up in the church when the minister asks if there's anyone who knows why these two...etc. etc."

"But—"

"Shh. I love this part."

Kate relaxed into the familiarity of her gran's occasional chuckle as the movie played through to the final scene, where Cary Grant's mild-mannered paleontologist character confesses the day with the rambunctious Hepburn character was the most fun he'd ever had. Mismatched. But she found something immensely satisfying about their falling in love. As if each had exactly what the other really needed to be happy.

Her gran turned off the movie and moved to sit beside Kate. "I want you to move to my cabin for a couple of months. The change of scenery will do you good. There's an excellent acupuncturist in Felton I want you to see. She also teaches yoga. Rest. Study for the bar exam without distractions."

"Mother won't approve."

"Do this for me. Think of it as your screwball comedy where, how did you put it...you do silly, spontaneous things that make no sense, but in the end it all works out. If you decide the path your life is on is the right one, then embrace it with confidence and I will support you." Her face softened into the one that confirmed Kate was loved beyond measure. "So many choices have been made for you. Whom you marry must be your choice alone, one that makes you happy."

She'd never doubted her gran's wisdom. If she was honest, the thought of not having to make decisions about parties or marriage proposals, of not having to watch Todd and Nic start their careers ahead of her, was appealing. Two months. She'd return healthy, on track with studying for the bar exam, and raring to go. "All right," she said with a burst of confidence. Then she shook her head. Her mother would be furious.

"I will teach you your first yoga poses." Her gran stood and settled her body into an odd stance—legs spread front to back, front leg bent, back leg straight with her foot turned sideways, arms lifted straight over her head, palms together. "Warrior I." She took several deep breaths and then brought her arms down, holding them straight out from her shoulders, one reaching forward, one back, and turned her torso ninety degrees to face sideways. "Warrior II."

Kate clapped. There was something majestic about the poses. Like her gran was different, her body strong and serene. She wanted to know what that felt like.

Her gran motioned Kate to join her. "Nothing better for restoring the body and focusing the mind."

Chapter Two

Kate unlocked the door to her gran's cabin and stepped inside, greeted by the faint smell of wood smoke mingled with lemon furniture polish. Her body relaxed as if from memory. All the good times spent here as a child, she and Gran, weekends and summers. She hadn't been here since before law school.

"You're kidding," Nic said, coming in behind her. "Rustic seems too kind a word." She folded her arms, surveying the living room. Walls were original to the 1940s cabin. Clear, all-heart redwood that was almost unaffordable nowadays. "I feel like I've walked into an old Western."

"Stickley furniture is a hallmark of Craftsman—"

"Whatever." Nic waved her hand in a dismissive gesture.

"You have to admit the location is beautiful." The cabin was in Forest Lakes, a housing development dating back to the twenties, hundreds of homes nestled into the redwood forest of the Santa Cruz Mountains, about an hour and a half south of San Francisco. "There's a lake where I used to swim. And lots of trails I can run on." If her stamina ever returned.

"And so many really tall trees. Kind of spooky. Do they ever fall?" Born and raised in Las Vegas, Nic admitted she'd never been outside of it until arriving in Palo Alto to attend Stanford.

"Not when I've stayed here."

"And what was that ugly yellow thing sliming its way across the walkway out front?"

"Banana slug. Second largest slug in the world. UC Santa Cruz mascot. Simultaneous hermaphrodite." She smiled at the memory of her gran explaining the word hermaphrodite to her as a child, which had led to a discussion of sex long before her mother broached the subject. "Means—"

"I know what it means."

"As a child I memorized the names of the local flora and fauna."

"How useful for the future managing partner in a law firm. Seriously, sweetie, what are you going to do here? Count pinecones?"

"Rest and study." It sounded like a good idea when Gran said it, but a week of listening to her mother's arguments against it had eroded her confidence. *No one watching over you. Away from home without the benefit of their cook/housekeeper. Too far from a hospital. Unfair to Todd to move so far away.*

He'd listened with his usual patience and agreed that it might be good for her. How could she not be in love with a man who was understanding and supportive?

"I counted only two restaurants in that little town we passed through."

"Felton. Gran moved out here from New York in the sixties, bought this cabin, and lived here until she married my grandfather. She had an estate planning practice in Santa Cruz." Moving out here on her own, not knowing anyone, had always seemed mythic to Kate.

"Whatever. Limited takeout. No salon. No shopping."

"Television." Kate pointed to the small flat-screen. Giants games and there was a collection of old films. "Honestly? I'm looking forward to time away from Mother. I understand how difficult it's been for her since Father's death, but she's clingier the last few months."

"She almost lost you. You're everything to her." Nic seemed sad for a second. Kate often speculated on the family she refused to talk about. Blue-collar. That much she knew. Her near-genius IQ had landed her in Stanford Law School. Roommates and study partners had led to becoming best friends. With Nic deciding to take a job in the city and almost engaged to Brian, Todd's best friend, they'd have the kind of lifelong bond her mother had with many of her friends. "What time is Todd coming?"

"After his meeting with a new client." He was driving down from the city to spend the rest of the weekend. "I wish you'd stay." She'd seen Nic almost every day for the last three years. She was going to miss her.

The corners of her mouth turned up. Tall. Slender. Dark, thick hair loose around her shoulders today. "You offering to share?"

"Share what?"

"That gorgeous guy of—"

"Don't be crude." The one thing she didn't like about Nic, and she really didn't like it.

"One of us has to. You're always prim and proper." She slapped Kate's butt. "Don't worry. I'll have a good bang tonight. Or maybe I'll stop by the restaurant on my way back." Brian's family owned several in the city. "Sneak him into the men's room—"

"Stop!"

"Drag him into a stall, rub against his dick until—"

Kate hurried out the front door and down the brick walkway that bisected the small front yard. Irritated. Okay, jealous. She must be the only person on the planet who didn't love sex, not that she'd tell Nic and risk more crude comments. It hadn't mattered with Todd at Harvard for undergrad and then law school. Their relationship had been more talk and text than face-to-face. She'd thought it would get better when they had more time together. She pushed through the gate in the picket fence, opened the door of her BMW, and lifted a box of bar-exam study materials from the seat.

"Lighten up, sweetie." Nic bumped her shoulder before lifting another box from the car. Fifteen minutes later they brought in the last of Kate's things.

"I predict you'll be bored out of your mind and back in civilization before the month's up." Nic draped her arm over Kate's shoulders as they stood in the small kitchen at the rear of the house. "Gotta dash. Research to do." Nic had taken a job with a top criminal-defense firm in San Francisco. Since the day Kate met her, she'd never wavered in her obsession with criminal law. "I'll impress the hell out of the senior associate and win a spot on his team for the trial." She bobbed her head side to side. "Or I'll give him more of the cleavage he can't keep his eyes off of. Either way I'll get what I want. Men are so easy."

"You know I've got your back, right?" Nic asked as they walked to the front door, her mood shifting in an instant as only Nic's could. As moody as she was brilliant, passionate about law, driven to be the best, and more fun than anyone Kate had ever known. "That's what best friends are for."

"I'll come home rested and raring to go."

"I hope so." Nic tilted her head, studying Kate for a moment. She kissed Kate's cheek, then wiped away the lipstick with her thumb before sliding into Brian's black Porsche.

Kate shook her head as Nic gunned it down the street. Always an edge of reckless with her. Doubts surfaced as she walked back into the yard. What *was* she doing here? She knelt beside the banana slug who'd gamely made it across the moss under the Japanese maple flanking the walkway. She stroked the aptly named three-inch-long slug nestled into ferns planted against the cabin's dark-brown exterior. Perseverance. Fast and furious had been her pace but slow and steady had gotten the slug to its destination. Maybe it would work for her.

❖

Chris reached over the center console of her Ford F-150 to the back seat and grabbed a bottle of water from the cooler. She guzzled it as she drove up Highway 9 toward her home in Felton, letting some drip down her neck and drizzling the last of it down the back of her shirt. She'd busted her ass alongside her crew today to finish the two-week landscape project in Santa Cruz that had been one long headache. Cold beer. Shower. Leftover ribs she'd grilled last night. Then up to San Francisco for her friend Georgia's monthly all-women sex party. Now that made her smile. Sure, she had lovers she saw on a regular basis, but Georgia's parties were one of a kind. Her phone rang and she pressed the answer button on the steering wheel.

"How's my favorite daughter?" Her dad's deep voice sounded a bit echoey, which it always did when he called from his office in the old metal building that was home to the painting business he'd owned since before Chris was born. He'd always called her that, even though she was his only daughter. Only child. Her mother had died giving birth to her and he'd never remarried.

"Tell me again why self-employed is a good idea?" She'd dreamed of owning a business as far back as she could remember, but high-maintenance clients like this woman took the fun out of being a landscape contractor. "Why hire me if she doesn't trust me to do it right and on time for her party?"

"At the end of the day…"

"I'd rather be the one in charge." Chris finished in harmony with him.

"Did you land that new project?"

"I wish. Woman calls last night and asks me to come by this morning. Fourth time I've been there. Review the plans. Explain the same things. Answer the same questions. She doesn't sign the contract." Her voice rose with irritation. "Has to think about it more. The house is one of those million-plus homes in Capitola with an ocean view, and she wants to nickel-and-dime me over a twenty-thousand-dollar project?"

"When she calls again, say you'd like to refer her to another landscaper who might better meet her needs. She'll sign the contract. If she didn't want you to do the job she wouldn't keep bringing you back. She's looking for attention."

"Why didn't I figure that out?"

"You would have."

Probably not. Plants were so much easier than people, as she'd discovered doing yard work to earn money when she was in high school. She understood their needs and loved designing gardens and managing the installations. Dealing with clients was still a challenge after eight years in business.

"You up for a ride tomorrow? Meet at Alice's around nine?" Alice's Restaurant on Highway 35 in the Santa Cruz Mountains was famous as a stop for motorcyclists. She'd grown up riding on the back of her dad's Harley until she was old enough to handle her own. They made it a point to ride together a couple of times a month.

"Nine's too early. Georgia's party tonight." An all-night affair. "Eleven?"

"Fair enough. Ask Stacy to join us." One of Chris's oldest friends and also a landscape contractor. Her dad treated Stacy like a daughter. "She looked rocky." They'd had dinner with him earlier in the week.

"She deserves to be rocky." Chris worked her jaw. "What a shitty thing to do." Stacy's girlfriend of six months had gone back to her previous boyfriend. No warning. No discussion.

"Got some nice steaks. Plan on staying for dinner." Grilling. Riding motorcycles. Owning a business. He'd mentored her in all three. She'd won the lottery in the dad department. "Be safe tonight."

"Always." She rolled her shoulders, irritation fading as she made the turn into Forest Lakes and wound along the narrow roads, deeper into the dappled shade of the habitat she loved. Mixed evergreen forest, as she'd recently explained to a client. Specific to the coast of California up to Southern Oregon. She'd fallen in love with the forest on motorcycle rides with her dad through the Santa Cruz Mountains, especially the redwoods that seemed majestic and magical. Now she specialized in using native plants in her garden designs. A great niche, especially with the prolonged drought raising interest in using natives, but if she was going to grow her business, she'd have to expand outside of Santa Cruz. A challenging task and the goal for next year.

Another block and she started the turn into her driveway. Except she had no driveway. A red BMW Z4 blocked it. Sweet car, but couldn't the driver have parked somewhere else? She pulled her truck nose-to-nose with it and stepped out.

A Sears truck was in the driveway of the house next door, and a Comcast van was parked in front. She'd never seen so much activity at the house and hadn't seen the owner, Katherine, in months. Maybe she was here for a visit and she'd bake her delicious chocolate-chip cookies. A guy talked on his cell near the truck as another guy maneuvered a dolly down the ramp, a carton strapped to it. Kenmore on the box. Washer or dryer, by the size of it. At the bottom of the ramp he lost control and it tipped over.

Chris sprinted and caught the side before it hit the driveway, righting it as the guy yelled for his partner to get off the phone.

"Careful with that!" A woman bolted out the front door and trotted across the front yard. Definitely not Katherine, the older woman who spent weekends here occasionally. The granddaughter she'd talked about? Mid-twenties. Not too tall. Lean in all the right places. Curves in all the right places. Toned legs that disappeared far too soon into cargo shorts. Pink tank top. Chris tried to keep her eyes focused on the woman's face. Really tried. They refused to budge from her chest. Way-more-than-a-mouthful breasts bounced as she trotted. She felt like purring at the perfection that stopped in front of her.

"If there's a scratch on it, you're taking it back." The woman whipped a disobedient length of wavy hair behind her ear. Wavy *blond* hair. Beautiful seemed too generic a word for her.

Chris gave her sexiest grin, staring into the prettiest blue eyes. Aquamarine. Sparking with feistiness.

Blond and beautiful watched the guys push the dolly up the walkway and then turned on Chris. "It's about time. I've called your office four times. I'll show you where the water heater is."

"Um, actually I'm..." Chris forgot about speaking as the woman's backside came into view. She followed the blonde into the house as if attached by a leash. Damn, she had the cutest tight, round ass. She cupped her hands by her sides. Perfect handfuls.

"Be careful," the woman said to the guys inching the dolly across the hardwood floor around the closely packed furniture in the living room. Continuing through the kitchen and into the laundry room at the back of the house, she opened a door to a tiny closet. "Do whatever it takes to get it working."

Standing so close to a beautiful woman, Chris's body responded the way it automatically did in such situations. She leaned in for a kiss, barely stopping herself as reality reasserted itself. She shook her head, trying to restore blood flow to her brain. "What's the problem?" She wasn't sure why she was offering to help, but a lady in distress was a lady in distress.

"No. Hot. Water." The woman pinned her with those piercing blue eyes before walking away.

Okay, beautiful and bitchy. Chris felt the tank. Cold. She laughed when she realized the problem was an unlit pilot light. Katherine was smart enough to turn it off when she left the last time. Finding matches and a flashlight in a kitchen drawer, she lit the pilot at the base of the ancient water heater and waited to make sure it stayed on. Giving the two Sears employees a sympathetic smile as they maneuvered the washer into its tight space, she went in search of the lady in distress. She found her in the office down the hall, peering over the shoulder of the cable guy as he worked on a modem. Chris waited, indulging in the view of the woman's ass.

"Well?" She straightened to face Chris.

"You'll have hot water in about an hour." She took the woman's hand and set the matches on her palm. A diamond tennis bracelet hugged her wrist. "If the water gets cold again, light the damn pilot."

"That was rude." The woman followed her to the living room. "If you want to be paid—"

"I don't want to be paid." Chris faced the woman who was less attractive by the minute. "I want that car away from my driveway."

It took her a minute to process this. "You're not the plumber, are you?"

"I'm your neighbor who's had a hell of a long day."

"Oh, gosh, I'm sorry. I assumed whoever lived next door was gone for the weekend."

"Well, I'm home, and I'd really like to get to my shower." Chris softened in light of the apology. Okay, half a bitch. She wiped her hand on her jeans and held it out. "Chris Brent."

"Kate Dawson." Strong grip inside soft skin and perfectly manicured nails painted orange with a black "SF" on each.

"Katherine's granddaughter. And…" Reluctantly she let go of Kate's hand. "Giants fan. Watched games with Katherine. Takes her baseball pretty seriously. Recites stats from decades ago."

"You a Giants fan, too?"

"Absolutely. Go, orange." She held up a fist, pleased when Kate bumped it with hers. In fact she didn't care much about sports. Weekends were for motorcycling and working on the house she'd bought two years ago. But it didn't hurt to have something in common with a beautiful woman.

"Three-game series with the Dodgers starts Monday. Want to come over and watch? If we sweep, we'll be a game-and-a-half behind them going into the last weekend."

"It's a date. You here for the week?"

"Staying until Thanksgiving." Kate took keys from a purse on the dining table.

Two months. Chris pumped her fist and then tucked it in her pocket when Kate raised her eyebrows. "Um, it'll be nice to have a

neighbor." Her stomach did a back flip when Kate smiled. She wanted to run her tongue from corner to corner of those full lips and then—
"Katherine okay? Haven't seen her in months."
"Working too much." Kate took keys from a purse on the dining table and walked toward the front door.
"Weren't you taking the bar exam in July? Did you pass?" Chris held the front door open. Kate's shoulder brushed hers as she walked out. Nice-smelling. Girly. Mmmm…
"Got sick and missed it." Kate's voice chilled. "Spent ten days in the hospital."
"Ouch." That explained the bit of sunkenness in her cheeks and circles under her eyes. "But you're okay?"
"Doctor says I will be. Right now I have the concentration of a mosquito and the stamina of a marshmallow." Kate kicked a plastic water bottle that one of the delivery guys must have dropped. It skittered across the driveway. "Gran thinks a change in scenery will perk me up. Along with acupuncture and yoga with a woman in Felton."
"Janie. She's awesome." She'd hooked up with Janie a few times. Great body.
"Oh, so you've taken classes with her."
Chris snorted. "Me? I have the flexibility of a redwood tree." She bent forward. Her hands barely touched her ankles.
"Want to take a class with me?"
"You wear tight spandex pants to yoga, right? And those little…" Chris ran her fingers under her breasts. "Crop tops?"
"You don't have to. They'd let you in in jeans and a…" She pointed to Chris's shirt. "Polo shirt."
"501s." Not just jeans. "No, the pants would get me to class. Nothing I like better than a woman in tight, tight, tight…" She grinned when Kate looked at her as if she wasn't following the conversation. Waited.
"Are you a lesbian?" Kate's cheeks colored a bit. Adorable.
"Since I was twelve." Sleepover at her best friend's house. Fool-around kisses she liked way too much. "You're straight?"
"Seven-year boyfriend."
"You can't be perfect."

"Gran did not warn me about you." Kate opened the car door and slid onto the black leather seat.

"I'll trade you a ride on my Harley for a spin in this." Beautiful blonde with a red convertible. Yes!

"Motorcycle? I don't know."

"Katherine trusted me."

"Gran rode with you?"

"Yep." Say yes. Kate snugged up to her back...arms wrapped around her..."I'll throw in dinner at one of my favorite restaurants." She added another grin. You couldn't offer a beautiful woman too many smiles. "Shadowbrook. In Capitola." Lived up to its reputation as one of the most romantic restaurants in the country.

"I love Shadowbrook. Gran took me there often. Wonder if they still have that cable car that takes you down to the restaurant."

"Still there." So they had something in common. She could work with that. Straight. But she could work with that, too. Almost engaged...a deal breaker unless Kate and her boyfriend had an open relationship.

She watched Kate whip the car around and park across the street, then pulled into her driveway. After putting tools in the garage, she went to her kitchen for the cold beer that was her after-work ritual. She tipped the pale ale into a glass she took from her freezer, downed half, and returned it to the refrigerator. She headed across the living room to the hallway that led to the bathroom and two bedrooms, one of which she used as an office, peeling off her polo shirt and sports bra as she went. Work boots, socks, 501s, then boxers came off into a heap on the bathroom floor.

Hot water pelted her back as she took a brush and worked the dirt from under her nails, then scrubbed away the day's grime from the rest of her. Spreading her legs, she rubbed soap-slicked fingers along either side of her clit. Shower masturbation. The best. A picture of Kate filled her mind and she let the fantasy roam. Naked in front of her, water cascading down her body. She'd take one of those luscious breasts in her mouth and coax the nipple into a peak while Kate moaned and asked her to suck harder. Her clit throbbed and tension built behind it as she imagined putting fingers inside Kate, fucking her, Kate crying out as she climaxed. Pushing two fingers inside, she fucked herself as she came. Withdrawing her fingers, she sucked them, imagining Kate's juices coating them. A beautiful woman deserved to be part of a fantasy.

❖

Kate stretched her calf, bracing against the picket fence that enclosed the small yard. She'd made it through the afternoon without a nap. Progress. A run before Todd arrived. She missed the endorphin high. A mile. No wimping out.

"Let me guess your favorite color." Chris walked toward her. Black Dockers and white button-down shirt, black leather vest. A good look on her broad shoulders and straight waist. The grin that seemed like part of her attire showed the dimples in her cheeks and softened her square face. Short, dark hair was parted on the side and slicked back, but with a chunk pulled forward over her forehead. Movie-star handsome was the phrase that came to mind. A bit like Cary Grant.

Kate tugged at the hem of her pink running shorts, a shade darker than her T-shirt. "You'd look good in pink."

"No yoga. No pink. Hot water?"

"So far."

"Let me know if you need help with anything else." Chris turned to go and then stopped. "Hey, do you like old movies like Katherine?"

"Grew up watching them with her." Kate pulled her heel to her butt to stretch her quad.

"Great! Took a film-appreciation course in college hoping for a date with the instructor. Didn't score the date, but fell in love with classic films. Don't have anyone who'll watch with me. Wanna have a movie night?"

"Depends. Favorite actor?" Kate stretched her other quad. Tight.

"Bogey by a hair over Cary Grant and Spencer Tracy."

"I can live with those choices." Cary Grant was her favorite. "Actress?"

"Katharine Hepburn. Is this a test?"

"Have to make sure we're compatible. Oh, gosh, that's not quite what I meant."

"So are we?" Chris took a step toward her, grinning again. "Compatible?"

"Um, Hepburn's my favorite, too." She didn't know how to react to Chris's flirtiness.

"You know what that means." She took another step, close enough that Kate smelled her cologne. Masculine. "Our first date will have to be *African Queen*."

"Only Bogey and Hepburn film." Surely she didn't mean date, date. She saw Todd's Lexus coming down the street. So much for her run.

He parked, opened the door, and came toward her, pushing his glasses up on his nose. "It's a maze in here and my GPS kept directing me to make turns where there wasn't one. Remote is an understatement." Brooks Brothers head to toe and all in shades of blue. Red-green color-blind, he wore blue most of the time. His boyish good looks, what her mother called his "Kennedy" looks, were an asset with women. His ability to appear intelligent without seeming arrogant an asset with men. He wanted to go into politics. A little shy, but she'd make up for that.

"Chris, this is my boyfriend, Todd." She put her arm around his waist. "My neighbor, Chris."

Chris extended her hand to Todd. "Off to a party up in San Francisco." She walked toward her truck and then turned back. "Katherine and I had a deal when we watched ball games or movies. I'd grill and she'd do a salad. Work for you?"

"Since salad is the extent of my cooking skills, no argument. See you Monday." Chris seemed likable, and it would be nice to have a friend here. She wasn't used to living alone. Alpha Chi sorority house her undergrad years at Stanford. With Nic and Bethany in a graduate housing apartment on campus through law school.

"You're not going for a run," Todd said, frowning.

"A walk."

"Are you up to—"

"Don't." She was tired of people hovering. She helped Todd carry his bags in and waited while he changed into pressed jeans and a short-sleeved shirt, his version of casual.

"Chris is a lesbian," she said as they set out down the street. A warm fall afternoon even in the shade cast by the tall trees. *Sequoia sempervirens*—coast redwood. *Acer macrophyllum*—bigleaf maple. *Arbutus menziesii*—Madrone. *Quercis agrifolia*—coast live oak. The names of the primary trees came back to her as they walked the neighborhood. It had changed since her last visit. Still a good number of small cabins like her gran's but more new-looking homes.

"Should I be worried?"

She swatted his shoulder. "Probably. I doubt you would have figured out the pilot light wasn't lit on the water heater."

"I'll never be the do-it-yourself husband. But you're happy with me anyway, right?"

She studied him, surprised by the question. He rarely seemed unsure of himself. Was this the opening to discuss the sex issue?

"Everyone says we're perfect together." He nodded as if for his own benefit as he took her hand. "We'll have a great life."

She breathed deep, pulling in the air that seemed to have a magic ability to energize as she listened to Todd talk about work. He'd joined his father's law firm, also an estate-planning firm, right after graduation. They would have a great life. All that romance stuff was pointless silliness.

Half an hour later they were home. A little winded, but her muscles felt loose and her skin had a pleasant tingle. She went to the kitchen for water. Stay hydrated, the doctor had instructed.

"Share the hot water?" Todd wrapped his arms around her.

Friends first, her mother said, made for a long relationship. Kate's parents had been perfect complements to each other. Her mother the outgoing one who kept her father's life energized with social events and projects. He the quiet, stable anchor to her exuberance. She'd inherited her mother's ease with people and his love of study and law. She pulled Todd's head down and kissed him. This she loved. The feel of him, solid and comforting. Yes, they were perfect together.

Her phone chirped. "Mother." She debated letting it go to voice mail. She was hurt by her disapproval. Not unexpected but still, it hurt. "I'll join you in a minute." Letting out a long breath, she went to the dining room for her phone.

"I've called twice in the last twenty minutes. I can't bear worrying about you, Kate, I simply can't bear it."

"Todd and I went for a walk. Forgot my phone."

"Anything might happen to you and you'd be in that awful hospital again." Her voice broke.

"I'm sorry." She wasn't the only one who'd been traumatized by her illness.

"I have good news. The massage therapist Marilyn Baxter raves about called. She had a cancellation Monday morning. You have an appointment at ten. She does restorative massage. Doesn't that sound perfect?"

"Means I have to leave here by eight."

"Seven would be better. Her office is near that new bakery I told you about. We can try pastries and decide whether to order their desserts for our party." The day-after-Thanksgiving party that Kate was determined to help with now that she was out of school.

Seven. For years she'd risen at five to run and then study. Since leaving the hospital she'd been sleeping until nine.

"Remember to coach Todd on what we talked about for the fund-raiser." Her mother had given her a list of things Todd and the county supervisor had in common. "I'll arrange for the right people to attend. You make sure Todd is prepared."

She could picture her at the secretary desk in her bedroom, from where she handled her social life. President of her Delta Zeta sorority alumnae chapter and head of the national membership committee. Active in several charitable foundations. On the board of an organization she'd established with her friend, Mrs. Cavanaugh, that promoted women-owned businesses. "I invited Nicole to meet us for lunch at that bistro on Geary. There's a dress shop nearby. I saw a divine Herve Ledger bandage dress that will be perfect for you for the fund-raiser."

"Won't it accentuate the weight I've lost?" Twelve pounds and she'd barely gained back five.

"You have a lovely figure. You want to look your best for Todd's big night and show everyone you're fully recovered. Speaking of which, I'm forwarding you an article on the dangers of mold for the immune system. Old cabin like Katherine's? In full shade and not properly ventilated? Probably infested with mold. It's frightening to think of—"

"I'll talk to Gran about it."

"Your health shouldn't be trifled with, Kate. See that she has it inspected. I have another call."

Kate went to the bathroom and stuck the thermometer in her mouth. Todd was humming in the shower. Her fever usually spiked in the late afternoon and again in the middle of the night. She pulled it out and pumped a fist in the air. Normal. And her most recent lab results were normal. Like she'd told Nic, she'd return home raring to go. Start working in the firm. Bar exam in February. Results mid-May. Officially start taking over her gran's duties. Summer wedding. She stepped into the shower and let the hot water pelt her chest as Todd soaped her back. Her life would be back on track soon.

Chapter Three

Chris wedged her Harley between two cars a block from Georgia's house in the Lower Haight district of San Francisco. She put her helmet in one of the saddlebags and took out the small canvas bag containing what she'd need for the night. Sex required the right attitude, the right equipment, and the right techniques. She had all, thanks to Georgia, her longtime lover and friend. Her boots pounded the street as she strode past typical San Francisco homes jammed against each other. Georgia. She let the name roll through her mind, as ripe and lush as the woman she'd met her first semester as a landscape-architecture major at Cal Poly, San Luis Obispo.

Walking across campus the first day, she saw the gorgeous blonde sitting on a bench, arms stretched across the back, face turned up toward the sun. Long, lustrous hair. Sleeveless, chocolate-brown blouse that showed plenty of cleavage. Hot. Make-me-come hot. She'd passed her when she stopped and turned around. Why not take a chance? This wasn't high school. Probably not a lesbian, but there were worse things than sitting next to such a beautiful woman for a few minutes. She plunked herself down next to said blonde. Unzipping her black leather motorcycle jacket, she stretched her legs out in front of her and crossed her booted ankles.

"Harley?"

Chris glanced at her, surprised. Looked more like the sports-car type. "Brand-new Softail Night Train. Anniversary edition." A graduation gift from her dad. "I'm Chris." She offered her best trying-to-impress smile.

"Georgia. As in the state. Ripe peaches and all that," she said in a faint Southern drawl, full lips tastefully painted with pink lipstick. Totally hot.

They ended up on her Harley after classes and in Georgia's studio apartment by evening. More than Chris dreamed possible with the woman five years her senior, at Cal Poly for an MBA.

"God, you're beautiful." Chris backed Georgia against the door and kissed her. Well, tried to kiss her.

"Take it slow, darlin'." Georgia restrained her with a palm to her chest. "Enjoy the journey." Her voice was as teasing and sensuous as the fingers trailing down Chris's abdomen. "First you set the scene. Tonight I'm in the mood for soft." She lit candles around the casually decorated room and put on mellow country music.

Chris was so horny from an afternoon with a Harley vibrating between her legs and Georgia pressed against her, it was hard to think straight. She captured Georgia, gripping the narrow waist that flared to curves snugged inside tight jeans. How fast could she back her to the bed and get down to the orgasms part?

"Not yet." Georgia lifted Chris's hands from her jeans. "Until you make me want to come from kissing, I'm not lying down with you."

Chris loved kissing and considered herself talented. This shouldn't take long. Should have known better. They kissed with the barest whisper of lips against lips. They kissed so hard her teeth felt bruised. They skated their tongues lightly over each other's and then thrust and parried as if dueling. They nibbled, bit, and tugged on lips and ears, cheeks and necks, more forcefully than Chris was used to, as Georgia taught her the art of exciting without leaving marks.

"How about a little one?" Chris grabbed her crotch, ready to get herself off. "Please? I'm dying."

Georgia brought Chris's hand to her mouth. "If you can come from this, you're welcome to it." She slid Chris's finger into her mouth and gave a sample of what her tongue was capable of. If she ever put it on the spot that throbbed. "That ache is a good thing, sugar. Those nerve endings are there for your pleasure. Let them please you." Georgia released her hand. "Like a great book, we need a tantalizing opening. Undress me."

Chris tugged at the top button. How fast could she remove the blouse?

"Slow—ly." Georgia covered her fingers. "Make me feel special, like a present you're unwrapping with great care." She guided Chris through a seductive unbuttoning coupled with kisses along the exposed skin. When Chris tugged at the button on Georgia's jeans, Georgia stopped her. "Not yet. We're still warming up. Play with my breasts. Find what arouses me."

Chris reached for the straps of the lacy black bra. Now they were getting somewhere.

"Not yet." That phrase again. "Make me want to let you see them. It's a privilege. Earn it. Pay attention. Read my body. Please me."

Chris had slept with a few women, but not anyone like Georgia. She figured obeying her rules was worth it. Pay attention. Okay. She circled Georgia's nipples with her palms, increasing the pressure until she saw a hitch in her breathing and tightening in her neck muscles. Then she massaged them, increasing the pressure until there was another hitch and Georgia sucked her lip between her teeth. Finally, she squeezed the nipples.

Georgia clasped her wrists. "All right, sugar. You're a fast study. Unclasp it." She smiled. "One-handed."

Chris reached behind Georgia and did just that. "Wow." Dumb thing to say, but the sight of lush breasts with pink nipples pointing right at her made speaking difficult.

Georgia linked Chris's arm and walked her to the bed. "My turn." She pulled Chris's T-shirt and tank top over her head, licking her skin along the rising hems. "Sit against the headboard. Let's heat things up." Straddling her legs, she sucked and licked Chris's breasts, gently and not so gently. "Some pain just hurts. Some pain also arouses. I want you to know the difference."

Chris's breath hitched as her usually not-very-sensitive breasts responded to Georgia's attention. "Gonna burst into flames." She pistoned her pelvis, desperate for enough friction to come, but it only made her clit ache more.

"Let's see what you learned," Georgia finally said, arching back onto straightened arms and closing her eyes.

Chris mimicked what Georgia had done, using her mouth, tongue, and teeth to arouse the woman who was way more responsive than any she'd been with. The pleasure of exploring a woman's body in new and sophisticated ways pulled her attention from the demanding ache in her clit.

"Mmm, that's so good." Georgia stopped her by holding her cheeks. "Let's take a break. I want to dance with you."

"Isn't it time for orgasms?"

"Let the parts cool down a bit. Don't worry. We'll heat them up again. Like cooking a meal. You have to know what to add, what your woman likes. Tonight we're adding a bit of romance to sweeten the taste." She snaked her arm around Chris's waist and pulled her tight, fitting her thigh between Chris's. "Bet you've never danced like this." She moved them in a sensuous bump-and-grind that was both arousing and relaxing. After sharing an iced-cold beer in a frosted glass, Georgia took Chris's hand and led her to the bed. "Now we're going to play with teasing."

"Isn't that what we've been doing?"

"Not like this." She directed Chris to sit against the headboard and tied her wrists behind her with leather straps. Standing over Chris, she lowered the zipper of her jeans inch by agonizing inch, blond pubic hair appearing as the fabric separated. When Georgia cupped her own breasts and thumbed her nipples, Chris growled deep in her throat.

"Easy, stud. Never lose control." Georgia straddled Chris's legs, then kissed her in a slow exploration of her mouth. When she moved her tongue to Chris's ear, duplicating what she'd done in her mouth, Chris jerked against the restraints. Georgia licked and kissed down her neck, then sucked her breasts before making her way down to her waistband, leaving a trail of aroused flesh.

"Gonna kill me." Chris moaned as the buttons on her 501s were opened way too slowly.

"You won't die from this. You'll be thanking me soon. Lift your hips." Georgia removed the 501s and traced her fingers up Chris's leg and inside the hem of her boxers.

"Ah, God. Don't tease. Gotta come so bad." She tried to catch Georgia's hand between her thighs.

"Teasing heats up the meal. I want you to feel how little it takes to spice things up. It's always about tension and release, needing and fulfilling. I won't leave you unsatisfied." Georgia stood beside the bed and peeled her jeans down her legs inch by agonizing inch. Finally, she stepped out of them, revealing trimmed curls above pink lips glistening with wetness. She again stood over Chris, this time with her pussy tantalizingly close to Chris's face, offering the intoxicating scent of arousal and sweet perfume. "Mix it up—the slow with the fast, the soft with the hard, the hot with the cool. Few women like a bland meal." She straddled Chris, waving her breasts across Chris's chest as she kissed her, slow and sensuous.

"Turn over, darlin'," Georgia whispered in her ear as she released the wrist straps. When Chris was on her stomach she refastened them. "Spread your legs. I'm going to make it safe for you to find out who you really are." Georgia whisked her boxers off and fastened her ankles to the bed.

Chris complied with curiosity and desire and a bit of fear. She trusted this unusual woman whom she'd spent the last twelve hours with. The more Georgia played with her, the more she realized the value of what she was being taught. This was carefully orchestrated sex, playful and arousing—okay, painfully arousing, but masterfully delivered.

"Restraint allows you to let go of everything but what's happening right now. The freedom to focus on every sensation." Georgia grazed her breasts down Chris's back to her ass, her hair tickling Chris's sides. She did it again, this time erect nipples moved like beads over Chris's skin. Then she stroked Chris's swollen labia, around her clit, and up her crack. "Surrender," she whispered in her ear. "Trust your body to give you pleasure."

At first Chris didn't like the lack of control, but gradually she relaxed. She became acutely aware of everything. The smells of perfume, and scented candles. Music. Soft bed. The straps. Georgia's touch became her world for what seemed like hours. Soft and gentle. Hard and painful. Every sensation became exciting and new and unexpected. Her entire body tingled with arousal.

"Now for the finale." Georgia entered her in a swift, deep plunge.

Chris arched her back and thrust toward the fingers, which stopped. She groaned in frustration and looked over her shoulder, almost coming from the sight of the candlelit woman, breasts undulating as Georgia fucked her. Slowly. Too slowly. "I'm dying here." She yanked hard on the straps.

"Shh, darlin'. Let the straps be your friend. Surrender."

Chris gave herself over to the fingers filling her and then leaving her wanting. Teeth bit along her neck, her back, her ass. Fingers caressed and massaged. The need to come and the frustration of not being allowed to morphed into a new sensation. Intensely pleasurable. She learned to ride that exquisite torture of opposites. She groaned and squirmed with the ache of it, sure she couldn't stand one more minute when Georgia slipped her other hand between her legs and circled her clit. It was so hard and sensitive it hurt. Every muscle in her body tensed as the hands took her higher, rubbing her clit while fucking her hard and fast. She didn't want them to stop.

"Time for release, sugar. Let it go."

She almost didn't want to. "Ahh, God. Gonna come so hard." Her sex burst, hot as fire, waves of heat racing down to her toes and up to her head. She rocked on those talented fingers as she kept coming and coming, the release longer than any she'd experienced. Restraints were released and she was turned onto her side, her head nestled against Georgia's breast. She drifted for what seemed like hours in the gentle embrace that made her feel safe.

She must have dozed because she woke to warmth and wetness against her thigh. She was on her back and Georgia was on top of her, taking her orgasm at last. Chris roused herself, pinching and twisting her nipples.

"Harder," Georgia rasped, her eyes closed, her face a picture in tension. Chris squeezed each breast, pulled on the nipples, as Georgia moaned and rocked faster. "Don't stop, sugar. Here we go… ahh…fucking good…yesss…" Georgia collapsed on top of her and nuzzled her neck as her rocking slowed. "You're a keeper," she said. "Now we rest, and then I show you how to top."

"What's that?"

"Taking the dominant role in sexual play. Like I've been doing with you. I'm a femme top. The way you dress and carry yourself, how you approached me, the way you've tried to take control…you're a natural butch top."

"We're not going to fall in love, are we?" She hated the drama she'd seen in too many of the romantic entanglements between kids in high school. Her dad had cautioned her to go slow, explaining that falling in love brought tremendous happiness but also the possibility of terrible heartache.

"And ruin a good thing? No, sugar. We'll have all the fun without any of the messiness."

That sounded great. She listened as Georgia explained about BDSM and role playing. A whole world she hadn't known existed. A world that intrigued her. By morning she was sure she wanted to know lots more about it.

"How do you know so much about sex?" Chris asked as they ate breakfast at a local diner, innocuously normal after the night's activities. Her crotch, ass, and thighs were so sore it hurt to sit.

Georgia studied Chris over her cup of coffee. "It's as essential as eating or breathing, yet most people don't know what they like." Her face took on a mischievous grin. "I learned the hard way what I didn't like and decided to spend the rest of my life indulging in what I do like." Georgia never elaborated on this cryptic comment, and Chris never pushed. All she knew was that Georgia was from Atlanta and had ended up on the central coast of California by following a woman.

"There are infinite ways to please. Know your strengths. You're butch and a top. Plenty of women will flock to your talents. Always make a woman feel welcome in your bed, sugar. You have to know what she wants before she does. You have to know what she wants even if she doesn't. It's all written on her body if you can read the signs."

They took rides on Chris's Harley, often ending up on a secluded beach or country road. They talked a lot and fucked a lot. By the end of the school year Chris had mastered a new way of having sex. No need for the messiness of emotions she wasn't good at. If she could please a woman like Georgia she could please anyone. And had pleased other women during those months.

She took Georgia on a weeklong trip on her Harley when the school year ended. They went where curiosity guided them, stopping to have sex whenever the mood struck. The trip ended at San Francisco, *where Georgia boarded a plane for Germany, having taken a job with a multinational cosmetics company. They parted with no regrets, no promises.*

She'd run into Georgia at a women-only BDSM party in San Francisco a couple of years ago. She'd instantly recognized the buxom blonde, hair still long and silky, body just as gorgeous. She'd walked up behind her, wrapped her arms around her, and mimicked a Southern accent. "You have to know what she wants before she does." They'd spent that night getting reacquainted and many nights together since.

Chris climbed the steps of Georgia's three-story Victorian, renovated into a work of architectural art, the exterior purple with lavender and blue accents. She opened the front door and walked into the foyer. Women everywhere. Talking. Laughing. Hugging. Kissing. She stood for a moment, inhaling the atmosphere. She loved it here. Hot, no-strings sex. The best kind. The only kind.

She walked to the living room on the right, furnished like the rest of the house in Victorian style skewed toward sensual with plush fabrics and subdued lighting. Georgia was talking to a tanned, exquisitely muscled brunette in a halter that barely concealed large breasts. Chris's stomach did a slow roll. She wouldn't mind tasting those breasts later.

Georgia caught her eye, kissed the brunette lightly on the lips, and came toward her, all hip sway and shoulder roll, champagne glass in hand. Chocolate-colored leather pants moved on her like a second skin. A gold silk shirt was open to the waist, revealing a satiny bra in the same color. "Hi, sugar." Georgia infused her voice with a trace of Southern drawl. She kissed Chris, tasting of Dom Perignon and the strawberry she always added. She ran her fingers down Chris's shirt, tugged the tie, and tucked her fingers in the waist of the pants. "Spend the night?"

Chris's sex contracted. It had been weeks since they'd found time to be together. She ran her hand up Georgia's back. "None of your lovers wanted to come?"

"Didn't invite them. You know how it is."

She'd had her share of women wanting more than she could give. "Who's that?" Chris nodded toward the muscled woman.

"First-timer. Making sure she knew the rules." Sex should be safe so it can be pleasurable. Georgia's nonnegotiable rule.

The front door opened and a woman stepped in, dressed head to toe in studded black leather. She unzipped the jacket and set her hands on her hips as she surveyed the foyer. Matching vest with nothing under it. Jet-black hair pulled into a tight ponytail. Pale skin with eyes as dark as her hair. Bloodred lipstick and nails.

"Trouble?" Chris asked when Georgia stiffened.

"Has a reputation for being reckless. Goes by the name Raven. Dom bottom. Hooks up privately for the most part. Came here last month and provoked an inexperienced top into playing rough with her. Really rough. The top was pretty shaken up. Told her not to do that again in my house."

Dominant bottoms were unusual in the BDSM lifestyle. Chris stayed away from them. She'd also had the experience of someone wanting more pain than she was comfortable providing.

The woman eyed Georgia for a moment, a hard, unyielding look, before turning her gaze to Chris.

"Be careful." Georgia squeezed Chris's bicep.

"Not interested." Chris broke eye contact. Drop-dead gorgeous, but she didn't like the hardness underlying the beauty. Feisty but soft was her style. Like Georgia. Like Kate. Ah, if only.

"Have fun." Georgia kissed her again. Her kisses always telegraphed her mood. Tonight she'd want a little rough play.

Chris went through the living room to the dining room, where food was set out on tables. Servers in short black skirts and lacy bras kept the plates filled and served drinks. She took a beer and walked around, greeting those she knew, introducing herself to those she'd like to know. Kissing and light petting. Anything more blatant was restricted to the bedrooms on the second floor.

Primed with arousal, Chris trucked up the stairs to the second floor, the center of the night's activities. She kissed several women standing in the hallway. No such thing as too much kissing. She went to the large bathroom where cocks and other sex toys, lubes, and condom packets were laid out on shelves. Experienced party attendees brought their own equipment, but Georgia made sure everyone had plenty to play with. She removed her shirt and vest but kept her pants on, locking them and her bag in one of the lockers.

"Nice body." A curvy redhead approached her as she finger-combed her hair in front of the full-length mirror. The woman ran her hands over Chris's shoulders and upper arms, then down her back. "Mmm. My girlfriend would really go for you. We're waiting for the private room. Join us?"

"What are you into?"

"Upright restraint. Whips. You do her while I watch. Then you fuck her."

"Maybe. Need to explore the action. Find me when you have the room." Used to be that was a scene she'd have sought out. In the last year she'd gone for tamer encounters she found easier and just as pleasurable. She needed a break from the hard-core edges of BDSM.

She walked to the first of three bedrooms used for public play. King-sized beds with satin sheets. Soft lighting. Couches for observers. A smaller room, outfitted with an array of BDSM equipment, was reserved for private use. A DO NOT DISTURB sign hung from the doorknob.

A threesome was in progress. A brunette with a tattoo across her upper back was fucking a redhead doggy style, large breasts moving as she pumped into her, while the redhead ate the pussy of a woman under her. A muddled parade of sounds came from the women. A blonde with large hoop earrings was on the couch, skirt hiked up to her waist, legs spread, hips rocking as one hand worked her pussy and the other fondled her breast. Neck muscles taut. Face flushed. The whole scene was too much of a turn-on to resist.

Chris went to the couch on the opposite side of the room. Unzipped her fly. Drove her hand inside her boxers and slid fingers on either side of her clit, avoiding direct contact or she'd shoot off. *Control the burn. Ride it. Let it please you.* So many lessons she credited to that year with Georgia.

The brunette fucked the redhead harder, breasts bouncing wildly. Sounds escalated. Chris locked eyes with the blonde on the couch as one of the women came with an extended, wailing moan. Then the other one came. Loudly. Chris scissored her clit and jerked herself off. Relief flowed through her body, like an infusion of warm liquid. The women on the bed tumbled into a kissing fest.

Chris stood and adjusted her boxers before zipping her fly. She walked to the blonde on the couch and bent over to kiss her. Ahh…the sweet taste of a woman's mouth.

With the edge taken off, she checked out the other rooms. A group of six played in the next one. The constant feel of skin on skin, anonymous tongues and hands all over her body...Maybe.

On to the next room, where two women wearing only black lace panties sat on the bed kissing. They stopped and looked at Chris. One blond. One brunette. Young. Femme. Both had large breasts and pierced nipples. Hot. Chris's clit contracted.

"Wanna join us?" one asked shyly. "We're new, but we know who you are."

Chris walked over and squatted at eye level with them. She had a reputation as a top to be trusted. A reputation she valued. "You a couple?"

"Kinda," the blonde said.

"Okay if you are, as long as you're sure this is what you want." Their gazes flicked to each other and then back to Chris.

"We've done it before," the brunette said, trying to act nonchalant, but her green eyes sparked with excitement and a bit of apprehension.

Chris cupped the brunette's head and kissed her. Then kissed the blonde. Great kissers. A plus. "Both want to be fucked?"

"Yes," they said at once.

"I want to be tied up." The brunette took her girlfriend's hand.

"Not rough." The blonde pushed bangs out of her eyes.

"I'm here to give you what you want. Any size you especially like?"

"Size?" They looked at each other.

"Cock." She didn't like the word dildo.

"Um, whatever you want to use," the blonde said.

Chris kissed each of them and went to retrieve her gear from the bathroom. Inexperienced but adventurous. She liked that. She'd make it good for them. Back in the playroom she stripped and set her harness and several cocks on the bedside table. "What shall I call you?"

"Brandy," the brunette said, "and this is Emma."

Chris kissed between them as she played with their breasts, testing their responsiveness. *Find what pleases her.* Georgia's lessons had given her the life she loved.

"Can you tie me up now?" Brandy asked when Chris finger-fucked her. "I'm ready." More than ready considering how wet she was.

Chris stopped sucking on Emma's breast with a final tug on her pierced nipple that brought another moan from the more vocal of the two. "Face up or down?"

"Up."

Chris fastened Brandy's wrists to the headboard with leather, fleece-lined cuffs. "Ankles?" she asked as two women wearing open robes with nothing on underneath entered and sat on the couch.

"Yes."

Okay, the full ride. After fastening Brandy's ankles to the bed, Chris put on her harness and fitted a medium-sized cock into it, then put a condom over it. Straddling Brandy's waist, her cock on the woman's abdomen, she turned her attention to Emma. This had to be good for her, too. She kissed Emma and worked her nipples erect. "Why don't you masturbate," she said to Emma as she guided her cock into Brandy.

The two on the couch fondled each other's breasts, locked in a heated kiss. Raven appeared in the doorway, pants and vest on, arms crossed. The woman was definitely hard.

Chris put her focus on the women she was playing with. Brandy seemed to like being fucked deep but not too fast. Emma lay on her side, knee bent, masturbating. She stilled inside Brandy and leaned over to suck Emma's breast, hoping to amp up Brandy's excitement. The brunette pulled hard on the restraints. Chris fucked her, backing off when she thought Brandy would come. Make her want it.

"I need to come," Brandy said, breathing hard, her eyes locked on the cock moving in and out of her.

Chris kept her thrusts shallow, building the tension, then fucked her deep and hard.

"I'm coming," Brandy cried out, arching her back.

"Me, too," Emma said, rolling onto her back, rubbing her clit vigorously.

Chris tilted her hips to find the perfect contact on her clit and let herself come as she stilled inside Brandy. Oh, yeah.

"God, that was good," Brandy said, her face sex-flushed.

Chris withdrew the cock and released the restraints. The women embraced and kissed. Raven was gone from the doorway.

"I want that one." Emma pointed to a thick, purple cock. "But don't tie me up."

Chris changed the cock, put a condom over it, and settled on top of Emma, who spread her legs wide. "Why don't you touch her breasts," she said to Brandy, who was looking uncertain.

Chris stroked between Emma's legs. Wouldn't need lube. She fisted her cock and put it against Emma's opening. Emma pushed onto it, wrapped her legs around Chris, and began thrusting. Chris braced on her arms and fucked her, finding the angle and fast rhythm that had her moaning. Emma came but didn't unwrap her legs. More. Okay. Chris fucked her to several more orgasms. Finally Emma's legs collapsed and she said, "No more. That was amazing." Chris left the bed as the two women curled around each other.

"Wanna play with us?" one of the women on the couch asked.

"Need to catch my breath. I'll find you in a bit." She took long kisses from each of them before gathering her gear and leaving the room.

She was in the shower when she noticed a woman leaning against the counter, watching her. Even through the frosted glass it was hard to miss the black hair and red lipstick. She lifted the towel from where she'd draped it over the top of the shower door and wrapped it around her waist before stepping out.

"You were pretty tame in there." Raven's voice had an edge of challenge in it.

"It's what they wanted." Chris dried her hair with another towel.

"Do you always give the client what they want?"

Interesting way to put it. She took her shirt from the locker and put it on. "Everyone should walk away happy." She dropped the towel to the floor with her back to Raven and put on her boxers. She felt the woman's eyes on her as she reached for her pants.

"I know who you are. We'd walk away happy." Raven moved behind Chris and cupped her ass. When Chris started to turn around, she squeezed hard, and moved her body to block Chris into the locker.

Chris relaxed but not for the reason she knew Raven wanted. All she had to do was take the hand pressed to her abdomen about to move inside her boxers and twist it into a wristlock, and Raven would be on her knees. Instead she spread her legs, unwilling to be provoked into becoming aggressive. Not her style.

Raven shoved her fingers inside Chris's boxers and pulled her pubic hair, but in the face of Chris's lack of hostility her excitement visibly deflated. She left the bathroom, her hands in fists at her sides. Yeah, that one was strung too tight.

Chris finished dressing and went downstairs. Danced, which she loved to do. A woman dressed could be as sexy as a woman naked. Warm, soft body in her arms. The tease of it. Breath against her cheek. A thigh between hers. Dancing was intermixed with trips to the second floor to play. As always, she had plenty of invitations from women wanting her to top them.

Raven seemed to always be on the periphery of wherever Chris was. It wasn't until after midnight that Chris saw her enter the private room with a petite brunette whose size belied her reputation as a top who liked the harsher BDSM paraphernalia—whips, in particular. Looked like Raven would get the rough she wanted. Pain to provoke pleasure was one thing. Pain for other reasons, and she suspected Raven had other reasons, was another. Chris stayed away from the more extreme BDSM practices.

Finally, around five in the morning, the party wound down and she waited in the living room as Georgia ushered out the last guests. "I don't know how you survive. All the sex happening and you don't participate," Chris said as they walked up to the second floor. Georgia stayed on hostess duty throughout the night, making sure everything ran smoothly, setting the stage for others' enjoyment.

"I make sure I have something special to look forward to." Georgia stopped outside a door at the end of the hall. She took a sip of champagne, passing the tingly liquid into Chris's mouth and then biting her lower lip and kissing her hard. Georgia opened the door and they climbed stairs to the third floor. Her private quarters, all in purple and blue tones, and every inch of it sensual in furnishings and art.

Chris stared at the painting above the bed of two naked women embracing. "New?"

"A gift on my last trip. I usually don't mix business and personal, but the Italians have no such qualms, and this woman..." Georgia shook her hand in a "she was way too hot" gesture. "If I were ever tempted to settle down..."

"You'd really—"

"Of course not." Georgia lit candles around the room. "I'll be thirty-five in a few weeks. Can you imagine?" She undid the buttons on Chris's vest and spread it. Fastening her mouth to Chris's breast, she sucked as only she could, taking Chris expertly to that point of pain/pleasure.

"Remember your birthday the year we met?" Chris tilted her head back and gripped Georgia's waist as arousal squirmed down to her clit. As much as she liked a steady diet of sex with new partners, she loved the familiarity and trust she had with Georgia. She let go in ways she never did as the butch top women expected her to be.

"Harness lesson. I let you fuck me. Best thing I ever did, taking you into my bed."

"Best thing for me." Meeting Georgia had been worth every penny of tuition.

"You had all the essentials. Just needed refining."

Chris put her palms to Georgia's satiny bra and circled her nipples, increasing the pressure until she saw the hitch in Georgia's breathing and the tightening in her neck muscles. *Read her body. Learn what pleases her.* She massaged the responsive breasts. Hard.

"You know what I thought when we parted company that year? That a beautiful femme would take you off the market."

Chris snorted. "Sounds like you're talking about falling in love. I'm like you, G. I want sex without the messiness of a relationship. No falling in love, no heartbreak." Like Stacy. Like too many friends over the years. She surrendered as Georgia undressed her, each touch of her hands or mouth designed to arouse. Her nipples became painfully hard. Her clit pulsed and wetness coated her upper thighs. Her blood pumped fast and hard with anticipation. It was always so good with Georgia.

"Lie facedown." Georgia's voice was like a caress.

Chris did and spread her arms and legs for the restraints she knew Georgia was in the mood for. After a night of topping, she was willing to let her take control.

"Let me please you," Georgia whispered as she tongued Chris's ear.

Chris's heart beat faster as Georgia fastened wrist and ankle straps. Always that moment of transition from freedom to captivity.

Surrender. Only with Georgia. Fingers filled her, expanded her, then withdrew to leave her wanting, over and over again as Georgia bit her neck, down her back, her ass. She was masterfully taken to the edge of release and then eased away. Tension built in her sex, in her muscles. Her mind went blank, her attention consumed by her body. The need to come became unbearable.

"Let go, sugar," Georgia finally said, riding Chris's leg as she fucked her hard and fast.

Chris moaned and clenched the restraints as they came together, her orgasm stronger than any she'd had all night. She drifted down slowly with Georgia draped over her back, kissing her neck.

Georgia released her and left the bed, returning with a harness and large cock. "Show me your stuff, stud."

Chris fucked Georgia, missionary, doggy, and variations in between, until she'd come as many times as she wanted. They slept in each other's arms for a few hours and then parted with tender kisses. She guided her Harley, the same black Softail Night Train from twelve years ago, through city streets, restored and refreshed in ways only sex supplied. Her clit was sensitive pressed against the crotch of the 501s, and she adjusted the seam to ease the discomfort, a small price to pay.

She headed south on Highway 280 toward San Jose, pulling off an hour later into Palo Alto. She'd pick Stacy up at her house, and they'd do the half-hour ride to Alice's Restaurant to meet her dad. Friends since the summer after Chris graduated from high school, they'd met in a lesbian motorcycle group based in San Jose, which they still rode with. The same age, both headed into landscaping, both Harley riders, and butch, they'd become instant friends. They'd slept together a few times that summer, but while Chris was happy without a relationship, Stacy stuck to her search for the love of her life. She'd seen Stacy through other breakups, but this recent one seemed to break her spirit. Why did people put themselves through that kind of hell?

Chapter Four

Kate looked up from the laptop, her attention caught by a repetitive knocking sound coming from the hillside behind her gran's cabin. Great that it took something to break her concentration rather than it wandering off like a puppy. It took her a minute to find the acorn woodpecker amidst all the trees, plunging its pointy beak into the redwood bark like a jackhammer. The bird darted off in a flash of black wings, red head, and Woody Woodpecker call.

She checked the time on her laptop and closed it. She'd promised the acupuncturist she wouldn't overdo. An hour of decent studying was progress. Standing up from one of the Adirondack chairs she'd re-stained earlier in the week, she went through several sequences of sun-salutation yoga poses, deck boards warm on her bare feet. With plenty of time on her hands she'd looked for ways to take care of the cabin. Chris had suggested staining the deck and furniture as part of winter prepping. She seemed to know a lot about that kind of stuff.

Sitting again, she picked up Nic's romance novel from the side table and sipped more of the nasty tasting herb tea the acupuncturist had her drinking to help with deficient chi and weakened immune system. She'd found the paperback last night in a box of law books, still packed from when they'd moved out of the graduate apartment. Nic's two addictions—romance novels and M&Ms. Red M&Ms in particular. She'd never understand the point of wasting time on these kinds of books. *Passion Untethered*. Ridiculous storyline about good vampires trying to save humans from bad vampires. Beautiful women. Hunky men. All sex crazed. So Nic's style.

She opened to where she'd left off, skimming pages until she came to another sex scene. A female vampire was impaled on the hard maleness of her consort, riding him—Her eyebrows shot up. While she sucked the nipple of a human female locked in her thrall who begged her to do it harder. Kate shook her head. Begging Todd to suck harder? No. She tugged her nipple through her T-shirt and bra. Tugged harder. Then even harder. A pleasant tingle remained when she let go. Would Todd think she was weird if she asked? They never talked about sex. Everything else but not that.

The vampire dragged her fingers between the woman's dripping-wet folds. Oh, please. Women did not get dripping wet. Then plunged them inside the woman's tight, velvety enclosure. The scene played out with everyone having mind-blowing orgasms with lots of crying out their passion. She snapped the book shut. Holding up her left hand she tried to imagine an engagement ring on her finger. A diamond solitaire. Simple. Elegant. That's what she hoped Todd chose. She gathered her things and went inside. Time for a run. Well, walk/run, but she was up to a mile in the week and a half she'd been here. Progress.

She was trying to close the latch on the front gate when Chris pulled into her driveway. Home earlier than usual.

"Problem?" Chris set a cooler down and walked toward her, 501s and green polo shirt dirt-stained.

"Won't latch."

"Screws are stripped from the post," Chris said after examining it. "I'll reset it."

"You shouldn't have to keep helping me." Leaky kitchen faucet. Installing a new showerhead. Unsticking a window. Didn't seem to be anything Chris couldn't fix.

"And miss the opportunity to use power tools?" Chris strode up her driveway and disappeared into her garage. She returned wearing a worn-looking tool belt and carrying a drill. She smiled that easy smile that filled her eyes, a warm milk-chocolate brown. She handed Kate the drill. "Keep pressure on the screw but let the drill do the work." She covered Kate's hand on the first one and then let her remove the rest. After setting the gate against the fence, she showed Kate how to mark new holes in the post. "You drive the screws in," she said, holding the gate in position. Next, they reset the latch.

"I see how this could be addictive." Kate handed the drill to Chris as she latched the gate with a satisfying click.

"Princess learns fast."

"Princess?"

"You know. Because you wear pink so much." Chris pointed at Kate's new Asics. Pink with green stripes.

"Let's break you in with pink shoelaces."

"No. Pink." She pointed to Kate's hair, nodding. "New highlights. More gold tones. Nice. And you've put on a couple of pounds. Must be my cooking." As much as Chris teased her about wearing pink, she also complimented her. Different than Todd's general "you look great" or her mother's fussiness about Kate's clothes and hair. Like Chris really saw her.

"Can we take a spin on the bike?" They'd gone for short rides several evenings as preparation for an all-day outing this Sunday. Riding motorcycles might also become addictive. More fun than she'd imagined, with an undercurrent of risk she liked. "Down to Shadowbrook? You still owe me dinner."

"Friend coming over. Tomorrow after the playoff game?" Day game against Washington in the NLDS opener. "Go, Giants!" Chris fist-bumped her.

"Sure."

One of the best parts of moving here was meeting Chris, Kate thought as she headed down the street at a fast walk. She had a relaxed way about her that Kate found easy to be around. She obviously worked hard, but not obsessively. Had real-world experience, which had led to conversations about the challenges of running a business. Didn't take things as seriously as Kate. Or Nic, who was hounding her to increase her study time. Or her mother, who was driving her crazy with details about the cocktail fund-raiser next Friday, never failing to mention how hard she was working to make sure Todd's big night, his "political launch," went well. She wondered why Chris didn't have a partner. She seemed made for a relationship. Breaking into a run, she drank in the beauty of the forest around her, feeling close to her old self. Yes, her life was back on track.

❖

Chris poured a beer into the frosted glass. Kate's naïveté about house stuff was cute. Fun to teach her. Okay, and she had selfish reasons. Her body close while they worked. Girly smell. Mmm. And having Kate snugged up behind her on practice rides on her Harley. Best kind of torture. Rein it in, she warned her libido. The odds of their bodies sliding against each other were slim. Okay, nonexistent. Very straight. Very committed to Todd.

She headed for her shower. Date with Jennifer tonight. They'd met at a grocery store a couple of years ago where Jennifer flirted with her in the produce section and then invited her for coffee. Explaining that she and her husband had an open relationship and she liked sex with women, she'd asked if Chris was interested in hooking up occasionally. After meeting Jennifer's husband and confirming that it was fine with him, they'd begun to see each other a couple of times a month.

Towel around her waist, Chris was coming out of her bathroom when she smelled the rich, spicy perfume. Jennifer. Smiling, she traced the scent to the living room. A tingle coasted over her skin as she took in the sight before her. Gorgeous blonde stretched out on her brown leather couch. Blouse unbuttoned to show a black lace bra. Naked from the waist down. Fingers wrapped around a large cock, moving it in and out. In and out.

"Made myself at home." Bent-kneed, pussy open to the world, Jennifer fondled her breast with long fingers, nails red. "Driving here makes me horny."

"Don't let me interrupt." Fuck. Her clit throbbed. She loved to watch a woman masturbate.

"Come over here and eat me." The tip of Jennifer's tongue circled her lips. Round and round…

Chris strode across the room, pushed the coffee table out, and sat on the edge of the couch. Pulling the cock out she buried three fingers in Jennifer's pussy. Dripping wet. "You're early."

"Fantasizing about you had me squirming at my desk."

She pinched Jennifer's nipple hard, the way she liked. Kneeling beside the couch, she took Jennifer's clit in her mouth, using the flat of her tongue and a lot of pressure while she fucked her hard. Jennifer tightened around her fingers. Driving deeper, she lightened the pressure on her clit as Jennifer's orgasm started with a long moan.

Finally she lifted Chris's face from between her legs. "Now fuck me with the cock."

Chris hurried to the bedroom for her harness. In the living room she dropped the towel from around her waist, then put on the harness and cock. Lying on top of Jennifer, she drove deep into her as she kissed her.

"Sweet. So sweet..." Jennifer clamped her legs around Chris.

❖

Kate turned the temperature knob again and pressed the ignite button. Her first attempt at grilling. Chris made it look fun and easy. "Oh, come on...How blasted hard can it be to start a barbecue!" She tried several more times and then walked toward Chris's, wishing she didn't have to ask for help again.

About to knock on the slider, she froze and covered her mouth with her hand as she stared into the living room. Chris. Naked. On top of a woman on the couch. Kate's heart leapt into her throat. *Back up. Go home. Don't*—

"Fuck me harder." Kate heard the woman's voice through the open windows.

Back away. Back away. Feet. Would. Not. Move. Heat enveloped her skin as if suddenly in scorching sun.

"You're so damn hot..." Chris straightened her arms and pumped her pelvis faster. The woman's legs were around Chris, hands stroking her back, their movements in perfect sync. Time slowed. She stared, as if locked in thrall. Sexual. Intensely sexual. Uninhibited. Raw. Passionate.

"Like that...perfect...I'm coming!" The woman's voice rose to a long cry.

Kate stared at the woman's face, watching the tension and taut muscles melt into a smile of...what? Relaxation? No. Pure pleasure. Oh, God, she'd never had that look on her face. She had no idea how that felt. Everything inside her collapsed with the realization of what she was missing out on. She backed up. One step. Another. Barged into Chris's barbecue. Something clanged. Chris looked up. Their eyes locked. Kate turned and ran toward her yard.

She bounded up the stairs to her deck, across it, and into the kitchen. She was not a Peeping Tom. She'd been too shocked to leave. How was she going to explain—She jumped when her phone rang. Her mother.

"I called a few minutes ago. You promised you'd keep your phone with you. I can't worry like this, Kate. I simply can't."

"Barbecue. Trying to light the barbecue." Oh, God, why had she gone over there? She forced calm into her voice. "I'm fine." Her heart was beating fast. Okay. People have sex. She walked to the living room. No big deal. What would it feel like to have that look on her face?

"Kate!"

"What?" She walked back to the kitchen, unable to escape the image of—

"I don't like you living there. Not one bit. Anything unexpected and terrible might happen to you, like it did to your father." Her mother's voice caught. "I'd never see you again."

"Nothing's going to happen." Real women did cry out as they came. Was she the only one who didn't? She kept pacing.

"Lucille Cavanaugh offered me…"

What was Chris doing to the woman?

"Kate?"

"What."

"I said Lucille offered me her tickets to that new play everyone is talking about. Saturday night. I invited Todd and Nicole to come with us."

"Sure." That look on the woman's face. She'd give anything to know how it felt to—

"Kate?"

"Huh?"

"I said we'll do cocktails beforehand. At the Top of the Mark, of course. Discuss last-minute issues for the fund-raiser."

"Yes. Cocktails." She covered her eyes. Chris had seen her.

"I heard it on good authority I'll be nominated for president of the Delta Zeta national organization."

"Great news." She'd never thought about two women together. It was…beautiful.

"I need to call about dinner reservations. Come home Saturday morning, and we'll have our hair and nails done and shop for new outfits. Oh, this will be so much fun."

Kate walked back to the deck for the chicken breast she'd planned to grill. Microwave it. A sinking feeling settled over her. She'd never forget that look on the woman's face. Movies. Romance novels. They were based on a reality that *did* exist.

"Hey." Chris came through the gate between their backyards and up the stairs to her deck, dressed in 501s and a black polo, as if she hadn't just been—

"I'm so embarrassed. You said friend." Kate crossed her arms as a flush moved up her neck. "Barbecue won't light."

"No big deal. I'm not shy about sex. Join us for dinner. Jennifer wants to meet you now that she has clothes on."

"I'm not dressed." Really old Stanford sweats.

"You're fine."

"No. Really." Her cheeks burned. "Princess wants to master grilling."

Chris fiddled with the knobs. Didn't light. Lifting the propane tank from the bottom shelf she said, "Empty."

Kate pressed her palms to her forehead and scratched fingers through her hair. "You must think I'm an idiot. How do I fill it?"

"Gas station in town." Chris pointed at the skinless chicken breast on the plate. "I'm grilling chicken wings. Tweaked the BBQ sauce from Sunday. Hot and tangy but sweeter." She'd grilled ribs before they watched the final Giants game of the season. "Easy enough to add this."

"No! I'll microwave it."

Chris picked up the plate and narrowed her eyes. "Don't make me have to eat this breast."

Kate pushed the sleeves up on the sweatshirt as she followed Chris to her deck. Act natural. Pretend you didn't see them having sex. She jerked her gaze away when she realized she was looking at Chris's butt. What *was* she doing to that woman?

Jennifer was seated at the patio table. Silky green blouse over a short skirt. Highlighted, layered blond hair. An engaging smile. Pretty.

"I'm Kate." She buried her hands in the pockets of her sweatpants. "I'm so embarrassed."

Jennifer waved her hand in a never-mind gesture. "Voyeurism can be a turn-on. I hope you saw the best part."

"Sit." Chris pulled out a chair for Kate. "I'll put the chicken on."

Jennifer stopped Chris, pulling her close for a kiss.

Kate watched two squirrels chase each other through the trees, trying not to look at Chris and Jennifer, then realizing she was being ridiculous. Nic and Brian kissed like that in public. Hard. Possessive. Like they couldn't get enough of each other. She sat and crossed her legs, resigned to staying. Couldn't possibly get more uncomfortable than it already was.

"Kate loves classic films." Chris spread ash-edged coals over the grate. She grilled with charcoal instead of propane, like her dad, she'd explained. "Can you believe my luck? And I have her hooked on motorcycling."

"That's one thing of yours I'm never riding," Jennifer said, winking at Kate. "Did she tell you she named her Harley Lauren Katharine?"

"Lauren Bacall and Katharine Hepburn," Kate said, not sure what Jennifer's comment about riding meant. "My two favorite actresses."

"Favorite couple?" Chris asked.

"Oh, please. Is there any other choice than Bogey and Bacall?"

"Had to make sure we're still compatible." Chris grinned at her and then set about putting pieces of chicken on the grill.

"They fell in love on their first film. *To Have and Have Not*. 1938. You can see it in the onscreen chemistry between them."

"The whistle scene," Chris said, coming toward her, dimpled grin in place.

"You know how to whistle don't you, Steve? You just put your lips together and blow." Kate quoted the famous lines, imitating Bacall's deep, sultry voice and then laughing at her silliness.

Chris mimicked Bogart's whistle that ended the scene, striding into her house with a leisurely roll to her hips.

"So you and Chris date?" Kate asked Jennifer.

"Chris doesn't date. She doesn't believe in falling in love."

"How can she not?" Chris loved the same movies she did. Romantic movies about falling in love and happy-ever-afters.

"Why complicate things?" Chris returned with three beers and frosted glasses. "You can have the pleasure of sex without the messiness of broken hearts and all that nonsense."

"So you aren't looking for a long-term relationship?" Kate tilted the beer into the glass and took a long sip. The heck with the acupuncturist's suggestion to stay away from alcohol.

"She hooks up with lots of women," Jennifer said. "One of us wouldn't be enough for her." Jennifer slapped Chris playfully on the butt. "I'm married, but I wasn't as satisfied sexually as I wanted to be. Friends invited us to a swinging party. Saved our marriage and I discovered I like sex with women."

"Sex is one of life's greatest pleasures," Chris said, putting the lid on the barbecue. "If my partner doesn't have as many orgasms as she wants, I've failed as a lover. After all, we're the ones with that special bundle of nerve endings whose only function is pleasure."

"Here's to the clitoris." Jennifer raised her glass. "Women are so much better at knowing what to do with it than men. Have you ever had sex with a woman?" she asked Kate.

"No. No." She shook her head and ran her fingers up and down the glass of beer. "Longtime boyfriend. Almost engaged." Soon. Todd would pop the question soon. "Straight. Monogamous." She shrugged and drank more beer. "I'm…" Prim and proper, Nic would say. "Traditional."

"Aren't we all until we discover there are other options? Sometimes you don't know what you like until you try it. I like threesomes with my husband and another woman. If you and your boyfriend want to explore swinging, let me know," Jennifer said. "You can come to a party with us."

"Sure." Kate tried to sound nonchalant. Her and Todd and— Oh, gosh. Fortunately conversation drifted to other topics. She and Jennifer discovered they'd traveled to some of the same European countries. As soon as dinner was over, she went home. They probably wanted to resume whatever they did together. With clitorises. Oh, God, she was way too naïve.

Back in her living room she checked her phone, afraid she'd missed a call from her mother. Nic had texted.

Essay. Call.

She'd sent Nic her practice essay on a constitutional-law question this afternoon. She sat on the couch, wishing she had another beer as she called Nic. She felt amped up. "If I ask a question, will you not be a smart-ass?"

"Anything for you, sweetie."

"Do you know what swinging is?"

"Context?"

Kate let out a long breath. She had to talk to someone about it. "Parties where you have sex with multiple people."

"My, my. What have you been studying? Little Red Riding Hood moves to the deep, dark forest and—"

"Stop! I had dinner with my neighbor."

"Mountain Mary, the lesbian landscaper who rides a Harley?"

Kate bristled at the fake country accent. She didn't like this nasty, dismissive side of Nic. "A married friend of hers was there. She goes to swinging parties with her husband and also has sex with Chris."

"Which part are you thinking of trying?"

"God, Nic!" She should have known better than to open the subject. "Sorry you're stuck with a best friend who's so naive."

"Lighten up. I love you the way you are."

"I suppose you've experimented with women?"

"When I was younger. Want me to educate you?"

"Funny." The thought was too weird to entertain. Nic was gorgeous, but having sex with her? No. Wrong.

"Todd satisfies you in bed, right?"

"Yeah." She looked at the bouquet on the dining table. He'd sent her all pink flowers. Their relationship was based on solid things—careers, common interests and goals, family connections. Things that would be there long after a few minutes of sex.

"Because if you want to make sure before you marry him…"

"God, no." No! They were perfect for each other. They'd have a great life. A shudder caught her off guard. Jennifer's face as she—

"Then let's talk constitutional law. Essay was good but you can do better."

Kate listened, taking notes on a legal pad. "I've missed these discussions," she said when Nic finished.

"Me, too. Come up to the city tomorrow night. Stay with me. We'll go clubbing. Find your wild side." She had a knack for finding out-of-the-way, often bordering on sleazy, bars. But they always had fun.

"Sure." She owed Nic a night out. "Oh, darn. I can't." Motorcycle ride and Shadowbrook dinner with Chris.

"Your schedule's awfully full for someone with nothing to do but count pinecones."

"Don't be like that. I'll see you Saturday for the play."

"Whatever." Nic ended the call.

Too keyed up to sleep, she went to the office and opened her laptop. She typed "swinging" into the search engine, laughing when Wikipedia was the first reference. She tucked her leg under her as she read. And read. Good lord. A world she had no idea existed. About to close it, she typed in "orgasm." It was after midnight when she stopped reading. Ten percent of women were truly anorgasmic. The rest hadn't found what gave them one. She was not going to be one of the ten percent. Tonight she'd try masturbating. Maybe she needed more stimulation to her clitoris.

Foregoing her usual panties and tank top, she lay naked under the sheets and cupped her breasts. She never touched herself. It seemed too weird. She pulled on her nipple, then twisted it. Mmm... It hardened and she kept doing it, then put her hand between her legs. Not dripping wet. Not any kind of wet. She poked her finger inside her vagina and kept poking as she played with her breast. It didn't hurt like it did when Todd penetrated her, but it wasn't arousing her like in Nic's romance novel. She rocked her pelvis the way Jennifer had. Rubbed her clit. Where was the pleasure from those special nerve endings? Rubbed it a different way as she kept poking with her finger. Nothing was happening. She tried to imagine what it felt like to have an orgasm. Still nothing.

She yanked her hands away and sat up. She picked up *Untethered Passion* from the nightstand and hurled it across the room. It hit the wall with a satisfying slap. She reached for the Sudoku book and flipped to the page marked with her pen. Was Jennifer staying the night? *Five. That square has to be a five.* Would they have sex all night? Multiple orgasms? *Means that box must be a...*

Chapter Five

Chris set chips and homemade salsa on the table on her deck. Finally a Saturday where she wasn't working on an install. She'd convinced Stacy to join her for a ride from Santa Cruz north up Highway 1 along the coast to Half Moon Bay, then inland through the Santa Cruz Mountains. Warm, blue-sky, fall weather. Her dad had met them for the last part of the ride before splitting off toward his home in San Jose. "You look relaxed."

"Hard not to be after a day on the bike." Stacy dipped a chip in the salsa and ate it, chasing it with Corona beer she tipped from a bottle.

"Hibernating isn't good." Chris tossed chips in the direction of a squirrel eyeing them from the corner of the deck. "Plus I wanted to ride with you on your maiden voyage."

"She's a beaut." Stacy's eyes softened at the mention of her new Harley Softail Deluxe.

"Whatcha gonna name her?" Chris stretched out her legs and cupped her hands behind her head. Maybe one day she'd be able to afford a bike like that. "If it sits between your legs it should have a name."

Stacy's face darkened. "How 'bout Faith?"

"Let it go." Another squirrel ran down a Douglas fir, jumping branch to branch, then onto the picket fence between her yard and Kate's and down to the ground like a trapeze artist. She tossed a few more chips in their direction.

"I miss her like crazy." Stacy guzzled beer and banged the bottle down on the table. "I don't get it. Tells me I'm what she always wanted. Best sex she ever had. How special I make her feel. Then goes back to her boyfriend? Fucking straight women."

Chris popped her eyes open as Kate appeared on her deck. She strode across it, through the gate, then sashayed across Chris's deck runway-model style dressed head to toe in—she swallowed hard.

"I found my inner butch." Kate whisked the zipper down the black leather motorcycle jacket. Up just as fast, all the way to her chin, then down to below her breasts. The body-hugging jacket bunched cleavage in the *V* of her T-shirt. "Black isn't my color, but the stitching and rucked sleeves let me keep my outer femme." She twirled, arms held out.

Chris let out a long whistle as she went to Kate and circled her, running her hand over swirls of purple stitching on the arms and back of the jacket. The smell of new leather mixed with Kate's richly scented perfume…her clit contracted. "How did the fund-raiser go last night?"

"Wildly successful according to Mother. You should have come up for it."

"No yoga. No cocktail parties." She knelt and inspected the matching chaps, her face inches from Kate's crotch. Standing, she shoved her hands in her pockets, confining them from the temptation of soft leather wrapped over delicious curves.

"Want to dress right for tomorrow." Kate's first ride with the posse, the nickname for the motorcycle group Chris had been riding with for years. "Hi, I'm Kate," she said, walking to the table. "Salsa from the other night?" She scooped some onto a chip. "That was sooo good over the skirt steak."

"Neighbor with the red BMW." Stacy gave Chris a hard look before tilting back a long swig of beer.

"Stacy with the new red-and-black Harley. Pretty."

"Harleys aren't pretty." Stacy air-quoted the word pretty.

"Are you part of the posse?" Kate asked Stacy.

"Yes." Stacy folded her arms.

"Look what I found." Kate handed Chris a DVD. "The only Cary Grant film neither of us owns."

"*I Was a Male War Bride*," Chris said to Stacy. "He cross-dresses. Hilarious."

"Let's watch it after the game. Go, Giants! We'll take St. Louis, then on to the World Series!" She fist-bumped Chris. "Pregame's about to start. If you don't want to cook I can order pizza."

"Picked up salmon from the wharf. Easy to grill."

"You're welcome to watch the game, too," Kate said to Stacy.

"Not into male sports. Overpaid, drug-using wife beaters."

"That's like saying all Harley riders are Hell's Angels." Kate put her hands on her hips.

"Hardly the same—"

"Lighten up, Stace." Chris massaged Stacy's shoulders.

"Invitation stands." Kate sashayed across the deck. Damn nice fit on those chaps. Damn nice ass.

"What the hell?" Stacy glared at Chris. "You sleeping with her?"

"What? Of course not. She's straight."

"Hasn't stopped you before. She's fucking with you. All that ass-waving." Stacy stood and mimicked Kate's walk. "And what's with your flirting? Whistling? Touching? Ogling her ass?"

"Doing what I do around a beautiful woman." Kate was a recurring player in her fantasies, but that was as close as she'd get to scorching sheets with her.

"Seriously? You cook for her?"

"Show Stacy your inner femme," Kate hollered from her deck before disappearing inside.

"Inner femme? Neither of us has so much as a toenail that's femme."

Chris dropped her head and hefted her foot onto a chair. Unzipped her boot. Tugged off her sock.

"You're fucking kidding." Stacy tapped Chris's big toe. "Pink?"

"Lost a bet about what year the Bogey and Bacall film *The Big Sleep* was released." She pulled her sock on. "Anything new on the Portola project?" A large housing development Stacy was bidding on.

"Meeting with the developers again next week. Looks promising." Stacy dipped a chip in the salsa and ate it, chasing it with beer. "Been thinking. If they hire me I'll bring you in as a subcontractor. Your expertise with native plants would be an asset."

Chris lifted her brows. "Thanks."

"Gotta look out for each other. Want a lead on a job in Palo Alto? Time frame doesn't work for me. Woman wants a backyard put in for a party the weekend after Thanksgiving. Husband's a big real-estate broker. Could get your name out to the right people."

Palo Alto was an hour drive from Santa Cruz. Travel time to meet with the client. Gas expense. Logistics of sending her crew over there and using suppliers she wasn't familiar with. She'd been focusing on building the maintenance side of her business in Santa Cruz. Not what she loved but steady income. Her goal for next year was to expand the design side. Her long-term goal was to have a company as large as Stacy's. She'd have to work outside of Santa Cruz to do that. "Sure." No risk, no gain.

"Can you not bring her on the ride tomorrow?" Stacy pointed in the direction of Kate's home. "Don't need a rich, straight chick pretending to be one of us in my face all day. Jesus. That was Harley Davidson gear. Know how much it cost?"

"A lot less than your Softail." It was cool how Kate had taken to motorcycling.

"You know how you always say there's nothing that getting laid won't fix?" Stacy peeled the label on the Corona bottle.

"Have fun for a while before you go falling in love again." She knuckle-rubbed Stacy's helmet-flattened dark hair.

"I was thinking I'd spend the night. I need someone to make me feel special. Someone I trust." Stacy looked at her, the anger gone, replaced with a look of vulnerability Chris rarely saw from her.

"Um, yeah. Okay." Damn. She'd miss watching the game and this would be tricky. First time after the breakup. More than simply feeling good. This scene had the potential for too much emotion. But they'd always looked out for each other. She pulled Stacy up, held her waist, and kissed her gently.

Stacy sighed and rested her forehead against Chris's. "Do that again."

Chris kissed her until Stacy relaxed in her arms. "Lemme tell Kate I can't watch the game. You start the shower."

❖

The leather chaps creaked as Kate walked through her house to the bathroom. Wearing leather. Riding Harleys. Learning to grill and fix things around the house. The new-and-expanded Kate with an inner butch. She put the thermometer in her mouth and walked the hallway while she counted the seconds. Normal! She danced in a circle, pounding the new boots on the hardwood floor.

Her phone rang as she settled on the couch with the pregame on. "Hi, Gran."

"I made that picture you texted me the screen saver on my phone." Kate had asked the sales clerk at the Harley store to take a picture of her in the outfit.

"Don't let Mother see it." She hated motorcycling behind her back, but it was fun and she didn't want to worry her. She felt completely safe with Chris.

"What's your latest project?"

"How would you feel about your bedroom painted pink?"

"Careful. You might decide it's home. Call me when the game's over."

A few minutes later her phone signaled a text from Nic. She frowned at the response to the picture she'd also texted to her.

WTF!

Riding w Chris on her Harley.

Nic wore leather, and Kate had assumed she'd like the new outfit.

What the hell is wrong with u! Risking ur life w Mountain Mary??

Kate clenched her jaw. Nic never shied away from doing daring things.

Company tomorrow?

Damn. Why tomorrow? Nic had turned down all her invitations to visit. *Sorry. Plans.* Several minutes went by with no response.

Don't b like this. Only till TG. Then all back to normal.

Used to have BFF. Seen her?

Nic had texted a picture of the two of them at graduation.

The back door opened, and Chris appeared in the archway between the kitchen and living room, hands shoved in her pockets. "Have to bail on the game tonight. I can bring dinner."

"Stacy."

Chris shrugged one shoulder, looking uncomfortable.

"Why doesn't she like me?"

"Her girlfriend left her."

"What does that have to do with me?"

"The woman was straight before she hooked up with Stacy. Went back to her boyfriend. You riding with us tomorrow? She's kinda upset about it."

Kate finally understood. "I'm a straight woman invading her territory." She went to Chris. "Is that how you feel?"

"Me? No. You can't help that you're straight. You're fun to be with."

"So are you." She straightened the collar on Chris's polo shirt. "What do I get if I gracefully bow out of tomorrow?"

Chris dropped her head, but her dimpled grin showed.

"Yoga class?"

Chris nodded.

"Crop top?"

Chris jerked her head up, a look of genuine distress on her face.

"Okay. Too much. Pink polo shirt?"

Chris dropped her head again. "Princess will be a great lawyer."

"I know." She walked to the couch. "Yes to dinner. Soon. Princess is hungry." Impossible to be upset with Chris. She wanted to please everyone. She texted Nic.

Yes visit tomorrow.

There'd be another day to ride with the posse. She was curious what it would be like around a group of lesbians. Probably not much different than a group of straight women.

Chapter Six

Kate sprinted the last hundred yards down the street, quads burning. "Yes!" She raised her arms over her head as she crossed an imaginary finish line at Chris's driveway.

"Good run?" Chris was kneeling in her front yard, fiddling with a remote. A coffin lid swung up, and two bloodied hands crept over the edge to the sound of maniacal laughter. Skeletons and spiderwebs hung from trees. Black cats perched on branches.

"Great run!" She pulled in deep breaths as she took the long-sleeved Giants World Series T-shirt from around her waist and put it on. They'd won in the seventh game on Wednesday night. She'd gone home to watch it with her gran. And been pulled in to lunch and furniture shopping with her mother yesterday. "Trail past the lake. Ran most of it." Two miles. The longest she'd done since the illness. She dropped into Warrior II pose, still her favorite. It made her feel strong and balanced.

Chris mimicked her. "How's my inner femme?" She insisted yoga was girly.

She pulled Chris's shoulders back and lifted her arms parallel with the ground. "Bend your front leg more."

"Harder than it looks."

"We need to take you shopping for yoga tights and," Kate ran her hands under her breasts, "a crop top."

"Don't push it, Princess." Chris plucked at her pink Polo shirt. She arranged the legs on a knee-high, evil-looking plastic spider and set it next to the walkway.

"Don't you have enough decorations?"

"Can't resist a few more."

"That's what you said last night when we covered your living-room ceiling with spiderwebs. Ick." Kate waved her hands as if fending off the sticky material. "And then made me carve 'just six more pumpkins.' I'm sure I have carpal tunnel." She shook out her wrist for emphasis. In fact it was a blast tracing the elaborate patterns and using the tiny carving tools.

"Wish you'd change your mind about coming to my party. I want you to meet Georgia and some of my crew."

"I've never liked Halloween." She'd endured sorority parties but never understood the fun of wearing a costume and pretending to be someone you weren't.

"Attacked by a goblin once?" Chris lurched toward her, shoulders hunched and arms out like a scary monster.

Kate squealed and flailed her elbows when Chris grabbed her waist and tickled her. "I gave Billy Bates a bloody nose in kindergarten when he tickled me."

Chris stepped back and held her hands up in surrender. "Brainy with violent tendencies. I like that."

"Remember, I'm making sure you abide by the noise ordinance," Kate said as she walked to her yard. "Ten oh one and I'm reporting the wild lesbians next door."

"Bossy lawyer," Chris called after her.

"You betcha." She'd sent the application for the February bar exam in yesterday. She was studying six hours a day and rocking the essays and MBE practice questions. She. Was. Back. Kate the Invincible. Too bad that wasn't a Halloween costume.

❖

Kate turned the volume down on the TV and answered the phone.

"I'm at the hotel," Todd said. "Be glad you didn't come. Cold and rainy." He'd flown to Boston for a friend's wedding. He hadn't seemed upset she didn't go, but her mother had lectured her on priorities. "Are you up in the city?"

"No. Opted to stay home." She'd decided not to party with Nic, who treated Halloween like a national holiday, going to extravagant lengths with her costume and then dragging Kate and a bevy of friends barhopping until early in the morning. Nic was pissed, but then bitchy was her only channel lately.

"Yeah, I don't understand the whole dress-up thing either. I'll call you in the morning, honey."

Kate turned the volume up, her mind sliding away from the movie, *It Happened One Night*. True she hadn't wanted to give up one of her last weekends here, but it was more than that. She was afraid to go to a wedding with Todd. Afraid he'd drop to his knee and propose. Three weeks until she moved home. Then she'd be ready. She hoped. Anxiety pinched her stomach. She chalked it up to normal fears about such a huge life change. She recited the reasons marrying Todd was the right thing to do. Reasons her mother had reminded her of yesterday. Her heart beat unsteadily, as it always did at this point in her thinking.

She couldn't forget those few moments of passion she'd witnessed between Chris and Jennifer. Masturbating had proved futile. She'd worked up the courage to ask Todd to suck hard on her breasts. It felt good, but intercourse still hurt. At least she was doing a better job of faking orgasms, she thought sourly, after seeing Jennifer come. Obviously it was her problem. She was resigned to accepting that she wasn't capable of having orgasms.

Sadness settled over her as she watched the 1934 romantic comedy that usually made her feel lighthearted. Clark Gable and Claudette Colbert fell in love navigating a series of zany adventures. Maybe she was in love with Todd. Maybe it felt different for her. Softer. Less physical. She suddenly regretted not going with him. A wedding was exactly what she needed to remind her of what she'd always wanted—a solid partner to build a life with. Compatible. Good for each other. She was being ridiculous. She had all of that with Todd. When he proposed, she'd say yes and get on with her life.

Harleys roared up the street and she went to the front door. Like in a parade, two by two the posse made the turn into her driveway, setting off the motion-sensor lights Chris had helped her install. Wearing chaps, the dozen or so women took cowboy hats out of saddlebags and strapped on what Kate assumed were toy holsters and guns. She clapped when several of them doffed their hats in her direction. She'd finally met them last Sunday. Except for Stacy, they'd welcomed her with gracious teasing about being the token straight woman.

She watched the rest of the movie to the background of cars coming down the street, women laughing and talking as they arrived for Chris's party. Maybe she'd pop over for a while. Meet Georgia. She was curious about the woman Chris had been lovers with for longer than she'd been with Todd. Costume. Movie theme. What could she throw together? Pajamas? White sheet for a ghost? Childish. Surely she could find an old dress of her gran's that would do. Searching closets, she'd almost given up when she unzipped a suit bag. Chuckling, she lifted out a light-pink wool suit.

Fifteen minutes later, she walked into the boisterous crowd on Chris's deck. Pumpkins carved in scary faces glowed fiendishly. She joined several of the posse and was tilting a club soda to her lips when she saw Chris walking through the living room, kissing women every few steps. She froze. Gangster costume she knew about, but this wasn't what she'd expected. Perfectly tailored, thirties-style, black pinstripe suit. Black shirt with a white tie. Mustache penciled on her lip. Black fedora perched rakishly. Handsome with her own brand of charm. All she needed to complete the movie-star persona was a beautiful moll on her arm. Kate sauntered into the living room, using plenty of hip roll. Tonight she could be anyone. She gulped when Chris looked her way. If looks could singe…Her heart stuttered and she stopped rolling her hips.

"Who's the *Legally Blonde* chick?" a woman nearby asked.

Chris's eyes traveled from her face down to her pink high heels and back up. Cocky. But something more. Pure appreciation, as if memorizing every inch of what she was looking at. She swept her jacket open and hooked her thumbs in her waistband. "Wanna dance, doll?"

"It's Kate."

Chris's eyes widened and she leaned forward to examine Kate's face. "Next-door Kate?"

Kate took off the sunglasses.

"Um, nice costume." She pulled a cigar out of her breast pocket and puffed it without lighting it.

A woman dressed as Marilyn Monroe, in a replica of the full-skirted, plunging-neckline dress from *The Seven Year Itch*, joined them, complete with a mole on her cheek. She handed Chris a glass of beer. "Georgia," she said to Kate as she linked Chris's arm and sipped from a champagne flute, a strawberry at the bottom.

"My neighbor, Kate," Chris said.

"I've wanted to meet you. You'll have to tell me how you got her into—" Chris clamped her hand over Georgia's mouth and glowered at Kate.

"Wearing them tonight?" Kate smiled sweetly. Pink boxers.

"No! N. O."

"She can't resist a bet." Another movie trivia question bet she'd won. Thank God. Or she would have had to help polish the chrome on her Harley. Inner butch had its limits.

Chris took Kate's arm. "I'll introduce you to Regina, my crew supervisor." Georgia's laughter trailed after them as Chris steered her to a black woman dressed as Storm from *X-Men*. "Regina, my neighbor Kate. Have fun." Chris strode toward the kitchen, glancing over her shoulder once.

"So you're the neighbor who loves old movies," Regina said. "I swear some of these women come just to kiss her." She pointed to the kitchen, where a woman dressed as Cleopatra had Chris in a lip-lock.

"Not quite like sorority parties." Kate shook her head as the kiss went on and on…

"I don't know," Regina said. "My first time kissing a woman was at a sorority party. Delta Sigma Theta. UC Santa Cruz."

"Alpha Chi. Stanford." No kissing. Not even the thought of kissing. The woman dressed as Cleopatra stepped aside and a woman in a Zorro costume took her place, kissing Chris with a lot of enthusiasm. Geez, she should sell those kisses to pay for the party.

"Engaged at the time. Surprised the heck out of me. Spent another six months resisting the truth. I was all the way to the wedding before I stopped denying I'm a lesbian."

"That was cutting it close."

"You're telling me. Slept with my maid of honor the night before the wedding. Bachelorette party. Little too much champagne. Some feelings shook loose."

"You're kidding." Zorro was replaced by a woman dressed as a dance-hall girl. Chris kissed her with as much attention as she had the last two. How could she pour so much into kissing so many women?

"Nope. Next day wasn't fun, but I never regretted it."

"Have a girlfriend?"

"Still looking for the woman who makes me see stars when we kiss. I know, I know. Silly romantic idea." Regina lifted one shoulder.

She talked with Regina awhile. Mingled. Danced a few times. Finally, around midnight, someone rang a bell and women chanted, "Prizes! Prizes!" Kate squeezed into the living room next to Regina.

Chris stood in the center, waving envelopes above her head. "Judges have been mingling with you all night. First category, best-couple's costume." Women banged surfaces, imitating a drumroll. Chris made a big show of tearing open the envelope. "Thelma and Louise!"

Jan and Cara, who worked for Chris, went for their prizes, plastic rings Chris put on their fingers amid more clapping. "Kiss! Kiss! Kiss!" Chris dipped each to catcalls before kissing them. On the cheek. Good-natured boos replaced the cheers.

"Next prize. Sexiest costume." Chris opened the envelope. "Marilyn Monroe!"

Whistles erupted as Georgia walked through the room, perfectly imitating Marilyn Monroe down to the gestures and facial expressions. She wrapped her arms around Chris's neck and hiked her leg up her thigh as cheering escalated. They kissed. And kissed. And kissed. Wow. The intimacy between them was palpable.

A dozen more prizes were handed out, each with a long kiss. Finally Chris shouted, "Last winner. Best costume for a first-timer." She ripped the envelope open. "Elle from *Legally Blonde*!"

Kate's stomach dropped at the same time her heart jumped into her throat. Would Chris kiss her? Regina hugged her. Women parted as she walked on unsteady legs. She took the prize from Chris, a bottled virgin daiquiri.

"Kiss! Kiss! Kiss!"

Chris took her shoulders and kissed her lightly on the mouth, then stepped back.

"That wasn't a kiss," someone yelled. "Kiss! Kiss! Kiss!"

Chris's gaze locked on her mouth. She looked unsure for a second and then engulfed Kate in her arms, dipping her backward and melding their mouths together.

Kate dropped the bottle and gripped Chris's shoulders. Falling backward... Chris's strong arms supporting her...the softness of Chris's lips against hers...the warmth of her mouth as their tongues caressed. Cheering and whistling all around her. She closed her eyes. Stars danced across her eyelids. Heat shot from where their mouths joined and spiked through her body like erratic lightning. She wanted Chris to stop kissing her and never stop kissing her. A series of barking cracks from outside. Fireworks. And then the kiss was over and she was upright and light-headed. Best kiss of your life, a voice in her head shouted. She tried to pull away.

"Not so fast." Chris held her tight as music started.

Kate's body moved into dance position as if she had no control. She didn't. Not when Chris was gazing at her, brown eyes smoldering, holding her in a magnetic pull, the confident, powerful, gangster. She draped her arm over Chris's neck, their cheeks inches apart, her cologne musky and masculine. For this dance she'd be her moll. She shivered when her thigh touched Chris's crotch. A bulge. She forced herself not to look down. The shiver reversed its course and shot up her spine. First impulse was to back up. Second was to press into it. She did. "Is that a gun in your pocket?" She barely recognized her own breathy voice.

Chris's eyes burned deeper. "Yeah. And it's about to shoot off." She shifted her crotch away.

Kate's knees went weak. Was she joking? The grin said she was. Her eyes said she was serious.

"It's called packing," Chris said in her ear. Bodies closed around them as women joined in the dancing.

"Um—" Kate cleared her throat. She couldn't form a single question. She resisted the urge to press into Chris. Then didn't resist. She'd never, not once ever, done anything like this, but she couldn't help herself. "Sexy" shouted through her brain. She was dancing with a woman with a penis-like bulge in her pants while their breasts touched. Her body reacted. Hot. Skin tingling. Nipples taut. Sex throbbing. The song ended. No! More. They stared at each other, breathing hard. Kate ran her tongue over her lips when Chris's gaze dropped to her mouth. Chris's hand tensed on her back as she brought her mouth closer. "I need air." She disentangled herself from Chris's arms. She wasn't Elle from *Legally Blonde*. She was Kate. In a body she didn't recognize.

She pushed her way through the crowd out to the deck. Too hot. Then chilled as misty rain dusted her face.

"Did you enjoy it?"

Kate spun around. Stacy sat alone at a table, dressed as a gunslinger in all-black Western wear.

"You straight chicks always do. Dancing with us. Kissing us. Playing with us. Then you scurry back to your straight lives." She moved her fingers imitating someone running.

"I'm sorry about your girlfriend, but don't take it out on me." Kate forced herself to walk calmly across the deck and through the gate. In her house she stripped out of the suit and hurried into the shower. Tilting her head up, she let the hot water coast down her neck. She'd never reacted like that to a kiss, as if she'd never been kissed. Grabbing the bar of soap, she scrubbed off her makeup, reminding herself that she was Kate. With a boyfriend.

Bundled in sweats, she went to the office and settled at the desk. She opened her laptop. Packing. No, not packing as in shipping material. Packing as in phallus. She pulled a foot onto her lap, massaging it as she read one site after another, as if she'd fallen down the rabbit hole. Soft pack or hard pack? She thought back to the feel of it against her crotch. Seemed both pliable and hard. Well, not hard as in erect. If she was hard-packing, would she fuck—She snapped the MacBook closed. Too much to think about.

Her phone signaled a text from Nic. Selfie. Dressed as a super sexed-up vampire, one arm draped around Brian's neck in a crowded bar, her other arm bent in front of her to show—She put her hand to her chest. Engagement ring on her finger. Big. Gaudy. Everything Nic wanted. She texted a string of exclamation points. Her heart stopped for an instant. Oh, God. Did that mean Todd had her ring? A text came back.

Come home tomorrow! Celebrate!

She was supposed to help Chris take down Halloween decorations tomorrow. Motorcycle ride on Sunday. She texted in return.

Yes!

A couple of days away from Chris and this silly whatever-it-was feeling would disappear. No big deal. She knew what it felt like to kiss a woman. *Best kiss of your life.* "Yeah, so?" she asked aloud. "I was caught up in the moment."

In bed she worked Sudoku puzzles until around two. Then she called Todd, not caring if she woke him. She needed to hear his voice. "I love you," she said the instant he answered.

"What time is it?" he asked, sounding sleepy. He'd be looking for his glasses, which he tended to put down somewhere other than the nightstand.

"Brian proposed to Nic."

"So he went through with it."

"What does that mean?" They seemed well matched and he was Nic's dream guy—handsome, fun, and rich. Her sacred triad.

"They've been fighting lately. He thought a ring might settle her down."

Didn't seem like the right reason to propose. She almost asked if he'd bought her ring but couldn't force the question out. When he asked, she'd say yes.

Chapter Seven

Kate lifted her new sunglasses and fixed them on her head as she made the turn from Highway 9 into Forest Lakes. She zigzagged down the street, top down, shimmying her shoulders for no good reason other than it was Friday. A great weekend ahead. Dinner and a movie tonight. Motorcycle ride tomorrow.

She tooted her horn as she pulled into her driveway and waved to Chris. She stepped out of her car and held up a bag. "Surprise! Thai. My turn to cook."

Chris came over, cooler in hand. "New do." She wiggled her fingers at Kate's hair. "Like the bit of coppery color." She smelled like sweat and dirt and the remnants of her cologne. Someone should bottle that scent.

Kate twirled and lifted her hair, letting it sift through her fingers. "Tried a new stylist in Santa Cruz." Lowlights as well as highlights. Her mother would say it was too bold, but it would fade by the time she saw it.

Chris plucked the sunglasses from Kate's head. "You'd buy jumper cables if they were pink." Frames had a pinkish tint. "Did you fit in studying?" She set the sunglasses back on Kate's head.

"Gosh, that would have been a good idea." It was cute how Chris asked about it in an encouraging way. Versus Nic's bossiness, criticizing, and prodding. She'd thrived on their rivalry in law school, but this was annoying. "Three hours of civil procedure. On the bar exam for the first time in February. Yoga class." She moved into Warrior II. "More civil procedure." Balance, her acupuncturist kept telling her. A healthy life was about balance. "Shopping!" She twirled again.

"Wish I could hire people with your work ethic. Had to fire someone today." She lifted her ball cap and forked her fingers through her hair. "Gimme an hour to shower and do paperwork?"

"I'll go for a run." An uphill trail she'd wanted to try. She jogged in place. Chris's eyes flicked to her chest. Long enough to leave Kate with butterflies in her stomach. They seemed to have taken up residence since the Halloween party a week ago. Since the kiss. And they were now taking wing. So she had a little crush. Harmless. It would pass.

She gathered the bags from her shopping spree and went into the house, sashaying her butt as she walked to the bedroom. She dumped the contents of the bags on the bed. Two romance novels she set on the nightstand. New camisoles. Lacy black bra and panties. Just because. There was a knock at the front door. She went to open it and took a step back as her heart leapt into her throat. "Todd."

Suit bag slung over his shoulder and matching overnight bag in his hand, he walked past her. Dropping luggage on the couch he folded her against him and took her mouth in a gentle kiss. The way he always kissed.

"What are you doing here?" Kate leaned back in his arms.

"Came to surprise Little Red Riding Hood."

"I wish Nic hadn't started that nickname. She's bitchy beyond all reasonableness lately."

"Brian says she's working an insane amount of hours."

Just like Nic. More determination than common sense. Pushing too hard. Not sleeping enough. Not eating right. According to her acupuncturist that's exactly what had let the virus get such a stronghold.

"We closed the Jameson deal," he said, breaking into a smile. "We're now the attorneys for one of the largest real-estate developers in the north bay. Dad admitted I was right about diversifying our services. The other partners wanted to take me out to celebrate, but I wanted to see you. After next week I'll officially handle the account. That license is as good as framed." The July bar-exam results would be released next Friday.

She stepped away and closed the front window she'd unjammed yesterday. It slid down without a scrape or bind. Not an accomplishment that compared to his. No run. No Thai food. No movie. No motorcycle ride. She looked out to the street, adjusting her mood. He'd driven all the way down here. They'd have a great weekend.

"I thought we'd order takeout and have a picnic in bed. We're on our way, honey." He took a bottle of champagne from his overnight bag and went to the kitchen. "Oh, great. Takeout. Smells like Thai," he said opening the bag. "Enough for two?"

"Yes." All of Chris's favorites.

"I need a shower," he said, picking up his luggage. He laid his arm over her shoulders as they walked down the hallway toward the bedroom. Setting his bags on the bed he picked up her new panties. "Nice." He kissed her again before he stripped and headed to the bathroom with his shaving bag. "How's studying? Thought I'd quiz you." His electric razor buzzed.

"Ahead of schedule. Let's take a drive down the coast tomorrow." Kate picked up the suit bag. The internal battle erupted again. She loved Todd. Everything was great. Except. Maybe this was the time to talk to him about…what? She'd faked orgasms for seven years? No. It was her problem. She'd keep her focus on what she loved about him. About them.

The buzzing stopped and he turned on the shower. "All right."

She put the new underwear in a drawer. Unpacked his bag. It was only a weekend. Hung his suit bag in the closet and unzipped it. An entire weekend out of her last two weeks here. Resentment spiked. Then cooled. He'd chosen to celebrate with her, and she owed him a good mood. She took his navy suit from the bag and ran her hands down the front to smooth it. Stopped. A lump. A shudder ran through her; then trembling took up residence in her hands as she reached into the inside breast pocket. Box. Small. She took it out and held it in her palm as she walked to the bed on unsteady legs.

Sitting, she scooted up against the headboard and set the blue Tiffany box on her thigh. This was the moment. *The* moment. Okay. She nodded. Yes. Okay. Taking a deep breath she opened it. Stared at the diamond solitaire.

"This isn't how I'd planned to do this." Todd stood in the doorway, towel wrapped around his waist, hair wet and combed. He picked up his glasses from the dresser and came to sit facing her. Removing the ring from its velvet enclosure he put it on her finger. "Will you marry me, Kate?"

She stared at their joined hands. At the perfect ring. *Say it. One word. Say it.*

"Honey?"

Was this how every woman reacted to a marriage proposal? As if the room was too hot or too small or too…Her breath caught in her chest. She looked for sparks in his eyes under brows that creased as she held his gaze. Was it too much to want to feel singed? She hurried from the room.

"Kate?" He followed close behind her.

In the living room she turned to face him. *Say it. Say yes and step into the life you've planned.* She swallowed hard. The word stuck in her throat as the truth asserted itself, glaringly clear. It would break his heart. Perhaps hers. She took off the ring and laid it on his palm. "I can't."

"I don't understand."

She let tears fall as words poured out unedited. "I'm not in love with you. I'm so sorry. I thought I was. I want to be. I want to be so much."

"How can you not love me?" Anger tinged his voice.

"I do love you. I'm not *in love* with you." She took his hand and led him to the couch. Tugged him down next to her.

The towel fell open. He stood. "I need pants."

Kate tried to gather her thoughts. She couldn't marry him. She was certain of that. But the why was shadowy and illogical.

He returned. Navy pants. Blue shirt, unbuttoned.

Kate motioned him to sit beside her. "Marrying you…" Emotions turned to tears. Filled her eyes and flooded over, looking for escape. "Do I look at you like Susan looks at David?"

"What?"

"Katharine Hepburn and Cary Grant. *Bringing Up Baby*. The way she looks—"

"You're bringing up a ridiculous movie as justification not to marry me?"

"Or how Claudette Colbert looks at Clark Gable in *It Happened One Night*. Or…Bogey and Bacall in—"

"This?" He grabbed the paperback from the coffee table and held it up to her. A man held a woman possessively, their faces close, about to kiss. "*A Touch of Temptation?*" He slapped it down. "You move to this Hansel and Gretel cottage and get carried away in make-believe nonsense, and suddenly you won't marry me?" He stormed to the dining room and gripped a chair, his back to her. "You have to be in love with me. This is what we planned! We're supposed to be married. Supposed to have a great life."

His anger made sense. The edge of desperation didn't. She went to him. "Look at me." When he did, reluctantly, she studied his face. And saw the truth. She'd been so wrapped up in her own confusion, she'd missed his. "You don't have that look in your eyes, either. Like you can't breathe without me." She cupped his cheek. "Don't you want to know what that feels like?"

He set his glasses on the table and let out a long breath. The gaze that returned to her was bruised. Sad.

"I'm so sorry I hurt you. I thought what we had was enough."

"Don't apologize. I have no right to be angry with you. I'm so messed up. I didn't mean for it to happen."

It took her a minute to comprehend. "You're in love with someone else." The shock hit her like ice water and then morphed into an odd sense of relief. She hadn't broken his heart. Relief switched to fear. Who was she without him? Without the certainty of the life they'd planned? For an instant she wanted to grab the ring and shove it on her finger.

"I thought when I moved home, back in the life I'd planned, back with you, it would all go away." He sat and ran his hands through his hair, mussing it.

"Someone in Boston." That's why he'd seemed depressed and unhappy when he first moved home. She sat beside him. "Why didn't you ask her to marry you?"

"She's a waitress. Vietnamese. Has an eight-year-old son. My mother…" He looked at her, genuine anguish on his face. "Will never approve."

"What's her name?"

"Aimee." His voice sounded dreamy and he never sounded dreamy. "I feel guilty as hell. I wanted to tell you. Then I decided that wasn't fair to you. I stopped seeing her." He took Kate's hand. "We're great together."

"That's not enough, is it? We'd have the perfect marriage on the surface but it wouldn't be supported by the right feelings."

"That's the dilemma I've wrestled with for months. The wedding in Boston affected me. Hearing the 'I dos.' I came home sure about honoring my commitment to you."

"Do you want to be with Aimee?"

"So much it hurts."

"That's what matters." She put her hand over her chest as the truth took root deep inside. That burning desire was the heart of a relationship. It couldn't be rationalized or willed into existence. The stuff of romance movies and novels.

He shook his head. "Mother." The word filled the room with heaviness.

"Doesn't get a vote." They shared a look. His parents. Her mother. Would not take any of this well. "I have to tell you something." It was time for honesty between them. "I went to Chris's Halloween party. We kissed. I didn't mean to. It just happened. A joke. And then it was something else."

"You move here and turn lesbian? Oh, hell. I didn't mean that."

"I don't understand it. A crush. I don't know." She scooted her chair close and wrapped her arms around him. "I'm scared. I don't know who I am without you. Without the future we'd mapped out."

Todd gathered her close. Safe. Familiar. Comfortable. "We need to step off the paths preordained for us. Find our versions of happiness before it's too late."

"Gran told me everyone was meant for great passion. I didn't believe her." Butterflies fluttered in her stomach. "You found it. I want to know if I can find it."

❖

"How was your run?" Chris hollered as she closed Kate's back door. Date night. That's how she'd been thinking of it. Fantasizing wasn't a crime. Motorcycle ride tomorrow with Kate's body pressed against her. Bag of takeout was on the kitchen counter. She loved Thai food. She continued to the living room, holding the DVD. She'd bet Kate had never seen this one.

Kate was sitting on the couch, legs drawn up under her, wearing the girly jeans and pink top she'd come home in. She finally looked up, eyes red and cheeks blotchy. Uh-oh...Crying. Chris shoved her hand in her pocket. "What's wrong?"

"Todd came." She took a shuddering breath as she wound a Kleenex around her finger. "He proposed. I said no." Tears made their way partway down her cheeks before she swiped them away. "Sorry," she said in a nasally voice. "You probably hate crying."

No hot water would be a lot easier to fix. Geez. She wanted to say the right thing, but what was the right thing? "Um, should you call your mother? Katherine? Nicole?" More tears ran down Kate's cheeks. Geez. Setting the DVD on the coffee table she sat beside Kate and rubbed her hands on her 501s.

"What am I going to do?"

"I'd say you did it. If everything in you wasn't jumping up and down and cheering him on as he proposed, then you did the only right thing."

"Ever since I got sick it's like I'm not the same person. Like something was damaged and I can't fix it."

"Sounds like transplant shock. You put a plant in the ground. Return in an hour and it's wilted."

"Why?"

"Roots are damaged or it's too hot or for no good reason. With TLC, shade, and a shot of Super Thrive, it's usually okay in a week or so."

"Super Thrive? Is that a joke?"

"Vitamins for plants."

"So, if I take vitamins I'll be all right in a week?" Kate looked at her, a bit of humor behind the tears.

Chris grinned. "Maybe two." That's all the time Kate had here. She wanted her to go home all better. When Kate smiled, her heart did

• 93 •

a back flip. She contained the surge of desire. To hold Kate as she had at the Halloween party. To kiss her. She'd done it for show, and then it had become more. Intense. Passionate. Princess could sure kiss.

"What's it like not to be in a relationship?" Kate's smile faded. "No one to plan your future with." She folded her arms. "To share your dreams."

It's freedom. It's pleasure without messiness or heartbreak. That's not what Kate wanted to hear. Her gaze landed on the paperback on the coffee table. Romance novel. That's what Kate wanted.

"What's it like to have sex..." Kate looked away. "Outside a relationship."

"You do have a relationship. You're totally focused on pleasing each other." *I could show you. I could make you feel better.*

"But when those few minutes are over, what do you have?"

Chris's chest felt heavy, like a slab of concrete. "Why does there have to be more?" Sex and relationships were different things. Don't mix the two and you don't get hurt.

"We're quite a pair. You have sex without relationships and I had a relationship—" Kate cut her eyes to Chris. Something sparked in the pure blue for an instant, then dimmed to sadness. "Have you ever been in love?"

"No."

"Right. Too messy." Kate took the DVD from the coffee table. "*Sylvia Scarlett*. Never heard of it." She turned it over. "1935. First Cary Grant and Katharine Hepburn pairing. She dresses as a boy to escape the police." Smiled as she read more. "So Hepburn finds her outer butch." Kate laughed and kept laughing. She put her head on Chris's shoulder, wrapping her arms around her waist. "Thanks for being my friend."

Chris laid her hand on Kate's head. Stroked the beautiful soft waves of hair. Princess. And so much more. She stood. "I'll heat up the Thai and you start the movie."

They sat side by side on the couch, thighs touching, until the movie ended. Kate yawned. "Time for bed."

Chris's heart did a double beat. What would it be like to scoop Kate up and take her to bed? She shot that thought out of her head.

Because Kate wasn't marrying Todd didn't mean anything had changed. Straight. Friend. "Leave at eight tomorrow?"

"Can't." Kate looked like she might cry again. "Need to go home and tell my mother."

"My plan was to drive up to Sausalito. We'll swing by your mother's on our way home. You can't miss driving across the Golden Gate," she added when Kate looked uncertain. Something she could do for her. A day sightseeing on the bike. Best way to take your mind off problems.

Chapter Eight

Kate opened the front door to her mother's house and stepped onto the tiled entryway. She needed to make it to her bedroom to fix her hair before—

"Kate?" Her mother appeared at the banister on the landing at the top of the staircase. She'd darkened her hair to a deep chestnut color and was letting the pageboy grow out a bit. "Oh, Kate, I'm so happy for you. I heard the wonderful news." Her mother descended the stairs, one hand on the railing, wearing loose-fitting navy pants and top with her usual cardigan. "And you came home to show me the ring. Why are you dressed like that?" She frowned. "And what happened to your hair?"

"My neighbor Chris brought me. On her Harley." She fluffed her hair flattened by the helmet.

"Motorcycle? Why would you be so reckless? Where's Todd? His mother said he was spending the weekend."

"That's what I have to talk to you about." A sleepless night of rehearsing what to say and now words failed her. "I can't marry him." Not the well-thought-out opening argument in her first important case.

Her mother put her hand to her chest as she descended the last step. "I...oh, dear, that's not possible."

"I'm not in love with him." She wanted a different moment. A celebratory talk full of "oohs" and "aahs" and "what a lovely ring."

"Is that all?" Her mother's face softened. "I wish you'd come to me with this. After so long a time those feelings naturally fade and you're left with a relationship of substance, a solid bond that will hold you through life. I thought we'd spoken of such things."

"I was never in love with him."

"Being in love isn't the important issue. It's unreliable. Fleeting. You have responsibilities ahead of you. The law firm, as well as a sizable inheritance. You must choose a husband wisely. A man who understands your station in life. With whom you share the same values and expectations. A man you're compatible with."

"Marrying him…it won't make me happy."

"Happiness is a choice. You set your mind to what is important, and choose to be happy with it. Todd is everything you should want in a husband. Come. I was about to have my afternoon tea. I'll call Todd's mother tonight. We'll work this out."

The doorbell rang. Kate went to open the front door. Chris. "Something wrong with the bike?"

"I didn't want to leave you without…" Chris shrugged her shoulders. "I thought you should have a cheering section."

She threw herself into Chris's arms. Their leather jackets creaked as they hugged. Kate breathed in the smell of her—leather and cologne. "You and Gran make a cheering section of two."

"Not marrying Todd isn't ruining your life."

"Kate?" Her mother asked from behind her.

She stepped away from Chris. "Mother, this is Chris."

"It's nice to finally meet you, Mrs. Dawson."

"Well, yes." Her mother looked at the Harley parked on the circular driveway. She pulled her white cardigan around her and folded her arms. "Kate has told me you've been a help to her."

"Come in," Kate said to Chris. "We were about to—"

"Perhaps she would enjoy a stroll through the garden while we finish our conversation."

Kate stared at her mother. She was talking like Chris was an employee.

"I thought I heard a Harley." Kate's gran marched toward them from the gate at the side of the house. Garden gloves hung from the front pocket of faded cotton pants.

"I thought you had the ballet this afternoon," Kate's mother said.

"Decided to stay home. How was your ride?"

Kate watched her mother as Chris and her gran talked. Arms crossed. Lips pursed.

"Breakfast at Alice's Restaurant," Kate interjected. "It's a biker icon named for the Woody Guthrie song." Her mother's face tightened.

"I'll show you my garden," her gran said to Chris as she headed to the gate. "You know where I am if you need me," she said to Kate.

"You discussed this with Katherine." Her mother's tone was icy.

Kate watched Chris's confident stride, chaps snugged up to her butt, the outline of the wallet in her back pocket. Sexiest walk she'd ever seen. "I called her this morning."

"You should have spoken with me first."

"I didn't want to tell you over the phone." The gate closed and her cheering section disappeared. She went to her mother and hugged her, unable to stop the tears. "Please don't be upset with me." Her mother's hug was stiff. Brief.

"What has gotten into Katherine? Encouraging you to ride on a motorcycle. And you." She gave Kate a hard look. "Abandoning your friends. Nicole says she barely hears from you. You're not yourself. I will not have Katherine turning you into a…" She fluttered her arm. "A mountain person. You must move home. We'll sort this out."

"Todd's not in love with me either."

"Whatever ill-advised ideas you've both acquired regarding romantic love are incorrect. It's a fantasy that never lasts. It distracts you from what is important in a relationship. You must trust me on this."

"I can't marry a man I'm not in love with." The more times Kate said it, the more certain she was she'd done the right thing.

"You and Todd are—" Her mother let out a squeak and clutched her chest with both hands.

"Mother?" Kate rushed to her side and wrapped her arm around her waist. "Mother!" Her mother's face paled as Kate helped her to the nearest chair.

❖

"What do you think of my garden?" Katherine asked Chris as they walked along the path, plants tumbling over from both sides.

"You have a keen eye for plants and design." Chris pulled her attention from the two-story Greek-Revival home. Kate's home.

Opulent in a way she hadn't anticipated. Meeting her the way she had it was easy to forget that she came from this kind of money. They talked gardening as they continued on to the cottage at the back of the property.

Katherine held the front door open. "I baked the cookies you like. Let's eat them on my patio."

Chris sat on the wicker couch on Katherine's patio and helped herself to a chocolate-chip-pecan cookie from the plate on the table in the center of the seating area. Her gaze roamed the small garden behind the cottage, but her thoughts were on Kate. Was she giving her the right support? She knew nothing about relationships.

Katherine took the chair across from her. "I appreciate your looking out for Kate."

"I like teaching her things. We have fun."

"And common interests."

"Huh?" Chris stopped chewing. "Oh, yeah. Old movies."

"And motorcycling. Kate says you've helped her find her inner butch." Hard to tell from her expression if she approved. "I've been thinking about redesigning this part of my garden." She pointed toward the small yard that mimicked the front garden with a series of densely planted beds connected by paths. "I want something contemplative and simple back here."

"How about a labyrinth? I've installed a couple this year." She took another cookie.

"Delightful idea. Kate and I walked several on our trip to Europe some years ago. How soon can you bring me a plan?"

"I don't work up here."

"You do now."

Chris stood when Kate came through the back door of the cottage. She looked upset. Uh-oh.

"I need to stay. Mother isn't feeling well." She'd pulled her hair into a ponytail. Stanford sweatshirt instead of the Harley jacket.

Katherine frowned. Started to speak, then didn't.

"I'm sorry." Chris wanted to wrap Kate in a hug. "I should head out." She'd planned to take her home via Highway 1 along the coast. Stop for dinner in Half Moon Bay. Catch the sunset.

"We'll walk you out," Katherine said, standing.

When they were on the driveway, Chris zipped her jacket and put her helmet on. Then took it off and set it on the seat. She walked to Kate and wrapped her arms around her. Damn, it felt good to hold her. "I had a great time."

"Me, too." Kate stepped back and folded her arms.

She wanted to say more. She straddled the bike. Checked gauges. Waited for the words to form. She looked at Kate. Grinned. "Here's looking at you, kid."

Kate smiled, shaking her head. A smile to remember.

She drove away. Through congested city streets, then south on Highway 280 toward San Jose. She pulled off at one of the vista stops. The sun was an orange ball sliding into the Pacific. Damn. What a day. No doubt she had a major crush on Kate. And she'd agreed to renovate Katherine's garden. Dawson women were formidable. She took her cell phone from her pocket.

"Hey, Stace. You up for dinner…twenty minutes…great." She sat for a while, watching the sun disappear. The sky seemed empty without it.

❖

"What's wrong with Cecelia?" Kate's gran asked as the sound of Chris's Harley faded.

"She nearly fainted. It was frightening. One minute she was fine, the next I had to help her into a chair. I need to check on her."

"I hired Chris to redo the garden behind my cottage. She suggested a labyrinth. I like the idea. Outer journeys that represent inner journeys. Metaphorical significance."

Kate shivered, but not from the cool air. Walking the labyrinth in the cathedral at Chartres. She'd felt like she was walking through concrete from the minute she'd entered it. Trying to convince herself she was fine. That her imagination was caught up in the mystique from everything she'd read. Chilled, weak, and short of breath by the time she emerged. She'd collapsed into her gran's arms, sobbing, feeling like she'd been lost in the labyrinth for days rather than minutes. She'd been ill for several days after.

"That trip exposed you to new people and cultures. You came home changed. And I don't mean deciding to major in art history."

Kate ignored the unspoken implication that Felton was doing the same to her. "Mother asked me to move home."

"Which would be like exiting the labyrinth without completing it. Your illness started you on a journey. Don't you want to know what's at the end of it? Tonight, care for Cecelia. Tomorrow, return to Felton and care for yourself." She cupped Kate's cheek, steely blue eyes locked on hers. "You have responsibilities ahead of you. You must learn what is important to *you* in order to manage them wisely."

Kate hurried to the house and up to her mother's bedroom. She was sitting up against pillows in the center of the four-poster bed, fashion magazines at her side.

"I'm sorry I scared you. It was the shock of thinking I'd failed you. It's a mother's responsibility to always provide the best. You make any sacrifice you have to." Her gaze seemed focused on something far away; then she looked at Kate. "Call Nicole. Have dinner with her."

"I'd rather stay with you. If we had a barbecue I'd grill you the best steak ever. I know," Kate said when her mother looked surprised. "Me cooking. I like doing things for myself."

"You're so like I was. Determined to do for yourself." She patted the bed.

Kate sat, scooting up beside her. "I used to love sitting on this bed when I was a child, watching you dress for evenings out." She rested her head on her mother's shoulder. "Please don't be disappointed in me."

"Shh." She patted Kate's arm. "We Dawsons gather our wits and move on from disappointment. Plenty of eligible men will jump at the chance to date you."

"What does it feel like to be in love?"

"Certainty. That you're with the person who will always be there for you. Who will care for you no matter what. Now, next week we'll get your hair fixed and—"

"I'm going to Felton tomorrow."

"Haven't you had enough of that nonsense?"

"Two more weeks." Two weeks with Chris she wasn't willing to give up.

Chapter Nine

Kate's heart pounded as Chris walked toward her all sexy stride, brown eyes pinning her with a feral gaze as she snaked her arm around Kate's waist, holding her captive before plundering Kate's mouth with a sizzling kiss that went on and on and—she groaned as the image dissolved and her awareness snapped back to the computer screen in front of her. Not again! She shoved her palms against the desk and lifted her feet as the chair rolled backward until she bumped into the bookcase on the other side of her gran's office. She tapped her head against the shelf. Reality. Passing the bar exam. All. That. Mattered.

She shuffled her feet to roll the chair to the desk and checked the time. An hour. Minus untold minutes lost to fantasizing. Little crush. Ha! This weekend she'd move home. Surely the distance would squelch the attraction. It confused her. She'd never been attracted to a woman.

Tossing the pen down, she took the cup of cold decaf to the kitchen. She missed coffee buzz but had promised her acupuncturist she wouldn't get over-caffeinated again. Fifteen minutes of yoga poses. Then glue her butt to the chair and write the practice essay on torts. Nic had ripped her last one to shreds.

Rain pattered against the roof. She loved rain. She shoved through the back door and onto the deck, sucking in gobs of rain-freshened air as she looked up at the trees behind the cabin, a mass of dark silhouettes and drooping branches in the early morning gray.

"You might want to put on a jacket unless you're going for the wet-T-shirt look."

Kate spun around. Chris walked toward her in the way that made her stomach—*Stop. Stomachs do not really drop.* She tugged the long-sleeved T-shirt away from her body, hoping her nipples didn't go taut. Nipples did go taut and she wasn't wearing a bra. "You came home late last night." Lights in her house went out almost immediately. No movie. No sitting next to her on the couch. No hug before she went home.

"Dinner with Dad. Came over to see if my friend made it up yesterday to clear your gutters."

"Yes."

"Call the chimney-cleaning company?"

"Can't come until next week."

"Check to see if your firewood's dry?"

"I peeked under the tarp. Spiders." Kate shook her shoulders, aware her T-shirt was getting clingier by the minute. But Chris didn't seem interested in her chest this morning.

"Let's look." Chris walked toward the wood stacked behind the garage. After lifting the tarp she said, "There isn't enough. I'll have a cord delivered. Do you have flashlights and candles?"

"I don't know." Kate walked into the house. Grabbing a sweatshirt from the laundry room, she pulled it on. "Isn't a storm in drought conditions a good thing? We stay inside and watch movies and eat popcorn."

Chris stomped her boots on the mat before stepping into the kitchen and closing the door. "More like we sit in the cold and dark, play cards or read by candlelight, eat peanut butter and crackers, and pray that a tree doesn't fall and squish us. Predicting winds as high as sixty miles per hour and twenty inches of rain in three days. We'll probably lose power and this road may be closed. It's our only way out." Chris stared at her as if waiting for her to say more. "To things like food?"

"Oh." She didn't like being treated like a child, but maybe this time she deserved it. Gran had scolded her last night along similar lines, but at least she wasn't lobbying for Kate to come home, like her mother was.

"You should go home."

"No. I can take care of myself." She wasn't leaving because of a storm. She went to the hall closet and returned with a flashlight and several candles. She set them on the counter and rummaged in a drawer. "Here." She handed Chris a pen and pad of paper. "Make a list of what I need. I'll go shopping today. Add anything you need."

Chris wrote, tore off the paper, and handed it to her. "If I think of anything else I'll call. Probably won't make it home tonight."

"Hot date?" Kate hoped her tone sounded teasing as jealousy spiked. Someday, married with kids, she'd laugh about the crush.

"Busting my ass on that job in Palo Alto until the storm shuts us down. Completion clause and the client won't budge on it. Stacy brought a crew to help. Shorter drive from her house." Leaves blew in when Chris opened the door.

Kate watched from the kitchen window as she strode across the deck. She was not running home, but apparently she wouldn't see much of Chris either. She kicked the laundry basket. It skidded across the linoleum and thudded into the refrigerator. She hadn't seen her all weekend. Georgia's party Saturday night. Sex party. She kicked it again. Then she'd met up with the posse Sunday in San Francisco. Without her. She hurried through the house and out the front door, running to catch up to Chris as she backed out of the driveway.

Chris rolled down her window. "What?"

"I'm coming with you. I want to help."

"Absolutely not. Your mother will have me killed if I let you work in this weather. And you're supposed to be studying."

Kate gripped the edge of the door. "You've helped me for the last two months. If you don't take me I'll call Regina for the address and drive myself."

Chris worked her jaw and then lifted her fingers from the steering wheel in surrender. "Change. Quickly. Grubbiest jeans and several top layers. I have gloves for you."

"You think I care if my hands get dirty or I break a nail?"

"I care that one isn't ripped off."

"Oh." She hurried to change. She'd helped her gran in her garden. A day planting flowers would be fun. She'd see what Chris did and spend time with her. Takeout for dinner. Movie, snuggled up on the couch. By the time they turned out of Forest Lakes, cocooned in the warmth and earthy, leathery smell of the cab, Kate was lost in another fantasy.

An hour later Chris parked in front of a Tuscan-villa-style home. Obviously new, it looked out of place in the neighborhood of casual, Spanish-influenced homes. "I used to run in this neighborhood when I was at Stanford."

"Are you sure about this?" Chris had been silent on the drive.

She shoved out of the truck and walked beside Chris toward the house. Blue sky was spattered with innocent-looking chunky white clouds tumbling over each other like cubs. They reached the backyard. She stopped. This didn't look like planting flowers. Piles of dirt. Palettes of flagstones and wire-encased bins of rocks dotted the area. Activity everywhere. The sounds of hammers cracked through the air as women worked on a gazebo. Several others wrestled a huge piece of black rubber over a hole about midway in the yard. Pond? Other women were building a stone wall. Regina and women she'd met at the party were moving rocks in the far corner.

"Really sure?"

Kate grabbed the gloves from Chris's hand. "Suck it up and find your outer butch," she mumbled to herself as she pulled them on. You asked for this.

❖

Chris turned into Forest Lakes, relieved to be home. Tired and the drive had been hard once they hit Highway 17. High winds. Headlights shone through the rain that was pelting the truck, illuminating leaves and redwood needles that fell like confetti.

"I love rain," Kate said, "but this looks like something out of *Key Largo*." The Bogey and Bacall film about people trapped in a hurricane. She tucked her leg under her and turned in the seat to face Chris. "Say it again. Princess. Was. A." She twirled her fingers in a "complete the sentence" gesture. "Say it or Princess might find that her schedule is full tomorrow and she can't help you."

Chris narrowed her eyes at Kate and huffed out a breath. "Princess was a help." A surprisingly huge help.

"And in return for my help, Chris Brent will..." She twirled her fingers again.

Chris wanted to grab them, put them in her mouth, and suck each one. "Take a yoga class with you." She worked her jaw. "And wear tights. No crop top!" She adjusted her butt on the seat to ease the stiffness in her lower back from hauling rocks for the dry streambed. Against all odds, they'd finished it.

"Someone would be less sore if she'd—"

Chris growled. Yes, Princess was a help, but also a distraction. To her, and her crew, who undoubtedly all had crushes on Kate. Ass-hugging, low-riding jeans were bad enough, but that strip of skin that showed every time she bent over was too much. And she'd bent over plenty today helping to lay the streambed. That crazy knack she had for figuring out how to set the boulders to make it look natural. Rule of thirds. Rule of odds. Golden ratio. Leading the eye. Landscape-design principles Chris knew well, but Kate came at them from her art-history background. And her ability to arrange flagstones for the path faster than anyone she'd ever seen. Which was why Kate was returning tomorrow. She ran her fingers through her hair and massaged her neck.

"And your neck wouldn't—"

"Do not push your luck." A woman could take only so much, and for an instant she wanted to yank the truck to the side of the road and take Kate's mouth in a bruising kiss. Infuriatingly brilliant and sexy as hell, even dirt-stained and hair a mess. She made the turn into her driveway and jerked the truck to a stop.

"Movie?" Kate reached behind the seat for the shopping bag. She'd insisted Chris take her to buy work clothes. Army Surplus store where they'd also bought what they needed for the storm.

"No. Um…it's late and we have a long day tomorrow." No sitting close on the couch. No. She watched until Kate was safely in her house. She took the rest of the bags into her kitchen and then poured a beer into a frosted glass. God, she hoped the storm wasn't as bad as predicted. Katherine had called her this afternoon, and she'd promised to look out for Kate. The only good thing about this was the excuse it gave her not to sleep at Stacy's. Too clingy lately. Too "always there" every time Chris turned around today. She needed her help to finish the job she wished she hadn't taken. There was no pleasing Mrs. Cavanaugh. When it was over she'd back away from Stacy.

Chapter Ten

Kate turned on lights as she made her way to the bedroom. No movie. Fine. She'd knock out that essay on evidence and send it off to Nic. She dumped the contents of the Army Surplus store shopping bag onto her bed. She stripped out of her filthy clothes, pulled on the gray canvas carpenter pants, and stuck her hands in all the pockets. So stiff she could barely squat. Sitting on the chair she worked her feet into the work boots. Reddish-brown leather like Chris's. As she strutted around the room she imitated Chris's stride. Add the tool belt Chris was loaning her and a bandana around her neck, and tomorrow she'd fit in with the crew. Kate the Invincible.

Her cell phone rang and she hurried to answer it. "You won't believe what I did today, Gran. Worked with Chris and her crew. Now I know why you love gardening. Building from scratch. Creating something that wasn't there before."

"I knew you carried my genes."

"We built a dry streambed. Ingenious way to direct runoff. I used my art-composition knowledge to help lay it out. Then I gave suggestions on arranging flagstones for a path. Apparently I'm good at it. I'm helping tomorrow."

"And physically you're all right?"

"Sore muscles but I feel great." She paced, squatting or bending forward every few steps to adjust to the stiff pants. "I finished everything on your storm-prep list. With help from Chris."

"You two must take care of each other."

She grimaced and looked up. Something big had landed on the roof. "The project is for Mrs. Cavanaugh. Mother's friend. She was incredibly rude to Chris. I want to stick up for Chris, but I keep chickening out. I'm afraid the women I'm working with will think less of me because I know her."

"Class issues are never easy. I've been on both sides of them throughout my life. You'll have to decide what kind of person you are at your core. Then you'll know how and when to act."

"If I speak up I'm afraid she'll tell Mother I was there."

"That does put you in a difficult situation. When you're true to yourself, you always run the risk of someone disapproving. Call me tomorrow when you finish the project. And send pictures."

"Gran?"

"Yes, dear?"

"Nothing." *You're twenty-five years old. Do not ask if you should sleep with Chris.* "Good night."

She stripped and went to the bathroom, then stuck a thermometer in her mouth as she waited for the claw-foot tub to fill. Normal. Pumped a fist in the air and twirled, laughing when she caught sight of herself in the mirror. Hair a tangled disaster. Bruises on her forearms. A small cut on her cheek. Her nails had survived, but she had blisters on her palms.

She washed and then sat back with the water up to her chin. She was running out of time with Chris. She closed her eyes, covered her breasts, and pinched her nipples. What would it feel like if Chris touched them? If she had sex with Chris? She ran arguments for and against it until the water cooled. Stepping out of the tub she realized it came down to one fact. She was too embarrassed to admit to Ms. Lesbian Casanova she'd never had an orgasm.

❖

Chris rinsed shampoo from her hair. Now the good part. She let the hot water run down her back and spread her legs. Rubbing her clit as she fucked herself with her other hand, she let tension build, goaded by images of Kate in those ass-hugging jeans. She'd come up behind Kate as she bent over to lift a rock. Gripping her waist she'd pull Kate's ass into her, cupping her breasts through the sweatshirt, squeezing them as she thrust against her. Clit was hard...so hard... about to shoot off. She held back. She'd unzip Kate's jeans and drive her fingers into her sex as Kate begged to be fucked. Chris let the orgasm take her as she imagined Kate contracting around her fingers as she came. God, she'd needed that relief all day.

Make a move, part of her brain said as she dried off. Only a few days left. No. Kate was straight. Had recently ended a relationship. Not right to hit on her. But...damn. The way Kate looked at her sometimes. Intense. And acted around her. Flirty. No. You're seeing what you want to see. Reality—babysit her through the storm. Send her home in one piece.

She dressed commando style in tattered 501s and a long-sleeved T-shirt. Walking to the refrigerator for another beer, she adjusted the seam away from her clit. Still horny. Masturbating never satisfied the way sex did. And God, she'd had great sex at Georgia's party Saturday night. She frowned. Then why wasn't she fantasizing about those encounters?

She settled on the couch. Scrunching a pillow under her head, she picked up the book of lesbian erotica from the coffee table. Coming-out stories. She opened to one of her favorites. Undid the buttons on her fly. Oh, yeah...her abs tightened as she stroked her clit and drifted into the fantasy on the page. The orgasm collected deep in her belly... almost...almost...the blonde in the story arched her neck and cried out as she came. Chris let the book drop to her chest as she rocketed toward—She jerked up to a sit when the slider opened. The book toppled to the floor, and the orgasm stalled like a kite without wind.

Kate stood frozen in the doorway. "Didn't want to be alone. I should have—Um, I'll...um, leave." She pulled the jacket hood over her head and backed up.

Chris stood, fumbling to button her 501s. "It's okay." She tucked her T-shirt in as she walked toward Kate, her clit burning and oh so in need of release. "I'm done. Little five-finger relief." She went to the sink and washed her hands. "I thought you were headed for a bath and bed."

❖

Kate's body mutinied. Chris's hand down her jeans. Masturbating. About to—She didn't think. There was no thinking. There was only an urgent desire to kiss her. She threw her arms around Chris's neck as she pushed her tongue inside her mouth. Warm. Faintly bitter taste of beer. Her heart pounded as if to escape her chest. Passionate. Hot. The kiss was everything she'd craved.

Chris cupped her butt and then her legs were around Chris's waist. "That's it. Ride me. You're so hot."

Kate realized she was rocking her pelvis against Chris. Oh, God, what was she doing? She rocked harder, the seam of her jeans rubbing against her clit. It felt good. More than good. Could she orgasm this way? She focused on the kiss, on that magical point of contact that sent heat racing through her body. Please, please, please. Let this be the way I can—Angry frustration doused the hope. Fake it. Get it over with. She jerked her mouth from Chris's. Would she know?

She pulled out of Chris's grasp. If she succeeded in faking it this time, Chris would expect them to have sex. She'd know. Kate took a step back. Chris reached for her, brown eyes full of desire. Another step. She fled out the slider and hurried across Chris's deck, rain pouring down on her head. Wind roared through the trees.

"Kate! Wait!"

She stumbled climbing the stairs to her deck. Caught herself on the railing. Wind whipped her hair and blew her jacket open. She hurried across her deck. A loud crack above her was followed by a crashing sound. She looked up into the dark.

"Kate!" Chris tackled her and covered her.

Kate screamed as something smashed through the deck. Wood splintered.

"Are you hurt? Kate!" Chris's voice was frantic as she scrambled off and knelt beside her, a hand on her shoulder, face inches from Kate's.

"Okay." Her hair was plastered to her head and she was shivering. "Okay."

"Oh, God." Chris helped her to her knees and wrapped Kate in a hug so tight it was hard to breathe. "Let's get you in the house." Chris helped her stand and then scooped her into her arms.

She burrowed against Chris's chest. A massive limb, taller than she, was impaled through the deck right where she'd been standing.

She squeezed her eyes shut as Chris took careful steps to the back door. Opened it. Then Chris was carrying her through the kitchen and into the living room.

She set Kate on the couch and knelt in front of her. "Look at me." Chris gripped her shoulders. "Where are you hurt?"

Kate's teeth chattered as she tried to talk. She'd almost been struck by the limb. It might have killed her if—

"Kate!"

"Elbows. Knees. Cheek." She touched below her eye. Winced.

Chris tugged Kate's jacket off and wrapped a blanket around her. "Need to get you out of your wet clothes. Sweats?"

"Bedroom." She couldn't make her teeth stop chattering. She hugged the blanket around herself and pinched her eyes shut. The awful crashing sound. Not knowing where it was coming from.

Chris returned and set red Stanford sweats on the couch. "I'll make coffee to warm you up."

Kate's hands shook as she fumbled out of her clothes and into the sweats. Her mother was right. She shouldn't stay here. She curled her legs under her on the couch, blanket held close around her, listening to Chris moving about in the kitchen.

"Does Katherine have brandy?"

"Sideboard in the dining room if she does."

Chris chuckled when she opened the cabinet. "Leave it to Katherine to have Courvoisier." A minute later she sat beside Kate and handed her a mug. "Wanna quote dialogue from *Key Largo*?"

"Is there a Bogey and Bacall movie for everything?"

"I don't know," Chris said in a Bogart voice. And then they were laughing.

Warmth landed in Kate's stomach as she sipped coffee, followed a second later by the calming effects of the cognac. She drank more.

"I should take you to your mother's. I'd never forgive myself if anything happened to you."

"Princess seriously underestimated the storm."

"Finish your coffee. I'll start the truck and warm up the cab."

"No." She listened to the soundtrack of rain beating against the house and windows as she sorted out her feelings. "Since the illness I've been scared something else bad will happen. Something I have no control over. I want to stay and deal with the storm." She lifted one shoulder. "Crazy?"

"Nah." Chris grinned. "Well, a little. But I get it. You wanna know what you're capable of."

"Exactly." The lights flickered off. Once. Twice. But stayed on. "Will you stay with me?" Kate shivered, but not from cold. Chris's gaze was intense, like a beacon pulling her in. She could taste the kiss coming toward her. Chris's tongue parted her lips and then explored with gentle sweeps. So gentle and yet igniting the heat in her belly. She moaned when Chris cupped her breast and rubbed her nipple.

"Let's scorch the sheets," Chris said in her ear.

Kate tilted her head as Chris licked down the side of her neck. Her body tingled in response. This must be what it felt like to be aroused. Maybe it would be different with Chris. Fear stiffened her. Maybe not. She slid away. "I need to talk to you." She ran her finger around the rim of the mug. How to say it. "At Halloween, when we kissed, it affected me." *Oh, good, Kate, that sounded lame.* She forced herself to look at Chris. "It blew my socks off."

Chris looked surprised. Then a grin spread up her cheeks, deepening her dimples. "It kinda did for me, too."

"I can't stop thinking about kissing you again. About wanting to do more."

"Then—"

"Let me finish." Kate circled the mug with her finger again. "Sex isn't the same for me as it is for you."

"You've never slept with a woman."

Kate shook her head. Oh, the hell with it. She'd always been the "pull the Band-Aid off quickly" sort. "I've never had an orgasm."

"With a woman? I know."

"With anyone."

Chris blinked. Blinked again.

Kate took a long sip of coffee as her insides roiled. Her eyes filled. *Don't cry. Don't.* She brushed tears away with her sleeve.

"Hey. It's okay." Chris put her hand on Kate's shoulder.

"It's not. Lucky me. Part of the ten percent."

"Ten percent?"

"Of women who can't orgasm. I did research."

Chris smiled. It irritated her.

"God, what was I thinking? Having sex with Ms. Lesbian Casanova."

Chris's eyebrows shot up. "Ms.—"

"It's what I call you in my head." Kate looked away, feeling ridiculous. "I don't like you very much at the moment."

"Yes, you do. Took guts to admit that." Chris bowed slightly. "Ms. Lesbian Casanova at your service. You've let me help you with other things. Sex—"

"Isn't like unsqueaking a door. Or unsticking a window." She glared at Chris's amused expression. "Okay. I get your point." She slumped her shoulders. "I'm scared. The thought of living the rest of my life not knowing how it feels to have that look on my face."

"What look?"

"Jennifer."

"So you did see the best part."

"Not funny."

"I want to ask some questions." Chris scooted closer.

"Stay there. What questions?"

"Sex questions. You know that's my favorite topic."

Kate nodded but didn't look at Chris, sure her cheeks were as red as they felt.

"How do you know you've never had an orgasm? They're different for everyone."

"Isn't there supposed to be a buildup and then a big release? That doesn't happen."

"Not with intercourse or masturbating?"

"No."

"With a vibrator or dildo?"

"Never tried. Too weird. Like if I can't do it myself, why would I try it with one of those things. Especially not a dildo. Intercourse hurts. I knew it was supposed to hurt the first time, but it never got better."

"Oral sex?"

"Todd did it once, but nothing was happening. I made him stop because I was afraid he'd know I was faking it. He didn't seem to know when—What?" Chris was staring at her wide-eyed.

"Why didn't you tell him you weren't satisfied?"

"We're not all like you," Kate snapped. "Casually talking about sex. I've never heard my mother *say* the word. You can't let someone think you're enjoying it and then suddenly declare, oh, by the way, I'm not satisfied."

"Sorry. That was thoughtless. I wanna help. We'll play until we find what you like."

"I like kissing. Maybe we should stick to that."

"Not a chance. But we should begin with kissing." And then they were. Hot, wet kisses. Tongues exploring as if old friends. Intense. Finally Chris broke the kiss. "Your sheets or mine?"

It would feel weird to have sex in her gran's bed. Weirder in a bed where Chris had slept with many, many women. "Mine." She took Chris's hand as they walked down the hallway, praying Chris was the answer to her problem.

Chapter Eleven

"What do we do?" Kate stood by the bed, hands clasped, trying to ignore the tenseness that always came with sex.

"I don't have a lesson plan." Chris turned off the overhead light and walked to her. "No taking notes. No pop quiz. Relax and enjoy." She turned on the bedside lamp. "It's all about pleasure."

Pleasure. What did that feel like?

Wrapping her arms around Kate's waist, Chris kissed her, slow and deep. "May I?" She held the hem of Kate's sweatshirt.

Fear nudged Kate as she lifted her arms. Chris had seen many women naked. How would she compare?

Chris licked her lips as she stared at Kate's breasts. "Black lace. My favorite," she said, her voice low and sexy. She kissed along the bra, from shoulder to shoulder, heating Kate's skin everywhere her mouth touched. Cupping Kate's breasts she pressed her thumbs into her nipples, then circled them. "Tell me when something feels good. When it doesn't." Chris sucked below her ear in a way that made Kate want to purr.

"Good." It was already so good. Everything in her felt heavy and full and slow. Maybe this was what pleasure felt like. A dense, heavy-scented, thick jungle of sensation.

Chris pinched her nipples hard through the sheer material, then harder, as she continued to lick and suck along Kate's neck.

Fire shot to Kate's sex. "Okay, really good." She realized her hands weren't doing anything except resting on Chris's waist. In her fantasies Chris had done all the touching. *Relax and enjoy.* She burrowed her fingers under Chris's T-shirt and crawled them up her rib cage to the underside of her breasts. She hesitated. Another woman's breasts...like her own and yet different. *Relax and enjoy.* Expelling a breath, she covered them. Her sex contracted. She mimicked what Chris was doing and pinched the large nipples.

Chris tensed. "I like a light touch on my breasts."

Kate stopped, embarrassed.

"Saying what we like." Chris rubbed her fingers over Kate's cheek. "That's how we learn to please each other."

"I like hard." The words flew out of her mouth.

Chris unhooked Kate's bra one-handed, her eyes sparking with desire. She lowered her mouth to Kate's breast, biting and tugging her nipple while her fingers pinched and rolled the other. Every touch sent a fiery staccato pulse down Kate's torso and into her clit. Those special nerve endings came alive.

Chris stopped and rested her forehead against Kate's, breathing fast. "Time out." She rearranged her jeans at her crotch. "Need to let parts cool down."

"You're that excited?"

"Wanna feel?"

Kate shuddered. She did, but had no idea what to do. She nodded.

Chris tugged her fly open. Taking Kate's hand, she slid it against her abs, down, down...

Kate jerked her eyes to Chris's. No underwear. Her heart thudded against her ribs as her fingers grazed tight curls. She paused, wiggling her fingers through the full bush. Not shaved the way hers was. She slid lower and stopped. Wet. Really wet.

"Told you." Chris rubbed up and down Kate's forearm.

Kate spread her fingers, sliding them through Chris's sex. Labia. Soft. Sensual. She squeezed the ridge between her fingers. Clit. Heat crawled up her arm as she stroked slowly on either side of it. "It's hard."

"Lesbian version of a hard-on." She gripped Kate's forearm. "Stop."

"Did I do something wrong?"

"God, no. It's just...if you keep doing that, your fingers will get a lot wetter."

"You're going to orgasm?" She was stunned that the response was that quick and noticeable. She resumed stroking. "I want you to." Chris spread her legs. "Faster." Her abs tightened. "Harder." Kate pulled her gaze from her hand and looked at Chris's face. She had to see her face. She kept stroking.

Chris's fingers twitched on Kate's forearm. "Fuck…ahh…Jesus, I'm coming…" Her abs relaxed and her body seemed to melt as a smile bloomed, softening her face.

Kate wanted that look so bad. She stilled her fingers. "Was that okay?"

"Beyond okay." Chris pulled Kate's hand from her jeans. "Kiss me."

Thought disappeared into a symphony of sensation. Chris's tongue playing with hers. Chris's hands sliding inside her waistband and massaging her butt. Chris's thigh pressing into her sex. She felt hot and tingly everywhere.

"What if I can't—"

"You can."

Chris sounded so sure. Sure enough that Kate let it chase away the fear. And then they were under the covers, flannel sheets cool but soft. She was naked. With a woman.

Chris guided Kate onto her back and settled on top of her, scissoring their legs. "Okay?"

Kate nodded as she ran her hands up Chris's back, absorbing the feel of her body. Not too heavy. Firm muscles. Soft skin. She sucked in her breath when Chris took her breast in her mouth, tugging and biting her nipple, then soothing it with her tongue. Painful, but it felt good. Arousing. Chris seemed to know the perfect way to touch her. Lost in sensation, she floated until Chris stroked up her inner thigh and into her sex. She tensed.

"Trust me."

Thoughts bounced inside her head, their edges sharp. She wouldn't orgasm. Another failure in her life. Chris touched her labia and clit. She wasn't wet, and it didn't feel any different than when she touched herself.

Chris withdrew her hand and kissed her tenderly. "I need something from home. Lubrication. Promise it'll feel good. Keep the sheets warm."

Kate nodded. As soon as Chris left, she curled onto her side, knees drawn up. Disappointment claimed her. What had she been thinking? It wasn't going to work. She was part of the ten percent. Not even Chris could change that.

❖

Chris pulled on Kate's jacket and hurried as fast as was safe across the slippery deck, past the limb that had nearly landed on Kate. Rain came down in a torrent and trees swung wildly. Everything had happened so fast. The kiss. Kate's confession she'd never had an orgasm.

In her house she collected bottles of lube. Giving a woman her first orgasm was usually something she relished. But this was Kate. Her friend. Someone she felt responsible for. She didn't know how Kate would react, and it worried her. Angry? It had happened when women realized their lack of satisfaction wasn't because anything was wrong with them. Some cried. Or became dependent, as if Chris were now responsible for their sexual pleasure. Giving Kate an orgasm was the easy part. Dealing with the consequences…she tried not to think about it as she hurried back to Kate.

❖

Kate looked up when Chris appeared in the bedroom doorway. Doubt had killed the allover tingly sensation. And then Chris was walking toward her with that easy smile and tousled hair. So damn sexy. Her heart skipped beats as she stripped out of her clothes. Solidly built and flat-stomached like a guy. Small breasts with light-brown nipples. Androgynous. Handsome and beautiful. A shiver ran through her even though the bed was warm. She wanted to touch her.

She set a small nylon bag on the nightstand and scurried under the covers. "Warm me up."

Kate squealed when Chris pressed against her.

"Nothing I like better than cuddling with a beautiful woman on a blustery night. You okay?"

"What's in the bag?"

Chris sat up, pulled out several bottles, and set them on the covers. "Lube. Pick a flavor."

Kate sat and picked up a purple bottle. "I'm not a child and this isn't a lollipop. I know I don't get wet."

"Some women get wet as they get aroused. Some get wet after they come. Others have intense orgasms and never get wet."

"So there's nothing wrong with me?"

"God, no. But everything will feel better if it's slippery."

Her heart beat unsteadily. If she didn't have an orgasm with someone as experienced as Chris… "Do what you have to."

"Give me your hand." Chris squeezed lubricant across the tips of Kate's fingers. "Put it on your clit."

She hesitated. Did she want to go through with this? Then she lay back and bent her knees. She had to know. "It's…warm," she said as she rubbed her clit.

"Cinnamon." Chris feathered her fingers through Kate's hair and then cupped her cheek. "You're beautiful." Chris took her mouth in a kiss as tender as it was arousing. "Can I touch you?" When Kate nodded, Chris put lube on her fingers and lay on her side to face Kate, head propped on her bent arm.

She tried to relax as Chris circled her clit. Please, please…There. Was it hardening? Oh, God, please. "Nothing's happening."

"It doesn't have to happen fast."

"It does. It really, really does."

"Face me and kiss the hell out of me."

Kate let out the breath she'd been holding. They kissed and kissed and kissed, but nothing felt different between her legs. "I told you I can't orgasm."

"We've only begun to explore," Chris said, looking not the least bit worried. "Tell me what feels good."

"That." Kate popped her eyes open. Chris was touching her clit with light strokes along one side. "I like that."

"This?" Chris stroked harder.

"I like the other better."

She circled Kate's opening. "I want to go inside you."

Kate tensed the way she always did before Todd entered her, waiting for it to hurt. It didn't.

• 121 •

"Second finger."

"I like one."

"Going deeper."

Something soft shifted in Kate's belly as Chris moved in and out of her. Instead of hurting, it felt good. When Chris sucked her breast and bit her nipple, she groaned and dug her fingers into Chris's shoulders. Her focus narrowed. Chris's mouth. Chris's finger. So good. "Pressure…inside. Never felt that before." Fullness in her sex and deep in her abdomen.

"That's what it's like before you orgasm." Chris scraped her teeth across Kate's nipple. "I want to put my mouth on your clit."

"Yes." *Anything. Please make me come.* Then she was on her back. Chris was between her legs, her tongue stroking, circling, flicking her clit, her finger deep inside Kate.

Oh, God, what Chris was doing to her. The fullness in her abdomen expanded. Her breath hitched. She'd never been this aroused. "Ooooh…" Kate jerked up. Chris was doing something different with her finger. The fullness in her sex gathered to a point, like the tip of a tornado whirling inside her. Demanding release. Almost painful. And then the pressure exploded, like dynamite, blasting a million pieces of heat through her body, over her skin, up her spine, as if pushed by Chris's finger. Her brain turned to mush, and the most exquisite relief flowed in the aftermath of the explosion. She twirled strands of Chris's hair, the only motion her muscles would perform. She felt like crying. Then she felt like screaming with joy. She'd had an orgasm. A word formed inside the sensation of floating. Pleasure.

"Told you Princess could orgasm." Chris kissed her abdomen, then laid her head on it, finger still inside Kate.

"Feel like Jell-O." The words came out thick and slow past puffy lips. She giggled. "Cherry Jell-O." Her eyelids felt glued to each other. Her body was tingling and more relaxed than she'd ever felt. She let out a long breath as she opened her eyes. "Do I have that look on my face?"

Chris pulled her finger out and scooted up to lie beside Kate. Her eyes were soft, and she sported a ridiculously smug grin. "What do you think?"

"You earned this." Kate traced Chris's lips with her finger, soaking up the warmth in her eyes. Cupping Chris's head, she pulled their mouths together. The kiss was sensual and deep, oh so deep. Finally, she broke the kiss. "Thank you for…what's the term…making me a woman." She giggled again, unable to contain her joy. She threw her arms over her head. "That was amazing. Better than…I don't know…better than anything. I want to do it again. Do you think I can?"

"Oh, yeah. Maybe not right away, but you can definitely do it again."

"Now you'll have to marry me," Kate said, teasing, trying to let Chris know what this meant to her. The grin disappeared. A moment of sadness passed through her when she realized this didn't mean to Chris what it meant to her. She snapped herself back to reality. This night was special and it wasn't over yet. "My turn." She flipped Chris onto her back and lay on top of her. Hesitated. Touching a super-experienced woman was intimidating. She kissed her. That she was good at. Chris squirmed under her. "Am I hurting you?"

"No." Chris's face was tight.

Kate wanted to laugh. She knew that face. Turned on. She pushed her thigh into Chris's sex. "Ride me." She'd never been assertive in bed. She wasn't afraid of her body anymore. She didn't have to fake anything. The freedom was exhilarating.

Chris bent her knees and cupped Kate's butt as she thrust, coating her thigh with wetness. "Ah, God…not gonna last." Her face softened as she came. She nuzzled Kate's throat, bit gently on her skin. "Dangerous to lesbians."

Kate turned her face and their lips met. The tenderness went straight to her heart. She'd expected Chris to be a good lover, but not so tender. Desire surged through her. She wanted more of her. Sliding down, she took Chris's breast in her mouth and cupped her sex. She tried different things with her mouth and hands, reading Chris's responses. She finally dared to press against the entrance to the place she most wanted to feel. Chris stiffened, and for an instant she hesitated. This was personal and intimate in a way she'd never experienced. Then thought ceased and desire took over. She entered Chris, and a tunnel of soft, warm flesh encased her finger. She moved in and out, tentatively at first, then more aggressively.

Chris moved her pelvis to the rhythm Kate set. "Add another finger."

Kate kept her strokes slow and deep as she closed her mouth around the nipple she'd neglected. She stole a glance at Chris's face. Eyes closed, lips parted. Arms stretched over her head. Everything about her was open and inviting. She stroked harder. Chris tightened around her fingers.

"Don't stop…coming…ahh…so good."

All the fantasies, all the romance novels hadn't prepared Kate for the sensation of Chris contracting around her fingers. She laid her head on Chris's chest and pushed in as deep as she could. So beautiful. She kept her fingers inside Chris as she listened to her heartbeat.

"Come up here." Chris pulled on Kate's shoulders. "I need to kiss you."

She withdrew her fingers and shimmied up Chris's body. "Okay for a beginner?"

"More than okay." Chris cupped her cheek, an unusually serious expression on her face, before kissing her.

She snuggled into Chris. Content. Happy. She closed her eyes, her hand over Chris's breast.

❖

Chris lay on her side watching Kate sleep. Damn, she was beautiful all sex-flushed. She'd expected Kate to be careful and analytical. Instead she was bold, responsive, and attentive. Quick at reading her body. Confident when touching. She traced Kate's lips. Princess could kiss. That last orgasm had been a heck of a surprise. She didn't let anyone but Georgia penetrate her but hadn't wanted to make Kate self-conscious by stopping her.

But there were complications she didn't like. Her lovers didn't live next door. They weren't the granddaughter of a woman she considered a friend. She hoped Katherine wouldn't be upset with her for sleeping with Kate. Lovers never worked with her. How would Kate behave tomorrow? Expect to hold hands? Kiss? Her crew would tease her. Stacy would blow a gasket.

Chris feathered her fingers through the incredibly soft hair. She'd given Kate her first orgasm. No better feeling in the world than initiating a woman into the pleasure her body was capable of experiencing. She eased from the bed. She wanted to turn out the lights in the living room. Looked like she was spending the night.

She picked up a paperback on the nightstand. Straight romance novel, based on the hunk on the cover. She read the blurb on the back. Mega-millionaire has a night with a sexy escort. Falls in love against his better judgment. Etc. Etc. Etc. In the end, romance was romance. Always complications.

Chapter Twelve

The carpenter pants chafed as Kate hurried down the sidewalk to Mrs. Cavanaugh's house. She'd dropped Chris off and taken the truck to the small park three blocks away. Ridiculous that Mrs. Cavanaugh insisted they not "clutter the street with their vehicles." She zipped up the jacket against the biting cold, wind whipping her hair every which way. Menacing gray clouds hung heavy in the sky, but it wasn't raining.

"I'm bisexual." She liked the cosmopolitan sound of it. Her first orgasm and it was with a woman. She palmed her hands together in front of her chest in gratitude. New problem. Was it specific to Chris? Would she enjoy sex with a man? Did she care? "I'm a lesbian." Harder to say. Scary to say. Her thoughts were interrupted when she reached the driveway. Stacy. Uh-oh.

"Couldn't drag your ass out of bed?" Stacy continued past her after giving her a scathing look.

She'd forgotten to set the alarm and made them an hour late. Mindless. Sex with Chris had left her deliriously mindless. When she reached the backyard she hurried to join Regina and the crew. Chris was talking to Mrs. Cavanaugh on the patio.

"Put this on." Regina handed her a Brent Landscape ball cap. "No, over the sweatshirt hood. Keeps it from blowing off."

Kate tugged the cap into place and worked her hands into her gloves. Her fingers were stiff and achy, and the blisters on her feet hurt like hell. "What's up?" She pointed toward Mrs. Cavanaugh.

"Woman's a pain. Out bright and early inspecting the path. Demanding we finish it today. Stacy explained we shouldn't lay flagstone because the mortar won't set before it rains. She refuses to listen to reason. Stacy went to buy tarps. We lay and cover."

Chris strode toward them. Pissed written all over her face. She said nothing as she bent and helped Cara lift a flagstone.

Nice butt. Especially naked. Kate shook her head. Ten cups of coffee wouldn't clear the images of last night. Now she understood why women lined up to sleep with Chris. Pleasure, Chris had said. Nothing had ever been just about pleasure. Boy, had she been missing out.

The morning went by in back-aching lifting and moving flagstones. Kate's focus narrowed to visualizing how the peachy-colored flagstones would fit, blocking out the wind that wouldn't let up and the cold that wiggled down her neck. Occasionally she had to cut off a corner the way Regina had demonstrated. Lay it across a two-by-four, score it with a chisel, and tap it apart with a mallet. It always broke cleanly along the score line. Was her life now in two pieces? Before and after? It didn't seem as simple as having her first orgasm.

"Chris!" Mrs. Cavanaugh's drill-sergeant voice arced through the yard.

"Not again." Chris headed toward the house.

"She should help if she wants her yard finished under impossible conditions," Cara grumbled. "My flipping fingers are so cold I can barely move them."

Kate shoved to her feet and took off her gloves. She knew what kind of person she wanted to be. She hurried after Chris, stopping beside her in front of Mrs. Cavanaugh. Chris glanced at her, frowning.

"My party planner insists on seeing exactly what the space will look like," Mrs. Cavanaugh said.

"I can't put those trees in the ground." Chris pointed to the dozen boxed trees lined up along the fence. "They'll be matchsticks by the time the storm's over."

"Mrs. Cavanaugh." Kate took off the baseball cap and pushed the hood back. God, her hair undoubtedly looked awful. "Kate Dawson."

Mrs. Cavanaugh frowned, then looked puzzled. "Kate?" She looked her up and down. "What are you doing here?"

"Chris is my friend." She put her hand on Chris's shoulder, more for her benefit than anything else. "I'm helping her."

"You shouldn't be out in this weather."

Kate bristled. "You don't want to pay for replacement trees. What if they move them into place in the boxes and you take pictures? Then move them back where they're protected."

"Do you know how much time we'll waste moving those trees?" Stacy asked, stepping next to Chris. "Any idea how heavy they are?"

"We can make it work." Chris gave Kate a look somewhere between grateful and irritated. "Take about an hour. That okay with you?"

"I suppose it will have to be," Mrs. Cavanaugh said.

Chris strode toward the trees.

Stacy glared at Kate for a long moment, then ran after Chris.

Mrs. Cavanaugh put her hands on her hips, shaking her head. "I gave Chris the job because of my commitment to supporting women-owned businesses. I'm not—"

"And she came highly recommended, I'm sure."

"Well, yes."

"It's not her fault there's an early storm." Or that you delayed them by changing your mind about materials several times.

"Nor is it my fault." Mrs. Cavanaugh opened the door to the house. "Come inside where it's warm."

"I'm fine." Kate pulled her hood up and set the cap over it as she hurried back to work.

"Could have told me you know her," Chris said, intercepting her.

"I was embarrassed."

"Then why did you volunteer to help if—"

"No!" She held up her hands. "Not embarrassed to be working with you. Embarrassed about her behavior. I've never seen her act like that. I don't want you or your crew to think less of me because I know her."

"Oh." Chris let out a long breath. "She gonna tell your mother?"

"Probably." Pride at having done the right thing shriveled when she pictured her mother marching into the backyard and dragging Kate to her Mercedes. Everything felt overwhelming, as if she didn't know who she was anymore. Something had changed deep inside since she'd moved to Felton. It frightened her.

Chris shot her that grin that made everything all right and put her arm across Kate's shoulders. "That princess stuff? You know I'm teasing, right?"

"I know." She leaned into Chris, settled by her solid presence. Stacy watched them from over by the boxed trees. She did not look happy. Neither did the crew when she returned.

"Mrs. Cavanaugh is a friend of my mother," Kate said. "The way she's behaved isn't okay with me."

One by one the women clapped her on the shoulder, adding versions of, "You're nothing like her."

They worked through lunch, celebrating every additional ten feet, camaraderie a buffer to the cold and pain. Late afternoon the wind quieted. Spooky quiet. The sky darkened so much it was hard to see what they were doing. Twice she nicked a finger with the hammer, the pain made worse by the cold.

"Let's see if the lights work," Chris called to Stacy. A few minutes later, knee-high copper lights spewed weak light onto the path.

Stacy and her crew gathered around them. "Fifteen feet to go," someone called out after a while. Then, "Ten feet." Then, "Five feet."

"That one." Kate pointed to a large flagstone. "Then flip that one and ninety-degree it." She pointed to another. "I'll take the corner off this one." She tapped her foot on a third. Five minutes later, she and Chris lifted the last stone into place. Jan leveled it. Cara slapped mortar around it. Everyone cheered and high-fived.

Regina picked Kate up in a bear hug and twirled her around. The rest of the crew lined up to hug her. Today she belonged with these women and she was darn proud of it. Chris was the last. She expected a quick hug, but when Chris didn't let go, neither did she. Chris had let her become someone she didn't know she could be.

The first fat raindrops fell, and they scrambled to lay tarps and put tools under cover. Then they all ran toward the park and their vehicles. Kate sprinted the last hundred feet, blisters from the work boots be damned. She held up her arms when she reached Chris's truck. Kate the Invincible.

Chris unlocked the truck door and held it open for her. As she moved past her, Chris grabbed her around the waist and kissed her.

"I've needed to do this all day," she said against Kate's lips before burying her tongue in Kate's mouth again.

"Chris!" Stacy. Bearing down on them. "What the fuck! You're sleeping with her?" Stacy stopped inches from them. "How damn stupid can you be!"

Chris angled her body between Stacy and Kate. "It's none of your business."

Stacy turned on Kate. "Go back where you belong!"

"Don't tell me where I belong!"

Stacy looked between Chris and Kate. Anger melted into an anguished expression, and she took off running across the parking lot to her truck.

"She's in love with you," Kate said when they were in the cab. She might not know the feeling, but she recognized the look. Darn it. She didn't want to cause a rift between Chris and Stacy.

"No, she's not." Chris started the truck and drove out of the parking lot, her jaw tight.

"You have sex with her." It made her unreasonably angry.

"Recently. A few times. She was in a bad place, and I tried to make her feel better. It was just sex. She knew that. Why do people make it about more than that?"

"Most people want sex to be about more than that." Kate pulled her phone out of her purse, dreading what she'd see. Yep, a voice mail. She hesitated and then put it on speaker.

"Lucille Cavanaugh? You worked as a…a…"

"Landscaper," she whispered. Chris put her hand on her thigh. She grasped it.

"Of all people. She's the worst gossip. What were you thinking! Risking your health by doing manual labor in this weather? Staying in that cabin with a dangerous storm coming? Honestly, Kate. You're acting like a rebellious child. Enough of this nonsense. Come home. Tonight."

Kate tossed the phone in her purse. Rain pelted the cab, windshield wipers on high barely whisking it away. She wanted to crawl onto Chris's lap, center console be damned. She wanted Chris to hold her. "Let's pick up takeout and go home."

Chapter Thirteen

"Thank God," Kate said when Chris pulled into her driveway. Even through rolled up windows, the wind howled. The houses looked ill prepared for what was rampaging around them. Redwoods swayed in wild arcs. Rain battered the truck like gunfire and overflowed a section of the gutter on her house, creating a curtain of water.

"We'll be okay." Chris took her hand and they sat there. The drive home had been harrowing. "I'll be over after I shower."

Kate pulled the sweatshirt hood up and made a dash for her house, holding the takeout bag. When she opened her front door the wind blew her inside along with a spray of leaves and rain. She turned on lights as she made her way to the kitchen. First things first. Get a fire going in case they lost power. She lit the tiniest pieces of kindling. Patience, her gran had schooled her. She waited until they burned and then added larger pieces. Kindling. More kindling. Don't add logs until you have a bed of glowing coals.

The lights flickered, and she hurried to heed Chris's advice about taking a shower while there was hot water. It was heaven on her sore muscles and wind-chapped skin. Bundled in sweats and heavy wool socks, she added logs to the woodstove. She imagined her mother's home. Warm. Their cook would be serving dinner about now. How bad was the storm there?

Her phone signaled a call from Nic. She answered.

"I'm with Cecelia."

"Is she all right?" Her heart tripped over itself, praying she hadn't had another spell.

"She hasn't heard from you all day and worked herself into quite a state watching news reports about the storm. Where the hell are you?"

"Felton. I'll come home first thing in the morning. I don't want to drive in the dark. Let me talk to her."

"I finally convinced her to lie down. You worked with Mountain Mary? Little Red Riding Hood gave up two days of studying to—"

"Is bitch your new occupation?"

"No. Being a defense attorney is. What's yours?" She paused, and Kate pictured her tapping a finger against her lip. "Oh, yeah. Gardener."

"Landscaper. It's honorable work."

"Five months ago you gave a speech to hundreds as valedictorian of Stanford Law School. Now you're digging in the dirt. What is wrong with you?"

Valid question. Was she exploring options or on a detour to nowhere? "We'll celebrate tomorrow night when you get your bar-exam results. I'm sure you passed."

"Bet your sweet ass I did."

Yes. Home tomorrow morning. Her mother was right. Enough of this nonsense. She'd take her mother to lunch. Shopping. Manicure. No, she wouldn't be having sex again with Chris. She picked up her phone and called her gran. "Mother's in a state. I'm coming home in the morning." She sat down on the couch and tucked her legs under her. "I slept with Chris," she said, hoping for words of wisdom on what it meant.

"Self-discovery is never a bad thing. Confusing, I imagine, but not bad."

"I hate being confused." She wound her sweatshirt hem around her finger. "This thing with Chris…it's taking me to a place I'm not sure I want to go."

"Until you go there, how will you know?"

"I had a future I was certain of before that blasted virus."

"But did you know yourself?"

She tried to swat the question away. More wisdom than she wanted.

"You had a path. Much of it chosen for you. Finding out who you are is the only way to real happiness."

"Darn it. The lights went out." The living room was cast into darkness barely breached by the fire.

"I weathered many a storm in that house. You and Chris stay together."

Kate ended the call. The back door opened with a bang, and Chris burst into the kitchen carrying bags of ice they'd bought on the way home. "Damn, these are cold."

Kate hurried to shut the door. Rain poured onto the floor and the wind was deafening. She helped Chris squeeze the bags into the refrigerator and freezer, then stuffed a towel along the bottom of the door to soak up the water.

Chris took off her raincoat and hung it in the laundry room. She went to the woodstove and opened the door. Firelight danced across her face as she bent to tend the fire. 501s that seemed made for her frame. Long-sleeved black T-shirt snugged across her shoulders. Damp hair slicked back. Sexy. As. Hell.

Chris closed the woodstove door and adjusted the damper, then turned toward Kate. "What?"

She shook her head. "Nic called. Mother's upset about the storm. I told her I'd come home in the morning."

"I'll drive you. Your car isn't safe in these winds."

They lit candles and spread them around the living room. Pools of flickering light danced across the floor and furniture. Romantic. A fantasy sprang to her mind. Snowbound cabin. The two of them alone cuddled in a soft bed under quilts. Days of sex.

They sat on the couch eating cold Mexican food. She tried to contain her fear as the usually serene forest erupted with a cacophony of sound. Frightening sounds of wind moaning through trees, rain pelting the windows like BBs, stuff banging onto the roof and deck. She scooted closer. She wanted to curl up in Chris's arms.

"About last night," Chris said, after they'd finished eating.

"I know you've done that for other women." Not special, and she wanted it to be.

Chris looked at her, frowning. "I was going to say that it was special for me."

"Would you kiss me?" Just a kiss. When Chris's lips met hers, nothing existed but that point of soft contact.

Chris slid her fingers down Kate's neck and cupped her breast.

Kate clasped Chris's hand as confusion grew. This felt wonderful but—"I don't think we should have sex. Last night was about finding out if I could have an orgasm. I'm not sure what tonight would be."

"Sex is always about pleasure."

"I don't know if it's that simple for me. Sex has always happened within a relationship."

"It's okay. I'll go home." Chris stood.

"You don't have heat at your house. Gran said we should stay together." Kate patted the couch. "Pull-out bed. I'll get blankets and pillows." She hurried down the hall. When she returned, the couch was opened into a bed. It would be so easy to lie down with Chris. She handed the bedding to her. "Thank you for being my friend." Then she went to her bedroom.

❖

Chris heard the bedroom door close. Another night of sex would have been fun, but it was probably for the best. Must be confusing for Kate, her first orgasm, and first time with a woman. She hoped Kate never regretted last night. She blew out candles and undressed down to her boxers. Sliding beneath the covers, she lay watching the fire and listening to the storm, more interested than alarmed. She made her living taming nature, making it conform. These infrequent displays of rebellion reminded her she only had the illusion of control. She played with her breast, imagining Kate's hand on her. She'd masturbated in the shower, but kissing Kate was a green light to her libido. She slid her hand inside her boxers. Relief came quickly. Rolling onto her side, she scrunched the pillow and closed her eyes.

Chris stirred. Someone shaking her shoulder. Kate. Barely more than a silhouette in the dark room. The fire had burned down to embers. "Are you all right?" The wind seemed less, but the rain hadn't let up.

"I can't stop wondering...what if I die tonight? Crazy, maybe, but I'm denying myself sex with you because of silly rules about what I should or shouldn't do. I want to know if my orgasm was a fluke." She lay down and put her head on Chris's shoulder. "No.

That's only part of it. I want to indulge in pleasure like we did last night. Kiss me again? And this time don't stop." She handed Chris a bottle of lube.

Chris cupped Kate's neck and pulled her into a kiss. She'd meant it to be a gentle kiss, but Kate ramped it up to a sizzling-hot dueling of tongues. "Lemme get the fire going." When she returned to the bed Kate was under the covers. Sweats on the floor.

She removed her boxers and lay on top of Kate, kissing her until they were both breathing hard. Sliding down, she took Kate's breast in her mouth. Lush didn't begin to describe it. She smiled as the nipple hardened. She bit and tugged it. Princess liked it rough. A surprise. She worked her other nipple with her hand, and soon Kate was rocking her pelvis. After putting lube on her fingers, she teased Kate by poking her finger just inside her opening, then circling her clit. She wanted her plenty aroused.

"It's not happening."

"Not supposed to yet." Chris bit her nipple again, then flicked it with her tongue. "We don't have a deadline to meet."

"Easy for you to say. You'd probably come if someone blew on you." Kate played her fingers through Chris's hair.

"Wanna try?" Chris kept stroking around Kate's clit. It was swelling. "Not everyone comes quickly. It can be fun to deliberately hold back."

"I'll leave that to you. It's still not happening." Kate's body tensed.

Chris slid her finger into Kate, all the way in and then out.

"Ooooh…" Kate raked her nails up Chris's back.

"What were you saying about nothing happening? You set the rhythm." Chris wanted Kate to explore, to find what she liked in a way that gave her control. She didn't know if Kate could come this way, but she'd add her mouth if she had to.

"Feels good, but not as strong as last time." She spread her legs wider and bent her knees, obviously trying to find the perfect angle.

Chris pressed up on the quarter-sized area with a rougher texture than the surrounding flesh.

"That's it." She lifted her head and looked at Chris. "What did you do?"

"G-spot. Front wall of your vagina. Can make a woman crazy when it's stimulated." She rubbed it.

Kate pressed hard against Chris's finger, her face relaxing.

"Enjoy it." The spot swelled, and she knew it wouldn't be long. She went back to feasting on Kate's breast.

"Oh, God, don't stop…it's building up inside." Kate rocked faster and harder, digging her fingers into Chris's shoulders. "So good…ahh…so good." She cried out as she came, rocking on Chris's finger. Finally her legs collapsed onto the bed, trapping Chris inside her. Her chest rose and fell with rapid breaths. "Jell-O again." When Chris started to withdraw, she clamped harder while pulling Chris's face to hers.

Then they were kissing and Kate's hands roamed over her body, through her hair. "My turn." She rolled on top of Chris and slid her fingers inside her.

Chris started to resist. Then relaxed. Kate was enjoying herself. No point breaking the mood with rules about top and bottom.

Kate whipped around on the bed and looked toward the back of the house. Crashing sound, distinct from the other storm noises.

"Tree coming down."

Kate covered her face with her hands and burrowed against Chris's side. "Will it crush us?"

"Too far up the hillside." Seconds stretched as the crashing continued, one tree taking down others in its path.

"I'm really scared."

"We'll be all right tonight. Want me to distract you?" By way of answer, Kate rolled on top and kissed her as she slid fingers into her vagina.

Chapter Fourteen

Kate locked her front door, running through the checklist. Water-heater pilot off. Bedroom-furnace pilot off. Woodstove would burn down on its own. Laptop and study materials were in Chris's truck, along with her clothes. She'd return for the remainder of her things after the storm. She held her jacket hood up as she dashed to the truck, soaking her tennis shoes as she tried to jump over a stream of water pouring down her driveway.

She held Chris's hand as they drove through the neighborhood in the dreary gray daylight. So much worse than she'd imagined. Yards and vehicles covered by branches and leaves. Runoff streaming along the sides of the road, backing up behind mud and debris, flooding the road. She gasped as Chris braked to a stop. A redwood tree was sprawled across the road, branches protruding like dozens of giant spears from a trunk taller than several men standing by it. Kate looked to her left and put her hands to her mouth. Half of a house was buried under the redwood tree. "Oh, God, what if people were in there?" Windows had broken out, and wood and roof shingles lay all over the yard.

"Would have heard emergency vehicles."

"What do we do?"

"Go home. Wait till they clear it."

"How long will that take?"

"Tomorrow. Maybe Sunday."

"Not today?" Now that she'd set her mind to it, she wanted to go home. Away from the confusion that being with Chris brought up.

Last night. Butterflies took flight in her stomach. Little sleep. Lots and lots of sex. Multiple orgasms. Multiple. Chris teased her about making up for lost time. Now she needed to process what it meant.

"Doubt it. Not a main roadway."

"Mother's going to be beside herself, and I'll miss celebrating with Nic. Bar-exam results posted at six."

"Sorry your plans are disrupted," Chris said when they'd returned home and unpacked.

"Seems to be my trademark." Kate added kindling to revive the woodstove.

"Lucky you have a gas stove. Would pancakes and bacon help?"

"A lot. I had this funny image yesterday of being snowbound in a mountain cabin."

"That's a fantasy I can work with." Chris wrapped her in a gentle embrace.

Impossible not to fall into the mood telegraphed by those sexy bedroom eyes. Impossible not to—Their mouths came together. Tongues meeting as if relieved to be reunited.

"Ms. Lesbian Casanova at your service," Chris said.

"I can barely sit or walk, my crotch and thighs are so sore. More sex and I'll be a cripple."

"Think of it as exercise. We'll send you home in prime shape."

Might as well make the most of her captivity. Go home with lots of expertise. "I have to call Mother." She grabbed Chris's waistband and tugged her close. "In a minute." She was spoiled by the best kisses of her life.

Kate sat on the couch, trying to compose an easy way to break the news. Hell, there was no easy way. She punched in her gran's number instead. "A tree came down across the road. I can't stand the thought of what this will do to Mother."

"I'll pass the news along and do what I can to reassure her. Forced detours aren't always a bad thing. Remember your screwball comedies where unexpected occurrences turn out for the best."

Kate ended the call, feeling like a coward for leaving the task to her gran. The thought of another lecture from her mother was unbearable. Phone battery was almost dead. She'd have her fantasy of an isolated cabin in the mountains. With her own personal sex instructor. The windows rattled from a gust of wind. A downspout clattered. She sent a text to Nic.

Road closed. Sorry can't b there. Know u will pass. Love u.

She watched Chris, cooking bacon while she whisked eggs and water into pancake mix in a bowl. A total package, she seemed made for a relationship. Kate went to her and hugged her from behind, resting her cheek on Chris's shoulder. As content as possible looking out the kitchen window at a hillside of swaying trees, branches flailing in an exotic dance.

"I need to study while my laptop still has a charge," Kate said after breakfast.

"K. I'll go get a book to read." Chris returned a few minutes later with a small duffel. Taking a paperback from it, she joined Kate on the couch.

Kate read the title. "*Leather and Lace.*" Lesbian erotica. "No idea such a thing existed."

"I brought lesbian romances, too."

"Maybe later." She went to the office before she said yes. Before she set aside all boundaries. Passing the bar. First priority. Only priority. She lasted…twenty minutes. Twenty distracted, what-did-I-just read, minutes. Her mind and body had never been at cross-purposes. She couldn't force herself out of craving more sex with Chris. She hurried to the living room.

"Going well?" Chris lay stretched on her back on the couch.

Kate ran and jumped on her, straddling her. "You're a bad, bad influence."

Chris set the book aside and gripped her waist. "And I should apologize?"

She unbuttoned Chris's green-flannel shirt. "You're a dangerous distraction." Stared at the mounds inside the snug T-shirt. No bra. "I have to pass the bar exam."

"I think better after sex."

"Makes me a mindless blob of Jell-O."

"I can go home."

"Over my dead body. Every lesbian in five counties probably wants what I've got." Kate tunneled her hands under the T-shirt. "You. All. To. My. Self." She pinched Chris's nipples gently with each word. "Okay, Ms. Lesbian Casanova. More. Sex." Kate tugged on the fly of the 501s. Buttons popped. She pulled jeans and boxers off, then ran her hands up the inside of Chris's legs, kneading the muscles. "I like touching you."

"I'm all yours." Chris put her hands behind her head, dimpled grin in place.

Kneeling between Chris's legs, Kate studied her sex as she stroked around her labia. So beautiful. She circled her opening. Wet. Poked her finger inside and then brought it to Chris's clit, spreading the wetness as she rubbed it. Pressing another finger to her opening, she moved in and out, barely penetrating her.

"Someone likes to tease," Chris said after a while.

"Is that okay?" She'd never experienced sex as play. It was fun to try different ways of touching.

"It is with me. You have to learn what your partner likes."

"How about this?" She pushed two fingers deep inside Chris. "Do you like this?" She moved in and out slowly.

"What do you think?" She rocked her pelvis on Kate's fingers. "Make me come."

Desire overwhelmed her and she drove harder into Chris. Fucking her. She was fucking a woman.

"Oh, yeah," Chris breathed out as she arched her neck and closed her eyes. "That's perfect."

Kate lost herself in the rhythm of fucking and rubbing Chris's clit as she watched the orgasm gather. Everything about her was beautiful. Tightened abs and quads. Hard nipples. Arching her back as she thrust her pelvis. Chris snapped her eyes open as she tumbled over into the orgasm, a smile settling on her face. So beautiful. Kate would never again be able to live without the pleasure of sex.

❖

Chris drifted down from her orgasm as they kissed, Kate on top. The more they played, the more Kate took charge. Not surprising, given her preference for control. Some women were natural tops. Some natural bottoms. No mystery which Kate was, but she'd save that for a later lesson. Next lesson was masturbating.

"Wanna play a different way?" She picked up the duffel from beside the couch and emptied the contents onto the coffee table—vibrators and cocks. "Don't make that icky face. How do you know you won't like 'em?"

"True. Might as well take advantage of my expert." Kate picked up a purple silicone cock. It bobbed in her hand. She frowned and set it down. Picked up a pink one, wrapping her hand around it in a way that sent a jolt of arousal through Chris.

"You can stimulate your G-spot."

Kate set it down, picked up a teal-blue vibrator, and turned it on. She shook her head and turned it off.

"Think of them as a tongue on speed."

"Seems clinical."

"Let's masturbate. It's cool. You see your lover getting aroused while you arouse yourself. Amazing how the two amplify each other." Chris pulled the coffee table away from the couch. They moved cushions and pulled the bed out. "On three. Clothes off."

Undressed, they lay facing each other on top of the sheet. Kate still looked skeptical, turning the little pocket vibrator on, adjusting the speed up and down. Finally she bent her knee and put it between her legs. She jerked it away. "Oh, my. That's…oh…interesting." She held it to her clit again. "Do I need lube?"

"Some like it dry and some like it slippery."

"Lube."

"Allow me." Chris applied lube around Kate's labia and clit, forcing herself not to keep touching. She didn't want Kate to be dependent on anyone for sexual satisfaction. "Good spot?" Kate had a dreamy look on her face.

Chris mirrored Kate's position, using her hand to masturbate. A vibrator would send her over right away.

"I miss your finger. You know. On my G-spot."

"That's where a cock comes in handy."

"Funny."

"There's nothing better than sex with a lover, but learning to please yourself is important. Sometimes you need relief and no one's around." Chris put a condom over the slender, curved, pink cock and lubed the end of it. "If you don't like it, I have ten fingers you can choose from."

Kate looked skeptical as she lay back and slid it in her vagina. "Hurts a little."

"Relax. Play."

She moved it in and out a few times. "I don't like it." She started to pull it out.

Chris put her hand over Kate's. "Bend your knees and tilt your pelvis until you find the right angle."

"Ah, God, that's it." She snapped her gaze to Chris. Smiled. A wicked smile.

"You might come from that alone or add the vibrator." Watching Kate fuck herself was making it hard to hold back. She wanted to come. Bad.

Kate twisted the vibrator on. "Kiss me."

They kissed, hot and demanding, the sound of the storm a background to the buzzing of vibrators and sporadic moans. "Tell me when you're ready."

"Close. Almost…" Kate's eyes were intense blue and oh, that smile. "Yes. God, yes. I'm coming." She thrust her pelvis up and held the cock buried deep.

"You're so beautiful." Chris let go, coming with Kate. So good. So fucking good.

"That was intense." Kate set the toys aside and turned on her side to face Chris. "I don't like it as much as when you touch me. Guess I like my sex with a partner."

"So do I. Like I said, you totally have a relationship through sex."

Kate nodded, looking thoughtful. Then she curled into Chris, head on her shoulder, and closed her eyes. "Love that downed tree."

❖

Kate woke. Cold. Chris was on her side. Asleep. She ran her fingers through Chris's thick hair and pushed an unruly chunk off her forehead. Now she could give herself orgasms. Self-sufficient, and that should make her happy. Instead, it made her sad. She liked skin to skin. Fingers and mouths. Giving and taking. Relationship.

She pulled the covers over Chris, dressed, and stoked the fire before heading to the office. For the fun of it she ran down the hall and slid the last few feet, almost falling on her butt. God, she felt good. She opened her laptop and resumed where she'd left off studying. An hour later she went to check on Chris. Still asleep. *Leather and Lace* lay on the coffee table. A short break wouldn't hurt, and she was curious.

She settled in the wingback chair by the woodstove. Three stories later, she closed the book. Wow. Nic's romances were nothing compared to this. Another way to learn, and she liked reading about women having sex. Her breasts felt full and her nipples tight. She was turned on. Slipping her hand inside her sweats, she stroked her labia and around her clit. Not wet but it felt good. She kept touching herself as she read another story. More aroused. Aroused enough she wanted to come. She eyed the vibrator lying on the bed.

She took it, lube, and the book to her bedroom so she wouldn't wake Chris. Undressing except for her sweatshirt she crawled under the covers. She read another story and then set the book aside. She spread lube over her sex and set the vibrator against her clit. She tried to lock onto an image from the story, but her mind kept putting Chris into the action. In chaps with nothing on underneath, her dark bush and sex framed by black leather. Bare-chested. Handcuffs in one hand. Commanding look on her face.

"You're beautiful."

Kate opened her eyes. Chris stood in the doorway, naked except for boxers. A flush went up her neck. How long had she been watching? She turned the vibrator off. "This book's racy."

"Supposed to be. Any particular story you like?"

"Um. Talking about it's too weird."

Chris tapped her head as she walked across the room. "Brain's a huge source of arousal." She picked up the book and fanned the pages.

"Fourth one."

"Ahh…" Chris pulled the covers back and pinned Kate's hands above her head. "Princess likes the idea of being restrained."

Kate's clit contracted. She tried to imagine giving up control like the woman in the story. Not going there. "Princess needs to come. Help?"

"You're doing fine. I'll watch."

"I like it better when you touch me."

"Good. Ask for what you want." Chris lay beside her.

"You inside me while I use the vibrator. And I want you to suck on my breasts." She spread her legs and turned the vibrator on. Sensations multiplied as Chris took her breast, sucking hard and tugging the nipple. Good hurt that amped up her need for release. She circled her clit with the vibrator, and then Chris was inside her and it was perfect. Pinpoints of pain at her breast. Her clit pulsing. She tilted her pelvis, and Chris's finger hit her G-spot. The orgasm blossomed from that point of pressure, building until it surged through her, heat followed by the tingling, floating feeling. "So good." She lay there, spent, with Chris's finger inside her. Connected. Maybe sex was a relationship.

"Let's read aloud to each other," Chris said after a few minutes.

She snuggled against Chris. Embarrassed at first, but Chris made reading erotica aloud seem natural. She played with Chris's breasts as she listened, keeping her nipples in hard peaks. "My turn to watch," she said when the story ended. "Make yourself come."

"Anything for Princess." Chris held her gaze as she moved Kate's hand aside and touched her own breasts. "Kiss me."

Kate drove her tongue far into Chris's mouth, then sucked on her tongue. Every kiss was different and new, overwhelmingly exciting. Breaking the kiss, she watched Chris run her hand down her body, slow, like she wasn't dying to come and Kate knew she was.

Chris stroked her clit as she kept playing with her breast. Tension built in her body and Kate was sure she'd come. Then she'd take her hand from her sex and rub over her abs. Then back to her clit. Build up. Ease off. Her control was amazing. Just when Kate was so turned on she was about to touch herself, Chris said, "Gonna come."

Kate entered her. She had to be part of Chris's orgasm. "I love feeling you tighten around me." She laid her cheek on Chris's chest, absorbing her heartbeat.

"You cheated." She ran her fingers through Kate's hair.

"Complaining?"

"Nope."

Kate lay in Chris's arms, kissing along her neck, her fingers still inside Chris. None of the usual worries hounding her. Sex was magical in ways she'd never imagined. After a while she realized the storm had lessened.

Chris seemed to notice, also. "Okay, sex maniac, I need to do something vertical. Let's walk to the downed tree."

"Storm over?"

"Break for a couple of hours. Then it'll hit with a vengeance again."

Kate scrambled out of bed. She felt great. Okay, sore, but great. Relaxed. Happy. A walk and then lots more sex.

Chapter Fifteen

Kate jumped in the middle of a puddle, splashing water onto Chris's dark-green rain pants. She felt like a little kid in the yellow rain suit she'd found in the closet. Way too big for her, she'd had to roll up the cuffs on both pants and jacket.

Chris darted to another puddle and returned the favor.

"What's that noise?" Like a really loud lawnmower.

"Generator." Chris pointed to a house on the right. "That's why they have lights."

"Why don't you have one?"

"Too expensive."

"I'll ask Gran to put one in. If there's another bad storm you can stay in her cabin." They walked down the middle of the street that was in much the same shape as it had been earlier, covered in debris. Muddy water streamed along the edges of the road, around overturned trash cans in some places. The sky was a churning gray cap above them, but it wasn't raining, and the wind had quieted considerably. People were taking advantage of the lull to clean gutters or repair storm damage.

"Oh, my God." Kate stopped when the downed tree came into view, then ran toward it in the too-tight rubber boots. It looked monstrous. A car she hadn't noticed this morning was pinned beneath it. Like the urge to look at a wreck on the highway, it was impossible not to look at the demolished house on the left.

Two men in rain gear stood nearby. "Heard on my scanner Highway 9's closed in both directions because of mudslides," one of them said. "They've shut down 17. Can't get to Santa Cruz or San Jose. PG&E tower went down. Won't have electricity for days."

"Glad I put that generator in," the other man said. "Won't miss the football games tomorrow."

Kate put her arm around Chris as they walked home. If not for Chris she'd be scared. "Oh, my, gosh. I know her." She pointed to an older woman wearing a purple rain slicker and jeans tucked into knee-high rubber boots who was shoveling mud away from the side of her house. She hurried over. "Les?"

"Well, I'll be. Kate," the woman said. Wisps of gray hair sprouted from beneath a blue knit cap. "Is Katherine here?"

"No."

"This is Gran's friend Les," she said when Chris joined them. "My neighbor, Chris."

"The landscaper." Les pointed to Chris's ball cap.

"What happened?" Chris asked.

"Blasted retaining wall failed."

"We'll help. Extra shovels?" Kate zipped her jacket against the wind that was picking up.

"Shed in back." Les studied her for a moment. "You look like Katherine when she was your age."

"Let's do this before it pours again," Chris said, returning from the shed and handing Kate a shovel.

"Can you fit me into your schedule to repair that wall?" Les asked Chris an hour later when they'd cleared the mud away from the foundation and dug a gully to channel the next round of runoff away from the house.

"I'll try next week."

"Worst storm I've seen in forty years." Les looked up as it started to rain again. "Going to get worse."

"We'll check on you tomorrow." Kate pulled the rain suit hood over her head.

"Hold up a second." Les went into her house and came out a few minutes later holding a plastic bag. "Cookies. And a photo album you might enjoy looking through."

"Les and her roommate would come over for dinner when Gran and I stayed here." She stopped and looked back to Les's house. "Oh, geez. That wasn't her roommate. She's a lesbian and that was her partner."

"You think?" Chris asked, sounding innocent, her eyes wide.

"I deserve that. Princess has been naive about too many things. Lucky I met you." Life lessons she wouldn't forget. She took Chris's hand as they walked down the street.

❖

"I'll make coffee," Chris said from the kitchen. "Steaks for dinner. Okay with pan-fried instead of grilled?"

"Yeah, like I expect you to stand out in the rain." Kate stirred the coals in the woodstove and added two small logs.

"I would."

She went to the kitchen where Chris was setting a pan of water on the stove. She wrapped her arms around her from behind. "You're more thoughtful than I know what to do with." Chris turned. They moved into each other's arms, into the kiss that set the butterflies in Kate's stomach to fluttering.

As Chris started dinner, Kate went to the living room. She straightened the sheets and laid the Pendleton blanket on top. Lit candles and set them around the living room against the invading dark. The room took on a romantic mood. She fingered the blanket, wondering what would happen on this bed tonight.

Bending over to put more logs in the woodstove, she noticed Chris looking at her. Unguarded desire radiated from her, like heat off pavement. Kate closed the glass door, debating. Risqué seemed to be the theme of the day. Without turning around she swayed her butt.

"Fuck."

"Enjoying the view?" She moved her hands in circles over her butt as she kept swaying.

"Does it bother you? My looking at you?"

"I like it," Kate said, trying to sound sexy. She circled her hips and pumped her pelvis. She'd never done anything remotely like this, but it felt safe to do with Chris. No, more than that. She liked feeling desirable. Turning around she circled her hips the other direction as she squeezed her breasts, then unzipped her jeans and slid her hands inside.

"Keep doing that and I won't be responsible for my behavior."

The way Chris said it, dark and dangerous, made Kate's clit contract. She continued dancing, alternating between touching her breasts and putting her hands inside her jeans, urged on by the look on Chris's face. Appreciative laced with plenty of heat. Deciding to go for broke, she took the sweatshirt off in what she hoped was a sexy striptease, revealing the flesh-colored satin bra. Cupping her breasts, she pushed them together.

Chris's eyes locked on Kate's breasts with a feral look. "You're killing me." She ripped her jeans open and thrust her hand between her legs.

"Get your hand out of your pants." Kate hadn't meant to say that, but it felt right.

❖

Chris hesitated, surprised by the command. Did she want to let Kate take control again?

"Turn around." Kate walked toward her, low-riding jeans open at the fly.

Chris complied, deciding to let this play out. Kate's natural tendencies as a femme top were coming out.

Then Kate was behind her, rubbing her breasts against her back as she snaked her hands inside her 501s, cupping Chris's sex through her boxers. "Off." Kate yanked pants and boxers down to her ankles and pulled them off each leg. She pressed Chris into the counter and kissed her, thrusting her tongue into her mouth, then biting her lower lip.

"Spread your legs," Kate said as she kneed them apart. She licked below her ear before sucking on her earlobe. "Feels like water isn't the only thing about to boil," she said as she slid her fingers into Chris's sex.

"Jesus, Kate." Yeah, she was a natural top. When Kate's other hand undid buttons on her shirt, cupped her breast and flicked her nipple, Chris arched her head back. A moan came up from deep inside. She gripped the counter as her legs went weak.

"Do not come." Kate's fingers worked her clit in a perfect—

"You're killing me." Chris clenched her jaw as the fingers backed off. Her thighs and butt trembled with tension as Kate continued to play with her, taking her to the edge of orgasm and then easing away like she'd been doing it for years. She surrendered to the sensations, riding the burn in her clit, letting it become pleasure. The more she let go, the more she wanted to and the more the need for release built. Just when she was about to beg, Kate stroked her clit in that oh, so perfect, way.

"You can come now."

The orgasm shot like fire through her veins. "Yes, yes, yes…" More. She needed more. "Don't. Stop."

"Never." Kate wrapped an arm around her waist, holding her up, as she slid her hand to Chris's ass. "Turn around and bend over." Kate's fingers slid down her crack, past her anus, then plunged inside her vagina. In and out. Deep. Slow. Too slow.

The burn built again. Control it. Ride it. Enjoy it. "What are you doing to me…" She bit her lip.

Kate drove into her faster. Harder. "Come on my fingers."

Chris shoved back into Kate's hand as her orgasm rolled through her, softer than the first one. She was jelly, physically and mentally, trembling with the aftershocks of the orgasms and with the knowledge that a novice who probably didn't know the word had topped her. Again. Her mind was reeling in a million directions, but her body hummed contentedly. No one but Georgia had ever taken her like that. Damn.

"I've got you."

Chris let Kate hold her as she tried to recover. Strength returned in her legs, but her brain was still mush. Kate's actions had triggered something she hadn't expected. She'd enjoyed it.

Finally Kate let go and reached around her to move the pan of water and turn off the gas burner. "Sit and I'll make the coffee." Her face was as angelic now as it had been fierce a few minutes ago.

Chris put her clothes on and went to the chair by the woodstove, too flustered to know what to say.

❖

Kate's hands trembled as she poured boiling water into the cone filter filled with coffee. Taking Chris like that was heady and exhilarating. The clock on the wall said five. An hour, and Todd and Nic would log on to the bar-exam website and see their test results. Her cell phone was dead. She could idle her car and recharge it enough to call or text them. She should do that. She made no move for her phone. Contact with them would pull her toward the life she felt far away from at the moment. The world would have to wait another day for her return.

She made the other cup of coffee and went to the living room. Chris didn't meet her gaze when she set the mugs on the table next to the wingback chair. Sitting on the chair arm, she combed her fingers through Chris's hair. "Can we talk about it?"

"Do you know what you did?" Chris caught her hand and kissed it, sucking several fingers into her mouth.

Kate moved onto her lap, legs draped over the arm of the chair. "Took charge?"

"You topped me. You created an interaction that involved power dynamics. It's called a scene. You insisted, with words and with your body, that I submit, and I did." Her expression made it seem serious.

"Oh." She shrugged. "It just happened. I liked the power I had to excite you, to make you want me."

"You're a natural."

"You mean I'm bossy and controlling."

"It's okay to be yourself when you're having sex."

"I've never initiated sex, never teased or taken control. You make it safe for me to explore. Did I do something wrong?"

"You did everything right. It turned me on. Big-time. I don't usually do that."

"You don't let women top you?"

"Only Georgia."

"Is that a butch/femme thing?"

"Tops can be butch or femme."

Kate huffed out a breath in frustration. "I don't even know what the questions are. I did what felt good. Sorry if I violated a rule." She started to get up, embarrassed.

Chris wrapped her arms around Kate. "I want you to have the freedom to find out who you are sexually. Once you know what you like, you can find someone whose appetites are compatible with yours. It's more important than liking the same movies or food."

"You mean in relationships."

"Yeah."

"See, you know about relationships." Kate ran her fingers through Chris's hair again. "We like the same kind of movies. And food. And sex." She tried not to laugh at Chris's obvious discomfort. "If you decide to try a relationship, I'll be your practice partner." When Chris tensed she added, "I'm kidding." Kate picked up the mug and sipped coffee as she thought about what she'd done. "When I was taking charge I felt responsible for you. To honor the trust you were placing in me by being open and vulnerable. There's more to sex than the act itself. Because I didn't enjoy the act, I never thought about anything else."

"There can be all sorts of power dynamics, intentional and not. It's fun to deliberately explore them, but there has to be trust. At least for me there does. Do you know what role-playing is?"

"Is that what we did?"

"Unintentionally."

"Teach me to do it intentionally."

"Feed you first. Then we'll play."

Kate stood, pulling Chris up. "I'm your sous chef." She tingled with nervous excitement as they made dinner. She had tonight and part of tomorrow. She wanted to learn more about sex. Lots more.

Chapter Sixteen

"I'll miss your cooking." Kate took another bite of steak topped with melted blue cheese and sautéed onions. They were eating at the dining table, candles casting soft light on Les's photo album that lay open between them.

"You won't be able to stay away long." Chris put her arm across Kate's shoulders and kissed her.

Kate pointed to a photo. "Look how short Gran's hair was." She read the caption. *Move-In Day.*

"Look at the clothes."

"Sixties, I know."

"More than that." Chris pointed to other pictures on the page. "Cindy's always in a dress. Les in slacks and a shirt. Butch/femme was the model for lesbian relationships then."

Perhaps her gran's advocacy for gay rights started with her friendship with Les and Cindy. Kate studied more photos. Not a single one where her gran wore a dress. "Did you always know you were butch?"

"I didn't know the word until I met Georgia, but I knew I was a tomboy. Refused to wear dresses even when I was little. Wore my hair short. Jeans and polo shirts like my dad. Liked to help him work on his Harley."

"Do you think it was because you were raised by your dad?"

"Nah. It's who I am. Like you're naturally femme. Lucky for me he didn't try to change me."

"Lucky for me. Butch is so darn sexy. My favorite kind of lesbian."

Chris gave her a heart-melting smile.

Kate turned a page in the album. "Must have been hard for Les and Cindy when they were first together."

"It was illegal."

Kate scooped up a big bite of baked potato covered in sour cream and bacon. "I confess I didn't understand your lifestyle. After the last few days, I do. Sort of. Sex is everything you've said, but outside a relationship it seems like having dessert with no meal."

"If it's a great dessert, who cares?"

"I'd miss what Todd and I had. Knowing each other so well. Trust and security. A sense of a future."

"Then that's what you should look for. But do you look for it with a man or a woman?"

"Way too much to think about." The complications piled up into a train wreck. If she was a lesbian, the ripple effect would radiate into all aspects of her life. It seemed too big a jump from finding out she could orgasm and liked sex with Chris.

"Have it both ways. Like Jennifer."

Kate tried to picture herself doing that. She couldn't. They continued to look at the photo album as they ate. Her gran in a convertible with Les and Cindy. At the Santa Cruz Boardwalk with them and other women she didn't recognize. Planting the Japanese maple in the front yard.

"Coffee and Les's cookies for dessert?" Chris asked when they'd finished the meal.

Kate set the napkin on the table and scooted her chair back. "Let's have a different kind of dessert." Standing, she tugged Chris up and led her to the living room.

Chris put logs in the woodstove, and they sat beside each other on the bed. "You seem curious about role-playing. Wanna try the submissive role? Something along the lines of that story in my erotica book? Restraint?"

Anticipation jolted through her and left a tingly sensation in her body. If she got aroused reading about it…"Sure." She held out her wrists. "Show me your stuff, stud."

Chris took leather cuffs from a bag and set them on the bed.

Kate examined one of them. Lined with sheepskin. She put it around her wrist. Not uncomfortable. "What else will you do?"

"Telling would spoil the fun." Chris's grin changed into a serious expression. "We have to talk about safety and trust. You control how far we take it."

"But you're in charge."

"Only within the limits of what's pleasurable for you. You need a safe word. Something you won't accidentally say. Pink." Chris seemed too serious for a silly game. "If you want to stop, for any reason, say 'pink' and I stop instantly. Don't ever do anything that makes you uncomfortable or scares you."

Kate's pulse jumped. Risqué. Daring. The illusion of danger. She'd bet Nic had never done anything like this.

"Undress and lie on your back."

Kate set the Pendleton blanket on the chair and lay on the cool sheets. She watched as Chris fastened each wrist and then her ankles to the bedframe. She was different. Detached. Kate could barely move her limbs, but the cuffs didn't hurt. The room was warm, candles cast flickering light, but there wasn't the same air of romance. She felt vulnerable. Exposed. A funny sensation sprouted in her stomach.

"You're beautiful." Chris straddled her abdomen, 501s rough against Kate's skin. She unbuttoned her flannel shirt and played with her breasts, closing her eyes as if in her own world.

"I want to suck them." Kate tugged against the cuffs.

"Shh. No talking. Focus on your body. Feel what's happening. Desire to touch. Not being able to. There's an edge where those opposites meet. Want. Can't have. Feel the tension. Make it sexual."

All Kate felt was irritated at the silly game. The frustration grew when Chris opened her jeans and touched her sex, rocking her pelvis, again with eyes closed as if shutting Kate out.

"I'm going to blindfold you." Chris pulled a black scarf from the bag.

"Isn't it dark enough in here?"

Chris put her fingers to Kate's lips. "Shh." She tied the blindfold.

Kate's breath hitched as the soft material tightened. Pitch-black. Sounds amplified. Wind through trees. Dog barking. Rain pounding the roof. Where was Chris? *Calm down. Just a silly game.* She gasped when something cold touched the front of her neck. Ice. Then it was gone. Water dripped down her neck. It tickled. Sound took over. She pulled on the restraints. That funny sensation in her stomach hardened into a knot of panic.

Chris circled her nipple with the ice cube.

Kate sucked in a breath and shivered from the cold as fear niggled at the back of her throat.

"Let yourself absorb the moment of shock and discomfort. Don't fight it. Become sensitized by it." She did the same on Kate's other nipple. Around and around. So cold it hurt. Then down Kate's abdomen and each leg.

She tugged on the wrist cuffs. She wanted Chris's mouth on her, warm and arousing, not this impersonal nonsense. She took a deep breath. *Calm down. Education. See it through.* Water dripped down her sides and legs. Irritating. She cocked her head, trying to sense where Chris was. Her heart rate notched up as her chest tightened. *Say the word. No. You're not in danger. Tough it out.* She flinched when something hot hit her abdomen, above her navel. Then immediately another hot drop below her navel.

"Wax. Won't hurt you. Let go. Let the pain change into something else."

Kate's world narrowed to her body and the random sensations assaulting her. A hot drop on her abdomen made the muscles contract. Then ice immediately in her navel. She squirmed. Then several drops above her pubic bone. There's no pleasure, she wanted to say. More drops of wax. Frustration built like bubbling lava. She hated the unpredictability. *No. This won't beat me.* Hot. Cold. Periods of nothing as if Chris had left the room. Over and over. Her breathing quickened. No way to stop the pain. No control. No control. "Pink!" She yanked on the wrist cuffs. She couldn't catch her breath.

"It's okay," Chris said, and then the blindfold was off. She looked worried as she reached to remove the cuffs.

Kate bolted up to a sit, sucking in air, but her lungs wouldn't fill. She clutched at her chest. "Can't...breathe."

Chris took off her shirt, wrapped it around Kate. "You're hyperventilating."

She grabbed onto Chris as sobs welled up.

"Breathe in from your belly. Slowly. Count to six." Chris rubbed between her shoulder blades. "Now exhale out your mouth...count to ten. Good. Again."

Kate did as instructed, clutching Chris's shirt until finally her breathing relaxed and the panic receded.

"What happened?"

"It took me back to what it was like in the hospital. Dark. Pain. No control. People doing things to me." Fear and anger coalesced. "I couldn't do anything to make it better. I was stuck lying there with the pain. It was awful."

"I'm so sorry. We shouldn't have done this." Chris tucked hair behind Kate's ear and cupped her cheek.

"You didn't know what would happen."

"That kind of play can trigger emotional reactions."

"I'm not the first woman to fall apart on you?"

"I should have taken better care of you." Chris looked crestfallen.

"Can we lie down?"

"Absolutely."

Kate snuggled into Chris's warmth, head on her shoulder, her heart still pounding. "To feel that lack of control again...that's powerful stuff."

"You're a natural top. It's okay to stick with that."

"I don't want to be afraid of it any more than the storm or getting sick again."

"You don't have to prove anything."

"It's a chance for me to give up control in a way that doesn't have consequences. A way to learn about myself. Isn't that what the last few days have been about?" Kate waited, watching emotions shift across Chris's face—doubt, resistance, then acceptance.

"No blindfold. Wrists tied together but not to the bed. You can hold them over your head. No ankle cuffs. That's the only way I'll do it."

"Agreed." Kate lay in Chris's arms until she felt ready to confront the fear again. Taking off the shirt, she rolled onto her back and held out her hands.

❖

Chris kissed each of Kate's wrists before tying them together with the scarf and placing them above her head. What they were doing was tame by bondage standards, but she should have eased Kate into it with more finesse. She'd been too caught up in her excitement to try new things. Kate's distressing reaction sat squarely in her lap. She straddled Kate's abdomen, studying her.

"I'm sure." Kate's eyes held hers.

"Keep talking to me." She focused her attention on Kate's breasts, teasing with a feather-light touch. Then she pinched both nipples in a rhythmic motion, increasing the pressure, gauging Kate's reaction. Finally she pinched them harder than she had so far. Kate flinched. "Can you feel how at the edge of the pain there's other sensations?"

Kate closed her eyes, frowning, as Chris continued to pinch and tug her nipples. "Almost...pleasurable. Like how my lungs or quads burn when I run, but in a good way. Do the wax and ice cubes."

"You don't have to—"

Kate opened her eyes. Looked at Chris with trust and certainty.

Chris picked up the candle and lit it off another one. Tilting it over the inside of her wrist, she let wax drip. Hot, but not too. She held it over Kate's belly and drizzled some near her navel.

Kate gasped at the contact. Closed her eyes.

She continued to drip wax at random intervals onto Kate's abdomen and thighs, peeling it off and licking where it had landed.

"I hate not having control over what happens to me."

"You do have control. You have control over whether you fight it or change your focus and move beyond it. Own it. Choose to let go into your body."

Finally Kate's breathing slowed. "I'm beginning to look forward to what's next." Her leg jerked when Chris dribbled wax on it. "Oh, and then you take my focus to my breasts," she said as Chris pinched her nipples. "Don't have...to think..."

Chris knew the feeling. That moment when your brain stopped analyzing and your body was all there was, wrapped in a cocoon of sensations. She could barely keep from kissing Kate, from burying her fingers deep inside her.

"Pain..." Kate arched into the touch of the ice cube Chris trailed down her abdomen. "Lingers...fades. Anticipation. Urge to fight while I wait. Surrendering into the next sensation. New. Exciting."

Chris added touches to Kate's inner thighs and around her sex, enough to arouse but not satisfy. Her moans said she enjoyed it. The occasional groan voiced her frustration.

"God, I want it so bad." Kate rocked her sex against Chris's fingers.

"You get it when I'm ready." She continued to stroke, close to Kate's clit but never on it. She thought Kate could last a little longer, although she wasn't sure she could.

"Make me come. Please."

Chris gave in to the plea but more to her need to be inside Kate. She reached for the bottle of lube, squeezed some on her finger, and sighed with relief as she slid into her. Exactly where she wanted to be. She lowered her mouth to Kate's clit and gave her what she wanted.

❖

Kate opened her eyes. Blinked as she became aware of her surroundings. Chris was looking at her from between her legs, hair tousled, lips parted. "Slide up here, stud." When Chris was on top of her, she wrapped her arms around her, wrists still bound. "I can't imagine doing that with anyone I don't know well and trust." She took her arms from around Chris and let her untie her wrists.

"Complete strangers do it to each other all the time, but I know what you mean." Chris lay beside her, propped on her elbow, hand on Kate's belly.

"Have you?" Chris had probably done a lot of things she didn't even know existed.

"Yes." She traced lazy circles over Kate's abdomen.

"You're into BDSM, aren't you?" The pieces finally clicked.

"Yeah, but it's a big kingdom. I've done enough experimenting to know what I do and don't like. Ultimately, you're always in control of your experience, even if you temporarily give someone power over you."

"What we did isn't very risky, is it?"

"I gave you a sampling of the basics—restraint, pleasure/pain, letting go into the purely physical. Don't confuse novelty with pleasure."

"Did you like it?"

"I liked showing you something new, why what you did by instinct caught me off guard."

"When I was playing with you, I was trying to figure out what you might like, what to say and do to turn you on. I liked that. This was exciting, but something was missing. I didn't feel connected to you."

"I'm sorry. You wanted to know."

"It's not that I disliked it. At least I had an orgasm." She kissed Chris, gently at first, teasing her tongue over those soft lips, then sliding into the warmth of her mouth. They were soon dueling with their tongues, exploring each other with escalating passion. "This, I love," she said when they pulled apart, breathing heavily against each other's cheeks. "So, you're usually the top?"

"Yeah."

"What if I like both?"

"It's called switching."

"Why did you let me top you?"

"So you'd have the freedom to explore. I kind of liked it."

"Do you top Georgia?"

"It's different with her."

"You two switch." She liked Georgia but felt a moment of jealousy for the relationship they had. "Is it okay if I top you?" Her heart melted when Chris gave her that slow, cocky half grin she adored.

"Top away. I'm all yours." Chris lay back and spread her legs.

She grabbed both of her wrists and held them over her head as she feasted on Chris's breast. When Chris squirmed under her, she wiggled down between her legs. She took Chris's clit in her mouth as she entered her. It was so easy to—Her heart tumbled. Make love to Chris. She closed her eyes and blocked out thought as she dropped into the wonder of touching her.

Chapter Seventeen

Kate opened her eyes. Sore abs. Good sore. Light seeped into the living room around the curtains. No wind. No rain.

Chris was sitting on the bed looking at her, holding a mug of coffee. She handed it to Kate. She must have been up for a while. She was dressed in 501s and green-flannel shirt, and the logs in the woodstove were ablaze.

Kate guzzled half of it. "What time is it?"

"After two. Road's open. Princess has her freedom."

Freedom. It hit her like a shock. She had more freedom trapped here with Chris than she'd ever had. She tucked hair behind her ear. Her fingers smelled of Chris. Last night and this morning had been one long sensual exploration. Her topping. Chris topping. It didn't matter. Pleasure as if no limits existed. She set the mug on the end table and pulled Chris down on top of her. "Kiss me senseless."

"My favorite thing."

She couldn't imagine anyone kissing like Chris did. Or arousing her like Chris did. Or trusting anyone the way she did Chris. She tried not to let the next thought form. Or having sex with anyone but Chris. Yes, she had to get out of here. "Do we have power?" she asked, her lips tingling and puffy after the long kiss.

"Nope. There's a pot of hot water in the bathroom for you."

Kate trudged to the bathroom. Wash up. The first step to leaving. Pack. Load the car. Get in. Start the engine. Say good-bye to Chris... good-bye to Chris...She hurried to the living room, toothbrush in hand. "I want to take out the limb in the deck before I leave. How do I do it?"

"Chainsaw it into pieces." Chris looked her up and down, slow and lazy, like a long caress. "My shirt looks sexy on you, but you might consider pants with it."

Kate's body responded to that look with all the clichés of falling in love. Stomach dropping. Heart vaulting into her throat. And undoubtedly a starry-eyed look on her face. She wanted to throw Chris on the bed and make love. That's what it had become for her. She ran and jumped into Chris's arms, wrapped her legs around her, and kissed her. Then she let go and hurried to the bathroom. Reality check. Chris wasn't in love with her, and she wouldn't make her uncomfortable with an unwanted confession. Sex was the deal. Period. Five minutes later, dressed in carpenter pants and sweatshirt, she joined Chris on the deck.

After showing her how to check the chain oil and fill the chain saw with gas/oil mixture, Chris handed her safety goggles. She demonstrated how to start and hold it. Then she stood behind Kate, hands over Kate's as they made the first cut. A piece of the limb toppled to the deck with a thud.

Kate sawed through the limb again. "Take that!" The chain saw was heavy and a bit awkward, but she felt powerful. Cut by cut she demolished the limb that had almost demolished her. "I want one." Kate hefted the chain saw before turning it off and setting it on the deck.

"I'll get one for Princess." Chris removed the goggles and brushed sawdust from Kate's cheek, her eyes soft. "You're not like anyone I've ever known."

All the air rushed out of Kate's lungs. She was in big trouble where Chris was concerned. Big, big trouble. Her heart melted as Chris pulled her into her arms. She squealed when Chris dipped her backward the way she had the night of the Halloween party. Closed her eyes as Chris's mouth met hers, the kiss as sizzling as that first one.

Chris brought her upright and released her. "I'll help you load your car."

"I want to come back and repair the deck. Will you help me?" A viable reason for a weekend visit.

"Anytime." Chris put her arm over Kate's shoulders as they walked into the house.

Kate went to the bedroom, changed out of the work clothes, and carried bags to the living room.

"I'll wash sheets and towels when we have electricity."

The sight of Chris taking the sheets off the bed was unbearable, as if she were stripping away what had happened on those sheets. "No."

"You don't want me to wash them?" Chris looked up at her, holding the corner of a sheet.

She dropped the bags and went to sit on the bed. "I don't want to leave today."

Chris sat next to her. "Why not?"

She swallowed the truth. Telling Chris she was in love with her would ruin everything. It was an infatuation that would pass. It had to. "I want to celebrate." Yes. Celebrate her newfound sexual freedom. Her new sense of self. Kate who knew what passion felt like. "Fix dinner for us?" She waited. Maybe Chris had a date tonight now that the road was open.

Chris grinned. "A 'we survived the storm' dinner."

"Let's dress up. Like a—like a fancy dinner."

"I can do that." Chris's grin collapsed. "What about your mother?"

"I won't tell her the road's open if you don't." For tonight she'd choose what she wanted over what was expected of her.

Chris lifted Kate off the bed and twirled her around. Setting her back on her feet, she cupped Kate's cheeks and kissed her soundly. "I'll go to the store and come over about five."

Perfect. Time to make herself beautiful for the woman she was falling in love with. "One more thing. Would you pack?"

Chris looked surprised, and then that grin was back. "Anything for you."

❖

Chris walked through Kate's back door and set containers of food on the counter. Candles were set out in the kitchen and living room, but the house was quiet. Kate must still be getting ready. Dress-up. She definitely wanted to see her dressed up. After starting the grill and putting the stuffed beef tenderloin on, she returned to the kitchen and opened the bottle of red wine she'd bought. She poured two glasses.

"One of those for me?"

She turned to hand Kate a glass. Her legs almost forgot how to stand. Whoa! Royal-blue dress. Body-hugging. Spaghetti straps. Kate's hair fell in untamed, golden-blond waves over her shoulders. Earrings, a bar of small diamonds, hung from each ear. Her gaze went to Kate's cleavage. Whoa! She was sure she had a ridiculous grin on her face, but she couldn't help it.

Kate took the glass from her, diamond tennis bracelet around her wrist. "You look handsome." She stepped close and wrapped an arm around Chris's neck.

Black chinos, a starched white shirt with tuxedo front and stand-up collar, and black boots. Dress-up for her, but not a match for the classy woman in her arms. She shoved away the whisper in her head that said Kate was out of her league. For tonight, Kate was hers. "You, too." Chris shook her head. She couldn't think with all the blood gone to her crotch. "Beautiful. You look beautiful."

Kate took her mouth in a kiss so hot Chris had to lean against the kitchen counter for support. She smiled against Chris's lips and rubbed against her cock. "Sexy," she purred before devouring Chris's mouth again.

Chris wasn't sure if she was spinning or the room was spinning as the kiss went on, hotter and hotter. "Um, I need to check the..." What the hell did she need to check? "Meat. Grill." She hurried out the door, but the smell and feel of Kate wound around and through her, tying her up in a dangerous blend of desire and something else. Something that whispered she didn't want Kate to leave. Ever. Distracted, she almost stepped in the hole where the limb had been. Lifting the grill lid, she needlessly rearranged the meat as she tried to right herself.

When she went back inside, Kate had set the table—linen tablecloth, china and silverware, cloth napkins. She looked at Chris as she lit two purple tapers. Her eyes shimmered in the flickering light as she blew out the match.

"Um, dinner..." Chris shook her head. "About twenty minutes." Heat simmered in her center, and her clit was throbbing. She knew she was attracted to Kate, but this was more. She wasn't sure she liked it. No. Of course she liked it. She swallowed hard.

Kate slinked toward her. Well, walked, but the dress slinked. She handed Chris a glass of wine and held hers up. "To exploring sexual pleasure with a thoughtful and talented guide."

Chris's heart swelled, like it was too small for her chest. Kate looked happy. Really happy. She took a sip of wine, waiting for the confusing emotions to clear. "I've never done with anyone what we've done. I mean teaching you."

"I like that I'm your first. Student, that is." Humor radiated from Kate's smile, but sparks flared in her eyes.

Too close. Kate was too close. Like a gasoline-soaked cloth waiting for a match. Chris wanted to be that match. She wanted to ignite Kate. Her stomach did a somersault. She took a step back. And another. Expensive jewelry. Soon to be partner in her family's law firm. Big house in Pacific Heights. Dial it down. Possibilities she hadn't realized she was entertaining dropped to the floor, shattering like breaking crystal. Kate was not going to be one of her regular lovers. Sex education. Period. Yeah, okay. She grinned, finding herself again, and gathered Kate to her. She kissed from the corner of her mouth to her ear, then tongued around and inside it the way that made Kate crazy.

"You're very, very good at that," Kate said in a breathy voice. "Dance with me?"

"Without music?" Chris nipped her way down Kate's neck, then out to the thin shoulder strap. She tugged it with her teeth.

"You underestimate me." Kate went to the living room and soft music began. "Battery-powered docking station." She turned toward Chris and held out her hand.

Chris took Kate in her arms. Their eyes met as they moved, a vertical version of what they'd been doing horizontally. The moment was so full of emotion it was overwhelming. An ache grew in her sex as Kate's thigh moved against her cock. She wanted to fuck Kate so badly her body growled with need.

Chris twirled Kate around and dipped her as the song came to its end. "And now, I'm your chef." She tucked Kate's hand to her elbow, walked her to the dining table, and pulled out the chair for her. Snapping the napkin open, she laid it on Kate's lap. "Tonight's specials are French onion soup, followed by beef tenderloin stuffed with hazelnut and sage dressing, and grilled vegetables." Chris bowed and retreated to the kitchen for the food and a chance to catch her breath. Kate was way more than she'd bargained for.

❖

"Not another bite." Kate folded her napkin and set it on the table. So far, the night was everything she'd hoped for. In spite of her efforts to keep her butch cool, Chris was obviously affected by her dress. Her eyes kept roaming over Kate's body, often ending at her breasts. Good. She intended to leave Chris well aware of what she'd be missing.

"I'll clean up." Chris took plates to the kitchen. "Coffee?"

Kate followed and wrapped her arms around Chris from behind, running her hands up and down the tailored, starched shirt. No bra, and Chris's nipples had been hard all evening. She cupped the bulge in Chris's pants. "I want to touch you."

Chris stiffened and turned to face her. "Do you know what you're asking?"

"Topping you?"

"More than that."

"Ahh. You don't give women access to this part of you." She took her hand away, disappointed.

Chris grabbed her hand and brought it back to her crotch. "My clit's hard. Go easy on me."

Kate draped an arm around Chris's neck and rubbed her palm lightly up and down the bulge, watching Chris's expression shift from hesitant to aroused in the flickering shadows from the candlelight. "Why are you hard?"

Chris raised her eyebrows. "Yeah, like you don't know how sexy you look."

"Busted." She kissed Chris as she loosened her belt and unzipped her pants. Sliding her hand inside the fly, she groaned at what met her. The cock was warm and pliable and felt like a part of Chris's body. Working her fingers inside the boxers, she fingered the realistic-feeling balls and held the shaft. Sexy didn't begin to cover it. Fear nosed its way into her thoughts. She liked to do things that she hadn't known existed until a few days ago. Things most people would find strange.

Chris held Kate's waist, her head tilted, as if trying to figure something out. "You like doing this?"

Kate nodded as emotions clutched at her heart. It felt like the most natural thing in the world to touch Chris this way. "You're the sexiest person I've ever met." *And I don't want to let you go.* She lifted Chris's hand to her breast, smiling as Chris caressed her, bringing her nipple to a peak.

"Beautiful." Chris tugged on one of her earrings with her teeth and then dragged her lips down Kate's throat, lingering at the soft place between her collarbones.

"I need to kiss you." She lifted Chris's head, running her fingers through her hair. Their eyes met for an instant, and Kate wanted to climb into Chris's soft, inviting gaze. They brought their mouths together, explored each other gently, as if meeting for the first time. She pressed into Chris's crotch. After days of noise from the storm, the quiet seemed like a soft blanket around them. The night was romantic and special and she'd never forget it.

"I want to fuck you," Chris whispered in her ear before she did that thing with her tongue.

"Anything."

She cupped Kate's ass and thrust against her. "I mean really fuck you."

Kate sucked in a breath as Chris's meaning became clear. She pulled back and stared at her.

"I'll make it good for you." Chris zipped her pants and took Kate into her arms, lifting her off the floor in one swift motion and carrying her to the sofa bed. She set her down and knelt in front of her, then slid the zipper down the back of the dress as she kissed between Kate's breasts. Sliding her dress down to her waist, she ran her tongue along the edge of the lacy black bra, then bit Kate's nipples to hardness. Removing Kate's heels, she ran her hands up the inside of her legs, then slid the dress and pantyhose off. She stared at Kate's black thong panties.

Everything was perfect. The room warm from the woodstove. Candles. The romance Kate craved. She slipped the shirt off Chris's shoulders. When Chris's eyes met hers, she melted at the raw desire, like steam coming off a pool. Taking her breast in her mouth, she sucked on the soft flesh while she rubbed her palm over Chris's cock.

Chris removed Kate's bra and panties, then guided Kate onto her back. She removed her pants and boxers, standing naked by the bed.

Kate stared at the cock sticking out from Chris's body, held in place by a black leather harness. Flesh-colored. Not too thick. Not too long. Her clit contracted. She wanted this connection with Chris.

Chris lay on top of her, the cock against Kate's thigh.

She opened her legs, realizing this was what Chris was doing that day with Jennifer. "Yes," she breathed against Chris's lips.

Chris handed her a condom packet. "Put it on me."

Kate slid it over the cock as she held Chris's gaze, seeing her own arousal reflected back to her. She spread lube over it, watching in fascination. Chris responded as if she felt every touch.

"Put it to your opening," Chris said, her voice heavy.

Kate did as a moment of fear surfaced. Then Chris was inside her.

"Okay?"

She nodded. It felt full in a good way. They stayed that way, Chris deep inside her. Connected. What she saw in Chris's uncensored gaze took her breath away, as if she were fully herself. Confident. Stunning in her androgynous beauty. A woman, yet something more complex. Impossible to define, but easy to feel the effect. Then Chris moved the cock. In. Out. Slowly. Kate bent her knees and tilted her hips, a smile spreading as she realized it felt really, really good. She wrapped her arms around Chris and pressed her heels to Chris's butt, consumed by the exquisite pleasure. The cock hitting her G-spot…their breasts grazing as they moved together in perfect sync.

Kate was afraid she'd break apart from the emotions building with her orgasm. She tried to wait. Tried to prolong the feel of Chris sliding in and out of her, faster now. She looked down her body. Chris's hard abs and the cock disappearing inside her was too beautiful. She dug her fingers into Chris's back, surrendering to the waves of orgasm that flowed from that point of union, carrying her away into unknown territory. She grasped Chris's hips and held her deep inside as she continued to contract around the cock.

"That was so hot." Chris studied her face as if memorizing it.

Kate's throat tightened as words threatened to push their way up from her heart. Words Chris didn't want to hear. She buried her face against her neck. Chris made her happier than she'd thought possible. And she had to let her go. But not yet. She tucked her emotions away. "Did you come?"

"No."

"Good." At Chris's raised eyebrow she asked, "What have you always fantasized about doing that you haven't?" A flicker of excitement crossed Chris's face. Oh, yeah. There was something. "Tell me."

She hesitated and then said, "To be sucked off."

"Your lucky night, stud." She took a deep breath, basking in the fullness of Chris inside her. Then she slid up until the cock popped out and stood erect between them. She peeled off the condom. "Lie back." When Chris looked uncertain she said, "Trust me."

Kate knelt between Chris's legs and licked her inner thighs, then around the harness straps. Chris was so wet it rolled down her thighs. Locking eyes with Chris, she ran the tip of her tongue up the shaft, around the head, and back down. Warm. Artificial, yes, but somehow part of Chris. Her eyes darkened. She kept doing it, teasing her mercilessly, enjoying every moment of Chris squirming and jerking her hips.

"Ahhh, God..." Chris let out a long moan when Kate took her in, all the way to the base, withdrew slowly, tongued the head, took all of her in again. "What are you doing to me?" She was propped up on her elbows, eyes glued to the cock as Kate kept sucking and licking, swirling her tongue around the head.

She put her fingers to Chris's opening. Surprise on Chris's face, and then she nodded. Her abs went rigid and she clenched around Kate's fingers before throwing her head back and pumping the cock into her mouth.

"Kate...Kate..." Chris cried out as she came. "So good..." She stopped pumping and held Kate's cheeks to stop her. "You wasted me."

She snuggled against Chris, her emotions shredded. What was she supposed to do with all this feeling? The turmoil dissolved as Chris kissed her. Hard. Deep. Possessive. She'd worry about it tomorrow. Tonight, Chris was hers.

Chapter Eighteen

Go away, Kate thought. Who was pounding on her front door in the middle of the night?

"Kate." Chris gripped her shoulder. "Wake up."

"Make them go away."

"Kate? Kate!"

She jerked to a sit as her heart rate skyrocketed. "Mother."

Chris scrambled off the bed. "Um, I should...yeah, I'll just..." She grabbed her pants and held them over her chest, staring at the front door.

"Kate!" Another insistent knock.

Her stomach bunched as she scrambled for her...dress...shit. She couldn't open the door in a dress. She looked in horror at the doorknob as it turned. She never locked it if she was home. "Get under the covers." She scooped her dress and nylons off the chair and sprinted to the bedroom, where she scrambled into sweats.

When she returned to the living room she didn't know whether to laugh or cry at the tableau. Chris. Covers gripped tightly under her chin, hair disheveled, eyes wide. Her mother. Two steps into the living room, hand to her chest, staring at Chris with a mixture of surprise and confusion. Nic beside her. Arms crossed, eyes hard on Chris. Only Todd looked friendly as he shot Kate a sympathetic look. She saw her bra and panties on the floor and nudged them under the bed with her foot.

"Oh, Kate, oh, Kate!" Her mother flew at her, arms out, clasping her in a breath-squeezing hug. "You're all right. Thank God. I've been sick with worry. And when we passed that awful tree and... and...that house..."

Kate tried to extract herself from the hug. Chris was staring at Nic, her face tight.

"We've been calling the local fire department several times a day. The road was opened yesterday afternoon." Her mother had circles under her eyes and was wearing pants and a sweater in blues that didn't match. "Why didn't you come home? Or call?"

"No power. Phones were dead."

"Oh, Kate. You could have been—"

"Cecelia." Todd put his hands on her shoulders. "Let's go outside so Chris can dress."

"Yes. Well. The important thing is that Kate's all right." She looked at Chris, clasping her sweater around her. "Why are you here?"

"I asked her to stay with me." Kate walked to the bed. Chris's gaze was glued on her. Distress.

"I need to use the bathroom." Nic headed toward the hallway.

Kate guided her mother toward the front door. "Outside? Please?"

"Oh, Kate. Don't ever worry me like this again." She crushed Kate in another hug. "You're all I have. All I have. I can't lose you, too. You must leave with us now."

"Come along, Cecelia." Todd ushered her out the door.

The toilet flushed and Nic returned to the living room. She stared at Kate, head tilted, an odd expression on her face.

"Nic, this is my friend, Chris."

She shot a hard look at Chris and walked out the door.

Kate locked the front door, irritated by Nic's rudeness. A laugh bubbled up as she collapsed on the bed. Tears stung her eyes. She rolled into Chris and held tight.

"That woman is your friend Nicole?"

"Yes."

"My cock is on the bathroom counter. Washed it after you fell asleep."

Kate snapped her head up. Another laugh bubbled up as she buried her face against Chris's neck. At least it was only Nic who'd seen it. "Last night..." She cleared her throat, fighting a swell of emotion. "I'll never forget it. I love...loved every minute of it." She hurried off the bed. If she kissed Chris she'd never be able to leave.

She went to the bathroom. The cock lay on a green towel. She reached for it. Dropped her arm to her side. Last night it had seemed part of Chris. Now it looked artificial. She covered it with another towel. Washed her face. Brushed her teeth. Finger-combed her hair. Didn't bother with makeup.

She dressed in jeans and a T-shirt, then pulled Chris's flannel shirt on over it. She held the collar against her cheeks, absorbing the smell of her. She took her bags to the living room. Chris had brought out the boxes of books and study materials from the office. The couch was put together and the furniture straightened. Sheets were piled on the chair. Sadness smothered her. "Can I take these?" She held up the book of erotica they'd read to each other and lifted the collar of the shirt.

Chris smiled. Not the cocky grin. A heartbreakingly tender smile. "Sure. You gonna be all right?" She was dressed in last night's clothes, shirt buttoned wrong and hanging askew over her pants. Hair disheveled. Still sexy as hell.

Kate shook her head. Every cell in her body cried out for Chris's arms. Words logjammed in her throat. *I want you. I love you.*

Chris stepped close. "Last night was amazing. Last few days were amazing." She fingered the ends of Kate's hair. "My beautiful Kate." Cupping Kate's cheeks, she brought their lips together in a gentle kiss.

Kate cleared her throat. "Stay here until the power comes on." She buttoned the shirt as she went to the front door. Taking a deep breath she opened it. Her mother sat in Todd's Lexus, the door ajar. Nic leaned against the car, arms folded, talking to her mother while staring at the cabin. She heard Chris close the back door.

Todd came to her and hugged her. "When I couldn't reach you this morning I called Cecelia to find out if you made it home. She was in quite a state. Said they were leaving to come here. I insisted on being part of the rescue party, as she called it. Are you all right?"

"Something happened with Chris."

"Obviously."

"Do you think Mother figured it out?"

"Definitely not. Do you want to talk about it?"

"Not now." What was there to say? *I had mind-blowing sex and fell in love for the first time with someone who doesn't believe in* love? They loaded her things into his car and hers. She closed the front door without looking inside. Locked it. Forced herself to walk to her car instead of to Chris's house for one more hug. One more kiss.

"I'll ride with you." Nic stood beside Kate's BMW. "Want me to drive?"

Kate shook her head. She hated Nic's driving, and she needed something to focus on other than the ache in her chest. Sliding into the car, she started it and backed out, wishing Nic had gone with Todd. She wanted to be alone with her thoughts, not explaining the cock. She wasn't ready to talk about Chris. She tried not to be obvious as she stared in the rearview mirror until she couldn't see Chris's house anymore. She wanted Chris to walk out, wave, blow her a kiss. Ask her to stay.

"Don't you care if I passed?" Nic crossed her legs. Designer jeans. Red cowl-neck sweater.

"Oh, gosh. I'm sorry."

Nic looked at her and lifted one corner of her mouth. Her version of a smile. She'd never seen her really smile. Not like Chris. "Todd passed, too."

"Congratulations." She waved to Les, who was raking leaves in her front yard. She wanted to be working with Chris to clean up their yards. She slowed as she drove between the cut ends of the downed tree, the exposed wood a pinkish-brown color and sawdust on the road. The windows on the crushed house were boarded up.

"Did you really not know the road was open?"

"Can you please take it easy on me?" If you looked up, it was as if the storm had never happened. Blue sky. Chunky white clouds drifted by as if in no hurry. Sunlight filtered through the perfectly still forest.

Nic put her hand on Kate's shoulder. "I don't want to fight with you. I've been a raving bitch. Stressed to the max over the bar-exam results and work. Let's kiss and make up over shopping and dinner today. If I don't get you out of the house, Cecelia might lock you in your room."

"She looks exhausted."

"I'm worried. She has to stop and catch her breath climbing stairs."

"I can't convince her to see her doctor."

"Stay home. Spend time with her. She was barely over your illness, and you take off and leave her alone. You don't know how lucky you are that she cares so much." Nic gave her a searching look. There was always something dark and lonely in her eyes when issues of family came up.

Kate squeezed the steering wheel, trying to pull her mind from thoughts of Chris. Her chest ached. Like she couldn't breathe right. Reminders of their lovemaking remained in her sore crotch and lips that felt bruised. She sucked in a breath, remembering the feel of Chris's cock inside her, their bodies moving together. She wanted it again. God, she wanted it again.

"You had an interesting weekend." Nic's tone was nonchalant, but she was drumming her fingers on her thigh. Annoyed. "Did you like it?"

Heat rose to her cheeks. Did she like it? Not that simple. She stopped when the road ended at Highway 9.

"Who else can you talk to about it?"

She stared at the old billboard on the right, Forest Lakes in faded yellow letters against the brown background. She turned left and sent the BMW away from Felton. Toward San Francisco. Away from Chris. "If I did like it, would that shock you?"

"Nothing shocks me. So she's a good fuck?"

"Don't be crude." Not about this.

Nic was quiet, looking out the window, her red-tipped fingers still drumming her thigh. "Bisexual's popular these days." After a minute she looked at Kate, frowning. "Surely you're not considering dating Mountain Mary."

"If you're going to be a bitch you can ride with Todd."

"Sorry." She squeezed Kate's shoulder.

"It started out playing around. I'm afraid it ended as more."

"There are plenty of appropriate women in the city you can date. Stay in your zip code, sweetie."

"What if I found a zip code I like better?"

"Treat it like a vacation. You're beautiful, rich, and successful. You can have your pick of women, but there's a limit to what you'll be able to sell to your mother."

"Happiness shouldn't be a compromise."

"Everything's a compromise. Have you considered it's an infatuation? I had a crush on a female professor in college. It passes."

"Honestly, I hope that's what it is."

"At least fall for a woman who looks like a woman."

"I like her the way she is." Tears filled her eyes. Talking about it made it hurt more. "I'm so messed up. I want Chris." She wiped her eyes on the soft shirtsleeve. "What am I going to do?"

"Exactly what you're doing. Move home. Get distance. I'll keep you so busy you won't have time to think. We need to ramp up your study schedule. We'll shop for my wedding gown and bridesmaids' dresses. You can help me choose invitations, flowers, cake, all that stuff you're better at than I am. In fact, why don't you move in with me until the wedding?"

They talked on the hour-and-a-half drive to San Francisco. About her study schedule. Nic's work. The wedding. Her life back to how it had been before the illness. Except it wasn't. She wasn't the same person who'd moved to Felton two months ago.

❖

Chris stood at the kitchen counter, still reeling, as she heard Kate drive away. Damn. What a disaster. She took her phone and went to her truck. Starting the engine she attached the phone to the charger and called Georgia.

"You all right, sugar? Your area was the hardest hit."

"You're not gonna believe this. Raven? The woman at your parties? Real name's Nicole." The icy, I'm-better-than-you look still pissed her off.

"I know. Works at a criminal-defense firm. Engaged to the heir of a restaurant dynasty."

"She's Kate's best friend." Chris explained what had happened.

"Now that's an interesting twist. Does Kate know about her Raven persona?"

"Pretty sure she doesn't." She rested her head on the steering wheel. How could Raven be Kate's best friend?

"You planning to tell Kate?"

"No matter how much I dislike Raven or Nicole or whatever, I won't violate her privacy."

"I wouldn't either. If she comes to my party next Saturday I'll suggest she find another venue."

"She'll blame me. If she isn't already bad-mouthing me to Kate, she will then."

"Why would—"

"She saw my cock when she used the bathroom. I don't think Kate's mother caught on to what was happening, but Nicole sure as hell did." Those eyes, dark and hard, boring into her.

"How was it with Kate?"

Great. Beyond great. A series of images flashed across her mind…Kate coming for the first time…Kate masturbating…Kate taking her from behind in the kitchen…Kate spread naked on the bed in cuffs.

"You still there?"

"Good. It was good. And confusing. But in a good way. Oh, hell." Chris ran her hand through her hair. She could still feel and smell Kate. Last night… She couldn't get it out of her mind. Kate dressed up…dancing with her…touching her cock…being inside Kate the first time…"It was great sex."

"It's all right if it was something else, Chris."

She didn't like the softness in Georgia's voice. "Have to go. Lot of cleanup." She looked at Kate's house. Couldn't stay there until the power came on, as Kate had suggested. Not without her. "Leaving for Christmas?"

"Don't I always?" Georgia chuckled. "Back to Italy."

"It's okay if it was something else with that woman."

"Touché."

"Can I spend the night next Saturday?"

"We'll see, sugar. In the meantime, I will see you Thursday." Thanksgiving at her dad's.

Chris disconnected her phone from the charger and stepped out of the truck. A trickle of smoke rose from the chimney of Katherine's cabin. Kate was safely on her way home. Back to her life. She started toward her garage for a ladder. Gutters first on both their houses. Then yards.

❖

Kate pulled into her mother's driveway but left the engine on.

"I'll pick you up in an hour." Nic plucked at Kate's shirt. "Lose the flannel."

She sat in her car after Nic drove away in Brian's Porsche. Todd's car was gone. She reached for her cell phone, charged on the drive. She wanted to hear Chris's voice so much it hurt. She put the phone in her purse and got out of the car. Nic was right. Probably a temporary crush. Her gran came through the gate from the yard and strode toward her as her mother stepped out the front door onto the landing.

"Come in and have lunch," her mother said. "I had the cook make your favorite soup."

"Be right there."

Her gran gripped her shoulders and studied her face. "Are you all right?"

"Yes. No. I'm so confused."

"Confused or afraid of the truth?" Her gaze was kind but, as always, demanded honesty.

"It's complicated."

"Love must be complicated. There's too much at stake for it to be otherwise."

It was complicated and it was very, very simple. She didn't have a shred of evidence that Chris felt the same about her. Maybe they'd hook up once in a while for sex. Kate's heart dropped. She'd be one of many. Not special.

"Kate. Come now. Lunch is ready."

Kate backed out of her gran's grip. She'd experienced the stuff of romance movies. She knew what passion felt like. But life wasn't a movie. There'd be no happy-ever-after. She walked to the landing and linked her arm through her mother's as she walked into the house.

Chapter Nineteen

Chris walked out of her dad's packed living room to the less crowded patio, leaving behind the cheering football fans gathered around the big-screen TV. She needed a break from Stacy's hovering—bringing her food, joining whatever group Chris was talking with, touching her, and generally acting like her girlfriend. She went to the dessert table and bypassed another slice of pie in favor of persimmon cookies. She was stuffed from the afternoon meal, but what was Thanksgiving without over-indulging.

"Smart we added that third bird." Her father joined her and cut a huge piece of pumpkin pie. This year they'd had to barbecue three turkeys besides the two hams. Her dad had started the open-house tradition before Chris was born as a way to thank his employees. It had grown to include friends and neighbors and Chris's employees. "Maybe we should have it catered next year."

"No!" Every year he suggested it, although she knew he wasn't serious. She loved coming over the night before. They'd eat pizza, bake pies and cookies, and do the prep work for the side dishes.

"Good." He put his arm across her shoulder as they walked to one of the many plastic tables they'd set up outside. "Stacy seems like her old self. Said she helped you finish up that Palo Alto job yesterday."

Mrs. Cavanaugh. The woman was a pain right up until the last plant went in the ground. Stacy had been there every day with several employees, acting like the blowup over Kate never happened. Help Chris wished she hadn't needed.

She sat beside her dad. Several of the posse were having a good-natured argument with two of her dad's employees about best Harley models. Taking her phone from her pocket she checked for a text from Kate. Nothing. They'd talked a few times and texted daily. Kate hadn't returned to help with Mrs. Cavanaugh's project. Studying. Shopping. Helping her mother with tomorrow night's party. And spending a lot of time with Nicole. Yeah, Kate was back in her life.

She joined the conversation for a while and then took more cookies and went to the bench beside the koi pond in the middle of her dad's yard. Her phone rang. She smiled as she answered it. Kate.

"Happy Thanksgiving. How's your barbecue?"

"Great food. Warm weather."

"I'll be right there," she said to someone. "Housecleaners."

"Sounds like a production." Kate had described the party tomorrow night as a formal affair, complete with lobster flown in from the East Coast, French champagne, and a string quartet. Based on names she'd mentioned, the guest list was heavy on San Francisco's social upper crust and people from business and entertainment.

"You have no idea. Arrrgh. Right away, Mother. I have to take care of something, Chris. I'll see you Saturday." She ended the call.

She was meeting with Katherine on Saturday to present the plans for her garden renovation. Maybe she and Kate could have dinner before Kate went to Mrs. Cavanaugh's party and she went to Georgia's party. At a hotel where—No, Kate wasn't one of her lovers. She put her phone in her pocket as Stacy approached.

"I remember when we put this yard in. We were a great team then. Still are." Stacy handed Chris a glass of beer and sat beside her. "We showed that snooty Mrs. Cavanaugh. She didn't get to hold the completion clause against you." Stacy held her hand up to high-five Chris. "Where should we go with our football-pool winnings?"

Chris kept her gaze on the pond, waiting for the irritation to pass. Stacy had entered them without telling her. Now she expected the two of them to go away for a weekend. "You should take someone else."

"Nah. We need a road trip. No better way to relax, right? Remember when we took the bikes up the coast to Mendocino the summer we met? Stayed in that crummy hotel and fucked our brains out? We'll stay in one of those fancy B and Bs this time." Stacy took a long drink of beer.

"May be time to switch to soda." She inched away so their thighs weren't touching.

"I need extra courage." Stacy angled her body toward Chris. "I'll know soon about the Portola project. I was thinking. Instead of bringing you in as a subcontractor, what if we partnered?"

Chris hesitated. She had a bad feeling about this.

"Oh, hell. I'm not saying this right." Stacy twirled the beer on the seat. "We're thirty, Chris. I'm tired of coming home to an empty house. Tired of chasing women who use me. And the business is getting to be more than I can handle on my own. Let's partner up."

"Partner how?"

"You gonna make me spell it out?"

Chris closed her eyes. Please don't.

"The last couple of months have been good, yeah?" Stacy took her hand. "We could have a solid thing. Work our asses off all day. Fuck our asses off all night. Motorcycle on weekends. I want to be with you. I'll do it on your terms." She entwined their fingers. "I'm falling in love with you."

Chris tried to pull away, but Stacy tightened her grip. "You're on the rebound. I'm not the solution."

"Come on, Chris. Don't tell me you don't feel anything. Let's date. Try it out. What have you got to lose?"

"I'm not in love with you." The words sounded cold, but she wasn't in the mood to soften them. Stacy knew the rules.

"Since when do you care about being in love?" Stacy's voice rose. "You can have all the sex you want. We can do threesomes. I'll go to Georgia's parties with you."

"You care about love."

"They always leave! They promise they're in love with me and then they leave. With you I won't have false hopes. We're compatible. We understand each other."

"It's not what I want."

"Everyone wants a relationship. Deep down inside we all want to belong. We can have it all." Stacy cupped her cheek and leaned in for a kiss.

Chris stood and shoved her hands in her 501s. She hated being the cause of the hurt in Stacy's eyes. "I can't, Stace. I can't."

"Because of Kate?" Stacy stood. "You think you can have something with her? What can she give you? She doesn't know you. She's playing around at—"

"Stop!"

Stacy's face went hard. "So that's how it is? Throw me over for her?"

"That's not how it is," she said, but Stacy was already hurrying toward the house. Damn it. She sat and closed her eyes. Sex was just sex, she repeated in her head. She startled when someone wrapped her arms around her from behind.

"You have to know what she wants before she does." Georgia laid her cheek against Chris's, then came around and sat hip-to-hip. "You need to talk out what's making you mope."

"Not moping." She ducked her head, knowing she couldn't hide from the woman who knew her so well. "Want company tonight?"

"Sex isn't the antidote to everything, sugar."

"So I'm finding out." She relayed the conversation with Stacy.

"Sex opens people up to feeling. That lets in other emotions. Falling in love is popular because it feels good."

"So I've heard."

Her phone signaled a text from Kate. She swallowed hard as she looked at the two pictures. Kate's reflection in a full-length mirror in different dresses and a question. "Which?"

"Neither," she typed. "Why cover up what's beneath?" She smiled at the "LOL" that came back and typed, "LBD." Kate gave a whole new meaning to little black dress.

Georgia peeked over at the picture. "Too bad she's not your type." She tapped a finger to her lips. "Oh, wait. She is your type. Bonus package, she likes Harleys and classic films."

Another text. Two more pictures. Kate in the LBD with two different sets of jewelry. Chris texted, "First one." The jewelry she'd worn Saturday night for their dinner. Fluttery sensations erupted from her stomach. What a night.

"That's a woman worth falling in love with."

Chris jerked her head up. "Why are you changing your tune? You showed me how to be happy without love."

"I didn't teach you that you couldn't be happy *with* love. Did you and Kate talk about what last week meant?"

"It was just sex."

"Hmm. You engage in days of sex with the same woman."

"Trapped."

"You allowed her to top you."

"Education."

"Are you more afraid to find out she does want to date you or more afraid she doesn't?"

"You want me to admit it's different with her? Okay. I can't stop thinking about her. Not only about having sex. I miss dinners with her. And movies. And motorcycling." Chris stopped as emotions filled her. "It wouldn't work. Can you see me at that fancy restaurant with her tonight? Or the fancy party tomorrow night? Making small talk with the likes of Nicole? Or her mother?"

"You're looking for excuses. Maybe what you have to offer is exactly what Kate wants. Don't miss out on something special because you're afraid. Talk to her."

"Chris!" Her dad hurried toward them. He didn't look happy. "Stacy locked herself in the bathroom. Won't talk to anyone but you."

"Drunk?"

"'Fraid so."

"This is why love is a bad idea," Chris said to Georgia as she stood. "Bad. Idea." It turned normally stable people into basket cases.

❖

"You looked lovely tonight. Black is always in style," Kate's mother said as they walked into the house.

Kate didn't tell her Chris had chosen it. She'd texted the pictures deliberately, hoping for the reaction she'd received. She yawned. Almost midnight. Dinner at the French restaurant, their Thanksgiving tradition, was always a drawn-out event. Last year her mother had cried through most of it, the first Thanksgiving without her father. This year Nic and Brian joined them. Her gran refused to come after last year's disaster. She took off the heels Nic had talked her in to buying. Higher than she usually wore, and her feet were killing her. "I'll see you in the morning."

"Join me for a cup of tea."

"I'm tired." She'd have to be up at five to study and get in a run before the party preparations began.

"We'll review the schedule for tomorrow. Great party planning is about timing and details." Caterers. Florists. Sound check for the quartet. The crew that was stringing white holiday lights through trees in the garden. Another crew that was delivering a Christmas tree and decorating it.

Kate walked in stocking feet beside her through the formal living room that tomorrow would be packed with guests. Her mother stopped to move an antique vase a few inches on the new rococo cabinet that had finally arrived after weeks of haggling with a dealer in France. "You're lucky to have Nicole. She cares about what's best for you. You've chosen your friends wisely. They'll be a help to you as you move into greater responsibilities."

"Sit," Kate said when they reached the dining room. "I'll fix your tea." Her mother looked pale. She tired easily, took the stairs slowly, and sometimes sat down abruptly, holding her palm to her chest. She cheerfully insisted she was fine. Good to be home where she could keep an eye on her. After the party she'd make her see a doctor.

In the kitchen, she set her purse on the center island in the all-white-and-stainless-steel kitchen. She set water to boil and checked her phone. Closing her eyes she willed there to be a text from Chris. Nothing. So far the crush wasn't dissipating. Todd was sympathetic. Nic cut her off and changed the conversation if she brought it up. When the tea had steeped, Kate set up the china tea service on the silver tray and took it to the dining room.

"I'm so happy you're home." Her mother filled two cups and set one in front of Kate. "So grateful you weren't harmed in that awful storm. You're all I have." She dabbed her eyes with the napkin as she went to the cabinet and took a black jewelry box from a drawer. "A thank-you for helping me with my party."

Kate lifted the lid. A large teardrop-shaped sapphire pendant set in gold and ringed in diamonds. Matching earrings. She lifted her eyes to meet her mother's. "They're beautiful."

Her mother lifted the necklace and put it around Kate's neck. "You'll have your own home. Your own parties. You must remember that your social and business activities will intertwine. Maintain an active role in society, and the firm will continue to attract appropriate clients. You're my pride and joy." Her eyes filled with tears again. The anniversary of her father's death was next month, but even with that she seemed unusually fragile lately. "Your father and I spoke often of your future. We wanted the best for you."

Kate wondered if his ideas about her future matched her mother's. She'd spent many hours with him in his study, talking about school and law and the firm, but seldom of personal things. She missed his quiet, thoughtful approach to problems.

Her mother stirred sugar into her tea. "Do you remember Karen Kingsley's son Stephen?"

"The kid who threw up on the cake at his birthday party?"

Her mother pursed her lips. "He's a cardiac resident at UCSF Medical Center. His mother told me in confidence that he always liked you. He's coming with them tomorrow night. Don't look distressed." She patted Kate's hand. "He's one possibility. I won't give up until I see you married to a man worthy of you."

"I'm tired." Kate stood and kissed her cheek.

In her bedroom, she removed the jewelry and flopped on the bed. Stephen Kingsley. She shuddered, trying to imagine kissing him. Kissing anyone but Chris. She took her phone from her purse and called before she lost her nerve. "If I come to Felton next weekend, will you help me repair the deck?" *Please say yes.*

"Sure. Would you spend the weekend?"

"Yes." Kate wanted to believe that was the answer Chris hoped for.

"Um, we could talk about what happened. You know. During the storm? In case you have questions. About sex. Or anything."

"Graduate course with my sex-education teacher?"

"I'd planned to send a vibrator home with you."

"I like your tongue better." Maybe there was a way to sneak in a tryst with Chris this Saturday before Mrs. Cavanaugh's party. Chris was meeting with her gran about the garden renovation. Hotel room? No. She'd never be able to explain why she was leaving for a few hours before the party. She should take Nic up on the offer to move in with her until her wedding. More freedom to see Chris.

"I'll have it fully charged for you. Nite."

"Nite." Kate plastered her palm to her chest as her heart skipped a beat. Only Chris would think to make sure she was taken care of sexually. She'd tried masturbating with her hand, fantasizing about Chris. She couldn't come. Every night she went to sleep frustrated, wanting Chris. It scared her that it wasn't only the sex that made her miss Chris. No, it was so much more.

Chapter Twenty

Chris held the tube containing the garden-renovation plans as she walked up the steps to Katherine's cottage and looked to the two-story main house. Kate was in there, probably dressing for Mrs. Cavanaugh's party. What was she wearing tonight? Maybe the black dress—She stopped the train of thought that was headed toward a fantasy of having sex with Kate. She was here on business. She ran through the pertinent points in the plan before knocking on the door painted sky-blue like the trim on the white cottage. Presentations were always nerve-wracking, even to a client she knew.

Katherine opened the door, looking festive in a red sweater and an apron with a Christmas tree on it. "You can lay out the plans there." She pointed to an oval-shaped oak dining table as she walked past it to a galley kitchen. "I talked to an editor I know at *Sunset* magazine. She's asked to do an article on my garden for years. She was impressed with your portfolio on your website. She's sending a photographer next week to take before shots."

"*Sunset?*" Chris whistled. Couldn't buy that kind of publicity.

"Eat while they're warm." Katherine set a plate of cookies on the table, helping herself to one. "I was once a poor judge of character, and it cost me dearly. I've trained myself to be an excellent judge of character. I approve of your relationship with Kate."

Chris spread the plans out, wondering what Kate had told her. "I like her." Okay, that sounded ridiculous. "I mean…"

"I know what you mean." Katherine gave a wry smile and went to the kitchen, where she slid another tray of cookies into the oven.

The front door opened and Kate stepped into the living room, a coat pulled around her. "Hi, Gran," she said, her eyes on Chris.

Chris absently smoothed out the plans, drinking Kate in as she walked toward the table, her high heels clicking on the hardwood floor.

Kate put her arms around her. "I missed you."

Chris let out a long breath as she absorbed all the curves that settled against her and breathed in Kate's perfume. She wanted to kiss her. Bad. She stepped back. "Missed you, too."

Kate pulled Chris's leather jacket open. "You look sexy," she whispered as she ran her palm down the white dress shirt and tugged on the waistband of the black Dockers.

"So do you," she said when Kate removed her coat to reveal the dress. Shiny gold fabric bunched across her upper body, showing tasteful cleavage, and cinched in around her waist. Probably a fashion word for the style of dress, but she didn't know what it was. "Beautiful necklace." She stared at the sapphire and diamond pendant resting between Kate's breasts. Probably cost as much as one of her company trucks.

"A gift from Mother."

"Want to grab dinner before your party? I'll take you somewhere—" Fancy. But she didn't have a reservation. "Um, somewhere."

"I wish. Mother has reservations at a new restaurant in Palo Alto."

"I regret interrupting this reunion." Katherine wiped her hands on her apron as she came toward them, looking amused. Picking up her glasses from the table she said, "I'd like to see my new garden."

Right. Chris forced herself into business mode. It was hard to think with Kate so close. "This is a site plan. Shows existing structures—cottage, the fence, trees, slopes, summer and winter sun patterns, etc." Chris moved the top paper aside to reveal the next. "Now this is the plot plan. What the garden will look like when I'm finished. You should keep the camellias along the fence. I propose a small pond at the edge of your patio by the seating area." She circled the spot. "Berm behind it." She moved her finger across the kidney-shaped area. "*Arctostaphylos* 'Sentinel' in the center, underplanted with *Heucheras* and *Deschampsia*."

"Translation, please, for the one who doesn't know botanical Latin," Kate said.

"Manzanita." Chris looked at her. Heart-stopping beautiful. So tempting to run her fingers through Kate's hair. "The mahogany bark and twisty branches provide year-round interest. Tiny bell-shaped flowers in the winter. Food source for wildlife." She lost her train of thought as she fell into Kate's eyes. They seemed a softer blue today.

"*Heucheras*?" Kate prompted in a soft voice, as if they were alone.

"Um, yeah. Perennial known as coral bells. Stalks of pink flowers in the spring." Kate's gaze drifted to her mouth, and Chris restrained the urge to kiss her. She wanted to smear the pink lipstick all over—.

"*Deschampsia*. Tufted hair grass," Katherine said, humor in her voice. "Evergreen with beautiful seed heads in summer. Fine choices. All natives and drought tolerant, once established."

"You'll have simplicity while still enjoying a beautiful garden." Chris pulled her attention from Kate. Focus. Katherine was the client. "We have about thirty square feet in the center for the labyrinth if you're sure about removing the existing plants." Kate's breast grazed her arm as she leaned over to study the plan. Her clit contracted.

"I'm sure," Katherine said.

"I've used a company that sells labyrinth templates. I recommend we choose from their catalogue."

"Can't you do something else?" Kate folded her arms.

"I like the symbolism." Katherine folded her arms also. "At my age, journeys, whether inner or outer, are a precious thing."

"You don't like the labyrinth?" Chris asked Kate.

"I had a bad experience at Chartres." Kate's face tightened. "Became ill walking it."

"If you have a bad experience walking this labyrinth, I will personally dismantle it."

Kate's face softened, and she wrapped her arm around Chris's waist. "I suppose if you protected me from that falling limb, a labyrinth stands no chance of hurting me."

"Limb?" Katherine asked.

"Didn't want to worry you," Kate said. "It plunged through the deck where I would have been standing if Chris hadn't tackled me. I took revenge. I chainsawed it into firewood. What's so funny?"

"Nothing." Chris suppressed the urge to laugh. Kate wielding the chain saw and Kate standing beside her in the gorgeous dress were hard to merge. "I love your inner butch."

"Tell Gran about your inner femme. Speaking of which." Kate took something from her coat pocket and set it on the plans. "Present." A few inches tall, wrapped in pink tissue paper and ribbon.

Chris ducked her head. She knew that shape. She peeled back the paper to reveal a bottle of bright-red nail polish.

"Great color for Christmas."

"Oh, you two are priceless." Katherine pressed her palms together, smiling broadly.

Chris felt Katherine's gaze on her, sure her cheeks had turned the exact color of the nail polish. "Materials for the labyrinth." She pulled her mind away from visions of sitting naked in bed with Kate, having her nails painted. "Decomposed granite would be the easiest to maintain, but we could do—"

"Flagstone," Kate and Katherine said in unison.

"I want to help build it," Kate said.

"It's not like the path. It involves turnarounds." Chris moved her hands in a semicircle. "Rounded? Hard to cut and fit?"

"I know what a turnaround is." Kate mimicked Chris's motion. "Teach me how to do it."

Chris held up her hands. "Okay." Not smart to argue with one headstrong Dawson, let alone two.

"When can you start?" Katherine asked.

"Don't you want to see the estimate?" Chris held up the printout.

Katherine flipped to the final page and signed the contract.

"I'll have to think about when I can get my crew—"

"Can't you and I do it?" Kate asked.

"Excellent idea," Katherine said from the kitchen as she lifted the lid on a large pot on the stove and stirred the contents.

"Um, sure. It'll take longer because I can only work on weekends."

"We'll have so much fun." She hugged Chris. "I have to increase my studying after the first of the year. Can we finish it before then?"

"It'll take a couple of weekends." Chris put her hands in her pockets before she swept Kate into her arms and kissed her senseless. Control. She'd learned to control her body's reactions to sex. This was different. Sexual but something more. Something that scared her. She didn't know how to control it.

"Remember Cecelia's New Year's Eve party," Katherine said. "She won't like materials stacked in the driveway."

"Next weekend, deck repair," Kate said. "And lots of sex," she whispered against Chris's ear. "Then we build Gran's garden. Mother travels to New York the week before Christmas. We'll make sure the driveway's clear before she returns." Her phone sounded. She took it from her coat pocket and read a text. "Have to go."

"I have a present for you, too," Chris said. "In my truck." She rolled up the plans and accepted the plate of cookies Katherine offered her.

"What if I swing by Georgia's party on my way home tonight?" Kate asked as they walked side by side through the garden toward the driveway.

"Really?" A rush of conflicting emotions surged through Chris. Surprise. Excitement. Then worry. Seeing people having sex could be a shock if you weren't prepared for it. If Nicole was there...The hell with her. Respecting her privacy was one thing, but protecting her from Kate finding out wasn't her problem.

"I can spend time with you and meet lesbians."

"You plan to date women?" An ugly thought surfaced. What if Kate had sex with other women at the party? She shoved it aside. She didn't have exclusive rights to Kate.

"Nic suggested I do both. She's been really sweet. I needed to talk about it, and she didn't seem at all shocked about us. Said I should go out with Stephen to keep Mother happy while I explore the idea of dating women."

Chris tried to imagine Nicole slash Raven as sweet. She must have a softer side if she and Kate were friends.

"Maybe I'm bisexual. Or maybe I'll discover I want to live like you. Sex without relationships."

This was a lot to digest. Kate hooking up with men and women. Kate at Georgia's. "These parties can be intense if you're not used to them."

"You'll be there. My personal guide." She bumped Chris's shoulder with her own. "I'm not naive, but now that I'm exploring my sexuality, I should really explore it."

Chris's head was spinning by the time they reached the driveway. She opened the truck door and handed a small package to Kate. "Open it later. In private."

"Why?"

"Bzzz."

It took Kate a second and then her eyes sparked. "You're a lifesaver. But tonight *you* take care of me."

Chris's libido happily amped up.

The front door opened and Cecelia and Nicole stepped out, chatting, dressed up as fancy as Kate. Both stopped when they saw Chris. Cecelia looked surprised. Nicole folded her arms and glared at Chris.

"Nic, you remember Chris," Kate said.

Nicole uncoiled. Arms dropped to her side. Shoulders relaxed. By the time she'd walked to them she'd added a smile. "Pleasure." She extended her hand.

Chris took it. The transformation was spooky, but maybe she'd misjudged the woman.

Nicole's eyes sparked and she tightened her grip, hard enough to hurt. Then she relaxed it. "Let's do lunch." She strode toward a black Porsche.

"Kate, come along," Cecelia said from beside a white Mercedes. "We mustn't keep Stephen waiting."

"Date?" Chris turned her attention to Kate.

"We knew each other as kids. He's doing his residency at UCSF. I'll see you later, stud," she whispered before walking toward the Mercedes.

The warm glow of being with Kate faded as she headed toward her truck. She'd known Kate would date men. Yeah, okay. Keep it simple. They'd be lovers until Kate figured out what she wanted. The black Porsche peeled onto the street. She had a bad feeling about tonight.

Chapter Twenty-one

"I feel like I'm driving the getaway car in a kidnapping." Todd punched the accelerator for emphasis as he drove his Lexus away from Mrs. Cavanaugh's house. "Cecelia didn't look happy."

"She's upset I'm leaving the party with you instead of Stephen," Kate said. "I have to admit he's a nice guy."

"We're not settling for nice."

A shudder of excitement whisked up her body. Half an hour and she'd be with Chris.

"Why was Nic pissed?"

"She springs this plan on me to have drinks at a new bar she found in the city and spend the night at her apartment. Promised it would be a night I'd never forget. She finds the trashiest bars imaginable and takes pride in it. I should have gone with her. I don't like lying or upsetting people I care about." She'd told them Todd needed to talk to her.

"We're being the rebellious children we never were and pursuing happiness at all costs."

"Pursuing happiness never put me at odds with Mother before." Kate removed the uncomfortable heels and wiggled her toes by the heater vent. "She scolded me for taking Stephen on a tour of Mrs. Cavanaugh's garden and showing him the streambed and path that I helped build. It hurts that she doesn't understand how much it mattered to me."

"You've never deviated from the punch list before." Only Todd could nail it so precisely. "Expectations we grew up with, so subtle we didn't know they were expectations."

"She complained that was no way to impress him on a first date."

"Ouch." Todd put his hand over his heart. "How easily she's replaced me."

"Stephen said it was our second date. Apparently we went to the movies in third grade. *Parent Trap* and ice cream afterward. He remembered that I had a caramel sundae with banana-nut ice cream."

"Sounds like love."

Kate smacked his shoulder. "I like your hair longer." She fingered where it lay over his collar. "And the mustache."

"Do I look dashing and dangerous?"

"Definitely." She tucked one leg under her on the leather seat, tilted her head back against the headrest, and closed her eyes, remembering the heat in Chris's eyes when she'd seen the dress. "Let's park at one of the rest stops along the freeway and smoke a joint."

Todd barked a laugh. "You have one?"

Kate rolled her head to look at him. "Wouldn't even know where to buy one. Some rebellious pair we are."

Todd took her hand. "Going to a sex party is enough daring for one night."

"Stop calling it that." A shiver went up her spine as nervousness pushed aside excitement. "It's a party. Where sex may be happening." Would women be walking around naked? She hoped not.

"Orgy. Orgy. Orgy." Todd tapped the steering wheel with each chanted syllable.

"I don't know what I was thinking. I lose my mind around Chris. They should put a warning sign on falling in love. Park your rational, logical self here, and prepare to enter the land of ruled-by-your-clit."

Todd shook his head. "Now I know you've lost it. Old Kate never talked like that."

"Sorry. That was insensitive."

"I get it. Saying Aimee's name is like a secret word that transports me to the land of goofy. And horny."

"Aimee. Aimee. Aimee."

Todd swerved the car playfully. "We came pretty close to missing out on all the fun." He guided the car onto the onramp to Highway 280 and headed north toward San Francisco. "Going to tell Chris you're in love with her?"

"No." Kate let out a long breath. "I feel like Julie Andrews in *The Sound of Music* wanting to run through the hills and sing because I'm happy." She sang a long "laaaa" note and spread her arms in front of her. "Then reality sets in. It would upset Chris, and maybe Nic's right that I'm caught up in the novelty and clandestine quality of it."

"Do you think it's temporary?"

"How would I know? It's not a subject I can research, and it seems my life experience is confined to what can be studied. I won't risk my friendship with Chris over a crush that might fade."

"If it doesn't?"

The surge of love swelled, rolling up from the butterflies in her stomach to the fullness in her chest that made her want to kiss Chris in the worst way. "When did you know it was the real thing with Aimee?"

"Don't be upset with me." He looked over at her. "When I bought your engagement ring and almost had a panic attack. I would have known sooner if I hadn't been caught up in the right or wrong of it. Being with her makes me feel like my best self, my happiest self. No matter how many times I explain that to my parents, it's like I'm speaking Greek."

"Bet coming out as a lesbian trumps your marrying Aimee."

"Aw, shucks. Stealing my thunder. Are you a lesbian?"

"Yes." It felt like the big-picture truth even if the details were complicated. "I've been hedging my bet by wondering if I'm bisexual. I'm not attracted to anyone but Chris, but if I were, I think it would be to another woman. If that makes sense."

"I'm a fan of being attracted to women."

"Butch women are sexy as hell."

Todd sputtered a laugh. "I like femmes."

"Nic insists I should, too. Says I can sell that to Mother, but not a woman like Chris. It's annoying. All week when we've gone out she points out feminine women and asks, 'What about her?' Stephen invited me to dinner next week. I have to tell him I can't date him. Regardless of what happens with Chris, I don't want to date men. How am I going to explain it to Mother?" All the expectations seemed to swoop down on her, pressing her into the seat and tightening the seat belt.

"She has gay friends."

"I'm noticing a difference between what she insists she believes in and what she tolerates when it's personal. Like how she advocates supporting women in business but it's not all right for me to work with Chris, especially if someone like Mrs. Cavanaugh finds out."

"Perhaps it's coming home after being away at school for so many years, but our parents' social circle doesn't look the way it did—close-knit and supportive. More like who can outshine who in the most-expensive-wedding category, or the best-attended-party category, or the whose-child-got-what-prestigious-job category."

"Mother hired a woman-owned catering company for the party last night, but when she found me in the kitchen talking to two of the servers while they cleaned up, she suggested I shouldn't keep them from their work. Translation, the hostess doesn't chitchat with the staff. Do you know what we were talking about? Law school. They both attend USF."

"Ah, yes. I'm getting plenty of lectures, and not only from my parents. Friends I thought I could count on have chimed in against Aimee. What do bank balances and pedigrees have to do with who you should love?"

They talked of Todd's work and her studying for the bar exam as he drove toward San Francisco. Finally he turned onto Fillmore Street in the Lower Haight neighborhood. A block. Another. She checked addresses and pointed to a three-story purple Victorian. "There."

Todd double-parked and set the emergency flashers. He came around to Kate's side and opened her door. Hugging her he said, "Have fun. Be safe. Text when you're ready to leave."

Kate watched him drive away, then stared at the smartly painted house. Two women walked arm-in-arm up to the lavender door, opened it, and disappeared inside. Chris is in there, she reminded herself as she walked up the stairs, shedding responsible Kate with each step.

Chapter Twenty-two

Kate paused on the landing lit up by two ornate fixtures. Laughter came from inside. What if she ran into someone she knew? Stop being ridiculous, she chided herself. About to push the doorbell, she heard a voice from behind her say, "Walk on in, honey."

A woman about her age with red hair framing her face sashayed up the steps. She opened the door and waited for Kate.

No backing out now. She entered, darting glances around the foyer and what she could see of the living room to the right. Women everywhere. Long hair. Short hair. Dresses. Revealing tops. Slacks and shirts. Suits. Lots and lots of leather. But no Chris. Several women turned to look at her, their eyes sweeping over her in the kind of look she craved from Chris. Their attention made her uncomfortable.

"Hang your coat in here." The redhead opened a door. "I'm Nora. Well, for tonight I am." Her eyes had mischief in them as she smiled. "Haven't seen you before."

"First time." Kate hung her coat in the closet, wondering again if this was a good idea.

"Shall I show you around?"

"I'm meeting someone. Chris? Short dark hair, little taller than me?" She tried not to stare at two women kissing while they caressed each other's breasts. They weren't the only ones. A lot of women touched each other or kissed. Sensuality was definitely the theme of this party, with a dash of holiday spirit from the decorations and high percentage of red clothing.

"Lucky you." Nora eyed her with new respect.

"Kate." Chris hurried from the living room off to the right. "I was watching for you and then went to get a beer." She handed the glass to Kate. "Nora." She tipped her head in the woman's direction.

Nora put her hand on Chris's shoulder and moved to kiss her.

"Maybe later." Chris cut her eyes to Kate.

Nora arched a brow. "If you want a threesome, find me." She winked at Kate before walking away.

"Are you sure it's okay I'm here?"

"Yeah." Chris swept her gaze all the way up and down Kate's body, pausing at her breasts, that roguish grin spreading up her cheeks. "You look beautiful."

Kate's breath hitched. The hell with where they were or whether she should have come. She was with Chris, and the butterflies in her stomach burst into fluttering. Wrapping her arms around Chris's neck, she kissed her. Gentle passionate, then demanding passionate. "I want you. Bad."

Chris smiled against her lips. "Play rooms are upstairs."

Play rooms. She imagined numbered doors like a hotel.

Chris took her hand as they walked across the foyer to the stairway. Women turned to look at them, or rather at Kate, like she'd won a prize.

Georgia came down the stairs toward them. Slowly. Hips and shoulders rolling in perfect counterpoint. Women looked up to stare at her. Impossible not to. Form-fitting silver dress. Mid-thigh. Sleeveless. V-cut to the navel. Sequined red belt and spiked heels. Red lipstick and nails.

"Welcome to our soiree." Georgia kissed each of them on the cheek. "Relax," she whispered to Kate. "It's all about pleasure."

Kate wanted to fan herself. Suddenly the house was too hot. "Your home is incredible," she forced herself to say instead of— "Your body is incredible." Chris had touched that body. Hundreds of times. Maybe thousands. The reality sent the butterflies into their cocoons. She was way out of her league here.

"A labor of love. I'll give you a tour later, if you like. Have fun."

Kate clutched Chris's hand as they continued up the stairs, or she would flee out the front door. They walked across the landing and stopped at the entrance to a hallway that went toward the back of the house in typical long, narrow Victorian style. Women talked in couples or groups in the hallway, some kissing or touching each other. Others stood in front of open doors, watching something inside. Most were topless. Many completely naked or wearing open robes. A flush swept up her cheeks as she tried not to look at breasts or crotches.

"The rooms on the right are public. Anyone can watch. Kind of like the real version of reading erotica." Chris smiled as if that should be reassuring. "There's one private room."

"Can we go in there?" The thought of being watched scared her. She'd do it wrong. Women would laugh at her. She'd be too self-conscious to orgasm.

"Whatever you want. Let's put your purse in my locker."

They walked to a bathroom. Kate stared at two women in the shower. The frosted glass did little to hide what they were doing. One's leg was hiked up while the other's arm pumped in and out of her crotch. Kate's ears burned with embarrassment. She hoped Chris didn't want to do anything so public. She looked at the array of things on shelves beside the vanity. Cocks and vibrators and harnesses, but other things she couldn't identify.

"Purse?" Chris opened a lock on one of the lockers.

Kate handed over the purse. "Can I keep my dress on?"

"Absolutely." Chris took a small nylon bag from the locker. Kate recognized it from the weekend. Sex toys were probably inside.

She gripped Chris's waist and pulled their bodies together, kissing her, reminding herself why she was here. She focused on that as they walked down the hall. Several women looked at their clasped hands and nodded at Kate, again with an expression of respect such as Nora had given her. It irritated her. How many of these women had come from Chris's fingers or mouth or cock? She tightened her grip. *Mine, and I'm not sharing.* She heard moans and cries before they reached the first room on the right.

"Do you want to go in?" Chris stopped in the doorway.

Kate shook her head as she took in what was happening. She'd expected it to be beautiful in a cinematic way. It wasn't. Three women were on a bed. One wore a harness and cock, but she didn't bother sorting out who was doing what to whom as she scanned the room.

Women watched, sitting or standing. Two masturbated, robes open and legs spread. Someone was coming, screaming out, begging for more. She looked at Chris. Did this turn her on? Of course it did or she wouldn't be here.

In a daze, Kate let Chris lead her to the next room. Five, no, six bodies on the bed, moving, writhing, some crying out or moaning. Again, women watching or masturbating.

"It can be fun," Chris said. "You relax into sensory overload."

Kate tried to imagine being touched by women she didn't know. She couldn't. The smell of sex and body odor and perfumes congealed in a way that made her stomach clench. She moved away from the doorway. Anonymous fucking. She'd imagined it like the erotica. Context. Okay, romance. She forced lightness into her voice. "It's uh...interesting." She wouldn't insult what Chris found appealing.

"We can go downstairs." Chris took her elbow and guided her toward the staircase. "Dance. I can introduce you around."

"I came here to be with you." She kissed Chris, long and deep, immersing herself in the kiss and only the kiss, but images of Chris in these rooms circled the perimeter of her awareness. She broke the kiss.

Chris took her hand. "Your private quarters await."

She kept her gaze on the floor and tried to ignore the sounds coming from the rooms as they walked to a door at the end of the hallway.

Chris shut the door behind them. Sounds diminished but didn't disappear. "You and me." She tossed her bag on the large bed with metal railings at the head and foot and pulled Kate close. "Like during the storm." She traced her tongue around Kate's ear and then kissed across her cheek. She sucked Kate's bottom lip and pushed her tongue into Kate's mouth.

Kate responded because she needed to, letting the familiar cologne and the taste of Chris's mouth erase the other sights and sounds and smells. She waited for the butterfly explosion in her stomach, but it didn't happen.

Chris went to the bag and unzipped it. "What's your preference?"

Kate folded her arms as she let her gaze dart around the room dimly lit by sconces. A number of rings were attached to one of the chocolate-brown walls. Cabinets and racks lined another wall.

Handcuffs. Ropes. Chains. Things she didn't have names for. Like a gym for sex. She walked to a rack of whip-like things.

"Floggers."

"You've used them?"

"Yes." Chris wrapped her arms around Kate from behind and nuzzled her ear.

"You top women with these...things." She spread her arm out to indicate the entire room.

"I have." Chris stopped nuzzling and stood beside her, shoving her hands in her pockets. "I've done a lot of things. Isn't that why you're here? Testing boundaries? Exploring?"

"What we did with the hot wax and ice...it was kindergarten level." To her it had been exciting and daring.

"This isn't school where you rank things in order of difficulty. Sex isn't like that." Chris sounded irritated.

"Do you bring women into this room?" When Chris walked away she wished she hadn't asked.

"I've never lied to you about who I am."

"Please don't be upset with me." To her embarrassment, tears filled her eyes. She waited until she could trust her voice. "I wanted to be with you in your world. I thought it would be like working with you. A little awkward at first. Learning new skills. But then I'd like it." She heard Chris zip the bag. Then she was in Chris's arms. She laid her head on her shoulder.

"I should have prepared you better so you could decide if it was your scene. You caught me off guard, and I confess that the thrill of being with you tonight made me forget it's my job to take care of you. I'll take you home."

Kate held tight. She wanted to stay so much. Maybe if she kept her eyes closed or if they dimmed the lights more. She took Chris's mouth in a hard kiss, willing the butterflies to take flight, willing desire to blot out anything else. She broke the kiss, ducking her head so Chris wouldn't see the tears. Crying upset Chris, and this wasn't her fault. She followed her out of the room.

Downstairs, she took out her phone and texted Todd to pick her up. "Mother thinks I'm with him," she said to Chris. "I don't want to explain why you brought me home."

"Yeah. Okay." They sat in the living room, sharing a beer. Women came over to greet Chris, most moving in for a kiss the way Nora had, obviously surprised when Chris declined.

Kate watched women move about the room, wondering how they could be so casual about touching strangers. Having sex with strangers. Any fantasies that she could be like Chris disappeared. She wanted sex inside a relationship, and the only woman she wanted didn't do relationships. What a mess.

"That's Todd," she said fifteen minutes later when her phone signaled a text. She curled into Chris and kissed her. A few butterflies fluttered.

Chris walked her to Todd's car and opened the door for her. "Thanks for taking her home," she said to Todd.

"Still on for next weekend?" Kate asked.

"You bet. I'll warm up my power tools." Chris smiled, not quite cocky, but enough to make Kate's heart feel hopeful.

She closed the car door and caught a final glimpse of Chris in the side-view mirror. Impossible to stay, but so hard to leave. "Can you pull over?" she asked when the house was out of sight.

"What's the matter?" Todd pulled to the curb.

Kate released her seat belt and fell against Todd. "I want Chris so much it hurts."

"I know." Todd held her.

Finally cried out, Kate sat up and brushed tears from her cheeks. Those rooms. That's what Chris liked. God, she was naive. Chris would never give that up. "Can we stop for a drink on the way home?"

"Sure."

She stared out the window, not caring where they ended up. Her heart cried out for Chris. Her mind repeated why she couldn't have her.

At home, she took her heels off and went upstairs, hoping her mother was asleep. In her bedroom she undressed, putting the necklace and earrings in the jewelry box. She sat naked on the bed and unwrapped the present Chris had given her. She held the vibrator, identical to the one she'd used with Chris. She'd included a bottle of lube. Sliding under the covers, she put some on her clit and moved the vibrator against herself as she fantasized about the night she'd imagined—making love, alone, on a soft bed. Sweet and romantic.

Why had she thought she could get that at a sex party? The pressure built and she let it. Fast. She needed to come fast.

Her bedroom door opened. "Kate?" her mother asked.

She turned the vibrator off and brought her legs together as the orgasm shrank away.

Her mother turned on the light and came toward the bed. "Eileen Bryant's daughter swooped in on Stephen after you left." She sat beside Kate, her blue bathrobe buttoned to her chin. "Don't worry. I told him about that unfortunate situation she had with the married man. I invited him to dinner Thursday night. I'll make a Wednesday appointment at the salon for us." She patted Kate's arm.

Kate waited for the door to close. She turned on her side and hugged a pillow. Chris was probably still at the party. In one of those rooms. She squeezed her eyes shut, trying to block out the images.

❖

Chris stood on the street until Todd's car was out of sight. She dropped her head. Damn it. She went inside, searching for Georgia to say good night. She wasn't in the mood to be here. She found her on the couch in the living room, kissing a full-figured blonde on her lap.

"Excuse me," Georgia said to the woman, meeting Chris's gaze.

"You all right, sugar?" Georgia put an arm around her waist.

"Everything's fucked up, G. I shouldn't have let her come."

Georgia linked her arm and led her up to her bedroom on the third floor. A whip and leather cuffs lay on the bed. Chris almost asked if she could spend the night. She wanted to be who she'd been before Kate.

"You've never brought anyone here. You've never been upset when someone decided it wasn't her scene. Why don't you take a break from all this? Spend time with Kate. See where it goes. What do you have to lose?"

Chris knew exactly what she had to lose if it didn't work out. She'd be like Stacy. Heartbroken because…Realization hit her like a stab to her chest. She shot her eyes to Georgia.

"Congratulations, sugar. I was afraid you didn't know you're in love with Kate."

"I don't want to be in love. It's messy."

"Messy doesn't make it wrong. I turned away from love because I realized it didn't matter to my happiness. You're turning away before you know if it makes you happy."

Chris started to argue but couldn't. She wanted Kate so much. She didn't resist when Georgia held her.

"I'm here for you." Georgia kissed her cheek. "We'll find a night for dinner before I leave for Italy."

They walked down to the second floor, where Chris retrieved her stuff from the locker. She'd closed it when someone slammed the bathroom door shut and locked it.

"What the hell is wrong with you!" Before Chris could cut around her, Nicole was in front of her, boxing her in. Inches from Chris's face, her eyes pinpricks of fury. "You'd let her risk everything? For a common butch who fucks anything with tits? Who the hell do you think you are?! If she prefers pussy she can have it with a woman worthy of her." Her voice shimmered with anger.

"These parties are fine for you but not for her?" Chris asked, taunting her. She tried to duck under her arm.

Nicole blocked her. "You might know her body, but you know nothing about her life. You're not what she needs. Get this straight, Mountain Mary. Stay away from Kate, or I'll fill her mother in on what's been going on. You think the storm was vicious? Cecelia will make that look like a spring shower."

"Kate's an adult. She can make her own choices."

"Are you really that naive? You have nothing to lose. She has everything." With lightning speed she slammed her knee into Chris's sex as she took her lower lip and bit, hard enough to draw blood. Then she stormed out of the bathroom.

Chris plastered her palms against the lockers as shock and anger flooded her. Try as she might to deny it, Nicole was right. What was she doing, getting involved with the likes of Kate? An image of the sapphire and diamond necklace flashed across her mind. Out of her league. Way out of her league.

Chapter Twenty-three

Chris stood in the living room of Katherine's cabin, running through her checklist. Kate was coming for the weekend. Hot-water heater pilot lit. Woodstove started to heat up the house. Refrigerator stocked with her favorite snacks. Sheets washed and put on the foldout couch. Clean towels in the bathroom. Fresh candles set out. Two bouquets of flowers. Too much? No. Nothing was too much for Kate.

"I love you," she whispered. Words she'd never say to Kate. She shoved her hands in her pockets, mentally fighting against Nicole's angry words when she'd confronted her last Saturday at Georgia's party. Defeat settled over her. Nicole was right. She didn't fit in Kate's world, and being in love didn't change that. She'd settle for what she could have. This weekend, Kate was hers.

She went home and spent the next two hours working on the design for a new residential project in Palo Alto. She had Kate to thank for it. The woman had attended Mrs. Cavanaugh's party and liked the garden. She hadn't talked to Stacy since the disaster at Thanksgiving and was pretty sure Stacy wouldn't bring her in on the Portola project. Probably for the best. Partnerships of any kind were messy. If the *Sunset* magazine article happened, it could be the key to expanding her business.

She went to her kitchen and started prepping for breakfast. Omelets with fresh crab she'd bought on the wharf. She chopped veggies, mixed dough for biscuits, and squeezed orange juice. Nine o'clock. She made coffee. Nine fifteen. Still no Kate. Her heart stopped as she realized she could have been in an accident. Her phone chimed a text from her.

Sorry. Had to take care of something for the party. On my way.

K.

Kate's sorority Christmas party next Friday. More important than spending time with her. Fine. She put the breakfast fixings in the refrigerator. Might as well pick up the materials at the lumberyard. She deliberately left her phone behind. Best not to be tempted to text her irritation. She had no claim on Kate's time. Keep it light and simple. Occasional lovers. Period.

❖

Kate lowered the window and inhaled as she made the turn from Highway 9 into Forest Lakes. Home, her body said, finally relaxing. She had the weekend with Chris. Bravo, Todd had said. Inconsiderate to leave again, her mother had said. Risky, Nic had said. She didn't care. She had to be with her. Things had been awkward at Georgia's party, but here Chris would be all hers.

Other than the cut ends of the redwood tree, she saw little evidence of the storm. One more block and she'd be—she took her foot off the accelerator and let the car slow to a stop. No. Her heart landed hard in her stomach. A Prius was parked in front of Chris's house. She hadn't said anything about having a date last night, but it looked like she had company. One of many, she repeated as she shoved the car into gear, gunned it into her driveway, and jerked the parking brake on. She sat in the car, schooling herself on reality. Multiple lovers with whom she did things Kate couldn't have imagined until Georgia's party. That's who Chris was. And she was in love with her anyway.

She took her overnight bag and the plate of cookies Gran had sent and walked to her front door. Irritation melted when she saw that Chris had bought her flowers. Thoughtful. Also who Chris was. She took the cookies to the kitchen, surprised to see Chris on her deck beside a stack of lumber. She hurried out, forgetting everything but the joy of seeing her. She stopped when she reached her. What if the other woman's perfume was on her clothing? "Whose Prius out front?" She tried to sound nonchalant.

"Andersons across the street had a party last night. Guess someone left their car."

What an idiot. She grabbed Chris's red-flannel shirt and yanked her close, moving fast to capture her mouth. Want. Want. Want. She unleashed her heart into Chris's strong embrace and the heat of the kiss.

"I'm making breakfast for you."

"I'm hungry for something else." She took off Chris's ball cap and ruffled her hair.

Chris's face spread slowly into the grin that melted Kate's insides. "Didn't my little present take care of that?"

Kate put Chris's hand on her breast. "Make—Make me come?" How easily she'd almost blurted out "make love to me."

"Sex stud at your service," Chris said, an odd flatness to her voice where Kate wanted hot and passionate.

She pulled back to look at Chris. Cocky grin. Warm eyes. No, she must have misinterpreted. Taking Chris's hand, she hurried into the house, to the couch, pulling Chris down on top of her. Driving her fingers through Chris's hair, she pulled their mouths together. She couldn't get enough of kissing her. She yanked Chris's jeans open, shoving her fingers inside denim, then inside boxers, cupping her sex. "I've missed this."

"Me, too." Chris closed her eyes and arched as she thrust against Kate's fingers.

Kate pushed inside her, deep and hard the way Chris liked. She slid her hand under the T-shirt and played with Chris's breast. She'd missed this so much, as if she hadn't been able to breathe right since leaving Felton.

"Gonna...come." Chris groaned as she rode Kate's fingers.

She stilled inside Chris. Loved to feel her contract around her fingers as she came. She nuzzled Chris's neck, their hearts beating against each other.

"Okay, let's get to the deck," Chris said after a long kiss, her expression serious before softening into a smile.

She wrapped her arms around Chris. "Just try to leave this couch."

"Would I leave you unsatisfied?" Chris thrust her crotch into Kate as if fucking her. "Let's take some clothes off you." She pulled Kate's tennis shoes and jeans off and knelt beside the couch, staring at the black-lace panties. Her gaze lifted to Kate's. Heat darkened the brown eyes. Slowly she lowered her mouth and covered Kate's clit through the panties. Licked. Tugged. Bit.

"Lube. Duffel." Kate's body was on fire. Seconds later Chris slid the panties off and entered her as she put her mouth to her clit. She dug her fingers into Chris's shoulders and scrunched the flannel shirt, surging toward release. She needed it so bad. Chris pinched her nipple. Pain. Pleasure. Curled her fingers, owning the spot that made Kate crazy, driving her up and over into a long, surging orgasm.

"Don't stop." *Don't. Ever. Stop.* Love welled up from the place in Kate's heart that belonged to Chris. What came out was an unintelligible mix of sounds packed with "more" and "so good." "I love you" stayed locked in her heart. She held tight to Chris as she floated down from her orgasm. Sadness nipped at the edge of the pleasure. Orgasms were no longer the point. Now she wanted them wrapped in words of love and a future she'd never have with Chris.

Time seemed to stop as they stared into each other's eyes. Finally Kate sat up, afraid she'd blurt out the last thing Chris wanted to hear, the words that would ruin the weekend so precious to her. "Feed me. Then deck-repair lesson."

Chris stood and pulled her up. "I held off putting up Christmas decorations so you could help."

"As long as we're done in time to make our reservation at Shadowbrook. I'm taking you on a—out to dinner as a thank-you for helping me with the deck." A romantic dinner. She put her head on Chris's shoulder, afraid her heart would burst from all the love encased within it.

❖

After breakfast where there'd been as much kissing as eating, Chris carried tools to Kate's deck along with the surprise she had for her. Cold but clear blue sky. Tomorrow they were hooking up with the posse for a ride. She could imagine every weekend being like this. Sex and meals and doing projects and motorcycling. If only...

"Ta dah."

Chris stared at Kate, moving the surprise behind her back. She was wearing canvas pants and work boots. And a tool belt. "It's pink."

"A bonus. Tomboy Tools. Ergonomically designed for women. Found them on the Internet."

Chris brought her hand from behind her and held up the tool belt she'd bought for Kate. "Um, yeah. I'll, um...put this one away." Apparently Kate didn't need her for anything but sex.

Kate grabbed her arm. "I want yours." She unclipped the pink tool belt and dropped it to the deck. "Put it on me." She held out her arms.

"It's the same as mine." Chris fitted it around Kate's waist and clipped it in back. She tugged it low on her hips. "Thirteen-ounce hammer. Better weight for you than mine. Twenty-five-foot tape measure. Carpenter's pencil. I loaded it with the screws we'll use for the deck." She picked up the Tomboy tool belt and moved the pink torpedo level from it to Kate's belt. "A bit of pink never hurts."

"You're the most thoughtful person." Kate wrapped her arms around Chris.

Their tool belts pressed into each other as Chris held her, inhaling her smell, absorbing the feel of her. Finally she let go or she wouldn't be able to. "I took the old blade off the circular saw. I'll show you how to put the new one on."

"I know how. YouTube videos." Kate peeled the protective rubber covering from around the tips of the blade. "Set it on the bolt shaft," she said as she did it. "Put the flange over the blade and then the bolt on the shaft. Where's the key thingy that tightens the bolt?"

"This saw doesn't have one. Have to do it the old-fashioned way."

"Oh."

Chris knelt beside her. "Clamp vise grips on the blade near the safety guard so it doesn't move while you're tightening the bolt with the wrench." Chris waited while she did. "We'll cut out the damaged boards back to a—"

"Joist. We stagger the cuts so the new boards aren't all the same length."

"Yeah." Chris frowned as she handed Kate a cordless drill. "Take out the—"

"Screws in the board several feet farther back along the length of it. Then lift the board and put a piece of wood under it to hold it up while we cut it."

"I can show you how to cut the board in place. Or we can do it your way."

She lowered the drill. "I didn't want to be the total dumb girl."

"You could never be the dumb girl." Chris tugged Kate's tool belt, pulling their bodies together. "I like teaching you." She could imagine a lifetime of teaching her and taking care of her. She let go. "Let's finish this so we can put up decorations."

Chapter Twenty-four

"I wish I'd known you then," Kate said as they approached the arbor-covered entrance to Shadowbrook, pointing to two teenaged couples exiting a limousine. They were dressed in tuxedos and fancy dresses. Apparently there was a high school dance tonight. "Would have saved me years of confusion."

"Your mother would never have let you go to a high school dance with me."

Kate didn't like the dismissive tone. She liked even less that it was true. Her mother wasn't homophobic, but based on her reaction to Melanie, a prep-school friend of Kate's who'd come to the Thanksgiving party with her girlfriend, lesbian was not on a par with straight. She'd made the case that gays would always be seen as different, equal under the law, but outsiders, subject to prejudices, subtle and not so subtle, which would affect their lives.

She linked her arm through Chris's as they waited their turn for the red cable car that ferried diners from the street to the restaurant down the hill. She wished they were truly a couple out on a date.

"You decided about dating men or women?" Not the first time today she'd asked.

"Can we not talk about it?" Tonight she'd pretend she was dating Chris and only Chris.

"I'll check us in," Chris said when they'd stepped from the cable car. "Bar's packed. I'll bring drinks for us. Beer?"

"Please." She watched Chris work her way up to the hostess stand. Black slacks and boots, white dress shirt with the black skinny tie, black leather vest. Packing. Sex-y. She frowned when the hostess hugged Chris and…yes, kissed her. She resisted the urge to march inside and claim Chris with a kiss.

She turned around and, seeing a space open up on a nearby bench, went to sit beside a teenaged couple. The young woman was beautiful in a peach-colored satiny dress with shoulder-length red hair. It wasn't until her date looked up that she realized it was a woman in a black tux, hair dark and shorter than Chris's. "I'm Kate," she said, standing in front of them. "Okay if I sit with you while my girlfriend's getting our drinks?"

"Sure." The woman in the tux shot to her feet. "I'm Syd and this is Elaine."

Kate sat beside Elaine. "Have you eaten here before?"

"First time. Elaine's always wanted to." Syd took her hand.

Kate was about to launch into Shadowbrook's long history when a stocky teenaged boy in a white tux approached the bench.

"You turn me down and then show up with her?" The kid stood in front of Elaine, his face hard with anger. "You're not a lezzie. What the hell!"

"Don't make a scene, Ty," Elaine said softly, meeting his gaze.

"Everyone knows I asked you first."

Syd stood and stepped between Ty and Elaine. She barely came to his shoulder.

Kate stood also. "Calm down," she said to the boy.

"Look at you." Ty flipped Syd's jacket open. "You like this shit?" he asked Elaine. Other people had turned in their direction as Ty's voice rose.

"Leave her alone," Syd said.

Chris strode quickly toward them, her face hard. She set the glasses of beer on a table and moved between Ty and Syd. "What she likes isn't any of your damn business."

"Ho, ho, ho. Another one." Ty reached for Chris's vest.

Chris snapped her hand onto Ty's wrist and squeezed. "Leave them alone or I talk to my hostess friend. Then your reservation disappears and you take your date to McDonalds."

Ty yanked his wrist free.

Kate stifled a laugh. Chris released her grip with perfect timing so his tug sent him off balance and he had to take an awkward step to regain it.

"Bitch," he growled as he strode away from them.

Kate put a restraining hand on Chris's arm when she made a move to follow Ty. "Meet Syd and Elaine. Our guests for dinner. If that's all right with you," she said to the teenagers.

"We'd like that." Elaine stood and clasped Syd's hand.

Kate's heart melted at their obvious affection for each other. "Talk to your hostess friend," she said to Chris, oozing sweetness into her voice, "and arrange a table for four."

"I'll get us Cokes." Syd walked off with Chris.

"You all right?" Kate asked Elaine as they both sat. That boy had looked angry enough to take a punch.

"I'm worried about Syd. She takes it hard when people treat her like that. I talked her into taking me to the dance. I didn't like how kids treated her last year after she came out. I made a point of making friends with her this year." Elaine's expression softened. "Little did I know I'd fall for her. She's the nicest person I've ever known, and beautiful, too. Don't tell her I called her beautiful. She'll get embarrassed."

"I painted Chris's toenails."

Elaine laughed. "How long have you been with Chris?"

"Not long enough." Chris and Syd returned. She vaguely listened to the conversation as she tried to imagine her life if she'd known Chris at their age. Tried to imagine her life as an outsider, subject to that kind of attack.

Dinner was superb and conversation lively. They left the restaurant, parting company with hugs.

Kate linked her arm through Chris's as they walked to the car. "Want to explain why Ms. Cool and Calm lost her cool with Ty?"

"It's not right."

"Nor was what Mrs. Cavanaugh did, but you didn't come close to blows with her."

Chris was quiet for a while. "Same thing happened to me at senior prom." Her voice was hard and distant. "Took a girl. Wore a tux. Got hassled."

"What's the rest of it?" She asked after several minutes.

Chris let out a long breath. "The girl's ex-boyfriend and his buddies caught me in the hallway. He pinned me. Pushed his crotch into me. Called me cunt and other things." She worked her jaw. "Fucker gut-punched me. His buddies laughed and clapped."

"I wish I'd been with you." Kate stopped Chris and stepped so their bodies were snug against each other. "I'm going to rub against you and tell you how much I want you inside me." She ground her crotch against Chris's. Slowly. So slowly. Closed her eyes and rested her cheek against Chris's. "I love you" rose up like champagne bubbles seeking escape.

"I've never known anyone like you." Chris looked at her. Need. Desire. Those she'd seen before. Something soft and tender lurked beneath that she hadn't seen. "I..." Chris shook her head and then she was Chris again, grin in place. She pressed her crotch against Kate's and kissed her.

Kate melted into her. Let herself be soft against Chris's strength. Drove her tongue into Chris's mouth. Lifted her leg around Chris's thigh. Did not care who saw them. *I dare you to say something. I. Don't. Care.* Breathing hard, she broke the kiss. "Let's take a drive and park along West Cliff so I can hear the ocean while you fuck me."

Chris sucked in a breath. She picked Kate up and spun her around before opening the passenger door for her. "Your wish is my command."

Ten minutes later, Chris nosed the BMW up to the curb facing the ocean. A full moon hovered, casting a streak of light across the rolling ocean. "Is this the best night ever?" She took Chris's hand and entwined their fingers. Romantic. Perfect.

"Beautiful woman. Beautiful scenery." Chris stroked the dash. "Beautiful car."

"Cad." Kate punched Chris's shoulder. "I swear. I don't know why I lo—like you. Kiss me senseless." *Mine for tonight.* Their lips met. Their tongues met. Familiar. Like she'd been waiting for this her whole life. She unbuttoned Chris's shirt enough to slide her hand inside. Soft breast. Nipple that peaked as she circled it. Then Chris's fingers were on her thigh, working their way under her dress and up to her sex. She took a bottle of lube from the glove compartment. "Take me." She spread her legs.

"Had this planned?" Chris teased Kate's clit on the outside of her panties.

"Orgasm. Now." Yes, she'd planned this. The night was everything she wanted. And it was far from over.

Chris slid her fingers inside the panties, slick against Kate's clit.

Yes. Yes. Yes. She fisted Chris's shirt and pulled her into a kiss. She couldn't speak, couldn't think as Chris entered her fast and hard. She hadn't been sure she could come like this. Now she was about to come too soon. Close. Close. And then she was tumbling over... Chris's arm tightened around her as she came, rocking her gently. Time seemed to stop as they held each other for a long time, the ocean crashing against the cliffs nearby.

Kate tugged Chris's zipper down. "Your turn."

"I'd rather wait till we're home so I can be inside you."

They held hands on the drive home, bantering over movie trivia, and Kate felt like a teenager in love for the first time. Her phone rang as Chris pulled into the driveway. She closed her eyes. Mother.

"Oh, Kate, thank goodness you answered. I fell coming down the stairs."

"What!" Mother, she mouthed to Chris.

"I hurt my ankle. It's swollen and I can't put weight on it because of the pain. I don't know what to do. I'm afraid I need an X-ray."

Kate clenched the phone. She knew what was coming.

"Can you come home? It's my right ankle. I can't drive."

"Isn't Gran home?" Surely her ACLU meeting was over.

"I don't know. Please?" Her voice cracked. "I'm scared. What if I broke it?"

"Yes. All right. Lie down on the couch and put ice on it." She ended the call. "Mother fell and hurt her ankle. I have to go home."

"She can't call Katherine? Paramedics?"

"It's not like I want to leave," Kate said, irritated.

"I get it." Chris shoved the door open and stepped out.

No, you don't. You don't get that it breaks my heart to leave you.

Chris opened her car door and walked Kate to her front door, hands in her pockets.

Kate hesitated, giving Chris time to kiss her. Then she opened her door and shut it hard behind her. Angry at her mother. Angry at Chris. She changed into jeans and took her bag to the car. She sat for several minutes, hoping Chris would come to her. Finally she put the car in gear and drove away, putting her hand over her heart as if she could keep it from shattering.

❖

Chris stood in her kitchen as Kate drove away. Kate was upset with her, but damn it, she was upset, too. She didn't understand why Kate gave in to her mother all the time. Didn't matter. She was gone.

She grabbed a beer and plopped on her couch, still in her dress clothes and wearing her cock. Damn, with Kate in her arms in the car, she'd almost blurted out "I love you." She closed her eyes and replayed the evening. Kate taking her arm, like on a real date. Standing up for those kids. Easy to forget she was only a sex-education teacher to Kate. She put in *Casablanca*. Fitting. Her phone rang. Stacy. She let it go to voice mail and then checked the message. She called her. "Yeah, it's okay if you come tomorrow." Why not? Kate wouldn't be with her.

"I miss you. Riding and stuff we used to do. I'm sorry about everything. I went a little crazy. I don't want to lose your friendship."

"Come here and we'll ride down to Santa Cruz together." She ended the call. Stacy's friendship mattered to her. She and Stacy understood each other in ways Kate never would.

Chapter Twenty-five

Kate set the paper down beside her half-eaten breakfast and sipped decaf coffee, staring out at the fog-shrouded garden and beyond it to her gran's cottage. An hour and Chris would be here for the garden project. They'd talked on the phone once since she'd left Felton. *I'm sorry. No, I'm sorry. How's studying? Fine. How's work? Fine. Well, I guess I'll see you Saturday.* She hated the awkwardness.

"Did you have fun last night?" Her mother limped as she walked to her place at the dining table. Mild sprain, the doctor had diagnosed after a two-hour wait in the ER.

"Yes," she said, lying. A double date. She and Stephen with Nic and Brian. Nic's idea.

"Did you talk to Veronica about the plans we discussed for future fund-raising and recruiting events?" Veronica was the alumni chapter president of Kate's Alpha Chi sorority.

Their cook brought a tray to the table. Tea and her mother's usual breakfast. Oatmeal with cream and brown sugar.

"Yes." Kate picked up the paper, hoping to put an end to the conversation. It wasn't fair, but she was still irritated at her for costing her the weekend with Chris. "We're having lunch after New Year's to discuss in more detail."

"We'll have you chapter vice president next year and ready to move into Veronica's shoes when she steps down. I'm so proud of you." She patted Kate's arm. "While I'm in New York remember to talk to the florist about the changes we decided on for New Year's Eve. It's too bad Stephen's on duty that night, but you'll have a chance to

· 221 ·

explore other options. Todd's mother called last night. She felt she owed me the courtesy of forewarning me he would be bringing a girlfriend to the party. I don't want to upset you, but it's a woman he knew in Boston. His poor parents. A waitress? And she has a son..." She shook her head.

"What difference does it make, if they love each other?"

Her mother set her teacup on the saucer. "It makes a great deal of difference. You can argue that it shouldn't matter, but it does. Our kind of society is conservative. Social connections are important, and people won't accept him the way they would if he'd married you."

"I don't believe that." She didn't want to, but Todd was already living the reality.

"It's subtle, but it's there...the clients he won't acquire, the deals he won't be offered, the parties he won't be invited to. You can't be too careful about such things if you expect the advantages that come with our position in the community. Marriage is a responsibility. Love is a choice, the importance of which cannot be underestimated."

The patio doors opened and Kate's gran walked in, dressed in faded jeans and gray-flannel shirt over a turtleneck. She tugged the door closed behind her. "Wonderful weather for installing a labyrinth," she said lightly.

"Honestly, Kate. This is beyond the requirements of friendship." Every day had been the same argument. She could get hurt. She was losing study time.

Half an hour later Kate stood beside her gran as the car service pulled out of the driveway to take her mother to the airport for her week of Christmas shopping in New York.

"Party!" her gran shouted, lifting her arms over her head and twirling. "And here's my other guest."

Kate's smile faded and her heart beat unsteadily as Chris drove her truck toward them.

Chris stepped from her truck, frowning. She looked around, her gaze settling on the empty pallets stacked by the garage. "Did you hire someone to move the materials?" she asked Katherine.

"Thought I'd make myself useful," Kate said.

"You shouldn't have." Chris looked at her, the frown deepening.

"Oh, for heaven's sake. I'm going to change into work gear." Kate strode to the house. Pissed. Her mother was upset with her. Chris was upset with her. Too damn bad. She was Kate the Invincible and it was time she acted like it. She was having dinner with her friend Melanie and her girlfriend tonight. She'd ask her to set her up on a date. As soon as her mother returned, she'd tell her she planned to date women.

❖

Chris shoved her hands in her 501s. Kate was pissed at her. Fine. She was pissed, too. At Kate. At the shitty week. She hadn't landed a big job she'd spent tons of hours preparing a proposal for. One of her company trucks needed expensive repairs. "I'm sorry," she said to Katherine. "I should have driven up and moved—"

"To quote my granddaughter, 'Oh, for heaven's sake.' You should have thanked her and moved on to more important things to disagree on." Katherine walked toward the gate into the garden.

Chris hurried to keep up with her, clenching her fists inside her 501s. *Focus on the project.* A lot was at stake with the *Sunset* article. She followed Katherine into the cottage and through it to the backyard. Materials were neatly laid out on brown tarps—two bins of Sonoma fieldstone for the pond, base rock and sand and six pallets of flagstone for the labyrinth. Hours of hauling, one wheelbarrow at a time. If Kate got hurt, or sick again, she'd never forgive herself.

The back door opened a few minutes later and Kate joined them on the patio. Damn, she looked hot in work clothes, hair pulled into a ponytail, Giants ball cap.

"Stand in front of those wonderfully neat piles of materials," Katherine said, holding a camera. "Arms around each other."

"Thanks for hauling." Chris put her arm over Kate's shoulders. It felt right. She didn't want it to, but it did.

"Smiles would be helpful." Katherine took several pictures. "I'll leave you to your work."

"What's the plan?" Kate's detached attitude was intimidating.

"We bring tools from my truck. Mark off the labyrinth and pond. You dig out plants while I dig the pond. That soil forms the berm. Tomorrow we'll lay the liner and rocks for the pond, install the pump, and fill it. If we have extra time we'll finish digging out for the labyrinth. Next weekend we start building it."

"You're the boss." Kate turned and walked away.

❖

Kate stepped hard on the shovel, driving it through the dirt, then pulling out the rosebush. She tossed it in the wheelbarrow and moved to the next plant. They worked without conversing. Her gran made intermittent appearances, watching for a bit and taking pictures, then shaking her head and going inside. She'd argued as much with her this week as her mother. No, she was not telling Chris she was in love with her. She turned so she wasn't facing Chris. She'd date other women. She would.

By the time her gran called a halt for lunch, they'd made decent progress. And hadn't spoken a word to each other that didn't have to do with work. They left their boots by the door and sat down to grilled-cheese sandwiches and split-pea soup. She glared at the table arrangement. She and Chris were placed beside each other.

"You two might age me ten years," her gran said when they'd finished. She set a plate of cookies on the table and settled again in her chair. "Are you enjoying yourselves today? Because I'm not. Being around you two is as much fun as having the flu."

"Gran—"

"I have a story for you." She was silent for several minutes, and when she spoke, her voice was different. Softer. "I was in love with someone before I met your grandfather. Someone whom I couldn't marry. A woman."

Kate swallowed her tea wrong. "You were involved with a woman?" she asked when she'd stopped coughing.

"I was."

"Why don't I know this?" She looked at Chris, who was studying her gran, head tilted. "Wait…when you lived in Felton?"

"No. Before I moved there. When I was at Columbia." She reached for a cookie, her expression thoughtful. "Olivia Jenkins. We were two of eleven women in our law class. We became study partners. We fell in love. I assumed that after graduation we would set up both a home and a practice together." Her face shifted. Sad. "Such was not to be. One of Olivia's friends told her parents about us. They were a well-to-do family. Liberal enough to allow Olivia to study law. Not liberal enough to embrace a lesbian daughter. They forbade Olivia from contacting me. I didn't see her for weeks. I was willing to risk anything to be with her. I thought the same was true for her."

Kate slumped against her chair, trying to fit this in with what she knew about her gran.

"She sent me a letter stating it had all been a mistake. I went to her home. It was ugly. Very ugly." Her gran straightened her shoulders. "When I realized she wouldn't stand up for me, for us, I left New York. Bought a bus ticket and stayed on until it stopped at the end of the line. Santa Cruz. I continued to write her, assuring her we could build a life here away from her family. I didn't know if she received my letters, but I kept hoping she'd find me once she had time to miss me. About a year later I received a letter from her. She'd married and had a son."

"Did Grandfather know?"

"Of course. He helped me overcome my heartbreak. He made me laugh again. He was much older. Never married. He wanted a partner—in his personal life and in his law practice. A family. I loved him. I accepted his proposal."

"You never saw her...Olivia...again?" Kate realized she'd grasped Chris's hand as her gran talked.

"Shortly before my wedding I received a letter. Her husband had died. She would move here with her son if I still wanted her. I never responded."

"You haven't spoken to her in all this time?"

"I have not." Her face hardened.

"Is she still alive?"

"I don't know. She taught at Columbia for many years. I saw articles she published." She looked tired, as if talking about the past had drained her. "So, as you can see, two women having both the freedom to be together and the support necessary to stay together matters greatly to me. I took a risk for happiness and lost, but I don't regret trying. Isn't your happiness worth taking a risk?" She looked at Kate.

Kate met the probing gaze. Gran had taken a risk for happiness. Todd had taken a risk for happiness. It was time she did. She looked at Chris. "I like you." And then down at her lap. "A lot." She turned in her chair to face Chris. Fine. Risk. Big risk. "I know it's not what you want to hear, but I think I'm in love with you."

"You are?" Chris frowned.

She dropped Chris's hand and clenched her jaw. She wouldn't cry.

"Your turn," Katherine said, her gaze now focused on Chris. "You owe Kate the truth, whatever that is."

"I think I'm in love with you, too." Chris took her hand.

"I can't be one of many lovers. I want a relationship with you."

"I'm not saying this right. I want you, too. Just you."

"You'd give up—"

"Kate," her gran said. "If this were a movie and the lead characters had finally declared their love for each other, what would happen next?"

Kate looked at Chris, sure she had a starry-eyed look on her face. She'd never dreamed Chris was in love with her. Her heart released the feelings bottled up and words poured out. "I love you." She grabbed Chris's shirt and pulled her nose-to-nose close. "I've been dying to do this all day." She kissed her.

"You really must do something about your communication skills." Her gran's chair scraped on the floor as she pushed it back. "I'm putting cookies in the oven. Don't get too carried away." She walked to the kitchen.

Chris pulled Kate onto her lap as the kiss went on and on. Claiming each other. They were still kissing when her gran cleared her throat.

"I don't wish to dull this moment, but we must face reality." She sat again. "I believe you are well suited to each other, but some may not. If you truly love each other, you must be willing to defend it against any who would criticize you."

"Aren't you being melodramatic, Gran?" She moved back to her chair.

"Katherine's right," Chris said. "You have more to lose than I do. Your mother won't approve. Your friends might not."

"They'll have to."

Chris took her hands. "There's more to love than saying the words. Felton. It was kind of a bubble. Now you're back in your life."

"I can't imagine a future without you. I won't give you up. Not for anything." She squeezed Chris's hands.

"You saw what happened at the restaurant." Chris looked way too serious. And a bit sad.

"We'll stand up for ourselves the way we stood up for Syd and Elaine. Why are you trying to talk me out of being with you?"

Chris let out a long breath, her face softening. "I'm in, if you're in."

"Excellent," her gran said. "I hope you two are more fun to be around this afternoon. Lunch break over."

"I'm having dinner with my friend Melanie and her girlfriend," Kate said as they sat on the wicker chairs and laced up their boots. "Come with me. Nic will be there, and you can get to know each other."

"I'm having dinner with Georgia. Just dinner."

"We'll all have dinner together. A coming-out party." Kate hurried to the door and opened it. "Gran! You're coming to dinner with us tonight."

"Fine, dear."

She sat on Chris's lap and wrapped her arms around her neck. "Stay with me tonight?"

"Here?" Chris eyes widened. She shook her head. "Bad idea."

Kate kissed the soft spot in front of Chris's ear. God, she smelled good. "Remember? Mother's in New York. I have the house to myself for a week." She placed feather-light kisses across Chris's cheek. "Don't you want to make love tonight?" That's what it would be. Candles. Her sexiest nightie. She kissed Chris, slow and tender. "Say yes." She wiggled her butt against Chris's crotch.

Chris pulled back, her eyes glazed. "I don't have..." She cleared her throat. "God, you're beautiful. What were we talking about? Oh, yeah. I don't have sex toys with me. I want it to be perfect for you."

Driving to Felton didn't make sense. An idea took shape. "We'll go shopping after dinner."

Chris groaned.

"Not that kind of shopping. Good Vibrations. We'll pick out toys." Kate wiggled her butt again, and the effect showed in Chris's gaze.

"Alone. Not with your friends."

"Okay. But Gran gets to—Kidding," she said at the shocked look on Chris's face. "You're kinda squeamish for a sex stud." She latched her mouth onto Chris's for a long, satisfying kiss.

Chapter Twenty-six

Chris woke, disoriented for a moment, in the unfamiliar room. Then she relaxed. Kate was snugged against her, breathing lightly, her head on Chris's shoulder. She rubbed her palm over the pink bedspread. Of course her room would be decorated in pink. She was still reeling from the day's events. Katherine's surprising disclosure. Kate telling her she was in love with her. Dinner. Kate holding her hand, touching her casually for anyone to see. Kissing her apparently without a second thought. Georgia's affectionate "I told you so." And the best part—the expression on Nicole's face when Kate announced they were a couple. Shock and anger she covered in an instant with a manufactured smile. Talkative at dinner, regaling them with stories from their Stanford days. Point taken. She had a past with Kate. But when they left the restaurant, Chris was the one who went home with Kate.

"I have a girlfriend," Chris said into the darkness.

"Yes, you do." Kate slid her hand up Chris's belly to fondle her breast. "Who's horny again."

"We should take care of that." Chris pulled Kate on top of her and cupped her ass. Then their mouths were moving toward each other with the force of magnets, tongues reaching for each other, diving into each other. Teasing. Demanding. The air around them was charged with sexual energy. Her clit throbbed with desire while her heart swelled with love and her mind said, "She's mine." She let Kate take control, spreading her legs as Kate entered her. "So good... so good..." She held back, prolonging release. Letting the incredible mix of sex and love take her higher. Finally she let go, calling out Kate's name as the orgasm thrust heat through her body.

Kate pushed her thigh against Chris's sex. "Again. Come again." She took Chris's mouth in a possessive kiss.

Chris's clit contracted and she gripped Kate's hips, thrusting against her thigh. Losing control and not able to do a thing about it. Kate owned her. "Fuuuuck." She came, a lightning bolt of pleasure that sliced through her body. Breathing hard, she kept her legs clamped around Kate's thigh as they kissed. So perfect.

"I want you inside me." Kate rolled off her and reached toward the bedside table. She handed Chris the harness and ribbed cock they'd bought at Good Vibrations. "Hurry."

Chris put the harness on, fumbling with the unfamiliar clasps, and fit the cock into it.

Kate knelt beside her, spreading lube on it and then on her sex. "I want to ride you." She lifted her leg over Chris and lowered herself until the cock was buried in her. She rocked, hands braced on Chris's shoulders, then circled her hips in a seductive roll that almost made Chris come again. "I love how full you are inside me." She straightened, pumping up and down as she fingered her clit.

Chris gripped Kate's waist, her pulse redlining as Kate's breasts bounced with her movements. "You're the most beautiful woman I've ever seen." The words blew into the room as if expelled from her heart. Kate was more than beautiful. More than a catalyst for desire. She made Chris's life complete. Made sex passionate and meaningful in a way she hadn't known was possible. Kate was who she wanted to be with for the rest of her life. The thought almost stopped her heart. What if she lost her the way Katherine lost the woman she loved?

Kate rode her, pumping faster. "Yes, yes, yes! I'm coming all over you." Kate threw her head back, breathing hard, a smile consuming her face. Then she collapsed into Chris's arms, the cock still inside her. "I'll never forget this night. I never dreamed you'd want to be with me. We owe Gran big-time. I was thinking at dinner…we should find Olivia. Maybe it's not too late for them."

"It's never too late for love."

"I'll bet Olivia's still in New York. If she doesn't want to see Gran, we won't tell her. But if she does, we'll set up a date."

Chris feathered her fingers through Kate's hair. "I'm worried about your mother." Terrified was more accurate.

"I'll handle her."

Chris couldn't shake the memory of Nic's warning that if Cecelia found out about them, she'd make the storm look like a spring shower. What had she stepped into? So many ways it could all crash down around her. Then Kate was kissing her and she couldn't think at all.

Chapter Twenty-seven

Chris trudged along beside Katherine as they walked through the garden from the cottage to the main house. Cecelia's New Year's Eve party she'd been dreading. She'd driven up this morning to put the finishing touches on the garden renovation. Kate had been helping her mother prepare for the party all day. Chris hadn't seen her other than a few brief visits. Stolen moments. She didn't like the secrecy, but Kate insisted on waiting until tomorrow. *She's wearing herself out on the party, and I can't tell her until it's over.*

The house looked festive, like a scene from a movie. *Great Gatsby*, perhaps. White Christmas lights in the trees around the patio. Men in tuxedos or suits and women in fancy dresses of every style and color moved about on the patio and inside the house. How many times would she be mistaken for part of the serving staff? What on earth would she say to any of them? She stopped and started to put her hands in her pockets. Except she had no pockets in the dressy pants.

"You must accept the parts of Kate that make you uncomfortable." Katherine looked elegant in a gray, long-sleeved dress, her hair done up in a style that probably had a name. "Wealth, social standing, her future with the firm...it's not fair to hold those against her. She's willingly spent time in your world, flourished in it, I might add. You have to make peace with hers."

"What will happen tomorrow?" Kate was telling Cecelia about them. New year. New me. Then she was spending the rest of the week in Felton. If Cecelia didn't keep her under house arrest. "Does she really believe she'll support us?"

"She's afraid to believe otherwise."

"I don't know if I can do this if I have to battle Cecelia's disapproval."

"I'm sorry to hear that. There are things in life worth fighting for."

She clenched her jaw, biting back the words. *It's not my fight. It's Kate's place to stand up for me. For us.*

Her dad and friends had been thrilled. No lack of support there. Well, except Stacy. Kate was not like Stacy's ex-girlfriend. Or Katherine's ex-lover. She would fight for their future. They continued to the house in silence, and then through the patio doors to the living room. Conversation and laughter replaced the pleasant quiet of the garden. Chris patted the couch as she walked past. They'd made love on it several times last week.

"Who would you like to meet first? Politician? Fashion designer? Opera singer?"

"Someone who likes gardening, old films, or Harleys?"

Katherine chuckled. "Don't I wish."

Chris appeared to be the only woman at the party wearing pants. No makeup. No fancy hairdo. No investment accounts at a brokerage firm. But Katherine was right. It wasn't fair to expect Kate to live solely in her world. Her confidence surged when Kate caught her eye. Damn. Stunning in a light-blue dress. *And all mine.* If only she could claim her publicly.

Kate excused herself from the man she was talking to and walked toward them. "Hi, handsome." She kissed Chris's cheek. She was wearing the sapphire necklace and earrings.

Don't go there, Chris reminded herself. *She doesn't want me for what I can buy her.* She startled when Kate patted her butt.

"I'll leave you in Kate's hands," Katherine said, smiling as she often did around them. Having her support mattered so much.

"Great party." She remembered Katherine's words about making peace with Kate's world.

"Liar. Come on. I'll show you to the food. That'll make you happy. And I snuck beer into the refrigerator for you and a glass in the freezer."

Ten minutes later, Kate had gone to talk to someone and she was headed to the food table when Cecelia came toward her. Bearing down on her would be more accurate, floor-length red gown flowing around her. She'd been trying to avoid her. Frankly, she was afraid of her influence over Kate.

Cecelia smiled as her eyes did a quick inventory of Chris's outfit. "I'm so pleased you could attend our party. What a pretty color on you."

"Um, thanks." Chris tugged on the jacket. Hunter green according to Kate. She flexed her toes inside the new dress shoes. Kate had taken her shopping. Women's clothing, but at least it was a suit. Kissing in dressing rooms had been an unexpected bonus.

"I peeked at the renovation. I'm so pleased Katherine realized she can't manage such a large garden. And thank you for making sure those ugly pallets were cleared from the driveway."

Nicole swooped toward them. Elegant black dress. Perfect hair and makeup. Chris wanted to laugh as she and Cecelia did the air-kiss thing. Then she felt a stab of jealousy. She'd never have that kind of relationship with Cecelia.

"Wherever did you find that dress?" Cecelia put her hands to her cheeks. "Brian should be here to fight off the men. You remember Kate's friend."

Nicole held out her hand. She didn't squeeze this time but held it too long, looking at it as if studying it.

No, I don't have a fancy manicure like you. Kate had offered to take her for one but her inner femme had limits.

"Come." Cecelia took Nicole's arm. "I'll introduce you to the senior partner at the investment company that handles my portfolio. It's never too soon to start planning your financial future."

Nicole wiggled her fingers over her shoulder at Chris.

"Bitch," Chris muttered.

"Occasionally," a male voice said from behind her. Todd. "Congratulations. Kate's the best. Nic can be a pill, but don't let her intimidate you."

"Easier said than done." She hated being stuck between wanting to tell Kate about Nicole's alternate persona as Raven and staying honorable to the code of behavior she'd lived by for years. She talked with Todd for a while and then drifted to a group discussing sports. She watched Kate mingle, seemingly at ease with everyone. A different side of Kate. Socialite Kate.

Two hours later she decided the party wasn't so bad. The food was spectacular. Katherine had introduced her around as a "highly in demand landscaper soon to be featured in *Sunset* magazine." As she listened to more and more conversations that seemed shallow, she realized these people weren't all that intimidating. Maybe she could make peace with Kate's world.

She went to the kitchen for another beer. Kate's thoughtfulness made her feel special and that's all that mattered. They loved each other and everything else was irrelevant. She wound her way through the crowd and went out to the patio, inhaled the cold air and stared across the garden to the tiny bit of the Golden Gate Bridge visible beyond. Heels tapped across the patio. Kate? She'd been surprising her all night with appearances at her side, always touching her briefly. Anticipation claimed her until the person walked close enough to smell her perfume. Not Kate.

"Beautiful view, isn't it?" Nicole stepped beside her. "Kiss and make up?" She moved so their shoulders touched.

Chris moved away.

"I don't bite," Nicole purred. "Nice suit. Are you packing?"

She clenched her jaw. *Don't react.*

"Big day for the lovebirds tomorrow."

She wished Kate hadn't confided in her. So far she must not have told Cecelia, but she couldn't forget the threat she'd made. She wouldn't put it past her to make trouble at the last minute. "Kate's happy. Can't you support her?"

"She's thinking with her clit. You might be a great fuck, but people don't live life in the bedroom. Look around. Do you fit in?"

"I was hoping to meet your fiancé tonight. Brian, right?"

"Lucky me to have it all," she said smoothly, folding her arms.

"Lying and cheating. Yeah, you have it all."

The smirk disappeared. Nicole shot Chris one of her dagger looks. Then turned and strode to the house.

"Don't leave mad," Chris called after her. Two could play this game.

❖

"Who manages your portfolio?" The man adjusted his tie knot for the umpteenth time.

"Excuse me?" Kate hoped her voice held the right amount of "it's none of your business" as she plucked a glass from the tray carried by a passing server. There wasn't enough champagne to endure this conversation, which should have ended minutes ago. Peter. Or was this Paul? Her mother had introduced her to more men than she could keep track of. This one kept following her, joining any group she stopped to chat with. *Go. Away.*

"I've done exceptionally well in the market this past year." Tug on the tie knot. "I'm expecting a big promotion next year." He checked his watch, making sure she saw the Rolex crown emblem. "Which begins in exactly fifty-nine minutes. I'm free next Friday. Dinner?"

"I'm not. Oh, I see someone I must talk to." Kate hurried away, forcing herself not to sprint. "Save me," she said when she reached Todd. She jerked her head in the direction she'd come from.

"Darling! Where have you been?" He pitched his voice loud enough to make Peter stop and veer in another direction.

"Have I told you how much I adore you?" Kate ignored her mother's gesture for her to join her. She had another candidate in tow. She searched the living room for the woman she loved. Ah, out on the patio talking to Nic. Excellent. Nic had promised she'd make friends with Chris.

"As a matter of fact, you have. Isn't love the best?"

Kate looked at Chris. Beautiful in her silk suit. Toenails painted red. Pink boxers with red hearts. All hers. *Happy. This is what happy feels like.*

"Kate, dear." Her mother came up beside her, barely acknowledging Todd. "Tony's looking for you. You promised him a dance."

"I'll be there in a minute." She should be dancing with Chris, but she couldn't bring herself to tell her mother before the party. She'd returned from New York more exhausted than before. Low iron, she'd said. Nothing to worry about. She'd taken to napping in the afternoons, and at moments she went pale and put her hand to her chest, trying to catch her breath. She'd finally agreed to see her doctor next week.

She went to meet Chris as she came in from the patio. "I'm so happy you and Nic are getting along. Underneath all her bravado and sarcasm she's fun and the best friend I've ever had."

"Um, yeah. I can see that."

"Meet me at the stairs in ten minutes. I have a surprise." Two dances later Kate excused herself and made her way toward the staircase. "You're late," she said, when Chris sauntered over. "Next year you're wearing a black tux. We'll have one custom-made for you." She started up the stairs, Chris at her side. "I wish we'd heard from Olivia. I had visions of inviting her out here and surprising Gran." In the absence of a Facebook page, Kate had emailed Columbia Law School and requested they forward her contact information to Olivia.

"What's my surprise?"

"If I told you it wouldn't be a surprise." They walked down the hallway to her bedroom. She opened the door and tugged Chris inside. Plastering her against the door, Kate fumbled with the lock as she fastened her lips to the mouth that had been torturing her all evening, so close yet untouchable. She ran her fingers through thick hair and cupped the back of Chris's head, lifting one leg to wrap it around Chris's waist. She pressed her tongue inside the soft lips, exploring every inch of her mouth. They finally pulled apart, breathless, Chris's lips covered with Kate's lipstick. "I couldn't go another minute without that." Kate wiped Chris's mouth with her thumb, her legs weakening when Chris sucked it into her mouth and bit. She pulled Chris to the bed and pointed to the cock and harness. "Your reward for putting up with my party."

Chris lifted her eyebrows. "Sex? Now?"

"Fifteen minutes. No one will miss us. We'll be downstairs when the clock chimes midnight." Kate put Chris's hand on her thigh under her dress, watching her eyes darken when she discovered the garter that held up her nylons. She'd purposely worn it, hoping for such a reaction. She groaned when Chris cupped her through her silk panties.

"Can't say no to that."

She helped Chris undress except for her shirt, then helped her fasten on the harness. "Lie on your back so I can straddle you." She stuffed pillows behind Chris's head, slipped her panties off and trailed them across Chris's face. She lubed her fingers and stroked the cock, watching Chris's face bloom with desire. Straddling Chris, she lowered herself until it was fully inside her. She arched and braced her hands behind her on the bed, adjusting to the fullness.

Chris slid her hands under Kate's dress and held her waist as she pumped slowly in and out of her. "God, that's sexy, baby. Let me have your breasts."

Kate sat up and moaned when Chris pinched her nipples in time with the fucking. She'd needed this all day. She closed her eyes and rode Chris's cock until the pressure built. "Close..."

"Touch your clit."

Kate spread lube and circled it. Pumped faster on the cock. Finally, she let out a long moan as her orgasm sprang from her G-spot. "So good...don't stop...you're making me come...ahh, God..."

The door opened, and noise from the party poured into the room. Kate jerked her head toward—

"Kate? What are you doing up here? Tony's leaving and you should say good—" Her mother's mouth froze. "What...what..." Her face went slack as her gaze flicked from Kate to Chris, Kate to Chris. Her hand shot to her chest, and her face tightened into a pained expression. She let out a choked scream and stumbled backward.

"Mother?" She scrambled off Chris and ran to the doorway in time to see her collapse, hitting her head against the wall.

"Mother!" Kate dropped to the floor beside her. "Mother!"

The red splotches on her cheeks disappeared, and her face went white in seconds. She tried to speak, but only gasps came out. She clamped her other hand to her chest, making sucking noises as she tried to breathe. Her eyes held Kate's. Shock. Panic. Fear.

"Call 9-1-1," Kate yelled at Chris when she appeared in the doorway, zipping up her pants. She grabbed her mother's hand. It was cold and limp. "Hurry!" Her mother's eyes held hers, full of disbelief. Then they closed. Oh please, oh please, oh please... "You'll be all right. You'll be all right. You have to be all right."

Chapter Twenty-eight

Chris jiggled her leg as she stood against the wall, her body still pumped full of adrenaline. No seat for her in the noisy emergency room. Kate was sitting beside Katherine, arms folded, looking often toward the door into the patient-care area. Nicole stood in front of her, as if guarding her, occasionally putting her hand on Kate's shoulder. Chris looked away when Nicole shot her another scathing look.

She felt queasy as she replayed those awful moments. The door that hadn't locked. Cecelia's look of shock before clutching her chest and collapsing. Kate scrambling off her. Her cock waving in the air. Fumbling to remove the harness and put her pants on. Kate's cries for help. Dashing for the door. Cecelia's face ghostly white against her red gown. Those awful seconds ticking by as she searched for Kate's phone. Dialing 9-1-1. Kate yelling at her to get help. Racing downstairs to the party. People staring at her in her untucked shirt and no jacket, barefoot.

Kate and her gran stood when a doctor with a disheveled mop of dark hair came through the door to the patient-care area. The conversation with him lasted several minutes, and he gave Kate a brief hug before hurrying back through the door.

She wanted to be part of the conversation. Part of the family. Not the outsider. The reason they were here. She shoved away from the wall when Kate walked toward her. She looked exhausted. Chris took off her jacket and slipped it around Kate's shoulders. The least she could do and probably the most that would be welcomed.

"Stephen says it's her heart."

So that was Stephen. "Heart attack?"

"Ventricular fibrillation. Heartbeat's irregular and too fast. Life-threatening. Trying to stabilize it with medication." Her gaze hopscotched around the waiting area, not once meeting Chris's eyes. She hadn't looked at Chris through the whole ordeal. "Then they'll decide on the next step."

"She'll be all right." Damn these pants with no pockets. If she couldn't hold Kate she had no idea what to do with her hands.

"She has to be." Tears filled Kate's eyes.

"I'm sorry."

"It's not your fault."

It *was* her fault. If she'd behaved as anything other than a sex-crazed, brainless—She wanted to wrap her arms around Kate, but she didn't have that privilege. Would probably never have that privilege now.

Kate's phone rang and she pulled it from her purse and answered. "Stephen's here, thank God…ventricular fibrillation. Oh, Todd, what will I do if she doesn't recover?"

Chris clenched her jaw.

"Thanks for staying until everyone left. Yes, come as soon as you can." Kate ended the call. "There's no point in your sticking around."

"Yeah. Okay." She didn't need to add to Kate's stress. "Call me when you know more?" *I love you.*

Kate nodded and handed her back the jacket before walking to Nicole, who hugged her as she glared at Chris.

Katherine came to Chris and walked with her out into the cold, drippy fog that blanketed the city. "I don't have any useful advice. I won't pretend this isn't a difficult situation. I'll do what I can to promote a favorable outcome."

Chris felt the first crack in her heart as the truth penetrated it like a spike. Katherine's voice was tight and flat. Full of doubt. By the time she reached her truck, her chest was filled with the shards of her shattered heart. It hurt to breathe. It hurt to think. She sat in her truck, shivering, searching for a way to undo what had been done. Hoping Kate would come for her, open the truck door, pull her into a hug, saying, "Of course I want you here. You're my partner." Five minutes. Ten.

She started her truck and drove away, slowly, checking the rearview mirror for any sign of Kate. When she reached the freeway she dialed her dad. She was about to hang up when he finally answered. "I need to stay with you tonight." She launched into an explanation of what had happened, pressing her hand over her chest as if to keep her heart from tumbling out.

"Don't be so quick with judgments. She's scared and in shock."

"She tossed me over, Dad." Resentment pushed aside the heartbreak.

"How would you react if it were me in the ER?"

"If she'd told Cecelia, none of this would be happening. She's chosen her mother over me." The distant look in Kate's eyes when she'd said, "There's no point in your sticking around." Like Chris wasn't there. Didn't matter.

"You don't know that. I'll put on coffee. We'll talk when you get here. Drive carefully."

She ended the call. Yeah, she did know that. She floored the accelerator, speeding down the freeway, passing few cars on the forty-minute drive. Replaying the night's events, emotions changing from hope before the party to the despair and guilt consuming her in the ER, ending now in heartbreak. She and Kate were over.

Chapter Twenty-nine

"I wish you'd go down to the dining room for breakfast." Kate set the breakfast tray over her mother's lap. The bedroom looked like a florist shop from the bouquets people had sent.

"I'm not strong enough yet." She was sitting up in the middle of the bed, the morning paper spread out around her. She'd been home from the hospital two weeks and rarely left her room. "Those medications make me feel funny. My legs are weak and I'm afraid I'll fall. Should we call Stephen?"

Not again. She'd called him numerous times to discuss this symptom or that. "Remember? He explained that it could take a while for your body to adjust to the meds."

"Oh, I'm such a bother." Her mother dabbed at her eyes with her napkin. "I've never cried so much in my life." She clasped Kate's hand. "I don't know what I'd do without you. When I think about what might have happened…No. I didn't die. I'll be fine. Stephen says I'll be fine." She lifted the lid on the plate. Egg-white omelet. Half a grapefruit. One slice of low-carb toast. "This isn't enough to keep a rabbit alive."

"Stephen expects you to lose thirty pounds. I talked to the physical therapist he recommended. Your first appointment is next week." Kate took her cup of coffee from the tray and sipped as her mother ate. Nauseous, as she had been often since New Year's. Her temperature was high most afternoons and she wasn't sleeping well. Stress. She'd be fine.

"I'm not ready for that."

"They'll start you off slowly."

"You'll go with me?"

"Of course. He suggested a walk around the block once a day."

"Invite him for dinner on his next night off."

"I don't have time."

"Please? For me?" Her mother took a bite of the omelet. "I'll do two walks a day if you'll give him a chance."

Kate smiled as her insides churned. Her mother acted like New Year's Eve had never happened. Like Chris had never happened. She'd never forgive herself for being reckless and thoughtless. Thinking with her clit, Nic had said with her typical bluntness. She couldn't believe how unreasonable her gran was being. She insisted Kate was making a mistake she'd regret for the rest of her life and that she was being unkind to Chris by not talking to her.

There was nothing to say. It was over. Love wasn't worth hurting people. She'd been in a fantasy where her actions didn't have consequences. Her mother was right. Love should be a choice, not an irresponsible yielding to desire. She pulled back the curtains to blue sky. Great weather for motorcycling. Was Chris riding with the posse today?

"It would make me so happy and I'd be less worried about everything." Stephen had said the heart condition was the reason for her fatigue, shortness of breath, and episodes of near fainting and that she was lucky to be alive. As soon as she was stabilized on the medication, he was recommending surgery to implant a device called an ICD that would restore normal heart rhythm if she had another attack.

"All right. I won't promise when, but we'll have dinner."

"Did you book our flight?"

"Yes." She'd agreed to accompany her to the Delta Zeta national convention in a couple of months.

Her mother fluttered her hand in front of her face. "You have no idea what it means to me that you'll be there when I'm inducted as president. One day you'll rise to president of your sorority."

"Nic's having lunch with us before your hair appointment." Her mother's first venture out of the house.

"I'm happy you two are close again. I still plan to help with her wedding. She's like a daughter to me."

"I'll come back in a few hours and help you dress." Kate kissed her mother's cheek and went downstairs to her father's study. Two hours of MBE practice questions. She'd be ready for the bar exam. She would pass and join the firm. Focus on what was important. By the end of the year, she wanted her gran to ease back into retirement.

❖

"Are you sure we should leave Mother alone?" Kate turned up the collar on her blazer as they walked out of the salon into the bitterly cold January wind that whipped leaves and papers across the sidewalk. Traffic rushed by on the busy downtown street.

"Alone with half a dozen people waiting to lavish attention and sympathy on her? Come on." Nic linked their arms as they walked down the street. "Let's buy something frivolous because we can."

"You're shameless."

"I've earned the privilege. Rags to riches. American cliché." Two cocktails at lunch had made her more sarcastic than usual.

When they passed a women's boutique, Kate stopped to stare at the leather jacket in the window. Caramel colored. Short waisted. It would look good on her and Chris would—Tears stung her eyes and she pulled in a shuddering breath. At the oddest moments the crushing ache in her heart would roar to the front of her attention. "I miss her."

"Think logically, sweetie. First crush. You'll barely remember her name in six months." Two men their age strolled past, giving them long looks. "Give Stephen a chance. He's a doctor. Knows anatomy." Nic used a singsong voice for the last sentence. "Bet he's great in bed. Now that you know what turns you on, you can train him."

The thought of anyone touching her but Chris made her stomach threaten to expel lunch.

"One of the senior associates is a dyke. Works to my advantage." They stopped at the corner, waiting to cross the street. "She won't make partner. Leaves a track open to me."

"It shouldn't matter."

"Welcome to the real world."

"You'd capitalize on someone else's—"

"You bet I would. Oh, I don't care about making partner. I want high-profile cases. That I win." She bobbed her head. "And a bunch of junior associates to order around. Five years and I open my own firm. You'll be my first recruit. Trusts and estates? Too tame. That mind of yours craves a bigger challenge." They resumed walking. "Let's talk civil procedure."

Nic fired questions and she answered. She glanced back toward the store. She wanted to buy that jacket.

Chapter Thirty

Chris backed her Harley to the curb across the street from Georgia's and shut the bike down. Party tonight. She removed her helmet and slapped it down in front of her on the seat, shoving aside the guilt. She was single. She belonged here. Tugging her gloves off with her teeth, she put them inside the helmet and unzipped her jacket. She took her phone from the inside pocket and opened Kate's voice mail from January third. Three weeks ago. Three oh two in the morning.

"Um, hi. It's me. Kate." Her voice had no trace of its usual animated quality.

"I'm outside Mother's hospital room." A pause was filled with ragged breathing, as if she were trying not to cry. *"I'm so scared. They shocked her heart today. No, yesterday. I'm so confused about what day it is. Twice. They stopped it. To reset normal rhythm. It worked, but it may not last. They're releasing her in the morning. No, tomorrow morning."* Another pause. More ragged breathing. *"She'll be on medications and might need surgery. I'm sorry. Maybe you don't want to know all this, but I said I'd update you. I should call you and talk to you...I can't, Chris. If I hear your voice it will break me. I miss you so much and this is so hard and it's all my fault. I thought there was a right time. An easier time. She barely looks at me, and when she does...it makes me cringe. Like she doesn't know who I am. I can't push. I can't. She's so fragile and frightened. I love you and I know I treated you badly in the ER. I was so scared and wanted it not

to have happened. I'm sorry. You deserve someone stronger than I am. I don't know how to be with you and not hurt other people I care about. I'm rambling. I want to talk to you. I want to curl up in your arms. I can't. Please don't hate me. Please."

Forty-nine seconds. Their love was worth forty-nine seconds.

Emotions tumbled through Chris, as they did every time she listened to the message. And she listened to it several times a day. To hear Kate's voice. Mostly to be angry with her. To remind herself that Kate hadn't stood up for them. The alternative was to miss her so damn bad she felt like she was living under water, everything dulled and distant. She tucked the phone inside her jacket, locked the helmet and gloves in a saddlebag, and pocketed her keys. She was single. She belonged here.

She strode across the street, carrying the duffel of sex toys. Through the front door. Up the stairs. She paused on the landing. *Don't change your mind.* She locked her bag and jacket in the locker in the bathroom. A woman in the shower opened the door. "Wanna join me?"

She'd played with the full-figured brunette a few times. She liked to be fucked. Hard. She could work off—She wasn't taking out her frustration like that. "Maybe later." She forced a smile. Didn't she used to have a cocky grin? She wet her hands and finger-combed her hair. Unbuttoned her white shirt to the waist of her black pants, exposing her bare chest. She sauntered down the hall, nodding at women who greeted her but not kissing them. Room to room to room. Watching. Waiting for a spark to entice her to join in. For her clit to tighten. Or her belly to bunch with desire for any of the naked women. She willed desire to capture her. She almost went into the last room. An orgy, Kate would have called it.

She whipped around and stormed down the hallway, head down, jaw clenched. She hurried down the stairs, grabbed a beer, downed most of it. Tense, that was all. She'd dance. Relax. She wound through the living room, stopped to hug several women, then headed down the hall to the dance room. Opening the door, she stepped into the dimly lit space. She didn't recognize the song but it had a danceable beat. She took a woman's hand and pulled her into her arms. Full breasts. Pulled her closer. Silky dress beneath her palms. Yes, this felt good.

The woman said her name and Chris ignored it. She needed curves and soft skin. Nothing more. Nothing less.

The dance ended. She ignored the woman's request for another, released her, and walked to someone else standing along the perimeter. Took her hand. Ignored the name and the wrong perfume. Focused on curves and skin and long hair that cascaded down the woman's back. She stepped back when the music stopped. Another song. Another woman. Then another. Finally she stopped thinking. Almost stopped remembering.

"What are you doing here, sugar?"

Without opening her eyes, she put her cheek on Georgia's shoulder, holding tight. "Where else would I be?"

Georgia took her hand and led her from the room. Up the stairs. Down the hall. Chris didn't look in the rooms. Her mind wanted what was inside. Her heart couldn't bear it. She'd play later. She would.

Georgia unlocked the door at the end of the hall, and they walked up to her bedroom.

"Don't send me away." *I belong here. I have to belong here.*

"Did you hear from Kate today?"

"I told you. She won't call." Chris shoved her hands in her pockets.

Georgia picked up a landline telephone from the desk and held it out to Chris. "Call her."

"What! No. No fucking way." She was probably on a date with Mr. Doctor Cardiologist from the ER. Or out with Nicole. That woman better not show up here tonight. She might give her the rough handling she'd been asking for.

"Isn't she worth fighting for?"

"Katherine asks me that every damn time we talk." She was sick of hearing it.

"Doesn't make it the wrong question. Kate loves you. She also loves her mother. People make bad choices when they're scared. Don't give up on her."

"It hurts so damn bad."

"I know, sugar." Georgia came to her and held her.

"Why wasn't I worth fighting for?"

"Tell her you miss her. That one thing. Do it for me."

"Can I stay with you tonight?"

Georgia released her and tucked the phone in Chris's waist. "You have to know what she wants before she does. Don't disappoint me." She walked out.

Chris went to the window and stared out, her reflection in the glass. Where was Kate? Did she ever miss her?

❖

"This isn't a good idea, Kate." Todd slowed as they approached the street.

"Then pull over and I'll walk." She had to know. She'd driven past Georgia's the last two Saturdays, not sure which night was her party. She had to know.

"Let's drive up to the lookout at the Golden Gate Bridge and smoke a joint."

"Know where we can get one?" She was pleasantly buzzed from the beers she'd had with dinner. The only way she could face doing this. Tonight must be party night. She didn't know if she hoped Chris was here or not. She wanted her to be happy, the way she was when they met. But she also wanted Chris at home, missing her. Her body tensed the closer they got.

"No, but give me a week. I like being the rebellious teenager I never was."

Rebellious. She'd had her few weeks of rebellious. All she'd achieved was almost killing her mother.

"Let's go to an all-night diner and drink insane amounts of coffee. I'll quiz you for the bar exam." He waited at the stop sign.

Bar exam. Four and a half weeks away. Nic had her studying eight hours a day, programmed down to the second. Three hours in the morning. Then breakfast with her mother and an hour or more handling her mother's extensive email communications. Then off to work in the law firm. Over to Nic's for more studying, usually while eating takeout. The pace was familiar. No time to think. Except she thought about Chris all the time.

A car behind them honked and Todd drove slowly through the intersection.

Kate tried to stay calm, but her heart was banging against her ribs. *Please don't be here.* A block and a half. A block. No sign of Chris's truck. She let out the breath she'd been holding. Then gasped as they passed Georgia's house. "Stop!" Todd did, and she stared at the black Harley. She pointed at it as tears filled her eyes. Chris was here. She'd lost her forever.

❖

Chris punched in Kate's number. She stared at the phone, willing herself to push the call button. Memories…Motorcycling and dinners and movies. The kiss at Halloween. Working at Mrs. Cavanaugh's. Kate's first orgasm. Taking care of each other during the storm. Kate saying, "I love you." Building the labyrinth. Her heart softened with each memory. Yes, she was worth fighting for.

Then other memories. Kate leaving Felton when her mother sprained her ankle. The disaster when she came to Georgia's. Nicole telling her she wasn't good enough. The ER. The voice mail. Her heart closed up with each memory.

She set the phone down and walked down to the second floor. Collected her things. She didn't belong here tonight. Next month. The month after. She'd be back.

She found Georgia in the living room, on the couch with a blonde on her lap. Jealousy surged as she watched them kiss and fondle each other. That could be her. It had been her. She'd given that up for what? Next month. The month after. It would be her again.

She'd intended to head home. Fifteen minutes later she found herself idling the bike across the street from Kate's house. She stared at her bedroom window for a long time. Dark, as was the rest of the house. Was she asleep? Out on a date? It didn't matter. Kate wasn't coming back to her. She'd moved on with her life. Time Chris did the same. She put the bike in gear and gunned it down the street.

Chapter Thirty-one

Chris closed the gate and walked through Katherine's garden that was in winter hibernation—bare-branched trees, perennials cut back to ground level, not a flower in sight. She turned up the collar of her jacket against the chill of the cold, heavy fog. She hated this bleak, dreary weather. She didn't look at the main house, half-expecting Cecelia to burst out the French doors and throw her off the property. She trudged up the steps to the porch and knocked on the door. Get this over with. Dinner with her dad tonight. Motorcycle ride tomorrow with the posse.

"Thank you for making time for me." Katherine held the door open, her voice friendly but her face absent the smile Chris was used to.

"Sorry I'm late. Tied up on a job." She was grateful for the increase in business that was making her run a crew most Saturdays. The new marketing strategy was paying off. Stacy had landed the Portola project and offered her work on it. She'd declined. Too many complications. She'd make it on her own. She always had. She followed Katherine through the cottage. No conversation. No offer of cookies.

On the patio she knelt beside the pond and dipped her hand into the cold water to lift the cover on the pump chamber. "Did the breaker trip before you turned off the pump?"

"No." Katherine peered over her shoulder.

"Did you turn the breaker off?" She looked up. "Okay, okay," she said. The withering "I'm not an idiot" look rivaled those Kate gave her. Used to give her. "Vapor-locked, most likely. Happens with new pumps. Turn the breaker on." Katherine went to the side of the house. When she came back, Chris started the pump and tilted it. That usually dislodged the air bubble causing the problem. Nothing. "One or both of the capacitors may have burned out. I need tools from my truck."

Chris was rummaging in the back of her truck for replacement capacitors and a voltmeter when a car peeled into the driveway. Sports car, by the sound of it. Her pulse jumped. *Don't look.* The car stopped. Doors opened. *Don't. Look.*

"You're kidding me! Can't you take a hint?"

Chris jerked her head toward the car. Black Porsche. Nicole marched toward her. As menacing as one could look in tight black jeans, red silk blouse, and heels. "Leave! Now!"

"I'll take care of it, Nic." Kate scampered around the car, holding a plastic bag.

She was captured by the same reaction as the day they'd met. Desire to let her gaze roam over Kate's body. Urge to kiss her. Instead of pink shorts and tank top, Kate wore leggings and a bulky sweater, both black. Her hair was longer over her shoulders, highlights less pronounced. God, she was beautiful. Chris brushed her hands on her 501s as her heart banged against her ribs.

Nicole stopped her and said something Chris couldn't hear. Then she went into the house.

"Hi." Kate stopped a few feet from her, holding the bag in front of her with both hands. French-manicured nails instead of her usual pink.

"Hi." She wanted to wrap her arms around Kate. She stuffed her hands in her pockets.

"Doing something for Gran?"

"Pond pump broke."

"I've been meaning to call. It's been hectic."

"Yeah. Me, too." Chris drank in every second of these few moments with Kate as hurt and resentment and sadness brewed inside intense longing. "How's Cecelia?"

"Getting stronger."

"Glad she's all right." Chris scuffed her boot on the driveway.

"I don't ever want to be that scared again."

She fisted her hands in her pockets. "Good luck on the bar exam."

"Gran told me the *Sunset* article comes out in April. Congratulations." Kate shifted her weight. "Chris, I—"

The front door opened. "We're waiting," Nicole hollered.

Kate held up the bag. "Better take Mother's lunch in to her. It was nice seeing you." Kate held her gaze for an instant. Circles under her eyes that makeup didn't hide. Must be studying a lot. Then she turned and walked toward the house. Didn't look back. Went inside. Nicole shut the door.

Anger knocked aside the longing. Cecelia's lunch was more important than talking to her lover. Ex-lover. And a lying, manipulative bitch was inside the house. Part of the family. While she was nothing more than hired help. *Not right, not right, not right.* Carrying her toolbox, Chris marched to the cottage, mentally daring Cecelia or Nicole to challenge her right to be there. She *was* the hired help today.

"I'm going up to the house," Katherine said when Chris reached the patio. "Don't leave until I return. We need to discuss details about the *Sunset* article."

"We can do that by phone."

Katherine fixed her with an odd look. Sympathy. Regret perhaps. "Walk the labyrinth. Some of the flagstones wobble. I'd like them fixed before you leave."

Chris focused on the pump repair. Fifteen minutes later, water flowed down the small waterfall. Katherine wasn't back. Damn it.

She went to the edge of the patio, the toes of her work boots right up to the entrance of the labyrinth. She hadn't walked it because it was dark by the time they'd finished it the night before Cecelia returned from New York. Fog swirled through the yard and the wind had picked up. Like something out of an old black-and-white film. *Wuthering Heights,* maybe. She shook off the eerie feeling of standing at the edge of a cliff. Silly. She stared at the first flagstone inside the labyrinth, the last one they'd laid, having worked out from the center. She and Kate jumping into each other's arms afterward, dirty and sweaty. A celebration dinner with Katherine followed by watching *The Philadelphia Story* and gorging on popcorn. Sneaking kisses. She'd spent the night with Kate. Inseparable lovers. Or so she'd thought.

She stared through the fog at the large boulder they'd placed in the center of the labyrinth. It seemed farther away than a mere fifteen feet. Fine. Walk it. Fix the wobbly stones. Make the client happy. Leave.

She lifted her right foot and set it on the flagstone, then set her left foot beside it. The stone was solid beneath her. She felt a tug in her chest and then warmth, like the sun had broken through the fog, but it hadn't. Right foot forward. Pause. Left foot placed beside it. She walked over several more stones. Pushed down on their edges. No wobble. The sound of the waterfall on the patio seemed to recede with each step, as if she were moving a great distance away. The fog was dense, but she couldn't shake the feeling of sun on her back. She made the first turn. And felt like she'd walked through a tight space. Pressure, like she was being squeezed.

She forced herself to keep walking, although her legs threatened to vault her out of this damn thing. Walk it. Fix the wobbly stones. Never have to see any of the Dawsons again. Step. Pause. Bring her other foot alongside. She continued, testing for uneven flagstones. This was a great design. Simple, but appropriate to the client's desires. It deserved to be in *Sunset*.

Reaching another turn, she followed the path as it wound back, feeling hotter, as if in noonday sun. She unzipped her jacket. Reaching the next turn she forced herself to keep moving, although she couldn't shake the feeling of being squeezed. Step. Pause. Stones were solid. This is what she did. Create landscapes to fit clients' desires. *You have to know what they want before they do.* She was good at it, and she would have the large, successful company she wanted.

Finally she reached the center and stepped on each flagstone. Solid. She dropped to the concave surface of the boulder. Exhausted as if she'd been walking for days. Kate. The smell of her. The feel of her. It seemed as if Kate were here with her, but that was crazy. She was in the main house. With her mother. With Nicole.

She stood. Tried to take a step. Couldn't, as if being held in place. She dropped to the boulder as sadness and loneliness encased her. Covering her eyes with the heels of her hands, she pressed them closed. She jiggled her leg, trying to dissipate the energy building inside like a flash flood. No. Not this much pain. Not the emptiness in her heart where Kate's love had been. She fought for control over the unwanted emotions, embarrassed by tears she couldn't stop, hoping Katherine hadn't come back. Her body tightened. She resisted...resisted...Then she did the only thing possible. She let go, surrendering to the emotions battering her. Hugging herself, she rocked, her heart breaking as she replayed moments with Kate as if watching a favorite movie. She sat there for a long time. Thinking. Crying. The warmth from outside retreated but now seemed generated from inside. In her heart.

The tears finally stopped and she dried her cheeks on her sleeve. The crushing pain in her chest changed to a dull ache. She placed her palm over her heart as she took deep breaths. She'd survive. She knew who she was. She knew what she wanted.

❖

Kate gulped back the sob building in her chest as Nic pulled her inside and shut the door. "It was nice seeing you?" She'd really said that? Tears filled her eyes, and she couldn't blink fast enough to contain them. Her chest felt like it was filled with icy daggers, and she couldn't catch her breath. A sob escaped, coming out as a strangled gasp.

"Pull yourself together," Nic hissed. "Do you want to upset Cecelia?"

Upset her mother or hurt Chris. The way Chris had looked at her. Trying to hide it, but she knew that face so well. Deeply hurt and rightfully so.

"She doesn't matter." Nic squeezed her arm.

"I don't want to give her up." The words came out in pieces separated by ragged breaths. She handed the bag to Nic. She had to talk to Chris.

"Kate?" her mother called from the dining room. "Did you remember extra dressing for my salad?"

She froze, her hand on the doorknob.

"Come have lunch." Nic pulled her away from the door. "Ignore Mountain Mary."

"Don't...call her...that." Kate tried to suck in air but only managed shallow puffs.

"You are over her."

"Not...over. Can't...breathe." She braced her hand against the credenza, light-headed. She struggled to breathe as Nic put her arm around her and walked her to the dining room.

"Sit. Take deep breaths." Nic pushed a chair back from the table with her leg.

Kate dropped to the chair and gripped the edges of it as panic escalated. Her chest burned as she gulped for air. Pinpricks of light danced across her vision.

"What's wrong?" her mother asked from her place at the dining table.

"Hyperventilating." Nic took containers out of the bag and put it in Kate's hand. "Hold it tight over your mouth and breathe into it."

Kate swatted it away. She wanted Chris. She'd talk her through this like she had that night during the storm when she'd panicked from the restraints.

"Kate! Oh, no, oh, no." Her mother hurried over, eyes wide, hands plastered to her chest.

Kate held up her hand, hoping to reassure her she was all right. She tried to remember what Chris had said. Breathe from her belly. In for a count of six. Out for ten. She wanted Chris beside her. In for six. Out for ten. Rubbing her back. In for six. Out for ten. Holding her.

"I...love her," she managed to say as she sucked in a labored breath.

"You don't." Nic gripped Kate's shoulder. "It was the shock of seeing her. I'll get rid of her."

"Rid of who?" Her mother patted Kate's back as if she were choking.

"Chris is here," Nic said.

"What! That can't be. I will not have that woman on my property."

"She's working for me." Everyone turned toward the menacingly low voice as Kate's gran came through the French doors from the patio. She looked spectral dressed all in gray, clothes and hair damp from the fog.

"I'll go tell her to—"

"You will not," her gran said, voice rising.

"I love Chris." Kate remained in the chair, afraid her legs wouldn't hold her. She searched her mother's face for any sign of understanding.

"That's absurd." She waved a hand dismissively through the air. "You'd been drinking. She took advantage of you. I will not have her bothering you!"

Kate forced herself to stand. Her legs felt wobbly as she walked to her gran. "You were right. I am meant for great passion, and I will regret losing Chris for the rest of my life." She fell into her arms, absorbing the reassurance in her hug. Then she turned to her mother and gripped the back of a chair. Still light-headed, but resolve pushed up from deep inside. From the place Chris had awoken. The place that knew happiness and passion. The place that needed Chris. "She didn't take advantage of me. I took her up to my room. We'd been romantically involved since before Thanksgiving."

"That's not possible. No daughter of mine would be so foolish." Her mother's expression hardened and her cheeks became blotchy red. "Or lie to me about it. Your future is at stake here!"

"I should have told you right away." She'd made a terrible mistake by keeping it secret, but losing Chris and abandoning her own happiness wouldn't undo what had happened.

"You don't love her."

"I do love her, Mother." Such a relief to finally own the words that had been trapped in her heart.

"It's your fault!" Her mother sent the accusation hurtling toward Katherine. "Sending her to that cabin."

"You're confused." Nic moved to stand beside Cecelia, arms crossed.

"Yes," her mother said, taking Nic's arm. "The stress of your illness. Moving away. Alone and vulnerable. I should never have allowed it."

Kate walked toward her mother, toward the hard look on her face. There had to be a way to melt that hardness. "You fell in love with Father. You must remember how it felt. Why can't you be happy for me?"

"Love is a choice! You must not choose someone inappropriate. You have no idea of the consequences."

Kate stopped in front of her. "I didn't plan this to hurt you. It just happened. Best thing that's ever happened to me."

"It's…an experiment. It can be excused. You haven't been yourself. We'll put all this behind us. I'll work harder to find the right husband for you."

"I found the right partner." She looked toward her gran's cottage as fear gripped her. What if Chris didn't want her?

"Romantic love isn't everything." Her mother's voice rose. "When life becomes hard, it's nothing. Nothing!" She crossed her arms, shoulders rigid. "It does not take care of you. It does not protect you. Your father would be so disappointed."

"No, he would not. He'd want Kate's happiness above all else. It's time for the truth, Cecelia. For Kate's sake." Her gran looked at Nic. "This doesn't concern you."

Nic started to speak and then stormed out of the room.

"It doesn't concern you, either, Katherine." Her mother's face had gone pale and she gripped the chair. "I've allowed you too much influence over my daughter. Allowed you to fill her head with silly notions about romance from those ridiculous movies of yours. Romantic love is unreliable!"

"I did think romantic love was reserved for movies," Kate said. "Because I'd never experienced it. It *is* real."

"Whatever infatuation you have will fade, and you'll be faced with the harsh reality. She is not a suitable partner for someone in your social position with important responsibilities ahead of you."

"Then I'll give up my position."

Her mother gasped and put her hand to her chest. "You wouldn't. Not after everything I've done to make sure my child would have an easy life. A perfect life."

"Cecelia," her gran said. "Kate needs to understand the source of your objections."

"This isn't the time."

"It's long past time."

"I won't talk about it." Her mother lifted her chin defiantly toward Katherine. "You never liked me. You thought I wasn't good enough for William."

"Phillip and I did try to talk William out of marrying you." Her gran walked toward Cecelia. "We had you investigated and discovered your background, which you hadn't shared with our son. Like you, we thought we were protecting him from making a mistake that would ruin his life. He never wavered in his love for you. Insisted he would marry you with or without our support."

Kate tried to grasp what was happening between her mother and her gran. She wanted to go to Chris, but this seemed important to resolve.

"It's so horrible." Her mother went to the French doors and stood with her back to them. She pulled the cardigan around her and folded her arms. Minutes went by before she spoke. "My father died when I was twelve. Momma had to work two jobs. I took care of my younger sisters and—"

"What? I have aunts?"

"I haven't seen them since I left for college. This is so hard for me."

Kate's gran came to stand beside her. She put her arm around Kate, her expression sad.

"We never had much money, but after he died, things worsened. Food. Clothes. School supplies. There was never enough. It was awful having to accept hand-me-downs from the church, then being teased about it at school. Going to bed hungry or cold. I wanted a better life so badly. Wanted to attend college. Our minister arranged for a wealthy woman in the church to pay my way at USF if I'd pledge her sorority." Her mother turned around, a smile on her face. "Everything changed. No one made fun of me. I had friends. Nice clothes. I loved living in the sorority house. Going to parties. On dates. And then I met William my senior year. He was everything I wanted in a husband."

Kate studied her, sadness curling up from inside as an ugly truth peeked through. "Did you marry Father for love or for money and social status?"

Her mother shook her head as she walked to the antique sideboard she'd bought earlier in the week and rubbed her hand over the surface.

"I'd like an answer," her gran said.

"I was a good wife to him. A good wife." She snapped her gaze to Kate. "You're dangerously naive if you think love is all that matters. It doesn't give you the important things in life. The right friends. The right opportunities. Security."

"I don't need it to. You're overreacting."

"There are consequences to frivolous decisions. I know. I suffered because Momma clung to her ridiculous obsession with her grand love!" She seemed to crumple. "I've said too much. You don't need to know this."

"Tell Kate the rest of it," her gran said, pulling out a chair. "Sit. I'll bring you tea."

Her mother slumped onto the chair, not looking at Kate as she fiddled with the corner of the placemat.

"Please." Kate sat and took her hand.

Her mother let out a long breath. "A few months after Daddy died, a woman drove up to our house in a Cadillac. Said she was my grandmother. Gave me and my sisters presents. Lots of presents. Took us out to dinner at a fancy restaurant. Momma was from a wealthy Charleston family. She'd run off with the gardener's son. My grandmother offered to take us back to Charleston if Momma admitted she'd been wrong to run off. Momma refused." She lifted her gaze to Kate, her expression pained, lost. "We could have had an easy life. A real home. Momma chose love over…I want you to have the future that will keep you comfortable and secure."

"You raised me to be like you." Kate had always known that, but it looked like the wrong path. A lonely path devoid of love. "It doesn't make me happy."

"Neither of us married for true love," her gran said, setting a cup of tea in front of Cecelia. "We made those choices knowingly, if for different reasons. I was afraid you'd take the same path, unknowingly. There's truth in those old movies. Romantic love is real. It is a choice. Perhaps a harder choice. A riskier choice. But I wanted you to know the difference. It's your life, Kate. I will support whatever decision you make."

Without Chris nothing else mattered. "Is Chris still here?"

"I believe so," her gran said.

Kate hurried toward the French doors.

"Kate!" Her mother gripped her arm as she passed. "Don't make the biggest mistake of your life."

Kate pulled away, opened the door, and sprinted toward the cottage.

❖

Kate burst onto her gran's patio, the screen door slapping shut behind her. Her heart jumped into her throat. No Chris. Then she saw the toolbox beside the pond. She looked around the yard shrouded in fog and spotted her in the center of the labyrinth, her back to the patio. "Chris!"

Chris sat still, elbows on her knees, as if she didn't hear Kate.

She hurried to the labyrinth. And froze. The frightening experience in Chartres Cathedral surged up in her mind. "Chris!" Still no response. Was Chris deliberately ignoring her? She considered running straight to the center, but that seemed like cheating. Missing out on a chance to conquer fear. Wasn't that what the last six months had been about? Fear of the unexpected? Fear of failure? Fear of sex? Her gran had sent her on a journey to find out who she was. This seemed like the culmination.

She stepped boldly into the labyrinth. Love was worth fighting for. Panic crescendoed with each step. Cold. As if the temperature had dropped twenty degrees. The fog seemed to thicken, almost obscuring the center. The yard became shades of black and white, as if she'd stepped into an old movie. Eerie.

Never taking her eyes from Chris she made her way around the labyrinth, the twisting path taking her closer to her and then farther away. She seemed lost in her own world, unaware of Kate's presence. She ignored the nausea and light-headedness as images from her life appeared and disappeared. A montage of how she'd come to be in this place. What seemed like days later, she stepped into the center.

Dropping to the flagstone, she knelt in front of Chris. "Hold me. I'm freezing." Chris's arms came around her and she burrowed into her warmth. "I love you."

"I love you," Chris said, but she had the wrong expression on her face. Frowning instead of her sexy grin. "Falling in love with you taught me that love does matter in spite of the messiness. In spite of the heartbreak when you sent me away in the ER. But I don't know that we have a future together."

"I know what you think." Kate sat back on her heels, her hands on Chris's thighs. "I'm a spoiled rich girl who played with you and then left when being with you became inconvenient."

"That's not what I think. You decided love was too risky. Not worth it if it upset people. Katherine's right. Love is worth fighting for. You let your mother take it out of your hands."

She gripped Chris's legs, searching for the right words. "You saved me from a life without passion. From living my mother's life. I hurt you. I'm so sorry. I've missed you every day."

"You left me a voice mail." Chris worked her jaw. "A voice mail."

"I was scared and—"

"What happens next time you're scared?" Chris looked heartbreakingly sad.

"Having you in the ER made me feel guiltier than I could bear. I thought I'd done something wrong and reckless and thoughtless. I didn't. I wanted to be with the woman I love at a party where we should have been a couple. Dancing. Holding hands. Every privilege other couples have. There was nothing reckless about taking you up to my bedroom. Reckless was not telling Mother about us. I told her I love you. That I won't give you up."

Chris took her hands from her jacket pockets and laid them on her thighs, inches from Kate's. She stared down, shaking her head. Still frowning. Not the cocky grin Kate needed.

She kept talking, presenting the most important argument of her life. "Because I'd never been in love I didn't realize there's more to it than the happy ending in movies. That's only the beginning. It takes commitment and attention. Like the gardens you create. Like this labyrinth we built. Fitting the stones together. Chipping off edges so things fit. Making it solid. Love needs tending, like plants, so it doesn't go into transplant shock." That earned her a tiny smile from Chris, and she moved her fingers closer to Kate's. "I drove by Georgia's last Saturday and saw your Harley."

"I went because I didn't know what else to do. I didn't stay. Couldn't be there. Not when all I thought about was you." Finally Chris's shoulders relaxed and her eyes softened.

Kate leaned forward for the kiss she desperately needed.

Chris gripped her shoulders. No kiss. "We come from different worlds."

"So we're like the characters in *Bringing Up Baby*. Mismatched in some ways but—"

"Life isn't a screwball comedy."

"It should be. I love the twists and turns that take the characters out of their usual lives and bring them together. I love the moment they realize they're in love and suddenly their life makes sense."

"Your friends...sorority...clients...will wonder what you're doing with me. Cecelia—"

"Doesn't get a vote. We can build a life together like we built this labyrinth. Give me one good reason why we can't be together."

"You know the first thing I thought about you? Beautiful."

"What's wrong with that?"

"Second thing? You're way out of my league."

"Chicken. So you have to dress up for parties. Or dinners with clients. Grow up, Chris." Kate took her hands from Chris's legs. "You've built an insulated world for yourself where you're never challenged or uncomfortable. Where life isn't messy."

Chris rubbed her finger over Kate's diamond tennis bracelet. "I can't buy you expensive jewelry or—"

"You think I care about any of that? What you give me, the freedom to be myself, the freedom to be sexual and passionate, is exactly what I want. I feel whole and alive when I'm with you."

"I'm scared." Chris covered Kate's hands. They were warm and callused. "Scared of how much I want you."

Kate turned her hands over and gripped Chris's. "Wanna take me up on my offer to be your practice partner?"

"Maybe." Finally the cocky grin.

"What have you got to lose?"

"Plenty."

"Good. Me, too." Kate stood and tugged Chris up. Wrapping her arms around her, she took the kiss she needed. Her heartbeat felt strong and steady for the first time in weeks. "Let's get out of this blasted thing. I'm freezing."

"I'm burning up."

"See? We're perfect together." She took Chris's hand and stepped from the center.

"Wait." Chris pulled her back. Taking a deep breath she settled into a perfect Warrior II pose. "One arm reaching toward the future." She pushed her arm forward. "One arm reaching into the past." She looked toward the hand extended behind her. "Centered in the present on a solid foundation." She met Kate's gaze. "Join me."

Love spilled from Kate's heart as she mirrored Chris, their bodies inches apart. "You've been taking classes."

"Had to keep up my inner femme." Sporting the sexiest grin ever, Chris leaned forward and kissed her, the warmth of it spreading through all the cold places in Kate's body.

❖

Chris stopped, pulling Kate into her arms and kissing her again. At this rate it would take days to make it through the garden to the main house. Fine by her. She didn't relish seeing Cecelia.

"You two might age me ten years."

Chris turned toward the voice. Katherine. Sitting on a bench beside the path. "Tell me something. Did the pond pump break on its own or did it have help?"

Katherine fixed her with a piercing look, perhaps laced with a spark of humor. "I'm clever, but not that clever."

"But you were clever enough to send Kate to Felton."

The corners of Katherine's mouth turned up. "I had a hunch your paths should cross."

Kate's mouth dropped open. Then she pulled her gran up and hugged her. "I love you. I love you. I love you."

"I've never been prouder of you." Her gran held Kate's shoulders. "Now go live the life you've chosen." She started for her cottage.

"I tried to contact Olivia," Kate said.

Katherine stopped. Her shoulders lifted as if taking a deep breath. She turned around. "I know."

"What?" Kate's look of surprise was adorable.

"She told me."

"And?"

"I'll let you know." She resumed walking toward her destination.

Kate squeezed Chris's hand. "Come up to my bedroom while I pack. Then take me home."

"Are you sure about—" Kate's mouth pressed against hers. God, she could kiss. "You need to pack fast." Her sex throbbed.

Chris tried to let go of her hand as they neared the house, but Kate held tight. She opened the French door and they stepped into the dining room. Nicole paced by the table. She cut her gaze toward Chris. Everything about her screamed "how dare you."

Chris strode to her. Gripped her shoulders. Kissed her cheek. "Thank you."

"For?" Nicole arched one eyebrow. Her makeup was subdued today. Not the exaggerated, overdone look she wore as Raven. How sad not to be yourself.

"Making me face my worst fear."

"I'm your worst fear?"

"People like you. People who make me feel I'm not good enough for whatever reason."

"This thing needs to end." Nicole's voice went hard as she turned toward Kate, who looked puzzled by their exchange. "Cecelia collapsed when you left. I had to help her upstairs."

"This thing," Kate said. "You mean the chance for a lifetime of happiness with the woman I love?"

"It's not love. You're infatuated with her sexual prowess."

"Believe that if it makes you feel superior," Chris said. "What I don't get is why you don't want Kate to be happy?"

"I'd like to know that, too," Kate said.

Nicole's eyes widened with surprise for an instant. "I do want you to be happy. That's why I'm trying to keep you from making a huge mistake."

Kate walked toward her. "As my best friend, shouldn't you be saying, 'I don't agree with this, but I'll support you?'"

"Truth is hard, but I wouldn't be your friend if I didn't raise the important issue." Nicole crossed her arms. "What kind of life would you have with her?"

"Someone who treats me like a princess? Who's been kind and attentive?" Kate spoke to Nicole, but her gaze locked on Chris, blue eyes feisty. "Who's shown her love for me in a hundred ways?"

"You can find someone more suitable. More—"

"Like you?" Chris almost laughed as the pieces fell into place.

"Exactly."

"This isn't about my not being good enough. This is about your wanting to be with Kate." Geez. This wasn't high-stakes class issues. This was common jealousy. Run off the competition.

"That is ridiculous." Nicole's voice was icy, but her eyes betrayed her with the way she looked at Kate. Hungry.

"Why would you say that?" Kate frowned.

Chris walked to Nicole. "You should tell her the truth."

"Don't threaten me."

"You think you're better than me. I'm not the one lying." She lifted Nicole's hand and looked from the engagement ring to Kate. "I left my toolbox by the pond. I'll be back in a few minutes." She walked toward the French doors. Then stopped and went back to Kate. Pulling her close, she kissed her as Nicole looked away.

❖

Kate watched Chris stride across the patio. The love of her life and she'd almost lost her. She nearly ran after her. Being away from her for even a few minutes was painful. But Nic was her best friend. "Talk to me." Silence. Head was down. What she could see of her eyes looked bruised and far away. "I love Chris. I love you, too."

"She deserves you. I don't," Nic said in a flat voice.

"Melodrama doesn't suit you." No smile. "What aren't you telling me?"

Slowly Nic lifted her head. Every muscle in her face was taut, her mouth a tight line, her eyes sparking with danger. Her fierce, go-away look.

"You're not chasing me off." Kate pulled out a chair and sat.

Finally Nic took the chair beside her and clasped her hands in her lap. "Before you…" She let out a long breath. "I never had a close friend. Hell, I never had a friend. Best three years of my life rooming with you. I thought I'd always have that connection. Then your illness. Scared me how close I came to losing you." She brushed her fingertips under her eyes. Tears. She'd never cried in front of Kate. "You were seeming like your old self, and then you moved away. I missed you," Nic said slowly, like she wasn't used to the words.

"Then I discovered you were involved with Chris." She met Kate's gaze. "Why not me?"

Kate felt crumpled by the hurt in Nic's eyes. "Oh, Nicki. I didn't know."

"There's more. Chris and I know each other from Georgia's parties."

"What!"

"Not like that. I go to Georgia's parties. I go to other parties like that."

"You're engaged to Brian."

"I do love Brian. But it's not enough. Sexually. I need…things. Different things…"

"BDSM things." Kate wanted to laugh that she knew the term, but there was nothing funny about this. "When you told me I could date men for cover and have women on the side…That's what you do, isn't it? And you wanted me to be the woman on the side?"

"Guilty on all counts, Counselor."

Kate tried to wrap her head around this. She should be angry. Nic had deceived her, but hadn't she deceived her mother by avoiding the truth? Love was complicated in ways she'd never imagined. "So you're bisexual?"

"I can't explain it. I won't explain it." Anger spiked in her voice and eyes.

"I'm not judging you. Why didn't Chris tell me?"

"There's an unwritten code. You don't talk about what happens at the parties. You don't out people. And I gave her a hard time when I realized she was your Chris. Threatened to go to Cecelia about—"

"You didn't send her up to—"

"God, no!" Nic looked shocked by the accusation.

"Don't mess with Chris. That would end our friendship. I'm going to Felton for a few days. We'll have dinner next week. You're still my bar-exam coach, and I'm your support system for work. I love you. Not the way you want me to, but I love you." She wrapped her arms around her.

Finally Nic hugged back, barely. "Tell Cecelia I had to leave." She strode from the room without looking back.

Chris set her toolbox on the table on the patio. Kate opened the door for her. Holding her hand, she walked through the house and up the stairs to her bedroom. Shutting the door she gripped Chris's jacket and pulled her close.

"Don't you want to check on Cecelia?"

"Kiss me."

"Kind of bossy." Chris's eyes sparked with desire.

"Not likely to change so get used to it."

"I can live with that. I love you." Chris cupped Kate's neck and pulled their mouths together for a long kiss.

"I know about Nic going to Georgia's parties. She explained why you didn't tell me."

"I won't keep anything from you again."

"And I should have stood up for us. The next person who hassles us will wish they—"

The door opened. "Kate, I want to—" Her mother froze. "What is she doing up here?"

"'She' is the woman I love. Chris. Who is here while I pack. Then we're going to Felton."

"Kate, please. You don't know the mistake you're making."

"I'll never be poor, Mother."

"Perhaps not, but you'll be ostracized for being gay. For being different." Her mother's face looked pained.

"I don't believe that. We'll live in a different world than yours. A world we build together. Based on love."

"Kate, you must—"

"Pack." Kate took her mother's arm and led her out of the bedroom. "Don't come into my bedroom again without knocking."

"I can't be alone. Not with my condition."

"We'll call your friends. Maybe Lucille Cavanaugh, to see if you can stay with her. Or I'll arrange for full-time nursing care."

She straightened her shoulders, fixing Kate with a puzzled look. "I'll manage." She walked slowly down the hall.

"What?" Chris was frowning when Kate returned to her.

"That seemed a little harsh. It matters to me that you stood up for us but—"

"I can't let her run my life."

"It must scare her to think she's losing you."

Kate wrapped her arms around Chris, soaking up the strength she needed. "When did you get so smart about relationships?"

"About a minute ago?"

"I'll talk to her, and then take me home, stud. Unless…" She tugged on Chris's fly. "Kidding," she said, when Chris looked shocked. Then she took Chris's mouth in a possessive, bruising, very long kiss. Sure of the life she wanted. The life with Chris that made her happier than she'd thought possible.

Epilogue

Chris handed her dad a glass of champagne and took her place beside Kate in the center of the foyer. Kate's big day. She was beautiful in her dusky-pink suit, looking every bit the new managing partner of Dawson Law Firm. Several dozen guests fell silent as Cecelia held up her glass.

"A toast to my daughter, my pride and joy, on this stupendous occasion. The end of a long journey..." Cecelia looked elegant in a black suit. She'd lost considerable weight and seemed healthy after the surgery to imbed the ICD pacemaker. She'd thrown herself into her position as president of her sorority's national organization with boundless energy. "Your father would be so proud of you," Cecelia said, concluding what for her was a restrained speech.

Chris sipped the French champagne as she watched Kate accept congratulations from one person after another. She was getting used to it—the champagne and Kate's role in society. She took her hand from her pocket and fingered the skinny tie, a gift from Kate this afternoon as they dressed for the party. Pink. Like her boxers. Like her toenails. Her heart pounded and her sex contracted behind the cock as she replayed what else they'd done while dressing.

Katherine came to stand beside her. "I looked over the lease and faxed them suggested changes." Katherine was legal counsel for her new Brent Landscape corporation. Chris had promoted Regina to project manager for jobs in Santa Cruz, while she opened the new office and handled the influx of business in the aftermath of the *Sunset* article. The lease was for office space in Palo Alto, where she and Kate lived during the week, spending most weekends in Felton.

"Having fun?" Kate asked, joining them and linking her arm through Chris's.

"Yes." Chris meant it. As with gardens, life was best as a balanced design. Motorcycling was a part of their life but so were social functions. As long as she was with Kate, she could handle anything.

"You sure you'll be all right?" Katherine asked Kate. "Two weeks is a—"

"Stop," Kate said. "You are getting on that plane tomorrow." A trip to New York. Kate had finally convinced her that love was worth the risk and she'd regret it if she didn't give the relationship with Olivia a chance.

"Uh-oh," Kate said, nodding at Cecelia bearing down on them. "Betcha she's coming for you." She nudged Chris in the ribs. "You haven't lived until you've been Mother's pet project."

Chris groaned but put a smile on her face. She wasn't rocking the boat with Cecelia.

"Christine, dear, you must come meet Mrs. Shepherd. She wants to renovate her backyard for their Fourth of July party. I told her I had just the right person. She sits on the board of the San Francisco botanical garden. You must make the right contacts, which will open doors for you."

Chris let Cecelia take her arm and lead her away. Another reason her business was flourishing. She'd never have believed it. Looking back over her shoulder she winked at Kate, who covered her mouth to stop from laughing.

After making the rounds with Cecelia, Chris came up behind Georgia and slipped her arm around her waist. "You have to know what she wants before she does." She handed her a glass of champagne.

"Love suits you, sugar."

"You knew it before I did."

"You had all the essentials. Just needed refining." Georgia motioned to Nic, who joined her. One of the biggest surprises of the last four months was the friendship between them. Neither would talk about it, but Nic seemed calmer and steadier.

"Dinner tomorrow night?" Nic asked Chris, wearing a black dress and her trademark red lipstick and nails. The engagement ring was gone.

"Giants game, but we can do lunch."

"Perfect. Shopping after?" The corners of Nic's mouth turned up as she sipped champagne.

"Don't push it," Chris said, returning the smile. She'd never fully trust her, but Nic was still Kate's best friend, and she respected their relationship.

Two hours later, everyone had left except her dad and Cecelia, who were engaged in a discussion over what precise shade of white to paint the exterior of Cecelia's house. She'd warned her dad what he was getting into by working for her, but he seemed more amused by Cecelia than put off by her.

"I called a cab for you," Chris said to Cecelia. "I'll walk you downstairs."

"Where's Kate?"

"Her office."

"I'll go—" Cecelia started in that direction and then stopped. "Well. Yes. I suppose it's been an exhausting day for her. Tell her I'll call in the morning."

"Still on for our Sunday ride?" her dad asked.

"Yep. We'll meet you at Alice's at nine."

"Honestly," Cecelia said, crossing her arms. "Must you ride those awful things?"

"Why don't you join us?" her dad asked Cecelia. "I'll pick you up."

"Oh, my, no." Cecelia pressed her hand to her chest. "I'd be terrified."

"I'll escort you downstairs," her dad said to Cecelia. "See if I can convince you to give it a try."

Cecelia took his arm. "I've been thinking that I'd like to spruce up the inside of the house. Perhaps you could make recommendations on…"

Chris shut the door behind them and went to the windows of the tenth-floor office. No matter how many times she'd been up here, the sun setting beyond the Golden Gate Bridge took her breath away. It still scared her how close she'd come to missing out on the best thing to ever happen to her. Yes, love could be messy, but it was more than worth the risk.

❖

Kate twirled her gold Cross pen as she looked out the window at the sun setting beyond the Golden Gate Bridge, sifting through the many emotions the day had brought. Joy she'd accomplished her lifelong goal. Worry about whether she'd be a good steward of the law firm. Sadness that her father wasn't here to share the moment. Or Todd. But then honeymooning…

She hadn't wanted an opulent party or the announcement in the *Chronicle*, but she couldn't begrudge her mother the celebration. Boundaries between them were a work in progress, but as Chris reminded her in moments when her patience was exhausted, all great designs took time to mature.

"You're beautiful and I'm the luckiest woman in the world."

Kate turned, her heart warming as Chris walked toward her, looking handsome in the custom-made, charcoal-gray suit. She still resisted Kate buying her things, but they were learning to compromise as they blended their lives. She fingered the skinny tie and used it to pull Chris close. "Kiss me senseless."

Chris took her in her arms, eyes shimmering with desire, and dipped her backward for a long kiss. "You all right?" Chris asked, bringing her upright.

"I am now." She wrapped her arms around Chris and then backed away, putting her hand to her chest as her heart jolted. There was something hard in the inside breast pocket. No, too big for a ring. Although when Chris asked her, she knew what she'd say.

"I'm proud of you and proud to be your partner." Chris handed her a small package.

Kate tore through the pink paper, opened the box, held up the gold nameplate.

"No office christening is complete without one."

"Nor is it complete without something else." She took Chris's hand and led her to the couch in her newly redecorated office. Her mother's project, although Kate had insisted on keeping some of her father's furniture. The burgundy leather couch and chairs were new.

"Sit." She pushed on Chris's shoulders, bending down for a long kiss. She closed the drapes and placed candles throughout the room, lighting them as she went, never taking her eyes from Chris. She locked the office door, took a bottle of lube from a drawer, and went to sit beside her. "Make love to me."

"Here?" Chris's eyes sparked with surprise and desire.

Kate brought Chris's hands to her breasts. "This day won't be complete without christening my office with you inside me." They undressed each other slowly, caressing, kissing, building their arousal. Kate lay back and guided Chris's cock to her opening, wrapping her legs around her. "So, Ms. Lesbian Casanova," she said as Chris moved inside her, slow and deep. "Sex was the deal. Did falling in love ruin everything?"

"Being in love makes sex better than I could have imagined." Chris stroked Kate's hair, sporting her cocky grin. "You were right. Sex is better inside a relationship, a future of shared dreams. We'll have a great life, my beautiful Kate."

"A life of passion and love." A life she hadn't known was waiting for her. Kate cupped Chris's face and pulled her down for the kiss that would last a lifetime.

About the Author

Julie Blair is a Goldie and Rainbow award-winning author of lesbian romances. From the time she was old enough to hold a book, escaping into fictional worlds where anything is possible and endings are usually happy has been a favorite pastime. Growing up a tomboy before it was fashionable, Julie attached herself to sports, especially softball, which culminated in her pitching in the Women's College World Series. She worked in restaurant management for a decade and has been a chiropractor for over twenty-five years. A Northern California native, she lives in the quiet of the redwoods in Boulder Creek with her partner, Pamela, and their two Labradors. She enjoys gardening, hiking, red wine, strong coffee, smooth jazz, and warm fall afternoons.

Contact information: http://www.julieblairauthor.com
Facebook: https://www.facebook.com/julie.blair.3720

Books Available from Bold Strokes Books

A Touch of Temptation by Julie Blair. Recent law school graduate Kate Dawson's ordained path to the perfect life gets thrown off course when handsome butch top Chris Brent initiates her to sexual pleasure. (978-1-62639-488-9)

Beneath the Waves by Ali Vali. Kai Merlin and Vivien Palmer love the water and the secrets trapped in the depths, but if Kai gives in to her feelings, it might come at a cost to her entire realm. (978-1-62639-609-8)

Girls on Campus edited by Sandy Lowe and Stacia Seaman. College: four years when rules are made to be broken. This collection is required reading for anyone looking to earn an A in sex ed. (978-1-62639-733-0)

Heart of the Pack by Jenny Frame. Human Selena Miller falls for the domineering Caden Wolfgang, but will their love survive Selena learning the Wolfgangs are werewolves? (978-1-62639-566-4)

Miss Match by Fiona Riley. Matchmaker Samantha Monteiro makes the impossible possible for everyone but herself. Is mysterious dancer Lucinda Moss her own perfect match? (978-1-62639-574-9)

Paladins of the Storm Lord by Barbara Ann Wright. Lieutenant Cordelia Ross must choose between duty and honor when a man with godlike powers forces her soldiers to provoke an alien threat. (978-1-62639-604-3)

Taking a Gamble by P.J. Trebelhorn. Storage auction buyer Cassidy Holmes and postal worker Erica Jacobs want different things out of life, but taking a gamble on love might prove lucky for them both. (978-1-62639-542-8)

The Copper Egg by Catherine Friend. Archeologist Claire Adams wants to find the buried treasure in Peru. Her ex, Sochi Castillo, wants to steal it. The last thing either of them wants is to still be in love. (978-1-62639-613-5)

The Iron Phoenix by Rebecca Harwell. Seventeen-year-old Nadya must master her unusual powers to stop a killer, prevent civil war, and rescue the girl she loves, while storms ravage her island city. (978-1-62639-744-6)

A Reunion to Remember by TJ Thomas. Reunited after a decade, Jo Adams and Rhonda Black must navigate a significant age difference, family dynamics, and their own desires and fears to explore an opportunity for love. (978-1-62639-534-3)

Built to Last by Aurora Rey. When Professor Olivia Bennett hires contractor Joss Bauer to restore her dilapidated farmhouse, she learns her heart, as much as her house, is in need of a renovation. (978-1-62639-552-7)

Capsized by Julie Cannon. What happens when a woman turns your life completely upside down? (978-1-62639-479-7)

Girls With Guns by Ali Vali, Carsen Taite, and Michelle Grubb. Three stories by three talented crime writers—Carsen Taite, Ali Vali, and Michelle Grubb—each packing her own special brand of heat. (978-1-62639-585-5)

Heartscapes by MJ Williamz. Will Odette ever recover her memory or is Jesse condemned to remember their love alone? (978-1-62639-532-9)

Murder on the Rocks by Clara Nipper. Detective Jill Rogers lives with two things on her mind: sex and murder. While an ice storm cripples Tulsa, two things stand in Jill's way: her lover and the DA. (978-1-62639-600-5)

Necromantia by Sheri Lewis Wohl. When seeing dead people is more than a movie tagline. (978-1-62639-611-1)

Salvation by I. Beacham. Claire's long-term partner now hates her, for all the wrong reasons, and she sees no future until she meets Regan, who challenges her to face the truth and find love. (978-1-62639-548-0)

Trigger by Jessica Webb. Dr. Kate Morrison races to discover how to defuse human bombs while learning to trust her increasingly strong feelings for the lead investigator, Sergeant Andy Wyles. (978-1-62639-669-2)

24/7 by Yolanda Wallace. When the trip of a lifetime becomes a pitched battle between life and death, will anyone survive? (978-1-62639-619-7)

A Return to Arms by Sheree Greer. When a police shooting makes national headlines, activists Folami and Toya struggle to balance their relationship and political allegiances, a struggle intensified after a fiery young artist enters their lives. (978-1-62639-681-4)

After the Fire by Emily Smith. Paramedic Connor Haus is convinced her time for love has come and gone, but when firefighter Logan Curtis comes into town, she learns it may not be too late after all. (978-1-62639-652-4)

Dian's Ghost by Justine Saracen. The road to genocide is paved with good intentions. (978-1-62639-594-7)

Fortunate Sum by M. Ullrich. Financial advisor Catherine Carter lives a calculated life, but after a collision with spunky Imogene Harris (her latest client) and unsolicited predictions, Catherine finds herself facing an unexpected variable: Love. (978-1-62639-530-5)

Soul to Keep by Rebekah Weatherspoon. What *won't* a vampire do for love… (978-1-62639-616-6)

When I Knew You by KE Payne. Eight letters, three friends, two lovers, one secret. Can the past ever be forgiven? (978-1-62639-562-6)

Wild Shores by Radclyffe. Can two women on opposite sides of an oil spill find a way to save both a wildlife sanctuary and their hearts? (978-1-62639-645-6)

Love on Tap by Karis Walsh. Beer and romance are brewing for Tace Lomond when archaeologist Berit Katsaros comes into her life. (987-1-62639-564-0)

Love on the Red Rocks by Lisa Moreau. An unexpected romance at a lesbian resort forces Malley to face her greatest fears where she must choose between playing it safe or taking a chance at true happiness. (987-1-62639-660-9)

Tracker and the Spy by D. Jackson Leigh. There are lessons for all when Captain Tanisha is assigned untried pyro Kyle and a lovesick dragon horse for a mission to track the leader of a dangerous cult. (987-1-62639-448-3)

Whirlwind Romance by Kris Bryant. Will chasing the girl break Tristan's heart or give her something she's never had before? (987-1-62639-581-7)

Whiskey Sunrise by Missouri Vaun. Culture and religion collide when Lovey Porter, daughter of a local Baptist minister, falls for the handsome thrill-seeking moonshine runner, Royal Duval. (987-1-62639-519-0)

Dyre: By Moon's Light by Rachel E. Bailey. A young werewolf, Des, guards the aging leader of all the Packs: the Dyre. Stable employment—nice work, if you can get it…at least until silver bullets start to fly. (978-1-62639-662-3)

Fragile Wings by Rebecca S. Buck. In Roaring Twenties London, can Evelyn Hopkins find love with Jos Singleton or will the scars of the Great War crush her dreams? (978-1-62639-546-6)

Live and Love Again by Jan Gayle. Jessica Whitney could be Sarah Jarret's second chance at love, but their differences and Sarah's grief continue to come between their budding relationship. (978-1-62639-517-6)

Starstruck by Lesley Davis. Actress Cassidy Hayes and writer Aiden Darrow find out the hard way not all life-threatening drama is confined to the TV screen or the pages of a manuscript. (978-1-62639-523-7)

Stealing Sunshine by Tina Michele. Under the Central Florida sun, two women struggle between fear and love as a dangerous plot of deception and revenge threatens to steal priceless art and lives. (978-1-62639-445-2)

The Fifth Gospel by Michelle Grubb. Hiding a Vatican secret is dangerous—sharing the secret suicidal—can Felicity survive a perilous book tour, and will her PR specialist, Anna, be there when it's all over? (978-1-62639-447-6)

Cold to the Touch by Cari Hunter. A drug addict's murder is the start of a dangerous investigation for Detective Sanne Jensen and Dr. Meg Fielding, as they try to stop a killer with no conscience. (978-1-62639-526-8)

Forsaken by Laydin Michaels. The hunt for a killer teaches one woman that she must overcome her fear in order to love, and another that success is meaningless without happiness. (978-1-62639-481-0)

Infiltration by Jackie D. When a CIA breach is imminent, a Marine instructor must stop the attack while protecting her heart from being disarmed by a recruit. (978-1-62639-521-3)

Midnight at the Orpheus by Alyssa Linn Palmer. Two women desperate to make their way in the world, a man hell-bent on revenge, and a cop risking his career: all in a day's work in Capone's Chicago. (978-1-62639-607-4)

Spirit of the Dance by Mardi Alexander. Major Sorla Reardon's return to her family farm to heal threatens Riley Johnson's safe life when small-town secrets are revealed, and love may not conquer all. (978-1-62639-583-1)